Frank Wakeley Gunsaulus

Monk and Knight - An Historical Study in Fiction

Vol. II

Frank Wakeley Gunsaulus

Monk and Knight - An Historical Study in Fiction
Vol. II

ISBN/EAN: 9783744641302

Printed in Europe, USA, Canada, Australia, Japan

Cover: Foto ©Andreas Hilbeck / pixelio.de

More available books at **www.hansebooks.com**

MONK AND KNIGHT

AN

Historical Study in Fiction

BY

FRANK W. GUNSAULUS

IN TWO VOLUMES

VOLUME II.

CHICAGO

A. C. McCLURG AND COMPANY

1891

CONTENTS.

MONK AND KNIGHT.

CHAPTER I.

TWO LETTERS.

"And whoso knoweth God indeed,
The fixed foundations of his creed
Know neither changing nor decay,
Though all creation pass away."

THE mountain torrents near La Torre were singing songs of spring; but the sweet voice of Alke was never more sad than when she called the little herd of goats and looked upon them as one by one on that morning in May, 1521, she saw them bound over the streamlet and come close to her very feet. A severe winter had just yielded to oncoming summer, and the spring-time appeared to be only a battle-ground on which now the glowing fires of an advancing June burned away the frigid chains of December, and then the chains grew more cold and solid, only reflecting the ineffectual light which struggled through frost and damp.

"It is somewhat like the life of humanity," said the maiden, as she drew about her shivering shoulders a coarse covering. "The patches of snow are like the drifts of ignorance and wrong which do not melt under the light of truth. Ah me! does the glacier grow from year to year? I never have seen snow upon these pastures in May until this day."

She looked up into the light, — irradiated, almost transfigured, — and mused again: "There is more light than warmth here." She seemed to feel the air with its contesting energies.

"That is the trouble with Master Erasmus. He is full of light, — light which illuminates every crag of ice, light which penetrates every cloud of gloom, — but he warms not; he will not melt the ice-bands. He is afraid of the avalanche. A great man afraid of the consequences of great actions, alas, how little he is!" and Alke took from her bosom a letter, which she read: —

ERASMUS to GASPAR PERRIN:

As to Luther, of whom you write so admiringly, I must say to you what I have said to the Most Blessed Father Leo X. I have no acquaintance with Luther, nor have I ever read his books, except perhaps ten or twelve pages, and that only by snatches. From what I then saw, I judged him to be well qualified for expounding the Scriptures in an age like this, which is so excessively given to mere subtleties to the neglect of really important questions. Accordingly I have favored Christ's glory in him. I was among the first to foresee the danger there was of this matter ending in violence, and no one ever hated violence more than I do. Indeed I even went so far as to threaten John Forben the printer, to prevent him printing his books. I wrote frequently and industriously to my friends, begging that they would admonish this man to observe Christian meekness in his writings, and do nothing to disturb the peace of the Church. And when he himself wrote to me two years ago, I lovingly admonished him what I wished him to avoid, and I would he had followed my advice. You have doubtless heard from Luther himself. Let me recite to you what I wrote him: " You have friends in England, and among them men of the greatest eminence, who think most highly of your writings. Even here there are some who favor you, and one of these is a man of distinction. For myself I am keeping such powers as I have to help the cause of the revival of letters. And more I think is gained by politeness and moderation than by violence. It was thus that Christ won the world to obedience to His authority. It was thus that Paul abrogated the Jewish law, putting an allegorical interpretation on its enactments. It is more expedient to declaim against those who abuse the Pope's authority than against the Popes themselves; and the same thing may be said of kings. Instead of holding the universe in contempt, we ought rather to endeavor to recall them to more sober studies; and regarding opinions which are too generally received to be rooted all at once from people's minds, it is better to reason upon them with close and convincing arguments than to deal in dogmatic assertions."

But I am more interested in the manuscript of which we talked so long since. I should like to see the little child whom I never could forget. If she reads some Greek, she must have found out much concerning the coins which I left with her. It appears too much to expect that those tiny fingers which grasped the coins should succeed in copying for me such a priceless manuscript. I shall think much of the writer as well as of the copy. Be sure that after this noisy quarrel of religion is passed by, we shall be rid of being called heretics, and nothing will be more valuable to me or the scholars than such a gift as your beloved daughter has proposed for me.

Half in anger, she folded it with graceless force, and was about to place it within her bosom again, when she paused.

"That is cold, cold light, if it is light at all. Ah! it is not so illumining as much that Erasmus did say, when he feared not the effects of the fires which make the light. A letter like that near my heart? No! it will make it yet more cold. Would that I could burn with a divine passion until the world should be inflamed! Poor daughter of a shepherd and peasant, a great life is not for me! I can only get manuscripts from disguised novices."

She was attracted by a footstep; then she saw her father approaching.

For the first time in many months, Gaspar Perrin was able to walk so far. Sickness, which had attacked him nearly a year before, had wasted his strong frame. But feeling now the inflow of strength from the lucent air, he had walked laboriously on, until he had made his way to the spot where his daughter stood; and breathing heavily, he stopped, leaned forward for an instant on his cane, as he said to the child whom he adored, —

" My dear one, you are not thinking about the goats, yet I do not blame you. That is the letter of Erasmus in your hand. One of the kids has fallen into the stream. It matters not, if things are going well with your mind; " and he commanded, as she suddenly started toward the stream, " Alke, stay, child ! "

Alke had entirely forgotten her task. Practical as she was, the severe commandments of what was and is called the impractical were upon her soul.

Is not the ideal, in whose presence what we call the practical must often be lost, a higher, broader sort of the practical?

At all events, this maiden had devoted one kid to the most practical problem of the Europe of her day; but the loss of that kid, so much like the many losses she had known, only made vivid the thought of her own life, with which she was struggling when Gaspar came near. The letter of Erasmus had come into her soul, like a great stone hurled into a placid pool; and the splashings had now gradually come to be a series of circles which were acquiring such order, as they broke one into the other, that out of it all she had fancied there might come a newly mirrored sky.

What was practical for Alke? Only the ideal.

Everybody loved her, because she was like an angel in that kind of saintliness which seems very distant to commonplace souls; everybody loved her quite as profoundly because she could do with so much more grace and gratefulness what everybody else in that community had to do, whether awkwardly and drudgingly or otherwise. Her sky was never so far above her earth that it did not communicate itself in starlight, sunlight, dewfall, and blue; and yet sometimes her earth never seemed as unsacred as when she looked away from it into the sky. Life, and not thought, solves this problem for every Alke; but she was then trying to think it out.

"No one," said the pale and weary father, whose strength rallied as he spoke to her, — "no one can sympathize with you as I do. You have in your soul the whole of this vast transformation which I feel is coming over all lands and peoples. Poor little girl, with an entire revolution in your bosom!" Gaspar's utterance was choked as they walked on together, — father and child.

He proceeded: "I have taught you, in this straitened life which you have had to live, the ideas which made Athens glorious and Rome imperial. They have come into your mind along with those sentiments which the monks could not kill, — the sentiments which made the Holy City of Jerusalem. Your life has been placed in a narrow vale, like a little field of rich ground; and now these rapid streams flow down from the ages upon it. Oh, my daughter, beloved! shall they entirely sweep the field away in their rush toward the sea, which even now they seem to have scented as no longer afar off, toward which they roll like wide rivers which have been long delayed?"

They were standing silently looking into each other's souls, through eyes glistening with tears. The goats were browsing among the flowers that had risen up to greet the sunshine, which lingered at the foot of a vast, snow-covered, frozen sea, whose gigantic edge dripped in tinkling drops into the mirror-like basin which held the

mountain shadows.   Alike felt it all, — the fine significance
of her father's sayings, and the infinite meaning of the
humblest life.

Latin and Greek, Cicero and Plato, had come to her
as to no other woman in the mountains.   Perhaps not a
half hundred men in all Southern Europe had so filled
their souls at classic fountains.   But she had something
else which these never gave her.   She had the intellectual outlook belonging to Christian culture.   Her deep
religious spirit had never allowed her to long for the
return of Europe to the pagan times.   Christianity without any crushing tyranny, religion without decaying for-
mularies, Christ without interposed barriers, had made
her thoroughly Christian.   Greece and Rome had given
to her soul a vision of the intellectual possibilities of
humanity, which lost none of its brilliant hopefulness
when she saw it all in the presence of the Christ.   Never
had she felt so surely that the next word for the world
was *reform*, as when she read the letter of Erasmus, and
saw his willingness to be content with merely intellectual
changes rather than have the world suffer a revolution, —
never since the hour in which her father had told her of
the report which some of the brethren had brought back
from Florence of Savonarola, who had allowed nothing
of the splendor of the Renaissance at Lorenzo's palace
to bewilder his moral eyesight.

But what could she do?

She had not forgotten her father's words as she begged
him to go homeward and rest.   As he turned to look
upon her before the mountain should hide her from his
gaze, his eyes saw not for tears.

"Poor girl!" he said, with a sigh which bore a hope.
"But she has spoken the truth.   Master Erasmus has
more interest in the manuscript of Virgil than in the
reform of the Church, unless it can come peaceably.
This cold world"—and the thin hand of Gaspar grasped

his walking-stick more tightly as he faltered upon the ice, — "ah, methinks this frozen world must have more light, but light with heat in it!"

Again he looked back. As Alke stood there, thinking of the huge movement which had already begun to make the proudest crowns tremble and the oldest institutions rock uneasily, she unconsciously made a suggestive picture. From the mighty glacier which ran backward amid the mountains for countless leagues, and which at any moment might desolate countless other leagues before it, there came a sharp report like the crack of doom. She looked upward to God through the murky sky which darkened the gray desolation of the crags; then she reached down and plucked a tender Lychnis flower which had been watered at the dripping edge of this awful sea of ice and snow. It was the picture of but one human career, with a power vast as that measureless glacier threatening to engulf it, while from the cold white breast its blooming life was inspired.

The Waldensian had but reached his cottage when two of the younger men of the fraternity, Gerard Pastre and Louis Savan, came up to the doorway, at whose approach Alke had with her own hands prepared, even in sight of the snow, a little garden-plot.

"Oh!" said Gaspar, "if my child had the sunshine which breaks from your faces, my brothers, this cold soil would grow food and blossoms at once."

"Do you think either of us looks as happy as we feel?" inquired Louis Savan, as he entered the home to which so often in Gaspar's time of sickness the councillors of the fraternity had come with news from the Reformers in Germany or Switzerland.

"You have come with thunder-clouds and winter on your faces so often," said the delighted peasant, as he drew near and searched the faces with renewed satisfaction, "that I look for the seeds in the pot yonder to break, and the trees outside to bloom at once if you looked upon them to-day. Where have you been with yourself, Gerard?"

As Gaspar addressed him, the young mountaineer, who had been in confidential relations with the Barbé, and had been the bearer of letters to and from the Reforming party in Germany, revealed his sense of special responsibility in his erect form; and as his lips parted, his very eye held within it the memory of a battle-field which, as it appeared, he had just left somewhere behind him.

"Here," said Gerard Pastre, "is a letter to you from God's noblest son, Martin Luther."

The hands which gave trembled quite as much as did the hands which received.

"And you saw him?" said Gaspar, with the emotions of a hero-worshipper struggling in his voice.

"Yes," answered Louis Savan, feeling glad to be able to contribute even second-hand items to the conversation, "he saw him, and he has come to tell us all about it; but our time is short. We must find our beloved Barbé. You may read the letter at your leisure. Much has happened since it was written. God bringeth forth nations in a day. Only a few of such days after the writing of the letter in your hand, and this same Martin Luther was at Worms; and long before that Gerard Pastre —"

"I was with Luther from the hour in which he received the summons from the emperor," said Gerard, who knew of the tremor in the soul of Louis Savan.

Gaspar was all attention. He could hear from the warm-hearted Luther at last! Erasmus was light, revealing the tinder and the need of its being burned up; Luther — so did Gaspar believe — was both light and fire. He saw in the flame within Gerard Pastre's eye, that that fire had communicated itself to at least one soul; there was a conflagration ahead. Oh, how cold seemed the letter of Erasmus, as, half afraid to speak, Gaspar thought of it, and the maiden down yonder at the foot of the glacier.

"I must have my daughter?" he averred in inquiring tones.

"Alke!" said both Gerard and Louis Savan. "Yes, truly."

"She must hear your story," said the father, fond, proud, and true. "She is down by the torrent with the goats. She must hear it all, — beloved one she is! I can walk the distance again;" and he rose only to sink back into the high-backed oaken chair, worn out by his illness, and exhausted in his felicity and hope.

As soon as Gaspar had revived, Louis Savan left the cottage, and hurried toward the glacier's edge to fetch the daughter to a cottage whose roof then seemed not far from the illimitable sky beyond.

Luther! — what a theme of conversation, what a star of hope, what a sword of triumph had that name been for months to the Waldensian household!

"I will read the letter to you now. They will come presently, and Alke may read it again for herself," said Gerard, anxious to behold the joy it was sure to give to the sick man.

"She knows the writing of the fiery Martin. Let us be thankful for fire as well as for light," added Gaspar. "Let me hear it."

To GASPAR PERRIN:

I am on my way to Charles V., Emperor. A safe conduct has been promised me, by request of God's servant, Frederic. I have no confidence in princes; for I remember the promises made to John Hus of Constance. But we journey onward. The imperial herald, who rides before us, often looks backward; and the Devil is in his eye. I cannot decline to go, for I believe God; and I believe, also, that this thing resolutely done will be for His glory.

I thank your minister for sending Gerard Pastre to me, with good news of your faith and good works. God will reward His saints. I am now out of sight of the loved towers of Wittenberg. Melancthon has promised me to stand by the truth. I am not out of sight of God Almighty; and He has promised protection and succor. Erasmus, whom you have ceased to follow, loses credit with me every day. Two years since, he wrote me exhorting quietude. God's cause cannot pause for his good taste. Friends can do much for my comfort. Gerard Pastre is a solace and a continual joy unto me. But it may be that he will have to leave me at Leipsic. I know not what may happen. God will not leave me. I write this to you, my faithful friend, feeling that if I die on my way to Charles V., you may know that I was killed on my way to heaven. Murderers can only hasten my appearance, by the sacrifice of His Son, at His throne.

In love of Christ,

MARTIN LUTHER.

CHAPTER II.

GERARD'S ACCOUNT OF WORMS.

"So lay the world.   So lie the frozen fields
 Before the dawning of the Arctic day,
 Sick for the sunshine, loathing wearily
 The cold, illusive gleam of fitful lights
 That toy with darkness ; then up leaps the sun,
 And routs those mocking lights, and changes all."

AS Gaspar touched the precious manuscript, — more precious to his soul than that manuscript of Virgil, — Alke, radiant and beautiful as a morning cloud, came to the side of her father.   Saluting Gerard Pastre as she kissed the tears out of Gaspar's hollow cheeks, she said, —

"I know it, I know it all, — all but the story of the Diet at Worms.   Tell me ! "

The great, deep, expectant eyes, reflecting the struggle of storm and sunlight, looked up into those of Gerard Pastre as he spoke.   Gerard's long fingers were often pushed through masses of almost yellow hair, and his feet moved as though he were repeating the long march from Wittenberg to Worms.   The suit he wore was stained and weather-worn.   His heavy boots contrasted with the less coarse foot-wear with which he had usually been seen in La Torre, as the rivers of Germany with the silvery splendor of the Pelice.   His voice seemed more masculine, and his great hands clinched whatever came in their way, as he proceeded with his story.

Every step was described. The rough but intelligent mountaineer was eloquent in his description. Now and then the clear blue eyes glistened, and the strong utterance faltered a little; and at the last no one had a tearless eye, as they found themselves standing breathless, each with attention riveted on the speaker, while his stalwart body looked like one of their own mountains smitten with thunderbolts yet defying the artillery of the skies; and concluding his tale, he placed one foot, as it seemed, upon the eternal truth; the other advanced into what appeared to be the certain future, and cried out, until the hills gave echo, —

" I cannot and I will not retract. Here I stand. I can do no other. May God help me ! " So Luther had spoken.

Everything about him seemed interesting; and each word concerning Martin Luther was an invaluable line that helped to complete the picture which each had made of the young Reformer.

" He is the fire," said Gaspar, as his swift-footed mind flitted along the route which had just been described to them as Luther's path to the Diet of Worms, — " Martin Luther is the fire, and woe to whatever may be consumed in its flame ! "

Louis Savan was a little inclined to be captious, even though his soul was entranced with the scene which Gerard had briefly recited to them. Fastidious and careful of proprieties, he had always urged his fellow-Waldensians to avoid violence. Luther was a trifle coarse in the picture which had just been made in his mind. He ventured to say to Gerard, —

" Did you not deem his sayings rough ? "

" As rough as a battle-axe in the hand of a single unprotected follower of Christ, when every friend of the

Devil, from the emperor to the theologian, was thirsting for his blood," said Gerard Pastre. "He never looked so godlike as when he sent a message saying to his absent friend: 'Christ lives, and I will go to Worms to brave the gates of hell and the powers of the air.'"

"And he never faltered?" inquired Alke, as she stopped cutting the loaf of acorn-bread which she was preparing for the hungry visitors.

"Never! Spalatin urged him to decline entering Worms. He told him of the peril; and Martin said only this: 'To Worms I was called, and to Worms I must go. And were there as many devils there as there are tiles upon the roofs, yet would I enter that city!'"

Louis Savan, a little anxious for the dignitaries, inquired again: "Did he respect those rulers whose power is always, as you know, from above?"

"And you a follower of Christ, whom the rulers of His time put to death! Ah, Louis Savan! Seckingen asked him to come to his castle at Ebernburg to do all and to answer all, through the confessor of the emperor. Luther replied: 'Not to Ebernburg, but to Worms have I been summoned. If the imperial confessor have aught to say to me, let him seek me there.'"

"Is not that enough for you, Louis?" asked Gaspar, with a smile.

"Nay," answered Louis; "I would convert unto us, rather than repel, even kings."

"Our cause is with men who think, and kings are usually ignorant," ventured Alke.

"The youth, the thought, the hope of the world are ours," added Gerard, as with his half-swallowed mouthful of bread he took some goat's milk, and proceeded dramatically: "Students shouted for him at Weimar, as old Leipsic and Nuremberg had greeted him. Forty horsemen came with Jonas Hessus and Crotus to take him to his old convent at Erfurt, where the prior welcomed him."

" But I want to feel that he has a heart as well as a head," urged Louis.

" Ah, Louis Savan! you would have wept full plenteously had you seen him, as I did, at Eisenach. His memory unsealed his heart. There his tears flowed in memory of the loved Cotta, and his great heart spoke tenderly."

" There is fire in that kind of light," interposed Gaspar, who was now lying on the couch near the window, looking out on the snow-clad heights, looking also into the future.

Louis Savan was not a conservative, if by that is meant a reactionary. He was only one of those persons whose minds never see truth unaccompanied with good society or unadorned with good taste without becoming just a little offended, either at the truth for appearing so unattended, or at the people and circumstances whose absence seems so unfortunate.

Gerard Pastre, on the contrary, like Gaspar, was a radical. He was never quite so sure that a proposition had truth in it as when everybody but the untitled had pounced upon it. He therefore took no little pleasure in saying to the listeners, — each of whom he knew to be right on the main question, —

" Even the barons seem to be with him. As Martin passed up the hall, a gauntlet touched his shoulder. Luther looked up into the face of a great fellow who was covered with steel. ' Pluck up thy spirit, little monk!' said the baron. ' Some of us here have seen warm work in our time ; but by my troth, nor I nor any knight in this company ever needed a stouter heart than thou needest at this time. If thou hast faith in these doctrines of thine, little monk, go on, in the name of God !' "

" Ha, ha !" laughed Gaspar, whose weakness made his humor more impressive.

" Did he appear *little ?* " asked Alke.

" Nay," answered Gerard, who stood over six feet at that moment ; " though he seemed little enough, often, as I walked by his side. But he was big enough when he replied to the baron and said, ' Yes, in the name of God, in the name of God, forward ! ' He seemed little enough when yonder, " — and Gerard pointed toward an old cupboard, which looked very little like a king's seat,— " yonder sat the emperor ; around him were knights and nobles without number. Closer still to the imperial Charles V. were archbishops and ministers of State ; at his right and left hand were princes of the empire. Martin looked little enough when he went up between the richly ornamented ranks. He had only a coarse, brown frock with which to outdazzle the gleaming armor. I tell you, Louis Savan, you would have been ashamed of his clothes. There he was, ' little ' enough, you must believe, — the son of a poor miner before a sovereign who rules half of this world ; but he was big enough when he said to me, who was a little worried : ' Gerard Pastre, I stand for what all your Waldensian fathers have believed and preached. God is with me. Fear not ! ' "

" Ah," said Louis Savan, " then even you winced a little. Ah, Gerard ! "

" Why," said Gerard, " I was afterward ashamed. The corrupt Church may always excel us in that kind of appearances. He was always majestic at majestic moments, and oftentimes he made the moment itself majestic. Everybody's eyes were on him. As we went through the city gate, I could hear them say, ' That is Luther, — that monk in the brown frock ! ' The court fool tried to be sarcastic, and waving his torch and crucifix, cried out, ' Ecce advenit quem expectamus in tenebris.' Alke, you know what it means? "

" Yes," said the maiden ; " ' Behold he comes whom in the darkness we have expected.' "

"Well," continued Gerard, "in every hour like that he was sublime. Crowds did not bewilder him, though the house-tops were filled. I saw him once silent, and methought tears were on his cheek, when an old soldier laid his hand upon his shoulder, and said: 'Poor monk, poor monk! thou art now going to make a nobler stand than I, or any other captain, has ever made on the bloodiest field. But if thy cause is just and thou art sure of it, go forward, in God's name, and fear nothing! God will not forsake thee.'"

"Nor will God forsake him, so long as he walks in that path," said Gaspar, wisely shaking his head in earnest affirmation.

Louis Savan was annoyingly silent. Alke busied herself at domestic duties, turning her fond eyes toward her father as he spoke, and often quitting her task inopportunely to get closer to the expressive glance of Gerard, who was now walking over the floor, and re-creating for the complete demolition of Louis Savan's doubt the scene of that memorable second day at the Diet of Worms. Gerard was somewhat irritated that Louis had not even yet, in the course of the relation of these events, cried out "Bravo!" and he had even begun to suspect that his description of the scene had suffered, because in his pointing to that antique cupboard as the throne of Charles V., Louis Savan had lost his vision of awe-inspiring princes and full-armored knights which he would have him imagine, among the saucepans and pots which lay in front, too prominent to require an effort of fancy to behold them.

"Courage?" cried out Gerard, so that every one attended upon the opening of his trembling lips, — "courage? Did you ask if his courage was lodged with a faith equal to a long strain and the opposition of the kings of the earth? I wish that every coward among us had been at Worms on that second day."

"What led Martin to postpone his reply which the king asked for on the first day, as you told me?" inquired Louis, still desirous of proof.

"Ah!" replied Gerard, "I can tell you there was never a bolder wisdom than his at that moment on the first day. He was asked two questions: 'Do you acknowledge these books?' and, 'Are you prepared to retract what they contain?' The first he answered with almost abrupt swiftness. It would have been grossly precipitant in even such a scholar, it would have seemed in such a presence as though passion lorded it over reason, had the monk as hastily answered the second question. It was a better wisdom than that which fears the lapse of time, and it ruled him. No one can say now that Martin Luther cannot hold his tongue. He has a temper of unusual heat, but his wisdom gave him such self-command that all the sparks from that flame went up the chimney. When everybody thought he had wavered, the next day he came back to give twice the power to his refusal to retract, because what they thought was irresolution or indecision was found to be deliberation and firmness in holding to his thought. I could see how it affected even the emperor. At the end of the first day's conference with the monk, his Majesty said, 'Truly that man will never persuade me to turn heretic!' and at the beginning of the conference of the second day, the emperor looked intently upon Martin, set his large, square underjaw, as if in determined opposition, looked over to the chancellor of the Elector of Treves, and shaking his head, confessed his astonishment. When Luther was done speaking, I, who stood only near enough to catch a few of his words, heard the emperor say, amid his wrath and awe, 'Unbroken courage! unquailing heart!'"

"But," said the chorus, — none more full of growing admiration than Louis Savan, — "tell us all, — the monk's speech, the reply, the —"

"Oh! he is light with fire behind it," added Gaspar Perrin, sure that he had a good, even if it were an over-worked figure of speech, whereat Louis Savan's enthusiasm roused Gerard, and he resumed his story.

"Martin Luther knew his audience. The chief personage within the walls was the emperor, master of the richest dominions, East and West. He had already treated the monk with insulting silence. Often on the route had Martin told me of the letter which he sent to his Serene Majesty, truly informing him of the greatness of his power and the hope which sat awaiting his august command. Martin had not forgotten that the emperor had left that letter unanswered, and that his Serene Majesty thought it a wiser statesmanship which led him to intercept Cardinal Wolsey and Henry VIII. on their way to feast with and flatter Francis I. on the Golden Field, than to attend to the demand of Europe for reform. I could not help thinking, as I stood there, within hearing, by the side of a bold man who had told me about the magnificence of what they say was 'a Field of the Cloth of Gold,' that Martin Luther remembered then how the kings of the earth do yet create tinselled pageants, and with tumultuous acclaim do yet lie to one another in the name of peace, while the kingdom of God cometh without observation. Ah! it did seem, as I once looked into the pale face of the young emperor, that he saw Somewhat in majesty behind the brown-frocked monk.

"It had been a great audience for Martin if the emperor had been solitary. The emperor had broken many a lance, but had never before met such a foe. But there was Aleander; his very presence made Martin pity his Majesty, who seemed to be looking, as he sat in thoughtful melancholy, first toward Elector Frederic, Luther's protector, from whom Charles V. had received the crown; and then toward Aleander, who had urged his Imperial Majesty to drag Luther to the Diet. Whenever Martin's eye flamed toward Aleander, he seemed to feel the embarrassment which could be known only to a papal nuncio, who on his way to that scene had beheld the growing triumph of the ideas whose condemnation he sought. Astonished at the influence of Luther, he had been unable often to find even an inn which would shelter him. But now the Roman courtier would look at the emperor with a proud hope, — a hope which seemed to decline on his face, as he remembered how nearly the confessor John Glapio had ruined his intolerant programme against Martin, and how often his Majesty had grown, cold in the cause of the prosecution. Martin appeared to seek his wandering eye as he entered ; indeed, Martin had told me that Aleander had pursued him with incredible fury. He called him that 'apostate' nuncio ; and yet Martin knew that he was very eloquent. Luther did not forget that in spite of the fact that on his way into the Diet Aleander had had the breath knocked out of him by the usher who hated his cause, the nuncio had swept that assembly with his passionate oratory. The monk seemed to be aware that the hour of another's eloquence had come.

"Before he began to speak he paused, as if becoming surer of his feet ; his self-command amazed me, as I saw him look upon those whose faces he recognized at once. Among dukes, landgraves, margraves, counts, and barons, he selected those to whom he was anxious to speak important words. There were as many archbishops as there were electors and dukes, sixty in all ; but he would turn swiftly as he thundered forth his words, from the Archbishop Albert, whom he knew to be hesitant and excited, toward Duke George of Saxony, who, he was aware, hated him with violence, and yet had spoken to the Diet against the indulgences and profanities of Rome without trembling in a single syllable. Guards and courtiers swelled the number of an auditory which leaned forward breathless, as the fearless Martin's eyes swept with a glance across the clouded countenances of the nuncios of his Holiness, who had flocked hither, and who fluttered about like foul birds disappointed of their carrion ; and Luther fixed their gaze for a moment upon the Archduke Ferdinand, the brother of the king. He fairly shook the building with a consciousness of the inevitable supremacy of the truth against all kings and popes, as he cried out : 'If I were to recant, what should I do but strengthen tyranny?' and he looked a thunderbolt into the open gaze of the Spanish grandees, who had come, as he saw, to institute in Luther's beloved Germany an inquisition as murderous as their own. It did seem that the Duke of Alva and his two sons would smite the agitated monk as he spoke.

"I was close to Bucer, the young Dominican, chaplain to the Elector ; and he was all a-trembling. He whispered, 'Would that Martin had come to Ebernburg and met the confessor of his Majesty !' Just then Martin, as if remembering, as I believe he did, that Paul of Armsdorf, confessor and grand chamberlain to Charles V., had, in his fear of Luther, tried to persuade him to confer, as Bucer did propose, in the castle of Ebernburg, — just then did the monk with a blazing phrase smite him and the one who sat next to him, the Bishop of Palermo and Chancellor of Flanders, who had desired the emperor to break every promise of safety ; and he shouted the words : 'I will defend myself, after the example of Jesus Christ !'"

"What then did Bucer say?" asked Alke, who was triumphing with Luther.

"Hush, my child ! Tell us all, Gerard !" said Gaspar, who was resting on his elbows and was entirely oblivious of pain.

"Every moment marked a victory, not more of language than of action, in this solid man's unpretentious eloquence. Without knowing it, he drew such a contrast between the power of the unattended truth and the weakness of decorated error as never one saw before. While the Pope's adherents were boiling with anger because the emperor, or at least the chancellor, did not interrupt him, Martin's eyes burned into the very soul of John Eck, the chancellor of the Archbishop of Treves, whose great voice had pronounced the charges against him, and who insisted that Luther should answer as an orator, not as a writer; so that, as the monk pleaded, 'Prove to me that I am in error,' the same John Eck looked as if he was wishing it had come in ink rather than in such startling eloquence.

"He feared nothing, though his friends were few. Chiefest was Spalatin, the trusted counsellor of the elector, who had informed Luther, at the first, of Frederic's friendship, who had sent him in advance a note of the articles which he might retract, who at last had become alarmed and had said, 'Abstain from entering Worms!' Once Martin looked straight at us all. Bugenhagen, who had joined us, having escaped death at Treptow; Amsdorff, and John Schurff, the law professor; Peter Suaven, the Dane, — a boy even yet is he; Justus Jonas, above us all, beloved by Luther, — it is not wonderful that Erasmus has spoken so well of him; — there we stood, as near as possible to the Duke Eric of Brunswick, who had provided in a silver vase some Eimbeck beer for Martin; while by him was Duke Brandeburg, who wanted Luther's ashes at once for the Rhine. Capito, the counsellor of the Archbishop of Mentz, who had played fast and loose with Aleander and our cause, was between. Martin saw his friends, then his half-hearted admirers, then his foes, like light shading off into darkness. He looked with supreme calm upon us all; and while we paused even in our attention to him, he looked over the deputies of the

free cities, beyond the imperial officers who had conducted him, and turned the volume of fire within those
eyes, which I shall never forget, upon three who stood
together, — the Imperial Herald, the Marshal of the
Empire, and Father Glapio.

"Gaspar Strum had presented himself at Wittenberg,
and summoned him to Worms; and on the way thither,
Luther had won his admiration, and the monk dreamed of
the conversion of this herald of Charles V. Ulric Pap-
penheim abided with the two counsellors of the elector at
the hotel of the Knight of Rhodes, saw Luther alight
from his wagon, and had told him amid confusion to
speak no word until questions were put ; and now Luther
saw that this hereditary Marshal of the Empire was under the thrall of his utterance.   Father Glapio, confessor
of the emperor, and most adroit of ecclesiastics, had been
frightened at the peril of the imperial throne, before this
monk ; Charles V. had trusted his policies, and now
Luther had astonished the Diet.   Luther saw the terror
upon the face of that awful monk.   Martin seemed to
have forgotten the emperor, who sat white-faced and agitated.   Luther's cause disdained monarchs ; it touched
the commonest of the crowd within, and Martin felt the
power of the greater crowd without.

"I marked him well when again it sounded without,
as though the Spanish troops had attacked the two thousand and more who ran by Luther's side as he entered
the city.   Still his eyes were on those three men, as the
Italians and Belgians swarmed against the town hall, crying out their impatience ; or when the people gazing from
the windows above the gardens or from the house-tops
defying all orders of the guards, caught up the hope or
fear that Luther had acceded to the scheme, and had
agreed to retract only what they termed his 'errors
in doctrine.'   At that moment these three men within
were enslaved to that piercing glance ; and Luther, dis-

daining a merely political reformation, was assuming command even of the emperor, as he at last said, with all the power of God in his utterance : ' I neither can nor will retract anything. I stand here. I can say no more. God help me ! Amen !' "

Gaspar was sitting bolt upright when Gerard concluded his story.

" Our leader — fiery, impetuous, wise, and fearless — our leader is the German monk ! Has the Barbé heard of this ? "

" Nay ! " said Gerard ; " I stopped to bring to you the letter. We are on our way to the Barbé at once."

" May God bless you and him together ! " said Gaspar.

" Gerard, the German monk's eloquence has made you an orator," remarked Alke, as she gave him some wine. " Be sure you tell this whole story to the Barbé ; the beloved man may have wit enough to choose you for coadjutor."

" Will you paint a parchment for me ? " asked the stalwart young Waldensian, as he bowed a farewell.

CHAPTER III.

A VICTORY AND A DEFEAT.

*A king's face
Should give grace.*
Favorite quotation of Henry VIII.

BEFORE the events just narrated had occurred, every sensitive soul at the French capital had detected one of those tremors running along the ground which indicate the action and interaction of forces of the first significance. Late one evening in 1522, Ami himself was standing alone in that vast open space in front of the Palais de Justice, lost in the thoughts which thronged his mind. The world of men and the world of books lay close together in his thinking, for they almost overlapped in his experience. His eyes had just beheld again the statue of Pharamond, standing with those of the rulers of France, beneath the Gothic vaulting of the Palais. He was on his way from those gilded walls to perform a service for Francis I. The past and the present were meeting in his imagination.

The spot which had almost fascinated him was that which an old monk told him had once been strewn with the fragments of one of the bulls which the industrious anti-pope Benedict was in the habit of fulminating at an hour less significant than this. Ami was almost a heretic.

Indeed, he was quite sure of being confirmed in his doubts as to the authority of the Holy See over his conscience, until that flood of hate which rose in him at the thought of Vian washed his convictions away, or until the report that Vian had himself dared to question the claims of his Holiness made him desire to remain a radical papist. At this juncture he had forgotten Vian; and he remembered only Benedict and his contemporaries.

" This, then," he said to his soul, " is the Holy Papacy in whose absolute authority I am to believe. When I first saw these huge buildings, and confessed the might of the Holy Church, I could not understand why my own father, if he were not an ignoramus, could have lived and died protesting. The soul, and the soul's right to its own powers are greater, however, than the Church. The Church is an institution. Institutions are meant to be servants, not masters of humanity. When I think of this, and reflect how many Benedicts and his like my father was expected to believe in and to reverence, I cannot understand why, if he were not an ignoramus, he could do anything but protest."

Ami had come near to pronouncing the word " protestant," — a word which, seven years later, at the Diet of Spires, should have its public birth-hour. He had no dream that it could ever signify such a revolution and such a history as lay immediately before him.

A self-respectful, intelligent soul alone with God, in the regal enjoyment of its own powers, clad with sovereignty over its own divinest energies, honest, fearless, and free, dwarfing the magnificence of a Palais de Justice, overshadowing the miraculous grace and chiselled grandeur of this superb structure by his own solitary and self-assertive manliness, — there is no such scene in the world. At such times one beholds the primacy of the soul.

> " For out of thought's interior sphere
> These wonders rose to upper air."

Here was man, richer, greater, and more authoritative than the splendid but enslaving circumstances which ancestors and predecessors had left to be his inspiration or his entanglement.   Here the Son of man was lord also of one of those revered institutions whose age or whose vastness always silences spiritual mediocrity.   Here was humanity finding in its own breast a court before which in a few years, as never before, tradition, relic, ecclesiastic, statesman, tiara, and crown should be fearlessly tried. In one soul at least the principle of Protestantism was born.

Not gifted, as was Vian, with philosophic prevision, Ami saw not the tendency within protesting toward individualism, which had frightened the English monk.   Not less, however, was there of certainty and sympathy in that faculty of historic imagination before whose eye the moon unveiled within the immense front of the building which he had just left, an incalculably valuable past.

No true child of the future underestimates the past, out of whose dark root and shaggy stem the blossoming future comes.   But Ami had other problems at hand.

"Have I been sent again to obtain a ring which shall rob another man of his wife and bring another Mme. de Chateaubriand hither?" queried he.

It could not be.   But the thought of Mme. de Chateaubriand led him to the indulgences.   That led him to the increasing sufferings of the Reformers, — Louis de Berquin, Lefevre, and Farel.   The moon again broke like a revelation upon the Palais de Justice.   It seemed very great.

As Ami looked at the colossal pile, and was conscious of the infantile freshness of his ideas, it occurred to him that beneath that shadow many a young man had foolishly set himself against what seemed obsolescent authority, and found it, instead, an ever-enlarging stream.

" This building," said he, " will probably echo with the

death-song of this movement, at whose head is only a German monk who once had to sing for his food."

Ami could not see that before 1619 the Palais de Justice would be an ash-heap, and the Reformation the conqueror of Europe.

Back again did his mind go to the serene confidence of Lefevre, Farel, and Louis de Berquin, the scholar. Then he remembered that he had just bent the knee and crossed himself in front of the figure of the Virgin, before which stood a statue of Louis XI. kneeling. In his new-found manhood and now, he would have stood on his feet, and deemed himself the more a man because of the man-child whom the Virgin bore. He wanted to return and to tell the few workmen who still lingered to admire those fine fantasies wrought in marble, with which the ornate chapel was being further enriched, that they need not return to toil and carve on the morrow.

"'And the veil of the temple was rent in twain from the top to the bottom,' — that," said Ami, "I have pondered over with Master Lefevre, Louis de Berquin, and William Farel. Ah, yes! when the Son of Man wrought man's redemption, the day of the temple had gone. Man alone became supremely sacred."

And Ami reflected upon that other word: "And I saw no temple there."

"Did not Luther's greatest teacher, Augustine, say, 'The true shekinah is man'? Heaven, wherever it may be, and whatever it may be, is that state in which man has found his rightful supremacy. Institutions are but instrumentalities wherewith to upbuild man. As the authority of man, on whose heart God has written His law in the love of Christ, grows, the institutions which he made for himself as he developed will fall away; and we shall see no temple there. Every institution from this time forth will be less material, more spiritual. The spirit of man will at last be God's only temple. I remember now

that Master Louis Berquin has quoted often to me,
'First, the natural; afterward, the spiritual.'"

There was a light around and within Ami more fascinating, more brilliant, than the moonlight.

Could it be that this errand upon which the king had
sent Ami was another Pandora's box of evils?

The feelings which led him to be anxious about it had
made him defiant in the presence of enormous buildings.
They had been inspired by the recollection that on that
day, one year before, the Sorbonne, under the leadership
of Beda, had ordered Luther's writings to be burned publicly.   That night the discouraged Ami had gone to sleep
upon Astrée's bosom, as they lingered too long in the balcony; and he awoke dreaming that the Syndics had compelled him to pile fagots about a beautiful woman who
was a heretic, whose scorched face at length he discovered to be Astrée's.

"May the saints preserve my soul from such another
dream as that!" said Ami, when a few hours after, he
met Nouvisset.   "But I am the king's friend, — yes, the
king's friend!"

"Do not expect to be happy," said the lame knight,
"so long as you tolerate that infernal passion of jealousy
in your bosom."

For hours these words echoed in the young knight's
breast.

"I am not jealous of Duprat, or Louise of Savoy, or
the Sorbonne; it is impossible," reassuringly mused the
young man.

But it was impossible.   Ami's unregulated soul was unable to permit another to influence one whom he loved
as Ami loved his king.

"So long as I love God, I must hate iniquity," said
the conscientious knight, who did not know how easily
conscience may be beguiled into service with self-
assertion.

Alone again in the moonlight, he thought of the king's disquieted realm; and it was not strange that his self-consciousness grew rather arrogant as he reflected that every tendency, which was leading the France of 1522 downward, had been met by his opposition.

As long ago as in the early months of 1516, shortly after the visit to Bologna, Francis I. had tried to persuade Ami that the Concordat was an unmixed blessing. The knight had never hesitated in his replies.

"The Chancellor Duprat sees ahead of him nothing but the ten archbishops, nearly a hundred bishops, and five times as many abbots, who must now supplicate the throne. Parliament — good Sire! be patient with me — "

"Only your service at Marignano and the saying of the astrologer keep me so, Ami!" said the king, who was greatly irritated. "Proceed about Parliament."

"Parliament," continued Ami, who never lost his temper with Francis I., "sees something else; and that is that your Majesty's powers are too nearly absolute."

"I will answer you, Ami, as I answered the deputies: 'I know that there are in my Parliament good sort of men, wise men; but I also know there are turbulent and rash fools. I have my eye upon them; and I am informed of the language they dare to hold about my conduct. I am king, as my predecessors were; and I mean to be obeyed, as they were.' "

"You have great confidence in the wisdom of your chancellor, Sire!"

"Did I not tell the deputies," vociferated Francis I., "that a hundred of their heads had been, seven months and more, painfully getting up these representations, which my chancellor blew to pieces in a few days? There is but one king in France. I have done all I could to

restore peace to my kingdom; and I will not allow nulli-
fication here of that which I brought about with so much
difficulty at Marignano and Bologna. My Parliament
would set up for a Venetian senate; let it confine its
meddling to the cause of justice, which is worse adminis-
tered than it has been for a hundred years. I ought,
perhaps, to drag it about at my heels, like the Grand
Council, and watch more closely over its conduct."

The outburst was medicinal. Ami was serene. From
that hour the King of France had begun to learn a better
wisdom; and as the knight thought again of the Concordat, he made a note of the fact that never did his
sovereign so much as now appear to desire his opinions
as to the real interests of France.

A little later, however, the king showed great ill-temper
at finding that Ami and the Duchesse d'Alençon had
been helping on the influence of Louis de Berquin the
scholar, and William Farel the preacher; also was he
provoked because they had given aid to Briconnet, who
had now become offensive to Louise of Savoy, in his
efforts to reform the Holy Church.

"You, Sire, have changed your attitude toward the
scholars," said Ami, who remembered the day when his
Majesty said: "I want to favor those who teach us. I
wish to have able men to live in my country."

"Not seriously," answered his Majesty. "Scholars
are harmless enough so long as they are in the minority;
but they are flocking about Louis Berquin and William
Farel in clouds."

"Shall the fact that truth and learning are growing
make you despise their champions?" asked the unnerved knight.

"Ami, your goodness is like the art of a virtuoso, as
the Italians say. I like our poet Clement Marot."

"So also do I; but he writes — "

"Love poems for our 'Marguerite of Marguerites'?"

" I see only the Psalms of David, which they translate and make into rhymes."

" Ah, Ami, do you really love Astrée ? "

The king laughed so coarsely that Ami heard within it a sneer at Reformers, and his Majesty's contempt for a pure affection. They separated.

" How far, for the sake of France, dare I stretch the tie which binds my king's soul to the astrologer's words ? " said Ami to Astrée, whom he sought instantly upon the king's departure. "How long may I count upon the friendship of the Duchesse d'Alençon, — his 'darling Marguerite'?   I will load every power with all that it may carry, in order to ally his Majesty with the cause of reform."

Astrée's eyes were soft and brilliant with happy tears. Her hand was unsteady, as she stood close to the tall knight and lost her white and jewelled fingers in his thick, long hair. She had trembled for their love often-times, as she followed his thoughts from place to place, and could determine from the stern eye of flame that they had reached that desolating spot, — " the Field of the Cloth of Gold."   Recently, however, Ami had been so under the influence of the simple eloquence of Farel, or the unaffected goodness of his teacher Louis Berquin, that it appeared improbable that ever again the word " Vian " could disturb his spirit.   Now she even believed it safe for her to tell him of what she felt he ought to know, since his mind was so set toward identifying itself with the Reformers.   They were beginning to suffer ignominy and outrage.   Ami's future course ought to be begun with the consciousness of everything which could bear upon it.

" Surely," she said, as the Duchesse d'Alençon told her of the letter of Erasmus to Francis I., — " surely there can be no plan to torture us. Vian a Reformer?   If it be true, Ami must know it."

Astrée read the letter for herself, over and over again. It was from Erasmus to Francis I. These words were only a portion of its message : —

"Of that most promising scholar, Vian, who was of Glastonbury Abbey, and of whom I wrote you, I must say this much, — while as a scholar he would serve admirably as professor in the University, it is to be considered also that other matters may unfit him for such a life. Master Thomas More writes me, that, since the meeting of your Majesty with the Sovereign of England at Guisnes, the monk has suffered from an hallucination, — such as young monks do have seldom, — the vision of a beauteous damsel. He has also looked so favorably upon the Reforming party that the abbot, if indeed Vian is yet at Glastonbury, anticipates in him at any time a turbulent Lutheran."

Within an hour after Astréc had read these words, the face of Ami was pressed against her own. It was hot, and his eyes were restless.

"I have just seen a most atrocious machine, — cruelty invented it," said Ami, as he sighed. "Duprat has made ready to send it to the mountains for the extirpation of heresy. One victim has already perished upon it. It is most incredible that men should seek to drag convictions out of the soul, as the bones are crushed, the muscles torn away, and human blood spurting over it all. Oh, it is an awful spectacle ! "

Ami had beheld only one of those engines of death which were so soon to be used by the Holy Church.

Astrée was calm, for she believed this to be the moment which she desired. "If," she thought, — "if he is so roused against the wrong done by the Church, he will not likely allow anything to unsettle his purpose. It may be that in this better passion of protesting zeal the ugly fiend which besets his soul — jealousy — will perish. The saints help me ! "

Slowly and painfully, even with the blushing embarrassment which a beautiful girl must feel at such a state of affairs, did she proceed to her task and perform it. She recited the letter concerning Vian.

"And you," cried Ami, his cheeks white with rage,— "and you knew it before this moment? Why?—why, Astrée—" Ami was transformed. His breath faltered at her name. "Why?" half whispered, half shrieked, hissed, and lingered in the palate of the knight. His fine teeth glistened, and his mobile lips quivered, as he still uttered the word "Why?" "Why should *you* have had to do with telling me of him?"

Ami's eyes were only the eyes of a jealous man. He could see nothing in the universe that did not connect itself with Vian, and depend upon the detested name. Vian had already ruined his life, as Ami believed. To complete the disaster, he had made the men of the Reform an abominable band, by his presence among them. There appeared no place for an explanation. Most hideous of all was the reflection that he was dreaming of Astrée,— an hallucination!

Astrée tried in vain to assure him. He could hear nothing but that clatter of horse's hoofs on the "Field of the Cloth of Gold."

"Do you not even see me?" cried Astrée.

He saw nothing but Vian saving Astrée there,— the dust, and Astrée in Vian's arms.

Probably she could touch his conscience. "What! Ami, you do not mean the less to despise the method of that cruel machine of torture, because one whom you hate has perhaps also despised it?" she said.

"Torture!" cried he, as he threw her slender loveliness aside,— "torture! If I go not with the Reform, the cruel machine is my weapon; if I go, the— I cannot think, Astrée."

No, Vian, no jealous man is able to think in straight lines. Reasonless, he seeks rest also, but finds none.

Two terrible things — Vian and that rack — were all he saw; and he was mute as his soul swayed between them. He took hold of the sobbing girl at his feet, and lifting her with tenderness, went out into the deep night, from which the moon hid herself with clouds.

Not long after that wretched night, Ami and Astrée were confronted with other questions. Did she find a solution for that earlier problem? Yes; and it lay in the self-respect which she urged upon Ami, — a self-respect which compelled in some ameliorating measure Ami's respect for her.

"Knight and friend of his Majesty that you are!" she said, as into the darkness he bore her, "never again shall those lips touch mine own, until I am assured that you trust me sufficiently to care nothing for Vian. Yes, I will pronounce his name. If I had not adored you, Ami, your injustice to him and your distrust of me had driven me to love its sound. You have distrusted me — "

"Never, Astrée, never!" Ami saw the flash of a radiant self-respect in the black eyes, — a flash whose gleam shot through the darkness.

"So long as you believe that Vian's imagined interest in me could possibly make a transformation in me or even interest me, you have failed to honor my love for you. Never " — Ami had lifted her nearer to his breast, and now he saw the trembling lips so near — "never, until you respect me, Ami," she whispered.

He had never known before the sorrow of not being able to manifest his love. It quickened his sense of Astrée's loveliness. She was a necessity to his existence. Oh, how lovable she seemed!

But nothing in love's armory is strong enough, until it is stronger than any foe it may meet. Astrée's eyes were telling him these things, — eyes so strongly commanding, intrenched behind tears. At length the victory was hers, and therefore his. In one long embrace they forgot Vian.

A victory, indeed, though only temporary; for no soul for whom the Infinite Love has not done more than this, is free from the marauding of such a passion.

CHAPTER IV.

A VIRTUOSO'S STATESMANSHIP.

" Never a thought o'er the boundary flying,
Never a thought as the clouds swing by."

DESPITE the fact that Ami's intense passion in this instance soon exhausted itself, leaving however, as it had each time before, a wider field in his soul for its fury when it should come again, his troubles of a less lawless and more personal kind were multiplying.

"A virtuoso!"—this was the only term of implied contempt which Francis I. had ever visited upon Ami's opinions of policies of State. It rankled like an arrow which still hung in his breast. He could scarcely trust himself to recall the temper of the king, as he spoke it, that day; and it was unsafe for him to utter it, even to Astrée, for she might pity him. A man capable of jealousy has a most sensitive pride, and often it is likely to behave worst when it is made the recipient of pity.

One man, beside Nouvisset, understood Ami; that was his earliest friend, Francesco. To him, at this juncture, Ami would most naturally go, because much that he had to complain of in the government concerned itself with the Italian ambassador and ally, who had been like a father to Francesco, — Admiral Andrea Doria.

This noble Genoese we have already met at the French capital. By this time, Louise of Savoy and Duprat were looking at him only as one who was able to perform certain most menial services for France. Generous as was the great admiral, filled as was his mind with memories of engagements successfully undertaken against Turk and Moor, he had never fancied, as the plans of Francis I. led him on into service, that the day was surely coming when the ill-concealed contempt of the courtiers toward him would ripen into insult. Ami, who did not undervalue the services of the admiral to his sovereign, was too knightly to intimate, even to Francesco, his dread of the miserable schemes of those at court who had grown jealous of Andrea Doria; but instead, he besieged Francis I. with protests against such a course as would exile this loyal ally and heroic servant.

It was very difficult for Ami so to confine his complaints as to omit Andrea Doria's name. Francesco and he walked together toward the lodgings of Louis Berquin the scholar, from whom Ami's conscience could not entirely detach itself. Just the day before, he had noted another triumph of Mme. de Chateaubriand over the will of the king.

"The patient queen," said Ami, "ought to demand her head."

Francesco thought a moment, confident that even Ami could hardly desire such a catastrophe to come so near to Astrée, whom, but for Mme. de Chateaubriand, Ami might never have seen.

"I know your thought," said the knight, bravely wrestling with his own; and then, as though he had detected a foul odor upon the air, which was otherwise fragrant with roses, he added: "The purest love here is sure to be blown upon by a stench— What is that, Francesco?"

"Only one of the peddlers," answered Francesco, as they turned about and followed the crowd, which had gathered about a noisy monk who, with a few hairs which he exhibited and certain bits of bones to which he asked reverence, began to preach, beating now and then upon a broken drum, and stopping his discourse for nothing else save the poor people who were buying indulgences.

Never before in the city had these men beheld a sale such as this. Once near Chilly, as they visited the peasant with Nouvisset, had they beheld a bellicose monk train the stubborn citizens into a credulity as to the value of the printed briefs of indulgence which he had to sell; and once, only once, had Louise of Savoy explained to Ami how courtiers and royal personages obtained such releases from the results even of prospective lapses from righteousness as under certain circumstances might be desirable even for him.

The instant the white lips of Louise soiled the name of Astrée in that connection, the young knight looked lightnings into her eyes; but the crafty woman only said, " Perhaps the heretics may make life more pleasant for you." The indignation which had grown up with that memory now seethed in Ami's soul, as the monk went on preaching about the blessed Leo X., and the huge fabric of St. Peter's at Rome which his Holiness was anxious to complete.

" The Holy Father appeals to his children, and his children must have the Pope's seal upon the briefs," mechanically sang out the monk, as he handed forth a bit of parchment to a coarse and well-known sinner, who smiled and said, —

" Eh? Three hundred years less of purgatory in exchange for my coins ! "

" Was there such indecency in the days of the first Pope, Saint Peter? " asked Francesco, who was never so conscious of small attainments in ecclesiastical history as when he was with Ami.

" No," answered the latter, rather aimlessly as it appeared; but he was determined to let church affairs alone for the present, and therefore added : "I am sure that money can be raised for almost anything, Francesco. The brother of Mme. de Chateaubriand is here from Lombardy."

"True, Lautrec was at court, intent on a rich marriage, — a marriage which Mme. de Chateaubriand had planned, — and intent also on taking back a large sum wherewith to pay the troops with which he had been trying to defend the Milanese since the battle of Marignano.

"We have costly indulgences at court," said Ami, sadly, "and an empty treasury."

"Mme. de Chateaubriand — " ventured Francesco, who was bright enough to reflect that every man desires to condemn his own relatives prospective, if condemnation is necessary.

"She ought to supply the necessities of Lautrec with the jewels which the king has given her."

"How much does a papal brief for such indulgences cost, Ami?" inquired Francesco, as they walked on toward Louis Berquin's lodgings.

"I am not acquainted with things ecclesiastical," said Ami, glad to get away from the torture of a dilemma, one of whose horns was named Vian; the other, corruption and torture. "This I do know about things political: the king's mother has worked out a scheme for Lautrec and herself. Of course, I am but a virtuoso! But I have been true to my king, and I told him of the peril which comes from an outraged people. Lautrec goes back with promises of money. Mark me, Francesco, he will be compelled to levy upon the duchy, and the Swiss army will dissolve. He is incapable enough with a rich court; he is imbecile in his plans without one."

Louis Berquin was absent, and the delightful hour which these two restless minds had promised themselves in his presence was lost to them. Deeper was the gathering darkness in which Ami felt that the sun of Francis I. might be going down.

"No sooner had Bourbon become wifeless, than Louise of Savoy began to claim the inheritance," said Ami.

"What inheritance?" asked Francesco.

"First, the inheritance of property, and then the man's heart."

"Oh," said the Italian, "she has been after Bourbon's heart since we were children, Ami. But Bourbon will never forget that the lovely Marguerite would have been his, but for her mother; and that Bonnivet — "

"Bonnivet would not have been shielded in his love for the Duchesse d'Alençon, if her mother had not hated Bourbon, whom she cannot rule even now."

"Things are at sword's-points, then? Bourbon detests Bonnivet."

"Did the constable not tell the king, when his Majesty showed him the plans of Bonnivet's palace, that the cage would be too magnificent for the bird?"

"What think you, Ami?"

"Is it treason to be true, Francesco? No? Then let me whisper it to you that the king's mother — I have said it to his Majesty — desires the ruin of the powerful Bourbon. *The king must not lose Bourbon.* Shall I say more?"

"If it be in your heart, poor burdened friend!" and Francesco pitied the conscientious servant of the unworthy king.

"William Farel — blessings on his name! — he must soon flee the city — "

"Ami!"

"I mean all I have said. The Duchesse d'Alençon is kind and true; but the king must not oppose his Holiness. Shall I say aught else?"

"Tell me all, Ami. Your king is not worthy of such suffering as you bear for him."

"Nay, my king has bad advisers. I look for brighter days. Astrée knows the schemes of Mme. de Chateaubriand. They will not fail at present; but afterward a better day will come. Let me say it, Francesco. Bourbon will be lost to France. Cardinal Wolsey will see to it, for he deceived my king at Calais. Lautrec cannot hide under the love of the king for his sister; he will fall."

"Ami, you have more to say. Tell me all!" impatiently begged Francesco.

"I shall be faithful to my king and friend. Soon Francis I. will find a stronger foe than any of these. But he must not allow Andrea Doria to be treated contemptuously by his courtiers, while Henry of England and the Emperor Charles V. are met together to devise against France."

"Nay, nay," said Francesco, who, as never before, saw that the king was becoming weak at home, and that the policies of Europe were massing themselves against him. "Nay," added he, "but why do you speak of Admiral Andrea Doria?"

A message from the king was just then placed in Ami's hand. Soon Astrée and the Duchesse d'Alençon joined him; and with the pale face of Francesco still in his thought, he was asked into the presence of his Majesty Francis I., who had an apology to make to the young and faithful knight.

CHAPTER V.

"AUREUS LIBELLUS."

Anglorum rex Henricus, Leo Decime, mittit
Hoc opus et fidei testem et amicitiæ.
Verses written in honor of Leo X. in the "Assertio."

WHAT would have been the agitation or wilful stolidity of Ami, the French knight, if, in July, 1521, he had been able to look across the Channel and see Vian, in Windsor Castle, still a monk, and never so much an Englishman as then, assisting his sovereign Henry VIII. in completing a book, famous before it was issued, entitled "Assertion of the Seven Sacraments. Against Martin Luther."

Ami's soul was being ruled by a phantom.

Vian's temper of mind had fitted him to remain long under the influence of Erasmus. Never, as yet, had any of the elements of the Reform gained access to his conscience. He had been kept pure, not by the Church or by the Reform, but by the vision of that little mate, now so nearly the dream of a woman.

Before he had been at Hampton Court three days, he had seen a letter from Erasmus, who asserted that he had no longer any friendship for Martin Luther. Greek literature was communicating to Vian such a desire for literary reform, that he even wondered why he had been interested at all in the German monk. Thomas More's oration at the reception of Cardinal Campeggio as papal legate, had been repeated to him; and the young monk was persuaded, for the nonce at least, that if the Holy Church went by the board, as it seemed sure to do if Lutheranism prevailed, that kind of individual opinion which the sub-prior had held before him as a peril, would produce anarchy everywhere. At least it appeared wise, if possible, to foster the movement of reform only from the inside. One of the first duties was the destruction of Lutheranism. Henry VIII. had enlisted himself; and the manuscript, parts of which were two years of age, needed only completion. Great, however, as was Henry's scholarship in other things, Wolsey was anxious that in his dealing with Luther's "De Captivitate Babylonica," he should be accurate and full on the history of the sacraments. He had therefore exhorted Vian to assist his Majesty; and the king had said, "My heart is quite gone out to your servant Vian."

When Vian objected to the bitterness of the king's expressions, Wolsey said: "You have nothing to do with his coarseness. Make sure that his Majesty is accurate with history, and hasten his publication."

Vian often hesitated; nay, he even attempted to dissuade his Majesty from issuing such an attack. Wolsey then called his attention to the fact that since 1518 Pace, and Wolsey himself, had been praising the incomplete work. Vian grew weary of Windsor Castle, and intimated that the court overestimated the force of Luther's volume, to which there was one reply. Tunstall would cry out again: "I pray God keep Luther's book from Englishmen. There is much strong opinion in it." At length Vian urged that England's sovereign should not so bemean himself as to bandy epithets with a belligerent monk. Then did the king himself tell him that he had already written to his Holiness about the matter, and had made large promises. At last Vian was silenced, and in

the course of the trial of Buckingham, he labored carefully upon the new book.

August 25th came, and it was finished. A copy covered
with cloth of gold, and signed by Henry VIII. was soon
in the Pope's hands; and even Vian was happy to have
done something toward bringing it forth, when the messenger returned from Rome to tell the court how he
kneeled before his Holiness and spoke to him eloquently;
how the Pope sat with his bishops, amid quadrants and
elegant cloths, looking pleasantly upon him; how he was
lovingly asked to kiss the cheeks of Leo X.; how the
head of the Church praised Henry VIII., and how he
desired five copies of so powerful an antidote to the
poisons of "the monster, Martin Luther."

Vian meditated on the word "monster." It seemed
entirely unnecessary to this monk, whose literary refinement had become so Hellenic, for even a pope, especially
for so cultivated an hierarch as Leo X., who was at that
time pontiff, to use so big a word for one whom they
all held to be so contemptible. "At least the whole
army of popes and kings fear him," thought he; and Vian
foresaw that Luther would surely make answer to
Henry VIII.

But Leo X. was never to be disturbed with a rejoinder
which quite equalled the attack of Henry VIII. in its
violence. That characteristic of this rejoinder was sufficient to one who, like Vian, was under the flattering
dominion of fancied refinement, to make him entirely
forgetful of the value of Luther's rough temperament, and
the nature of the gigantic blasphemies which he was to
overcome; and so this dignified monk and courtier at
the time of the appearance of Luther's rejoinder contented his fastidious taste with the reflection that he had
helped to wake up a barbarian. Luther's book appeared
from Wittenberg, July, 1522. Leo X. had died on
December 2 in the previous year.

"At last," remarked Vian to Giovanni, who often visited him at times when the Abbot of Glastonbury was in attendance upon Parliament, or when his lordship had occasion to consult, through another, the cardinal or the crown, — "at last my Lord Cardinal has the tiara in his grasp."

"Nothing is more improbable than his ever obtaining it," exclaimed Giovanni, sharply.

Vian could not understand the violent asseveration of his old friend, save that it proceeded from an Italian. "Surely Wolsey is the man for Supreme Pontiff," thought he. The monk had found in Wolsey no serious opposition to that state of agnostic indifference into which his own mind had fallen as to matters theological.

Of his great ability no man had doubt, — least of all men, Vian. He had been attached to Wolsey as to none other, for Wolsey was the one Englishman who had already set to work to make England a first-class power.

"Certainly the cardinal is luxurious enough," said he.

"He surpasses any pope in pomp," agreed Giovanni.

"He is favorable to our learning and philosophy," asserted Vian, with the self-confidence of the English Renaissance.

"Entirely so, at present," replied Giovanni. "But he will not be Pope. He has done as much as Luther may do, to destroy the awe with which the world has looked upon the papal chair, and — "

"How can it be? Cardinal Wolsey is not heretical."

"But he is powerful. Freshly grown power is always heresy in the presence of ancient power which has become weakness, Vian," said Giovanni. "Thomas Wolsey has posted no propositions on the cathedral at Wittenberg, has burned no papal bull, has defied no Diet at Worms; but he might as well have done these. He has made himself and Whitehall, in the room of the Pope and St. Peter's, the dictators of Europe. He has

taken the place of Gregory VII., and has ruled, while the
rest of the rulers were at one another's ears.   Not a king
or emperor, for the last five years, has known what he
wanted to do until Wolsey was consulted.   He has not
listened when the Pope has quoted councils and repeated
texts; neither did Luther.   The papal see is not of
essential supremacy any longer.   The power of two
energetic intellects has overshadowed it.   Wolsey is the
Luther of politics; Luther is the Wolsey of ecclesiastics.
You do not understand me?   You are going to Rome,
Vian; you will understand me at Rome."

Of one thing Vian was sure, — he had a growing admiration for the powerful cardinal, and wanted to see
him pope.   Naturally enough, the very influence which
at one time threatened to make Vian a contemner of
things papistical, now conspired with others to make him
restless to behold Wolsey in the papal chair.   That influence was none other than John Wycliffe.   Vapor in
some atmospheres becomes rain; in others, snow.

Out of one of those Wycliffe letters, out of the whole
story of his life, Vian had obtained a vivid conception of
the rights, privileges, and spirit of England, as a political
institution, which made him an intense Englishman.
Wycliffe had vindicated England against a dictator who
lived in Italy, — so it seemed to Vian, — when Urban was
made to yield in 1366.   All the workings of Wycliffe's
mind at that hour were exposed in the packet of his
letters which Vian's father had left to him.   With these
he had thoroughly sympathized, as he had stolen glances
at them at Glastonbury, and reflected upon their significance while he had been living with cardinal and king.
This Wycliffite ideal of the rights and prerogatives of
England was entering into the warm stream of his admiration for Wolsey; and as the cardinal had become
the typical self-respectful Englishman, that stream of admiration would have carried him to the papal throne.

Vian did not suspect that this same Wycliffite ardor for England might, in circumstances which could arise when England's king should find a grievance against a pope, create a sort of patriotism which would leave England popeless, except for the presence of a king who would serve as both sovereign political and sovereign ecclesiastical. "Cardinal Wolsey is the self-sufficient Englishman, — he is the England which I love. Let him be the Holy Father." This was as far as the impulse had gone at this time with Vian, in declaring itself. He ventured to say only this to the old man, in spite of his assurances of defeat, the eyes of the younger monk resting meanwhile upon an interesting letter from Clerk, then the ambassador at Rome, — a letter which lay topmost with many other papers of the cardinal, and which contained these words : —

"Every man here beginneth to shift for himself, because of such garboyle and business as out of all order is like to be committed here in this city, until such time as we be provided with another pope. I beseech Almighty God send us one to His pleasure."

"The *Opifex Deus !*" said the sly old child of the Renaissance, who through his cynical paganism had observed the religiosity of the ambassador's epistle. "He has had very little to do with finding Saint Peter's successors in the past. Let us trust, Vian, that in this case the cloud-compelling Jove may have more influence at Rome."

CHAPTER VI.

THE ETERNAL CITY.

> " A universal tumult, then a hush
> Worse than the tumult, — all eyes straining down
> To the arena's pit, all lips set close,
> All muscles strained, — and then that sudden yell,
> *Habet!* — That's Rome, says Lucius: so it is!
> That is, 't is *his* Rome, — 't is not yours and mine."

IT is Rome, Jan. 8, 1522. Near the wall of the Borgo, half-way between the Janiculum and the Vatican stood Vian; and looking straight into his eyes was a Neapolitan trooper, who insisted upon knowing the business of the former in Rome at that time. Clerk, the ambassador of Henry VIII., had already given up hope of making Vian's person safe in the Eternal City. Possessing nothing of Vian's enthusiasm for Trajan's Pillar or the ruins of the Temple of Bacchus, and caring even less for the Coliseum than for his luxurious couch in the palace, he did not understand the obvious recklessness with which Wolsey's young friend pushed his way about, through a city which was thronged with Spaniards, beneath whose glittering garments hid daggers for any who might be suspected of opposition to the will of Charles V., and with Neapolitan troopers who ravaged by day and slept at night in the galleys with which Civita Vecchia was crowded.

"An Englishman!" exclaimed the trooper, with a dash of petulance. "The election had been over long ago, had your cardinal not thrown an hundred thousand ducats in the scale."

"*My* cardinal?" observed the frightened monk, whose outer garment was a thin cloak guarded with lace, whose rich material contrasted strongly with the thick birrus worn by the servant at his side, and whose pearl-sown edge revealed, as it fell backward, a girdle exquisitely barred of silk and gold, and a doublet of satin, whose aiglets of silver shone almost as brightly as did the clasp of gold which fastened it, in which gleamed two gems.

"Indeed! You know how things are to issue yonder, do you?" said the Neapolitan, pointing to the Basilica.

"I am not the less an Englishman," retorted Vian.

"And a brave fellow, in no mischief as I can see," said the other, charmed with the courageous frankness of the stranger. "Dismiss your servant! I will give him my blade as a surety for you; and we will betake us to the Arch of Titus, for which I heard you making inquiry a short time since."

True, the Neapolitan, who was one of the army which Don Manuel the Spanish ambassador had ordered from Naples on learning that Leo X. was dead, had been following the footsteps of Vian for many hours. Every syllable which the Englishman had uttered was treasured in the Italian's heart. But luckily, Vian had said nothing of popes, conclaves, or kings. Instead, he had been garrulous with his servant about classical manners and Roman literature, — the old Italy which Vian assured the ignorant man was superior in every way to that of their poor, degenerate day. The trooper who had been set to the graceless task of apprehending conspirators against the will of Charles V., — a sovereign whom he abhorred, — was weary of listening to this rumor and that, which had proceeded from the Basilica or from the brain of a madman. The conclave had now been in session for thirteen days ; and infinitely perplexing had been the reports of conspiracies, briberies, frauds, and farces. Tired soldiers, who a fortnight before had begun to watch for foes with proud interest, now cared not whether Colonna de' Medici or Farnese was to be triumphant ; and this trooper, who was himself a hapless man of letters, pursuing the trade of a soldier that he might find bread, was fascinated at once with an Englishman of such evident rank, who cared for the ancient Rome when she was so illy represented by her vulgar successor, and so overwhelmed by soldiers and ecclesiastics. Vian, quite as delighted as was the Italian with his new acquaintance, immediately dismissed his servant, and soon they were standing under the Arch of Titus.

" You are living in the Rome of the Forum, not in the Rome of the Vatican," observed the soldier, who went on to utter sentiments which expressed themselves as though they had been delayed many days. " It is, as you explained to that slave of yours, the greater and truer Rome. I myself have written some verses upon the theme, and I fancy that when you have gone back to England you will hunt up the roads of Cæsar, which must yet be discoverable in Britain, while priests and kings wait for the newly elected pope to die, and while they wait conspire for the new wearer of the tiara. The only truly modern world, after all, is the ancient world ; and I am right glad to find an Englishman who at this moment might be dozing in the palace within reach of the late pontiff's wines, straying away to look up the laurel of Daphne. Have you ever loved ? "

" I," hesitated Vian, — " I have had a dream, — that is, a vision or — "

" Well, dream, vision, or actual love-affair, — it is all the same here in Rome. The more visonary the vision, the more real it is ; and the more actual your love-affair, the more certainly will it turn out to have been a dream. Why do I ask you? For the reason that I suspected it; no one will expose himself to robbers and soldiers, as you have done in Rome, without having on hand a love-affair, either with some woman or with the ancient city herself. You are really love-stricken. I could discern as much, when first, ten days ago, I followed you to the shrine of Apollo. But you are under the Greek god of love, Eros."

"I myself am a Pythagorean," said Vian.

The trooper exclaimed: "A Pythagorean! There can be no love of woman in you! You must vent your raptures on something whose soul has not transmigrated downward. The Eternal City will suffice. Even your dream of love — and I wish you would tell me about it — will vanish before the Pythagorean view of things. I had a friend, — a Pythagorean; and Rome was his dwelling-place. But he really lived in a world of old friends. He himself — so his philosophy taught him — had been a friend of the ancient poet Martial; and most of Martial's epigrams, especially the less decent, were on his tongue. He often explained to me why Martial, if he had passed through less than three transmigrations, — that is, if he had been born but twice, — would appear, not as a rhymester, but as a writer of prose. Such was his life at Rome that my friend, who in his other life had bandied witticisms with him, easily worked it out, with the aid of his Pythagorean charts which he himself made at that time and now remembers perfectly well, that Martial would reappear as a literary vagabond, learned enough and more humorous, as also he would be more licentious than ever. Hist!" — and the trooper pointed to a figure partially wrapped up in a faded and torn doctor's gown, his hair illy hidden by a worn cap. Bright eyes, full of laughter and scorching irony, were glistening upon the path which he was treading, and which led toward the Coliseum. "Hist!" said the Neapolitan, "there he is even now!"

"Your friend who knew Martial the poet in the other life?"

"No! Hist! It is Martial himself, or rather, Martial as he lives now in pontifical Rome. Oh, your Pythagoreanism would have confounded Minerva herself! Look at him! It is Martial as we see him now, — so my friend has told me."

"Why," observed Vian, who had been favored with an hour on the day before with the most characteristic man of the Renaissance of ancient Rome, — "why, that is the physician, Dr. François Rabelais!"

"The same, the same!" answered the Neapolitan. "Martial, — Rabelais! Ah, sir, you Pythagoreans live in a strange world. See! he is going to the Coliseum. Let us follow, after a while. Meantime," pursued the trooper, who appeared entirely inattentive to the fact that the English Pythagorean was attempting to solve the problem of Martial's metempsychosis, "let us talk on this matter of love for old Rome, which by the way is almost the only kind of love that monks can indulge in without an indulgence from the Pope— Oh, you must not smile at indulgences! St. Peter's had to be finished and ornamented; therefore his Holiness had to have money; therefore he had to offer indulgences for sale; therefore St. Peter's is glorified on the debauchery of Europe!"

"I perceive that you are heretical," broke in Vian.

"Well, I prefer Cæsar's Rome to Leo's Rome," replied the trooper, "and you are in love with the same ghost."

"That is not my vision." Vian remembered the dream of Lutterworth, Glastonbury, Whitehall, Rome, — for it had returned to him on the night before; and his lips moved with the whisper, "Dear little mate!" Then he saw her as a woman.

"No, perhaps not; but being a monk, — I saw you

take the crucifix from your breast as you stood in the great vault, — being a monk, as I said, and a Pythagorean, you have had to banish actual womankind out of your life and philosophy, and being a scholar as I see, you have fallen in love with the Eternal City. Well, she is in a sad plight ; but if you really love old Rome, you will disassociate her in your mind from her unfortunate circumstances. She lies, after being half breathless for many centuries, still alive under all the rags of her own former clothing. Basilicæ, statues, manuscripts, and arms, gems which she wore, lie tossed about from this cold portion of her still heaving breast to that ; and now those who for two hundred years have caught a whisper from her lips, or felt beneath the enwrapped loveliness of her form a heart beat, have been finding beneath the long silken tresses of her hair, the gracefulness of her strong arm, even the voluptuous splendor of her glorious eye. This gang of cardinals and princes — the ambassadors of all Europe gathered here to quarrel and perhaps choose a head for Christendom — do not reflect that the gorgeous ceremonial of the Church, the place which the papal chair occupies in the human mind, many of the doctrines of the councils and much of their power, are but fragments of the old clothes of this ancient political Rome, painted and laced by the ecclesiastical spirit which the Christian religion infused into the human soul. Your ' Ave Maria ' is in Latin, — the language of the sibyl of Cumæ. Even your Pope is Cæsar Imperator. The capital of the Church was the old capital of the State. Rome is still the world's centre. Still the dream of universal empire floats over these seven hills, and nowhere else. You have studied the doctrines? Well, the old Roman prayed for the dead who had neglected the gods of the Capitoline Hill. Candlemas is not more devoted to light than was the older festival of Lupercal. The nun is the Vestal Virgin. She is yet buried alive. The

Holy Virgin was enthroned in Diana's city, Ephesus, for the same reason that the Pope, Cæsar's successor in the human imagination, was and is enthroned in Rome. You will see torches wave there, when this election is done, as they once waved when Cæsar mounted the throne. The Pope began as *papa*, as you say; now he is the sole Prince over nations. Cæsar has come again. The festival of the resurrection occurs when the spring-time tempts the corn. The Virgin began as a woman who had borne a son; she is now the Queen of Heaven. Oh, I know you must go back to England in love with old Rome!"

By this time they had reached the Coliseum. Vian was conscious that he occupied an anomalous position, even to his own mind. Here he was a servant of his Lord Cardinal Wolsey, anxious to see him made pope, perfectly certain that he had been a defeated candidate from the first. Vian was trying to hold to the Rome of the Holy Father in 1522, while he was in love with the old Rome of pre-papal days.

At the conclave they had seen an illustration of the truth which the Neapolitan had been speaking. Vian had beheld it, as they passed the filthy huts which he saw were builded of fragments of marble porticos and decorated by entablatures from the peristyle. Cattle had looked out upon him from beneath roofs which overhung broken columns of exquisite workmanship, and slabs on whose immaculate strength beauty had dwelt for seventeen centuries. As they stood with that ignorant complacency with which a fat monk repeated his "Ave" or meditated upon the victory of Constantine, a horse, which might have been only a very remote and badly descended son of one of Cæsar's war-horses, was tied to a statue of the beautiful Apollo; and the beggars were exhibiting their sores, as they sat on bits of cornice which had once helped to support a graceful arch upon which

Horace and Augustus had gazed. Never had Vian been so sure of the composite character of the faith for which he stood. With one mighty effort, he still could compel himself to say, —

"And yet the one vitalizing fact which prevented barbarism from ruining this old Rome entirely, and has brought down to this day a stream of civilizing influence, is the Holy Catholic Church. Long live the Pope!"

The cool air came not unpleasantly from snow-crowned Soracte, fanning into motion the light edges of that growth of moss which far above the head of Vian clung to the enormous ruin, and driving into one of the cellars the wretches who besought strangers for an alms. The broken beams of light lingered upon the sharp corners of the ruined Forum and Capitol, toward which Vian looked, his eyes resting upon the spot where now, sixteen centuries after the last dance of the Muses, the followers of a peasant were selecting his Vicar.

The Coliseum and St. Peter's, — he was about comparing them for a moment, when the Neapolitan and Dr. François Rabelais engaged him in conversation.

"They are electing a pope yonder," said the witty physician, pointing to the domeless building in front of which was a huge scaffolding devised by Bramante; "and I have just written a dissertation on lettuces."

"Why did you not write on the authority of the Pope?" asked the Neapolitan.

"Because the authority of his Holiness is long ago spoiled. I wanted a fresh topic. Aha! lettuces are the only fresh things in Rome," answered the great wit.

"Here," observed the trooper, who was not unpleasantly jocose nor too familiar with Vian's name, "here is an Englishman, a Pythagorean, and a — "

"A friend of Thomas Wolsey also, I suppose, eh — "

"One who is to be disappointed, I fear," said Vian.

"Ah! I am not disappointed with popes when I examine their pedigrees and count their children."

Rabelais had not yet been asked by the Bishop of Maillerais to find out whether Farnese was the lawful son of a somewhat dissipated pope; but his mind was sufficiently full of such information concerning the Churchmen of the day to make him very loquacious whenever the topic of reform was introduced. Rabelais has left many testimonies as to his cleverness in understanding the real force of the Lutheran movement; and young as he was at that time, his conversation possessed many of the witticisms which afterward sparkled on his page. He was not long in finding out that Vian had held warm relationships to what was known in England as " the new learning." He saw the anomaly, — this engaging youth, stirred with the Renaissance and stolid against the Reformation, looking anxiously every now and then in the direction of the conclave. Rabelais soon discerned that Vian's refined objections to Luther and a great popular revolt against ecclesiastical Rome were founded upon exactly the same ideas and fears which had taken the warlike tone from Erasmus, and had made Thomas More timid.

The three — Vian, the trooper of Naples, Rabelais — sat together in the chilly air. The awful masses of stone overshadowed them, until the sun, finding openings through the arches and between the columns, gathered out of an unclouded sky sufficient warmth to make their corner in the broken amphitheatre fairly comfortable. Rabelais had already begun to spin for them the story of Pantagruel and Gargantua, with which the reader is familiar. Vian had been musing upon the vast audiences of the past, as his eye wandered up and down the stony flights of steps which burdened the huge pedestals. His soul was back again with Nero, as yonder the emperor walked in his gardens with Acte, when Vian recalled the epigram of Martial, and he thought, —

"Why, Martial is here, talking at my side!"

There was no mistaking him. Rabelais!—Martial!—it was confusing; but Rabelais was sketching the future of the Reform. He had reached this part of his story:—

"Whereupon Gargantua, fearful lest the child should hurt himself, caused four great chains of iron to be made to bind him, and so many strong wooden arches unto his cradle most firmly stacked and mortised in huge frames. Thus continued Pantagruel for a while, very calm and quiet, for he was not able so easily to break those chains, especially having no room in the cradle to give a swing with his arms. But see what happened once on a great holiday, that his father Gargantua made a sumptuous banquet to all the princes of his court. Hark what he did, good people! He strove and essayed to break the chains of the cradle with his arms, but could not, for they were too strong for him. Then did he keep with his feet such a stamping and so long that at last he beat out the lower end of his cradle, which notwithstanding was made of a great post five feet square; and as soon as he had gotten out his feet, he slid down as well as he could till he had got his soles to the ground, and then with a mighty force he rose up, carrying his cradle upon his back, like a tortoise that crawls up against a wall. In this manner he entered into the great hall where they were banqueting, and that very boldly, and did much affright the company; yet, because his arms were tied in, he could not reach anything to eat, but with great pain stooped now and then a little to take, with the whole flat of his tongue, some good lick, good bit, or morsel. Which, when his father saw, he saw well enough that they had left him without giving him anything to eat, and therefore commanded that he should be loosed from the said chains. When he was unchained they made him sit down, where, after he had fed very well, he took his cradle and broke it into more than five hundred thousand pieces with one blow of his fist, swearing he would never come into it again."

"Pantagruel is the Reformation!"—when Rabelais had concluded, Vian found within his mind this ugly element of discord,—"Pantagruel!"

CHAPTER VII.

A NEW POPE.

In times of decadence power always searches for minds of a niggardly temperament, — the undecided, and above all, those who have passed their lives in a sort of twilight. — EMILIO CASTELAR.

THE Neapolitan and Rabelais followed the English monk as he walked across the space and began to climb the steps.

"The future climbing upon the past!" said the wit.

"Yonder," said the soldier, pointing far through a giant arch toward St. Peter's imagined dome, — "yonder is the present! Let him rejoice in its grandeur while he may."

Vian now stood upon the loftiest step, and looked down upon the space which had been crowded at one time by nearly one hundred thousand Romans; then, without straining his gaze, his eye found in his own fancy the vast dome of St. Peter's. Was it not possible to lose sight of a noisy friar of Germany in the magnificent flood of memories which Vian saw piling up on the Campagna, until it rushed across the space between, and struck and swirled with a still more solemn sea of holy hopes and fears which came sweeping on from one of the crosses that glittered in the purple light? The ancient Rome had built the Coliseum at the hour when the old Roman spirit was dying; the mediæval Rome had built St. Peter's at the hour when the spirit of the Middle Ages was vanishing! Vian did not dare to adopt this view; it led to the suspicion that modern days would create a fane as different from St. Peter's as was St. Peter's from the Coliseum. He was, however, convinced that he had not the mental freedom which he supposed himself to possess.

Why should he be afraid of the suspicion that great changes were to come? In Wolsey's presence any kind of opinion on religion had hitherto seemed so tolerable that Vian supposed he had come to the intellectual liberty which he had yearned for at Glastonbury. But now, to him, standing where he could look over Roman arch and Christian temple, with the shout of the multi-tude in the amphitheatre mingling in his soul with the whispers of the cardinals in the conclave, it was evident that a human soul must get a freedom for its operations which a Wolsey could not give or take away, if the soul would realize its destiny.

Awhile ago he had been on the point of comparing the Coliseum with St. Peter's, — their memories, their architecture, their renown, their significance. That mo-ment occurred when he stood beneath the arches of the one, or before the steps leading into the other. He was now above both of them, and his feelings suggested the thoughts that the human soul could surmount and overawe its own creations; that in such moments those creatures attained their true proportions; that at such instants the future came into sight, and that after all there are but two great powers in the universe which have to do with the problems of mental freedom and its solution, — God and the human soul.

How long Vian remained upon that step he did not know. When he descended Rabelais smiled, told a humorous tale or two, and the three set out for the

Capitol. Vian was listening while they chattered of the affairs within the conclave. The wind was now sighing through the plane-trees and laurels; and the scantily clad Rabelais was glad to use the birrus of Vian's servant, who had come from the palace with a message to Vian from Clerk the ambassador.

"The emperor took the city by his soldiers, even before the Almighty could get here with His pious cardinals," said Rabelais, as they aimlessly wandered in front of the trenches out of which the workmen of Alexander VI. had brought some of the grotesques. "Some of the cardinals do not look like children of Minerva —"

"Nor of Venus," added the Neapolitan, "though I saw one of the least beautifully created tumble into the ditch at Porto d'Anza, where they found the Apollo of the Belvedere."

"He was doubtless a beautiful worshipper of Apollo in the other life, who had sinned, and therefore had been born ugly in this life, but was yet sufficiently united to his past to find the place of the image of Apollo," said Rabelais, looking at Vian. "Poor Antony, who doubtless is a cardinal in this life, ought to be apprehended where Julius found the statue of Cleopatra."

Soon they had reached an inn, at which they partook liberally of cakes and of wine, which induced plans for another series of visits to classical places. Between the pillars and modern churches, sarcophagi and temples, they talked of the election of the Pope.

"Every cardinal is a candidate," said the Neapolitan.

"So said Don Manuel," added Vian; "and it would seem that they are voting on one name at a time."

"Did your Lord Cardinal Wolsey ever really expect the papal throne?" asked the Neapolitan, bluntly.

Vian was somewhat annoyed at the question, for he had learned of the treachery of Charles V. It would

have been insulting from a soldier who had not the
Neapolitan's hatred for the emperor. Vian answered:

"It is an age of royal liars."

"What! not Henry VIII., who has crushed Luther!"
exclaimed Rabelais, knowing not that Vian had sometimes looked indifferently upon his part in the compo-
sition of Henry's book, especially since the story of
Pantagruel.

"It is an age of lying," said he, feeling that it was
a safer assertion; "and the chief of liars is Charles V.
He promised my Lord Cardinal his support at Bruges,
and repeated it through the ambassador, the Bishop of
Elna, whom I left speaking to his Eminence at Hampton
Court."

"There are too many Churchmen in the affair for
anybody to tell the truth," remarked Rabelais.

Vian continued: "Henry VIII. sent his ambassador
to the emperor to learn his choice — "

"And," interrupted the Neapolitan, who seemed to
know everything, "Henry VIII. also sent two letters, —
one in favor of Wolsey, to be used if he shall be elected;
and another in favor of De' Medici, if Wolsey shall fail."

Vian stoutly denied the truth of this statement; but
he saw that the Neapolitan was constant.

Rabelais simply said, "His Majesty would make a good
pope."

"The one hundred thousand ducats which Wolsey has
offered would indicate that Henry VIII. is ready to pay
for the tiara for another," said the soldier, with an implied assurance that some one in the conclave had been
carrying out news of importance.

It troubled Vian. "Every precaution has been taken
against such as you knowing too much."

"Oh, yes!" laughed the Neapolitan; "the army of
lords and prelates stop up the breathing-holes — "

"The Devil will get in anyhow," said Rabelais.

"The platters are washed over and over again when they come out; and holy noses smell about the meats which enter and the pots which return, to discover a syllable of simony, which the Pope's bull prevents, or to find a phrase of news from some cardinal, which by this time any of them is too weak to write. You"—looking into the calm eyes of Vian,—"you saw the turning-wheel which was invented, by which their food is delivered. Not even a cardinal could make it tell a tale."

"This is the thirteenth day?" inquired Rabelais. "Ah! they have had but one kind of meat for several days. Rabelais! thou wouldst make a good choice of popes, for thou hast gone many a day without any meat at all; but in these days hunger is not piety."

"From the first day," said the Neapolitan, "the Cardinal de' Medici was hopeless of election. Tokens and signs told his party of the fact."

"Who was the saint carried forth from the conclave a few days ago, half dead from foul air?" asked Rabelais.

"Gremani."

"Lucky dog! and pious cardinal also, I doubt not."

"Yes; everybody within the conclave is tired, suspicious. Why, when Farnese's servant asked for a larger pot of wine, they cried, 'Oh, it is a secret watchword,— 'More wine!'"

"Nonsense!" said Rabelais; "that has been the watchword of the whole series of conclaves for ages. The Cardinal of Ivrea,—poor old fellow!—who was taken prisoner on his way hither, must have wished the captors had killed him, so much does he dislike scarcity of meat and wine."

By this time the three found themselves looking into a lime-pit about whose edges lay broken statues, a bust of Mars, and innumerable fragments of the colonnade of Minerva, the most beautiful blocks of which had been long ago converted into lime. Vian never felt him-

self so much a pagan; and his mind flew at once to
Giovanni.

Vian felt it desirable to know more of the facts with
which the Neapolitan seemed perfectly familiar; and saying farewell to Rabelais, to whom he gave the cloak, and
to the Neapolitan, to whom he gave an invitation to visit
him if ever he should betake himself to England, Vian
was soon enjoying himself with a party of Wolsey's friends,
who had given up every hope of the advancement of the
cardinal if Richard Pace, whom now they anxiously expected, should not arrive before the dawn of the next
day.

January 9 had come. The air was resonant with rumor. Vian's imagination had been stimulated by a story
full of circumstantial accuracy, which he overheard while
gazing at the ruin of the temple of Jupiter, — a story
which led him to believe that Leo X. had been poisoned.
His officer, Paris de Grasis, had strangely omitted to
care for the late Pope in his sickness. The medical
attendants who made an examination were certain that
his Holiness had died by poison. A cup-bearer had
been taken to the castle of St. Angelo. Vian could see
the livid and swollen corpse. What could such a city
and such a conclave do toward selecting a suitable
successor?

Soldiers had crowded the streets since the day of Leo's
death. Cardinal Volterra, one of the foremost candi-
dates, had so insisted that the Imperialists had prejudiced
the issue of the conclave by the presence of Swiss arms,
that a thousand foot were added to their number to guard
the conclave. The city thronged about the Basilica of
St. Peter. It angered Vian to see the haughty Imperialists, as they denied every rumor which pleased the Roman populace, or spit upon the suggestion which once
lifted the crowd toward the window, that Wolsey had won

the throne. Vian had to persuade himself that probably at no time had Charles V. dreamed, as had Wolsey, of the use of force to consummate his purposes; that in such an event the outside ward was held by stout Roman nobles, the second by the ambassadors, the third by the prelates who kept the keys of the conclave.

Reports that of the thirty-nine who had gone into the conclave singing "Veni Creator," not one was now strong enough to speak at length, made the throng which surged up against the Chapel of Sixtus IV., demand that the life of this cardinal or that should be spared.

"Colonna sung the Mass," whispered an Italian, whose belated information stirred the crowd with such interest that shouts of the word "Colonna" gave to the multitude in the street the impression that that faction had prevailed. As soon as the falsity of the report was announced, the shout "Cardinal de' Medici" went up; and children on the Aventine were crying out the defeat of the Colonnas. At once Vian recognized the absolute necessity of the strong guard. Often, in spite of them, did it appear that the cardinals within the palace would be dispersed by the furious populace.

Almost every cardinal, fourteen days ago, had gone into his cell, — a room sixteen feet long and ten feet broad, — healthful and confident. Now every one was pale and weary. When twelve cardinals had voted for Farnese, Saint Quator, whose strength was stimulated by the prospect of an immediate decision, shouted, "Papem habemus."

Colonna rose at once.

"Papem habemus," cried out the Imperialists, led by Campeggio and De' Medici.

"Your reckoning is false," shrieked the haughty Colonna.

"Papem habemus! Papem habemus!" came from twelve throats.

"No!" and Colonna had vanquished the pretenders of the Farnese faction.

Out into the multitude came the word "Farnese," on wings unseen. On that instant the crowd broke into fragments. Soon the palace of Farnese was surrounded. Beyond the artillery and over the heads of the troops which defended it, the rough crowd saw within the splendid residence the testimonies to his luxurious taste. They paused; the troops were its defence; and leaving behind them the silent cannon, the throng pushed its way back again toward the Basilica.

Inside, the half-starved cardinals were listening to the nomination of Colonna; and as the wave went back which had brought that name forward, the name of the mightiest cardinal in Europe was pronounced.

"His youth! No!" shouted one after another.

"Too young," said an Imperialist who dreaded Wolsey's name.

"Nine votes," said the chalice which gleamed upon the altar.

De' Medici, Campeggio, and Volterra were pale, while Colonna and Farnese were wild with wrath. They could not help hearing the shoutings of the multitude without; but now they were far more intent upon the message to be given by those silent billets, which with so many genuflexions were being deposited within the chalice.

It is done: thirty-nine cardinals present; thirty-nine votes have been cast; all is orderly.

"Twelve votes," said the officer, with faltering voice.

"Not once have I received more than six," thought De' Medici, who was determined to stand well with Wolsey if his election should be accomplished, but was sure that the next scrutiny would not be so favorable to him.

"Too young," repeated the cardinals, who feared only his abilities.

"He is less than sixty and more than fifty," said Campeggio.

Again the chalice was the receptacle of votes, which were placed within with a trembling hand. Only the Medici faction was calm.

"Nineteen votes," said the officer, with evident consternation.

Oh, could Vian have known it as he stood there on the outside, laughing at Rabelais as he talked of his new cloak !

Inside, every face showed exhaustion but that of De' Medici. He, however, now saw that he could not be chosen. Wolsey was showing too much power. "Now let the Imperialists rally," whispered De' Medici.

Don Manuel had made De' Medici the lieutenant of Charles V. in the conclave. Henry VIII. and Wolsey must be defeated. Tortosa was to be the Imperial candidate if De' Medici could not obtain the tiara ; and now for ten times the chalice had registered the growing strength of another.

"Twenty-six votes ! " and this was the eleventh scrutiny.

"Tortosa ! Tortosa ! " they cried. Election by scrutiny was overthrown ; and by concurrence an aged and feeble man, schoolmaster long years ago to Charles V., was chosen to the throne of Leo X.

"The Holy Ghost did it ! " said the tired cardinals. The crowd repeated it.

Outside the Basilica, Rabelais said to Vian, "The Holy Ghost can do little enough, as we know, so long as they are in good health."

Then the crowd caught up the words of the wit. Screams greeted the cardinals as they came forth. The city was a laugh, a jeer, a peril which derided the conclave, and hated the name of the " stranger Pope," as they called him.

In the morning, when Vian set out from Civita Vecchia for London, the gray mist was still lingering above the Pontine marshes, and the quiet dawn which had now lit up the desolation of the Coliseum fell upon the ground, like the gold powder, which, with mixed carmine and minium, served to conceal the same blood-spattered soil when, centuries before, the roads which led to Rome were those of politics rather than of ecclesiastics, and when within that enclosure Rome shouted over the cruel spectacle of death in the amphitheatre.

CHAPTER VIII.

THE COURT AND THE VISION.

> Doth he use then on mules to ryde?
> Yea, and that with so shameful pryde
>   That to tell it is not possible:
> More like a God celestiall
> Than any creature mortall
>   With worldly pompe incredible.
>
> ROY.

VIAN had been sent to Rome to bear a special message to Don Manuel. He had failed to see his Lord Cardinal made pope; but there were other things for him to do.

Before Vian had been at Whitehall a single fortnight, Thomas Wolsey had recognized him as a young man of careful scholarship, fine business ability, and above all, of quick and accurate perception of the motives and character of the men around the chancellor. Wolsey himself was astonished at Vian's capacity for affairs associated so intimately with what seemed to him a daring genius for speculation in matters of religion and philosophy. His success on the "Field of the Cloth of Gold," in pleasing every one interested in the display, furnished proof enough of his ability.

"I want you always to be with me at Hampton Court, whither I shall often go for quietude and the fresh air. I shall not be troubled with much business there. I order that all business shall be done at Whitehall. I want Hampton Court for health and rest, and there we will talk over your 'new learning' and reforms in the Holy Church," said his Eminence.

There was a slight flavor of irony in these last words which almost assured Vian that while the Chancellor appreciated his fitness for diplomacy, he would make an effort to rid him of his heresies. Yet he believed that Wolsey's interest in heretics and heresies was political, not religious. Things had become so pressing that it was only a word now and then which was spoken upon these subjects. Only when the shrewd politician saw that something in the mind of his trusted young friend was taking the very soul out of that delicately formed body, — only when he saw that Vian was so influenced by some such weight upon him that, brilliant and powerful as he was, he had really exhibited but a small portion of his energy in politics, — was it that his Grace would chat with him about the progress, perilous enough to crowns and mitres, of the new opinions at Oxford, the attitude of the scholars toward the Greek philosophy which had been brought from Florentine academies, and more particularly the impossibility, as the cardinal saw it, of keeping a Church at all without a more comprehensive treatment or a severer discipline.

"Abbot Richard Beere may be right," said he; "the sword must go against the heretic."

Little as Thomas Wolsey could know of the demand for freedom which such a soul as Vian's was making, now and then the keen discernment of the eminent Churchman enabled him to meditate thus : —

"I say this young man needs no liberality of thought which he does not already possess, because I avow truly that I, as a faithful and important adherent of the Pope, need nothing for myself which I have not. Perhaps, however, the freedom which I use comes to me because the Holy Church has much open space in the direction of my desires, and there may be not a hand's-breadth of freedom in the direction of Vian's aspirations. There ought to be room on every side, for we are not all alike."

Only his profound love for the young ecclesiastic and the evident demands of policy would allow him to yield to better reasonings than those which ever come to any soul untouched by love. They detained his scheming intellect, however, but for a moment. Soon some brilliant plan for a short cut to the papal throne mastered him, and Vian's cry for freedom seemed both silly and wicked to the mind of the chancellor.

"Vian, my son," he would say, "the honor of your sovereign, Henry of England, the duties you owe to his Holiness, the loyalty you have pledged to me," — Wolsey always talked with such an ascending scale in mind, — "these ought to banish such whimperings from your breast."

One man at least partially understood Vian. Fra Giovanni, who was thoroughly at home at Hampton Court, whose absence from Glastonbury Abbey was productive of unalloyed delight in the minds of both the abbot and his sympathizing priors, had watched the contesting energies as they struggled within him. Much as the happy old friar was interested in Vian's fight for intellectual liberty, he was so sure that he would obtain it that he gave himself no special concern upon the point ; but rather did he devote his observations — for Fra Giovanni was a consummate detective, as had been proven in Italy and England — to what he saw was a battle between a vision and a philosophy.

He tried in vain to explain Vian's mental condition to Thomas More, who had begun to believe that the brilliant future of Vian as a scholar was overcast with clouds.

"Why," said the old friar, as they stood talking one morning at Hampton Court, to which More often came either as an honored guest or because Wolsey and the king's affairs required it, " the young man is in love with a vision, has loved the object of that vision for nearly fifteen years, and is trying to kill his love with the philosophy of Pythagoras."

" He will never be able to destroy a heart-beat with a theory of his brain," said the intrepid man, who honored love in his theories and in his experience.

" But what do you mean? Something, I know, is extracting the vigor from his soul."

" Well, let us go out where we may talk it all over. Vian is a noble young fellow, and we must cleave to him now."

" Vian must have the privilege of doing his own thinking if he be not badly heretical," said Thomas More, not at all conversant with the truth which Fra Giovanni had discovered, and never guessing that Vian had gone further toward the iconoclasm which More feared than the latter dreamed.

"'That is not what rocks his soul so uneasily now. I say to you that he is trying to abolish a passionate love for a fancied maiden, with a theory of the transmigration of souls."

" Impossible !" again remarked the statesman.

As the two were wending their way slowly across the red-brick court, beneath the latticed windows and through the awe-inspiring cloisters, the young man himself in whose career they had such interest was explaining to the chancellor's secretary, who was very tolerant of his religious or irreligious proclivities, why he could not wisely accomplish a mission to the court of Francis I., which had been proposed to him.

The secretary had insisted ; Vian was faithful to the interests of Wolsey, and refused to go.

Wolsey himself knew of the unpleasant meeting of Vian and Ami on the " Field of the Cloth of Gold ; "

but it had not occurred to him that at this juncture it might be important to consider its effect upon diplomacy. Vian had become almost indispensable in the service of his Grace. He had shown a comprehensive talent for statecraft, and brought a wonderful insight into association with his intimate acquaintance with the forces which were agitating the religious and literary world. Wolsey therefore had felt peculiar gratitude that Vian escaped the dagger of Ami.

Wolsey would willingly have trusted Vian with any message or task in England or France. Why was he not willing to go? It certainly could not mean insubordination. "Surely 'the new learning' has not entirely turned the head of Vian," thought the chancellor. His Grace also remembered the girl Astrée. He chuckled at the thought that Vian's fear of meeting her again — lovely creature that she was — might have saved for his Grace at this hour the skill and tried talents of his most brilliant servant.

Then the chancellor laughed, as he said to his secretary: "The young man Vian is mysterious. He is not in love. He cares nothing for the French girl whom he rescued. That abominable philosophy of Pythagoras has destroyed the charm of every female for Vian, except that of the intangible girl in his vision. Abbot Richard said he never could be a respectable monk with that beautiful little girl floating in his dreams. Mayhap I cannot make him a good politician until the vision fades. One thing is sure: the young man Vian has a clean soul, and pure. I wish all monks had some vision which, like Vian's, would keep them from mortal sin."

No other man in Wolsey's service at that hour would have dared to object to going to France. It was such an honor that even wisdom of the ordinary sort would have been deluded. It was a delicate situation for the monk who was now playing in politics, for the scholar

who was so successful at diplomacy. Vian was known to
have no great reverence for the papal chair. Cardinal
Wolsey had been offered, in 1520, the help of the
emperor by the Spanish envoys toward that position;
and at Bruges Charles V. had voluntarily indicated his
acquiescence in the scheme. Vian was known to have
regarded the " Field of the Cloth of Gold " as a magnificent farce considered by the side of Wycliffe's translation
of the New Testament. Could it be possible that he declined to go to France and represent Wolsey, because he
pretended to foresee that the demands of the Reformers
and the popularizing of intelligence would some day be
considered as the only worthy topics of the time for
kings, cardinals, and even their private advisers and
servants to interest themselves about?

The great effort at mediation at Calais had failed.
On Nov. 25, 1521, he had left the obstinate Emperor
Charles V. and the ambitious Francis, — the one to his
adviser; the other to a man whose strong intellect divided
honors with a passionate, jealous hate of Wolsey's young
friend Vian. This latter was the chosen friend of
Francis I., — Ami, who was always at his side, and who
at the moment when, to obtain even a temporary truce
with Charles V., the king would have surrendered Fonta-
rabia, said : " Sire, his Majesty the Emperor of Germany
has no equivalent to offer you. I beg you to accept
no brief truce from Charles V. through the hand of a
cardinal who desires the papacy."

From that hour Cardinal Wolsey had understood the
influence which this young knight Ami exercised upon
the mind of the French King. He knew that on the
" Field of the Cloth of Gold " Vian had met an antagonist of equal power. He now reflected that Vian might
have the best of reasons for declining to go upon the
proposed mission. Of one thing he was sure, — Vian
was not a coward.

That morning Wolsey had departed from Hampton Court, "desiring to be alone," as he said to More; and so was rowed down the Thames by eight trusty and stalwart oarsmen, to find, before he set foot upon the palace stairs at Whitehall, that Vian, the young monk, who had previously saved him from the hate of Leo X. by the discovery obtained from the ambassador of Charles V., had now, by his wise refusal to go to the court of France, exempted his plans with Francis I. from what would have been sure defeat. Vian had put a letter into the hands of the cardinal as he entered the boat, and in it all was explained.

"The Pythagorean philosopher may not be satisfactory to Glastonbury, but his political sagacity adorns Hampton Court," thought his Grace, as he tore the note to pieces, and threw its fragments into the river.

"My refusal to prejudice the cause of my Lord Chancellor by meeting him who is at once my bitterest foe and the trusted dæmon of Francis I., may bring upon me the contempt of his Grace for the present; but I will bide my time," was the remark made by Vian to the secretary at the same moment at Hampton Court.

In their long walk through the buildings already erected, and in sight of improvements already begun, More and Giovanni had resolved to put into operation some scheme which should, if possible, so relieve Vian's mind of some of its problems that he might achieve the high success as a man of political affairs which seemed possible for him.

"You ought not to be here simply revising the plans of James Bettes, even if he does call himself 'master of the works of Thomas, Cardinal of York,'" said More.

"I learned architecture of Richard Beere, Abbot of Glastonbury," replied Vian, as he proceeded to give instructions concerning the copings of the parapets and the forms of those chimney-shafts which have delighted Victoria in our own day.

"James Bettes is not some Angelo dead and born again," said Giovanni, trying to make Pythagoreanism appear in Vian's answer.

"No; if he had been an Angelo he would be laboring now at some St. Paul's School, or perhaps at building a great temple for heretics. A man who has been brave and good never finds himself born anew on a lower scale."

"Vian," said More, with a touch of friendship in his tone, "come with me for a holiday."

"I must not leave my Lord Cardinal. When he returns I must tell him again that I cannot go to France. That fiend Ami will upset his plans if he knows I have to do with them. I could not go. Would you explain it to his Grace? Fra Noglini, who knows the knight, avows that his jealousy of me is so great that he would join the heretic William Farel, and go body and soul with the Reformers themselves, had he not learned that you and Master Erasmus were my friends, that I loved to read the 'Praise of Folly,' and that if he became a heretic, he might find myself in the crowd."

"You are in politics now, and out of church quarrels," said Giovanni.

"Yes. But I want to feel free in my thought and faith, nevertheless; and he, the hypocritical Waldensian sucking sweets at the court of Francis I., pretends to have a conscience. He is an infernal scoundrel, but he hates the indulgences as much as does any true saint. He would break his Majesty's realm to pieces to defeat me. I want to be true to my Lord Cardinal, good friends, and I refuse to go to France on any mission for the sake of his Grace. I beg you explain to his Grace where I am. I did not try to steal the affections of the girl Astrée. I want no woman's love. My philosophy prevents my loving any man's beloved. Pythagoras teaches that woman is man who has done wrong in some previous life. I prefer men. But oh, I had a vision once — "

More thought he saw that the monk was on the verge of madness. He was standing, or trying to stand, where hurricanes were meeting.

" Perhaps you would better amuse yourself with helping his Grace to build and adorn Hampton Court," said Giovanni, full of sympathy.

This touched Vian's soul. ' He hated the life he had been living. He hated the struggle through which he had been led. He hated, most of all, the thought that he must actually abuse a mind made for higher things, by amusing it in this crisis with the magnificence of the court of Henry VIII. and the splendors of Wolsey's country palace. The society of one great truth, held honestly and defended with heroism, would have compensated him for the loss of all; but he was hedged on every side.

"It is all amusing," said he, "to have a mind unmoved with the greater facts of this life. I have a certain faculty of hearing the lies of kings and popes and cardinals, and arranging them so that my Lord Cardinal can beat them all at lying. I am here so long as the falsities of men are valuable to one another. I want the truth. No pageant can hide that desire." Then he added in a long laugh: "We had a pageant ludicrous enough here at Hampton Court. My Lord Cardinal was giving a dinner to an ambassador. He sat in the centre of the high table. Around him were the guests. Two ladies were very near to his Grace. Gold and silver vases stood where we could find room. The minstrels played; and the dinner being over, the maskers waited in the chamber for the procession. Everybody was disguised. The hoods had been made in France, Spain, and Italy. The laces of gold and the embroidered green satin came from Flanders. The waiters upon those who wished to gamble held the bowls full of ducats and dice, while the dance went on. Suddenly the king himself rushed in, masked and picturesque. Forty others followed attired as the hideous crew of a pirate. Consternation seized every one. The torch-bearers dropped their torches, the drums thundered, and the fifes screamed, until all was confusion. Then the king himself pulled down his visor, and laughed at my Lord Cardinal, whereat the king sat down and played on the harpsichord while he sang a laughable song. It was all very amusing; but I would rather have an hour with Erasmus. Then there are serious questions of statecraft here. Charles V. swears and breaks his oath; the Pope promises and forgets; Francis I. embraces his Majesty, my king and yours, and both of them have their ministers arranging another farce. It is all serious and amusing, good friends; but I have had a vision, as you know. That vision I have buried in philosophy; but I do not think that Pythagoras or even the Pope can bury the noisy demand of the Reformers. What think you?"

More said nothing. He was charmed, astonished, perplexed; and he rested not until, on the return of Wolsey, Vian was allowed two or three days as a holiday.

CHAPTER IX.

All things are but altered, nothing dies,
And here and there th' embodied spirit flies
By time and force and sickness dispossessed,
And lodges where it lights in man or beast.
  PYTHAGORAS *in* OVID (*Dryden's translation*).

"IT is a battle between a vision and a philosophy then," said More, looking upon Vian with his placid gray eyes.

"Alas! I am torn to shreds with the contest, whatever it may be," answered the Pythagorean monk, as he shook his head aimlessly.

They were standing together in the home which has become renowned in history for its refinement and affection. Hours were gliding by on wings of gold. It was impossible for Vian to escape the charm of the family life which made that house so heavenly. The intellectual impulse which was generated there moved Vian's mind toward love. He yearned for such mental and spiritual companionship as made the atmosphere ideal. Hearthunger never appeared so irrepressible. He remembered that More had once been pledged to the life of a monk. He could not avoid contrasting what would have been the loneliness and thirst of his soul with the delicious interchange of thought and feeling, the bright and glowing fires of mutual devotion, which characterized that home.

Love had made her sacred temple there. The altars of affection were covered with costly sacrifices so freely given. The fire from on high was consuming the offering. The incense-cloud of affection ascended to the great white throne.

"I have been pledged to a monastic life; I am an oath-bound celibate," thought Vian with a sigh, as the wife of More came near and placed her hand upon the shoulder of her illustrious companion.

They had a delicate topic to talk upon. More was anxious to deal with one problem at a time, and his wife was conscious that her presence would interfere seriously with the full expansion of a conversation on celibacy. One such beauteous planet suddenly coming into such a gloomy sky would unduly irradiate and might confuse a soul so embarrassed with the limitations which annoyed Vian. She soon found another task of love elsewhere.

"But your devotion to Pythagoras has more to do just now toward putting out the fires of love, than your attachments to the monastic life," said the wise friend.

"Alas, oftentimes my vision of my mate plays havoc with my philosophy, good sir!" observed Vian, painfully smiling.

More was determined to test him.

"You have had a beautiful vision, Vian; and Saint Paul, when he explains the glory of his own career, has said, 'I was not disobedient unto the heavenly vision.'"

"But, good friend!" urged Vian, "mine began as the vision of a child."

"Samuel's vision, so the Scripture tells us, was a child's vision. It must not be forgotten that the Saviour of the oldest of sinners makes him return to his childhood before he is saved. Except we become as little children, we cannot be saved," replied More.

"Yes; but," Vian said, as he felt the vision steal upon him again, and command him with its pristine charm, — " yes; but I have been taught that these desires for love and for being loved, this thirst for the one above all others whom I must love, whom I have never really seen, — I have had it all held before me as a temptation of the Devil. Against something of this sort saint after saint has struggled. To escape that pitfall, some of the more holy have cut their bodies with flints and rolled in tangled patches of briers, penetrated their flesh with thorns, and frozen their limbs in caves of ice. Oh, it seems so strange that this beautiful one, whom I never have lost out of my vision, should be the only power in my life to keep me pure and to make me hope for saintliness; and yet that all the custodians of religion should tell me, from the words of the Fathers and the lives of the saints, that the dream I have had of her is the Devil's own invention to drag me to hell ! "

" It cannot be," said More, firmly.

Vian, long hours before, had told the story. In spite of this vow, it had haunted him; and now, in spite of Pythagoreanism, which had been a sort of substitute for that faith in the Church which he had lost and which degraded woman, the vision came back upon his soul with a celestial beauty. He had an affectionate faith that Thomas More would get him into no difficulties. He had always been thankful that he had obeyed the statesman on that dusty roadway, when he followed him and Erasmus, and that he went back obediently to Glastonbury Abbey. He had told but three men of the vision which had followed him since childhood. He had told the sub-prior, on an occasion forever memorable to Vian, in explanation of his difficulties with the monastic life. He had related the story of his ideal love for his unseen mate to Fra Giovanni and Thomas More. Each had met him with a characteristic prescription. Monasticism, in the person of the sub-prior, regarded his vision as a Satanic device to damn him. Fra Giovanni looked upon it with the contempt inspired by a philosophy which made a woman to be but a man who had behaved badly in some other life, and was therefore punished in having to appear on earth as a female. Thomas More, looking out from the experiences of love itself, pitied the yearning heart of Vian, and being a Churchman who feared a little the revolutions which he had helped to incite, tried to be cautious even in his use of truth.

Everything was against his making such an impression upon Vian as would serve to abolish that passionate love. Here was a living woman of whom her husband had written an epigram, which has inspired an archbishop to translate it thus : —

> "With books she 'll time beguile,
> And make true bliss her own,
> Unbuoyed by Fortune's smile,
> Unbroken by her frown.
>
> .   .   .   .   .
>
> So left all meaner things,
> Thou 'lt on her breast recline,
> While to her lyre he sings
> Strains, Philomel, like thine."

Vian was a lover, a musician, and a man of literary talent. His ardor was not cooling in the presence of a beautiful woman, whose husband, by educating her in literature and particularly in music, had made the Pythagorean philosophy so ineffective in so far as it threw a shadow upon such womanhood. Not Holbein's famous picture in oil, nor those of Erasmus's " Colloquies " in words, so sympathetically reflected the love at the home of Sir Thomas More, as did Vian's growing thirst.

More shrugged his shoulder — Erasmus tells us that " his right shoulder always had the look of being higher than the left " — when Vian, fully intent on keeping his faith in the transmigration of souls, proceeded to tell him of a few of his Pythagorean experiences.

"I am sure that in some other life I have met our sovereign Henry VIII."

"Where did you encounter him?" queried the host.

"In Rome, on the Appian Way. Yesterday I caught in his words the same tones with which he spoke to his charioteer. In his laugh I know there is the guffaw of one of the Cæsars."

"Do you recognize anybody else about the throne or court as belonging to that age? Has anybody else's soul transmigrated?"

"Now, good sir," said Vian, trustfully, "you will grant me forgiveness. Master Erasmus would not find fault. I love him. The chains which bound me once to worn-out traditions he has partially broken for me. I am too thankful to do him dishonor. I know that he wrote the 'Praise of Folly,' or at least completed it, in this house. You need not blame me — "

"Vian, you need not be anxious; we both love Erasmus," said More, wistfully.

"Then let me say I do not doubt that Erasmus — or the man we know as Erasmus of Rotterdam — is really Lucian of Samostata. He has his old satire; his mind is keen with the same weapons of wit and irony; and he knows that the priests now require his sarcasms, as did the gods of Rome in the time of his previous existence."

"Well," said More, laughingly, "that is a bright and just literary judgment, at all events. Erasmus himself would appreciate that."

"So," said Vian, "I am sure that one of the sisters at the nunnery is one of the vestal virgins of Rome come again. She acknowledged to me that at night by the crucifix she finds her way back to Rome. The old Roman religion has begun to decay; a new faith breathes like a spring-time upon the altars, and a fresh enthusiasm glows in the eyes of the priests. She says it all seems to be reenacted again. Just as she stood, herself being one of the last of the vestal virgins, at altars from whence the mind of ancient Rome had been led by the decay of faith and the rise of a novel worship; so here on earth, in this new time, she beholds the attack on the papacy and the influence of 'the new learning,' with an ominous atmosphere around it all, indicating that a great transformation has come."

"You must live in a very strange world, Vian," said More, reflectively.

"Yes; I do indeed. The ghosts of the past are everywhere. I myself am one. If I knew all previous history, I could find out people and tell them their past. I could also tell whether they had done well or badly in their other lives. The very animals are but the incarnate souls of very vicious people. The saints and heroes are those who had done well and have been re-incarnate at a higher point in the scale. When I recognize a man, I can always see what his tendency is, downward or upward. One thing is a worry to me —"

"Ah !" said More, "only one?"

"No; would it were so ! Woman is a problem, — that is, some women are problems."

"Woman has always been a problem," said the pleasant host.

"Yes; but women — that is, all women — do not take their places in my philosophy as they ought, if they are what they seem to be, or if love is not a snare, or if Pythagorean doctrines of metempsychosis be true."

"That is a fierce trilemma. Each point is a spear," said More, with a smile.

"Well, what I mean is just this," — pointing to the monkey which appears in Holbein's famous canvas, "The Household of Sir Thomas More," — an animal which there nestles in the robes of Dame Alice Middleton, but which in actual life and at the moment spoken of was climbing upon the table before Vian, — "that monkey is doubtless the re-incarnation of some court-jester — "

"Or philosopher," whispered More.

"And Pythagoras teaches that he is what he is now because he was so bad in the other life. But Fra Giovanni has so explained Pythagoras that woman — "

"And you are a Pythagorean, having lost your faith in much that the Church teaches?" inquired More, reprovingly.

"I believe in God, in the Blessed Son our Lord, in the Holy Virgin — "

Vian hesitated with the words "Holy Virgin;" and then he said: "I believe the teachings of Pythagoras to be true. Some day they will be harmonized with true Christianity."

"But," said More, "you find it hard to think that such a woman as Dame Alice — " and just then Alice Middleton, who in no small measure had taken the place of "the gentle girl" whom More had lost, came near to them, and appeared, as she was, a most beautiful and affectionate woman — "you do not believe that she " — More placed his hand upon her white forehead — "is only a bad man reborn into a twenty fifth or sixth life."

Vian said, "No," with decision.

"What shall we say about your vision of that lovely maiden, your little mate at Lutterworth? It seems that if Pythagoras has spoken truth she must have been a bad — "

"Never! Not at all!" cried Vian. "I would annihilate all philosophies before I could believe that. She is as real to me as ever, — I believe that I love her."

"You are a sworn celibate too," observed Sir Thomas More, gravely.

"He is a beautiful lover," broke in Dame Alice.

"You are a Pythagorean," said More, with evident knowledge of the difficulties of Vian's heart and brain.

"I am nothing," replied the monk, — "nothing, if I do not love that vision of my soul's mate."

"Vian," — More began slowly, as they both stood up, and Dame Alice put her hands upon the gesticulating hand of Vian and that of her husband, — "you may know that when I was younger than I am now, I played at farces which I myself did compose. If I had to write one now, it would be simply the record of an imaginative young monk who has had a rapturous vision which has been too powerful to allow him contentment as a monk, and which is now too strong to let him remain a Pythagorean, believing in the transmigration of the soul. As I said to you, the battle is between a vision and a philosophy; and this sweet woman knows philosophy will not win the victory when love is in the vision."

"Oh!" said Vian, as he walked to the window and looked out where the children of Sir Thomas were learning the Greek alphabet by shooting arrows at the letters, "I am confident that it was a child's vision. I shall find myself always a Pythagorean and a Christian. I have believed that I should some day behold that same lovely face which has haunted my eye. But the abbot assured me that it is the temptation of the Devil; and I was once flogged when I spoke of it to a prior who had thought me heretical. Later on, as I lost my ability to have faithful care for the relics and fasts and feast-days at Glastonbury, the vision came back. I thought I should find her — O God, how often this unseen companion of my spirit has kept me from mortal sin! Then the first truths of Pythagorean philosophy became my meat and drink, instead of monks' tales and the exploits of saints. I accept that philosophy to-day."

"Of course it involves the doctrine of the soul's transmigration," said More.

"Yes," hesitated Vian. "I believed that this doctrine did shed a fair light upon the sweet face in my vision.

I thought that I must have known my mate in another life. I think that, beautiful as she is in my dream, she has been compelled to work out a ransom for herself somewhere. She lives probably in some corner of this big world. Oh, I dread, and yet I yearn to meet her if but for a moment! I will — I must be a Pythagorean. It is the only philosophy to harmonize with our holy religion. I will not — I cannot believe that this affection is born of Satan. That vision has kept me, I say, good friends, — it has kept me pure. I am glad enough to be away from Glastonbury, where the prior asked me daily if I did not want to be flogged because the face of my soul's mate still haunted me."

Dame Alice stood near him, wondering, breathing a prayer for Vian. It was at an hour when the currents of thought which preceded the Reformation swept before her, mingling, in this unique experience, the driftwood of the past with gleams which lay upon a tossing flood set toward the future.

CHAPTER X.

THE SACRIFICE OF BAYARD.

"Lost! an army in the hills of Genoa! The finder shall have a reward."

HARDLY had Pope Adrian VI. been enthroned by the intrigues of Charles V. through Don Manuel, before Don Manuel himself began to share the contempt which Rome expressed after the election.

His Holiness offended the men of the Renaissance, as he entered the Vatican. He remarked, as he saw the statuary, "Sunt idola Antiquorum!" and refused to enter the Belvedere, which he afterward walled up.

"The Holy Ghost," said the Spaniard, "was with the cardinals in the conclave, but the Devil has been with them since they came out."

His Holiness was not ready to hand over the tiara to the custody of the emperor; Adrian VI. even contended that Don Manuel had tried to prevent his election.

Charles V. and Cardinal Wolsey were soon beholding at Windsor a play, in which "Amity" (which they were expected to constitute) had sent "Prudence" and "Policy," who broke the horse "Force," or France, bitting him severely and reining him most carefully. France must be invaded; and the Pope, England, and the emperor were against her.

Grave as was the peril to Francis I., it had grown more terrible, when one morning Ami came to him and repeated the words of Bourbon: "It is too late."

"Where is his sword?" cried out the French monarch, who was wrathful beyond expression, as he looked into the calm face of Ami, who so often had urged him to be just with Bourbon,—"where is his sword?"

"Sire," answered Ami, with dignity and a graceful courtesy which tangled the king's thoughts, "he bids us say to your Majesty that his sword was taken away when his command was given to the husband of your darling sister Marguerite."

"The collar of Saint Michael?"

"Here, my gracious sovereign," said Ami, producing it. "It was under the head of his bed at Chantelle."

"Oh, Ami," said the king, whose heart was bursting with pain and foreboding, "forgive my tears, forgive my insults! I would give Duprat and Bonnivet, Lautrec and Lorraine,—all of them would I give for him, for Bourbon, if he had never fallen to be a traitor."

Ami knew that this was no time for reminding the king of his previously expressed anxieties and protests. No true knight ever said, in word or deed, "I told you so." He was sure that, if ever, the king needed his friendship now. Bourbon had been mistreated by the king, the Chancellor Duprat, and above all, by Louise of Savoy; but now Bourbon was a traitor. That fact was sufficient to warm Ami's spirit to enthusiasm against him.

Charles V. did not intend the conquest of France; he was simply making Henry VIII. pay for an army which would persuade Francis I. to give up Milan. Bourbon, in his flight, had eluded the eye of Francis; and soon Francis was again growing weary of Ami's pleas that Duprat's schemes for the capture of Bourbon should be superseded, when the item of news came,— Ami had to break it to his king,— "The Emperor Charles V. has made Bourbon Lieutenant-General."

While Francis I. and Mme. de Chateaubriand were

arranging all sorts of plans to tarnish the love of Astrée and Ami, and thus to reduce it to the level of their own, the young knight was gathering from the luminous darkness of Astrée's eyes, and from the soft pressure of her lovely hand, the courage and tenderness with which next day, having followed the king into his Majesty's chamber, he adjured him to prevent the sacrifice of Bayard to the ignorance of Admiral Bonnivet.

" *He* will not complain," said the king, who was full of spite over the failure of Mme. de Chateaubriand's latest scheme.

" *I* do not complain, Sire."

The rich divan upon which the king lay, was half hidden with the splendid garments which gave beauty to the sinewy strength of his Majesty's form. As the king rose to say, " The astrologer said it ! " Ami's eyes fell upon a jewel-box which he and Astrée had observed in the hands of Mme. de Chateaubriand ; and the knight turned away.

April 30, 1524. A stone sang through the air. Yonder was a puff of smoke from an arquebusier.

" Jesus, my God, I am slain ! "

" No," said the dying man later, to those who came up to hope against despair, — " no ; it is done." His trembling hand lowered his sword, and the glassy eyes were fixed upon the shining cross in its hilt.

" Let us carry him hence," exclaimed Ami.

" No ! In death I will not turn my back on the enemy. Charge ye ! "

It was Chevalier Bayard's last word of command. " Miserere mei, Deus Secundum magnam misericordiam tuam," murmured he again, as they gently placed him, the knight *sans peur et sans reproche,* under the whispering tree around which ran a clinging vine.

Through his tears Ami saw the dust-cloud. The

enemy was near. Mid the clatter of hoofs, Bayard was confessing to a young man, Jacques, —

"All I regret is not having done my duty as I ought to have done," he said.

"A quart of my blood were nothing!" said Pescara, the foe, as he commanded that Bayard's enemies should raise a tent above the agonizing man.

At that instant Ami saw a well-known figure near him. On his breast was the coat of arms of Charles V.; in his eye was pain. It was Bourbon.

. "I grieve for your disaster," said he, kneeling by the side of the greatest of knights.

Chivalry spoke again. Bourbon had risen. Through the branches above him sighed the spring. Prophecies of summer played and vanished upon his glittering armor.

A cloud came over the scene, as Bayard extended his finger, which seemed a sword tipped with scorn, and said : "My Lord, no pity for me! I have done my duty, and die. There is pity for you, who fight against your oath. your country, your king."

As Bourbon silently withdrew, Ami felt himself knit, in bonds never to be severed, to Francis I. and to France. He was, however, not less sure that Admiral Bonnivet had sacrificed Bayard.

October found Bourbon commanding Milan, which he had forsaken when his army was in such condition as would justify setting up in Rome such a pasquinade as has been printed at the beginning of this chapter, and to which city of Milan he had returned with thirteen thousand men.

Meantime Ami had urged Francis I. to pursue the disorganized Imperialists, until his Majesty, acting under Bonnivet's advice, had told him : "I have now no patience with you or with astrologers."

That iron entered Ami's soul. What should he do?

Astrée was far away; but he remembered her words. They sufficed to make him burn for an opportunity to prove himself a better soldier than Admiral Bonnivet. Ami could still hear Louise of Savoy say to him with stinging scorn: "The King of France allowed you to exchange the cap and plume of a page for halbert and helm." "No," had said Astrée, as she looked upon her knight in polished steel; "I have loved a knight, and Bayard said it."

The king himself solved Ami's problem. A last message to his Majesty, which had been lost for a time, had finally arrived. Bayard had so commended Ami to the King of France that Bonnivet's words went for naught; and Ami, Feb. 23, 1525, was made ready to serve his sovereign again.

CHAPTER XI.

PAVIA.

" Madame, tout est perdu fors l'honneur!"

NOVEMBER 8 had seen the king sacrifice more than two thousand Frenchmen in storming the town of Pavia. The river was a torrent; the skies were murky; and Bourbon and Pescara had strengthened the Imperialists by their arrival. Around the governor, Antonio de Leyva, were consolidated the viceroys and generals of Charles V. Francis, in obedience to Bonnivet, had continued the siege, in spite of the proposals of the enemy, the starved condition of his troops, and the peril of his situation. Continually on horseback, he rode about within sight of the garrison of his foe, sneering at the suggestions which he had received from the new Pope, Clement VII., and laughing with Bonnivet over Wolsey's second defeat at Rome.

Antonio de Leyva had converted all the sacred vessels of the churches into coin; and the gold chain which hung about his neck had been melted into ingots. The women were working in the trenches. Desperation had done its work in making the Imperialists courageous. Each army had agreed to fight next day. Night had come over the tower of Mirabello, from which Montmorency had made the bodies of its defenders dangle, because, as he said, "they had resisted a royal army in a hencoop." Darkness, broken in upon by the starlight, half concealed the great walls which surrounded the park.

As Ami sat there in the star-lit night watching with one whom he so deeply loved, filled with inspiring recollections of the night before the battle of Marignano, and impressed with the importance of what he foresaw was to be known in history as the battle of Pavia, the king suddenly turned to the young knight, and said, —

"You believe me to be surrounded by bad advisers."

"I have not said so much," was the swift reply. "But I have thought your knowledge of my loyalty and love would allow the truth to be spoken concerning the measures and methods proposed to you, Sire."

The moon looked clearly upon the fearless and affectionate honesty of the young knight. Francis I. was charmed with his superb appearance. Ami had resolved to remain in the saddle, even if the sovereign slept. He was mounted upon a noble charger, which was as unwearied as his gallant rider. One of the squires held the rein, which was at that instant relaxed. Ami was clad in complete armor. Every incidental word or motion indicated his readiness to dismount, as was the custom, and leave his horse in charge of one of the infantry, while he fought. The golden spurs and the white girdle, which latter Nouvisset had asked Astrée to place around his loins when he left Chambord, seemed instinct with a nervous vitality. His helmet detained the silvery light, as the beams played upon its glittering surface. Beneath his cuirass was beating a heart which now had but two impulses, then made one, — love for Astrée and loyalty to the king. Jealousy of the detested English monk had driven conscience from the field of his emotions; and jealousy had gone away after conscience in hot pursuit. He was not interested in Reformers or Reformations. The

Waldensian within him slept in the stalwart ambition of
the knight. As Francis I. gazed upon his companion,
he still believed that though Chevalier Bayard's race
had been run with this young Bayard, he could even yet
rekindle the expiring embers of chivalry.

"I did venture to say," remarked Ami, "that it appeared to me, Sire, that your soldiers should have been
drilled by their commanders."

"Drilled?" asked the king, — for at that hour in the
history of war it was a new idea that such a regulation
should be imposed upon officers — "drilled? Did you
say it?"

"Every man should know his pike or bow or arquebusier, — every man should be known for ill or good in a
crisis like this."

"You do not see victory — "

"Except in trained soldiers who have not been
gathered by force or by money," interjected the knight.
"Courage, my king, is born of love and loyalty; and
even courage needs to be trained to its task. We are
on the way to a new era in the history of military affairs, Sire."

"Ah!" said the king, betraying his somewhat sleepy
condition, "you and Nouvisset would make many revolutions. What else, Ami?"

"If the contest does not come at dawn, I would have
your Majesty's mercenaries so disposed that they would
not dare to abandon their king and the nobles of France,
even if they desired."

"I see," said the king, "you have lost faith in human
nature, — first, in the good sense and skill of commanders
such as mine; then, also, in the soldiers themselves."

"Nay, my king, nay! I never have had any faith to
lose in purchasable human nature."

"Nouvisset was a mercenary," said his Majesty,
sharply.

"His love for you, his loyalty to France, however, have never been purchasable," was the answer. "He loves the king and France."

"What else?" said Francis I., as he scowled upon Ami, and then yawned with royal earnestness.

Ami sat more knightly than before, peering out into the shadows which were a little disturbed by the starlight, and he said wistfully, —

"I hope the captains have not overestimated the number of men under the standard of your Majesty. Every man should have been counted."

"Still you distrust somebody!" said the tired king, with petulance. "It must appear to you that my captains have some interest in exaggerating the strength of my army."

"They have truly, Sire!" was the reply, — a reply which never left the mind of the King of France, until more than a year later, his army was placed under a finer military administration.

"You are peering into a bog of heavy shadows, Ami. Come, cheer up! This is another Marignano. We shall go to Bologna again and get another ring, I pledge you!" Upon the face of the king was a coerced smile.

Ami, by the instincts of his mind and by Nouvisset's culture, had a certain mastery of the science of war. He said nothing. The moon was hid again behind the clouds.

"Be careful of your person," urged Ami, as he strained his gaze far over to the wall of Mirabello, where he was now sure that what he had descried was only the light playing with the shadows.

"And you are a knight?"

"And a lover of my king!" was Ami's answer.

Nothing burdened the mind of Francis I. as did the defection of six thousand Grisons, upon whom he had relied.

While the king cursed them, Ami thought of the speech of Cardinal Sion to the Swiss, before the battle of Marignano, in which that fierce orator told them, "Ye are the distributors of sovereignty!"

Could it be that at length Europe had passed into the hands of a rising democracy?

Ami started, as again the lights and shadows moved yonder. It was two o'clock on the morning of February 24.

"Only the flashes of dawn," said Bonnivet, as he turned away.

"Nay!" exclaimed Ami. "They are soldiers!"

It was true. Pescara had broken down nearly fifty fathoms of the wall; and three thousand German and Spanish troops, — each man's armor covered with a white shirt, — trusting to the interval of darkness, had accompanied the vanguard under Guasto, and had stolen forth to save the garrison.

Instantly the French cannon poured a flame of death upon them.

"Scatter and flee!" cried Guasto, as the fire divided the columns.

"They flee! they flee!" shouted Francis, when he beheld the falling enemy. "Charge!" cried he, as he descried the foe clambering upon the bank.

Down upon them swept the impetuous sovereign of France. Ami alone urged him to refrain from exposing his person. Dead at the king's feet fell the Marquis Civita San Angelo. The enemy's advance-guard was broken. The men-at-arms about him were stung with indignation at Ami, who twice had prevented his sovereign from advancing beyond his own guard.

"The lanzknechts are unprotected!" cried Ami.

"Cut him down for his contumacy!" shouted Admiral Bonnivet, who struck at the knight.

"I would fain call myself 'Duke of Milan'!" said the

haughty king, as he broke through a corps, with the brother of Mme. de Chateaubriand, Lescun, at his side.

"The soldiers of his Majesty are between their guns and their foes!" said Ami; "this ought not to be."

Ami was as helpless and sorrowful as he was brave and faithful.

At that moment Pescara threw nearly two thousand of his arquebusiers upon the French. Horses and riders struggled in death, while the arquebusiers fell back to renew their attack upon the gendarmerie. The king and his troop now masked the French batteries by persistently fighting in front of them. The unprotected lanzknechts were cut to pieces by the Germans whom Pescara had hurled upon them. Montmorency was abandoned by the Swiss and captured by the vanguard of Guasto, who had now thrown his forces into the gap which the King of France had created.

Ami defied the hirelings of Bonnivet, as he urged the king to unmask his guns. All around the sovereign the foe was creating a bloody plain. Horses and knights, broken arms and bloody helmets, were piled about his Majesty. Antonio de Leyva soon joined Pescara with the garrison.

At length Duc d'Alençon, Marguerite's husband and Bourbon's puny successor, instead of coming to the rescue of Francis, left the field, and carried the rearguard of the king in retreat. Marot and Henry d'Albret were prisoners; La Pallisse, La Tremoille, Chabannes, Chaumont, and Francis de Duras were slain.

"My God!" said the king, "what is all this?"

"I cannot endure this disaster," cried Bonnivet, who raised his visor and fell mortally wounded.

"Ah, wretch!" hissed Bourbon, who on pressing near had forgotten all the other sins of Bonnivet in his remembrance that he had aspired to the love of Marguerite, and who at that moment saw his enemy's corpse. "Thou hast cheated me of making thee my prisoner; thou hast ruined France and me!"

The king's three wounds were bleeding profusely, but now and then he was able to cut down an assailant. His huge sword at length became heavy in his hands, though he compelled one of the foe's standard-bearers to groan in death beneath his Majesty's horse. The king's courage was, however, departing, while the intrepid Ami was defending his master on every side.

"You *are* a Bayard," said Francis, with gratitude; and then with sorrow he added, "Ah, Bayard! had you been here, this had not happened!"

They had turned toward the bridge over the Ticino. It was broken down. A blow on his horse's head made the beast reel and stagger to the earth. The Spaniards crowded about him, as the king stood by the side of his dying charger, and smote his face. The golden lilies blazed upon his coat of mail. In the storm of battle his thick plumes still nodded defiance. No one, save Ami, knew him, as he fought man after man, until Seigneur de Pomperan — a refugee with Bourbon — came near, and helping Ami to drive the rough soldiers from the king, urged him to surrender to Bourbon, who was in sight.

"I would rather die than honor a traitor!" replied the bleeding French Sovereign. "Send the Viceroy of Naples! I will surrender to him."

Francis I. was soon a prisoner. Lannoy held his sword.

"Oh, Ami," sobbed the great broken heart, as Francis commanded him to bear the words, "All is lost, save honor!" to his mother, Louise of Savoy, — "oh, Ami, if I had heeded your words! Do not avenge yourself on me, by preventing my frank speech. Ami, had I obeyed your words I had been a victor, and Bourbon had become my prisoner. Farewell! The astrologer said it!"

As Ami turned to go, — for the king's desire was not to be changed by Ami's pleading to accompany him, — another kind of message from the Abbot of Najara was placed in the hands of a courier, who was to bear it to the Emperor Charles V.

"Twenty-five years ago to-day," so ran the language, "your Majesty is said to have been born. It is the day of the Feast of the Apostle Saint Matthias. Twenty-five thousand times thanks and praise to God for His mercy! From this day, laws for Christians and Turks must be prescribed by you."

CHAPTER XII.

LA TORRE.

Thou, Lord, dost hold the thunder; the firm land
Tosses in billows when it feels thy hand;
Thou dashest nation against nation, then
Stillest the angry world to peace again.
Oh, touch their stony hearts who hunt thy sons, —
The murderers of our wives and little ones.

Yet, mighty God, yet shall thy frown look forth
Unveiled, and terribly shall shake the earth;
Then the foul power of priestly sin and all
Its long-upheld idolatries shall fall.
Thou shalt raise up the trampled and oppressed,
And thy delivered saints shall dwell in rest.

BRYANT.

WHILE, on the soil of Pavia, a haughty and un-intelligent king was passing into servitude unto Charles V., the cause whose demands he had at first invited, then forgotten, and at length scorned, was acquiring sovereignty throughout Europe. His Imperial Majesty Charles V. himself had not yet even measured swords with the Reformation, though he had fancied Francis I. to be the most important prisoner his armies might capture. Francis himself had not yet even awakened to the majestic power, the neglect of which was to make his reign a most brilliant failure, though he imagined himself to have been defeated by the most resistless force of the sixteenth century.

There, near La Torre, upon a maiden's face quivered a splendor more majestic than that upon the crown of the emperor; and yonder in the mountains of Switzerland was seen a glow which that Swiss army knew not, when in their presence the King of France was knighted by Bayard at Marignano.

> "Si el non vol cum la fe las obras acabar
> La corona de gloria nones degne le portar."

These dear old words, which had been repeated by her forefathers so often when they found themselves likely to forget that faith without works is dead, had just come from Alke's lips, as full of the rippling melodiousness of her soul as was the mountain brook of the harmonies of summer. She was passing under the heavy shadow of the great cliff to pluck another blossom which had attracted her eye.

The fever was raging in the neighborhood of Gaspar Perrin's cottage as never before. Every day the lay-representatives of the haughty Church repeated to the affrighted denizens of that hitherto lovely valley the assertions of the priesthood that this virulent disease would not abate until the Barbés and the fraternities yielded their submission to the Pope. Poor mothers, the bodies of whose children had been recently hidden from their sight, were met, as they fell to weeping at the graves, by these papistical emissaries, who assured them that the monks had the tenderest sympathy for them in their bereavement, but that nothing could be done to relieve the valley from the presence of the plague until the authority of the Vicar of God was recognized.

"You dare not claim the right to sacrifice your innocent children," said one of them to an affrighted woman who had stolen away from her cottage to visit a little grave under the hillock. "You know their lives are not yours to give as an offering to your wicked rebellion against the Holy Father. You may slaughter yourself only with peril to your soul, but with what more dreadful peril do you kill your little ones ! "

Many a mother's heart stopped beating while these implied maledictions hung over her head ; and many a strong man whose eyes had just looked into the yet livid face of his dead child for the last time, found himself asking questions of his soul such as never occurred to him before. The redactor — the senior Barbé — was absent, and Alke felt that a severe trial for their faith was coming.

Events and confessions of faith have often jostled uneasily against one another in the life of mankind ; and Alke, who was now a sort of high-priestess in the mind of the community, saw that the Waldensian spirit, which had endured much, needed a mighty strengthening against these horrible experiences and the sinister suggestions of the Churchmen, who now hung about the sorrowful and dying.

" Oh, sister and beloved ! " cried one poor woman, whose only son lay next the open window, with the shadow of death hovering over his scarlet cheeks, " oh, Alke, I could believe in God when I saw the priests burning his father in a swift flame ; must I believe in the priests when I behold God burning his child in the slower fire ? "

The spiritual crisis seemed more imminent when it was noticed that even Alke's face was strangely wan, and her eye, full of weariness, the true home of constant watchfulness and prayer, was becoming unsteady and sad.

Oh, how the infinite abysses of loveliness and faith within those eyes — vast deeps which entertained the Eternal One — appeared to have grown narrow and shallow, as she had looked upon the lustrous images of death in those children's faces ! Could it be that the

Lord God of the Waldensians had forsaken her, who sang like a Miriam in yonder cavern, who had blessed little ones and made that dedication of our Lord's Prayer at the communion which none could forget?

These awful doubts were multiplying. More recently, and especially on the day before, Alke's prolonged absences from the scenes of suffering had been noticed with an unholy dread.

Had God so forsaken her that she had forsaken them?

True, at evenfall she had brought more flowers into the homes of the dying than ever before. Never had the pillows on which the children gasped for breath been so irradiated with color; never had the low rooms been so fragrant as in the hours just gone. But death had been supreme all day, and she had been away so long!

"Oh, my children die, and the flowers wither as soon as you bring them!" sighed Jeane Ferson, as she, whom some called the "angel of the dawn," silently went out of that cottage upon that very morning again, a tear in her sad eye, and weariness in her uncertain step.

A knot of the stricken ones in the roadway — some leaning upon the breasts of big, silent men who looked perplexed, others looking away toward little graves which had been made by the side of the tombs of fathers and husbands slain for a faith which was now shaken — was seen to be deeply engaged in attending to a rather loquacious but good-hearted peasant-woman, who had believed in God and Alke up to that very hour. Her faith, however, was now quite gone.

What had she seen? Enough to prove to her that Alke had given up hope, had been overtaxed, was probably wandering in her mind, and had begun trying to hide her despair in aimless flower-gathering.

"Oh, I could see it!" she said.

Before this chattering woman could tell her story of Alke, a solemn son of thunder threw into their panic-stricken souls an account of an event quite calculated to make the conquest of doubt and superstition complete.

There is no such scepticism as that which is born of superstition, and there is no such credulity as that which nurses at the breasts of doubt.

"A child has been cured, — a child of Manel Janven," said he, with a voice betraying the state of mind into which that indubitable fact had placed him. Other hearts than his — even Manel Janven's — were wondering which was the direst calamity, — the loss of a child with still a fragment of faith left, or the cure of a child and all one's faith gone over to the enemy. That event brought with it this fearful dilemma. For every one knew that one of the priests had been muttering sentences and exhibiting relics over the little one; and now — they had heard it — the child was delivered from the plague.

Nobody asked a question. Many a mother listened to hear a baby's cry, and many a father felt a sickening possibility drinking the blood out of his heart. Only the mountaineer with grewsome look had spoken. Every one else wanted to speak. Each, however, seemed to feel that in matters of belief, as in affairs of practice, it is not what goeth in but what cometh out of one's soul that defileth. Silence is often the salvation of faith.

How desperately they struggled to keep the Waldensian faith! How, also, did each mother feel her babe's eye looking up into hers from the grave by the torrent or from yonder cradle!

Now, for the first time, they knew that French soldiers were not the strongest foes of belief. An unexplained fact, coming into one's creed from the larger equation of life; a babe's moan which finds no harmony amid all the tones of one's belief, — will do more to break up the accepted equation, or to destroy the accepted tonic theory, than the armies of a world. An army is usually the shadow of a phantom; but a fact, needing no army, must make a place for itself. No creed is strong enough to disdain the smallest fact.

"The child is nearly well, and laughs, as it toddles around about," repeated this man, hardy with his sense of reality. He was even harsh, as every soul possessing a fact which we cannot make to fit into our scheme seems to be.

"How was the little one made well?" inquired a brawny man, whose throat was full of tremors, as he tried to speak.

The answer was as pitilessly accurate, and therefore as thoroughly inaccurate, as is any response which worships what we call "the scientific method," — a method which has always illustrated its unscientific tendency by so stating the facts of which it does know that it discounts those of which it does not know.

This was his answer: "The priest said words over the sick child. The priest also showed relics to the little one."

It was a true account as to everything but the whole truth.

"Yes," cried Gaspar Perrin, who for a few moments had stopped with the circle, "I could tell you more than that. The priest fed the child day and night."

Gaspar turned toward his cottage wondering if he should find Alke. Silence again! Another fact, — therefore a necessity, perhaps, for another equation!

Think you, reader, that these knew how increasingly a genuine Protestantism must always have that experience? "Thy heart shall fear and be enlarged," must be written upon the soul of every man who reveres truth more than statements, who knows that institutions and constitutions are less large than man and human life. The bane of Churchmanship, inside of Catholicism and Protestantism alike, has been its vigorous necessity to crowd facts into predetermined theories; the work of Christianity is everywhere to respect facts by making theories accordant with them. It is a large universe which we inhabit; and so large and rich in facts it is, that the ultimate creed will never be written. The protester — sometimes by necessity a protester against Protestantism — will always have his work to do in this world.

In the bewilderment which Gaspar's words caused, the garrulous old woman began to tell of Alke's wanderings, as she had observed them, in a way entirely true to the facts which she saw, thoroughly untrue to the facts which she did not see. Nobody fancied then that the soul most agitated by the advent of all these facts, and indeed the soul most sure to find their meaning, and thus to discover their harmony with the old facts, was that of this very girl Alke, who was both gathering flowers, and holding her mind to the facts which she had and to the faith in which she held them, while she labored. Alke's un-churchly protestantism against an uncomprehensive creed was healthier far than theirs, because she had a dim, unspoken faith in truth, — that thing which guarantees that whenever one has discovered two facts between which there seems to be no connection, there is a certainty that a third exists somewhere which will relate them. Alke was more than a Waldensian. She had so read the Greek philosophy that her rationalism was Christian; and she felt that while she was thus waiting on truth, she was obeying the precept, "Wait on the Lord."

What was she doing in the defiles between the mountains? Gathering flowers for the pillows of the dying; gathering facts for the completion of her creed. How? By obeying a noble faith in truth and a noble impulse to help humanity.

One is never so sure of a complete and true creed as

when one has set out to do a completely and truly generous act.

All that the old woman saw was this: Alke had found a Golden Ball which her eye had seen in a dewy meadow. In that air above her, which for an hour had hung thick and murky with storms, she had gathered around that tuft of sunshine the harvest of beauty from the height and depth.

" Going mad ! " had whispered the woman, as she saw Alke digging under the anemones which swayed with the huge pines overhead, — pines in which just then the dazzling light, breaking through the gray gloom above, swept like a dream, and left every tree a shivered emerald. " Going mad ! going mad ! "

The eye of despair and assured wisdom followed Alke, as she grasped a bunch of ox-eyed daisies which were curiously defiant of the darkness when the sun was overcast ; and stopping only to dig again, as it seemed, Alke pushed on toward a rhododendron, which surpassed in depth of crimson even the Alpine roses which were held in her girdle.

" She is eating roots. Ah ! gone mad? Yes ; gone mad ! Alke has lost faith and has gone mad," averred the peasant-woman, shaking her gray locks like a despairing prisoner.

Still had the sad eyes of the peasant-woman followed Alke.

Far over the rocks, where the noisy torrent plunged into a tumultuous, wild cascade, flared the Kamblume, red like a torch, as if to light the rapid way of the dashing waters at night and to outrival the stream itself in power of attraction by day. There was Alke, her wan face and tired eyes seemingly uninterested in the glaring splendor. As she dug again beneath the blossom, and plucking up a root, tasted it, the woman on the rock behind the pines whispered, —

"Yes; poor Alke! Gone mad! Does the Barbé know it?"

Up and on Alke climbed, the eyes of the older woman's anxious and satisfied thought following her, until she and her flowers were half hidden midst the weird desolateness of the crags, or until she emerged again, like a lost spirit, bent on finding an old path, only to reach down into that summer snow-field of Edelweiss, even beneath the bloom, to the dark roots below, — the same eyes following her, tears gathering in the old sockets of the gray head, until Alke stood looking out over the valley beyond, where were health and rejoicing, where Alke saw girls radiant with bright ribbons and beautiful in white bodices, and whither she started. In a moment she had left the perilous crag on which she had been standing. She slowly withdrew from its loneliness; and there it stood out alone like a pedestal bereft of its glorious but pathetic figure.

This was all that the talkative woman, then almost despoiled of her own faith, could see. She had told it over again. Looking again through her eyes, as they huddled together, a band of stricken souls, baffled and perplexed in belief, this was all they saw as she told her tale. "Going mad! gone mad! Digging in the ground beneath the blossoms! Eating roots!" — these phrases they heard, as they silently parted and went away, listening to the crash of beliefs within their own breasts.

CHAPTER XIII.

A HEART'S DISCONTENT.

TWO sad weeks had gone. They had ended in a dawn-like revelation.

"Who said it?"

"Young Gerard Pastre," replied Louis Savan. "I ought to say our dear Barbé, I suppose; but we are Waldensians, and fear even a little priestcraft. Besides, Gerard is so young."

"And what said he, Louis? Do not keep us waiting!" urged a mountaineer.

"He went on to say, — Gerard is eloquent sometimes, good friends, — he went on to tell, as I cannot, how Alke herself a week ago was trembling for her own soul. You know it all. Every child was dying. Every mother looked at a grave, or at a little one who might leave her for its grave in a day. The heavens seemed to give no answer. Strong men among us doubted God's love. The priests swarmed about us, taunting the men and inducing the mothers to doubt the effacacy of our faith, and to believe that God was punishing us for rebellion against the Pope. Then came the cure of that child by the priest;" and Louis Savan placed his hand upon the head of Manel

Janven's little child, who stood before them. "Could Heaven have made a more awful trial of our faith?"

"And then," said Gaspar Perrin, who had been silent until he stumbled in his speech, — "then you thought my Alke was going mad."

"Then," pursued Louis, whose voice shook, as he looked about in vain for Alke, "she was in the hills hunting for herbs and roots, — God bless her!" and Louis could say no more.

The truth was that on that holy day to which Louis Savan referred, the service of thanksgiving and praise had been held. As he and those about him came homeward, they had met those who remained to guard the flocks and cottages; and Louis Savan was telling them of Gerard Pastre's sermon.

Gerard Pastre, who, when we met him last, was leaving ,Alke, as her quick wit bade him good-by, in the hope that he might become a Barbé, had soon finished his course at La Torre, and was now, as he had been for a year, Coadjutor. But they gratefully remembered that he was more than a minister. He had been a student of medicine for months before he was sent to Wittenburg to see Luther; and in the frightful crisis through which the faith of that plague-stricken community had just passed, he was Alke's constant companion and successful co-laborer.

How radiant appeared the day after such a night of gloom! Even the little graves seemed to respond in praise of this deliverance for their faith.

The facts may be easily guessed. The life of the child of Manel Janven had been spared, not because the priest had held before it a relic of Saint Ambrose, not because he had muttered before it the phrases which he did not understand, but because, knowing something of the disease peculiar to the region, and intelligent of the properties of the root which grew beneath the blossoms that decorated a certain narrow gulch in the rocks above, he had in secret fed the child the proper medicine, which he had craftily prepared. There had come a speedy cure. The priest had felt every confidence that the entire fraternity would soon forsake their opposition to the Church, and that relic-worship and obedience to the Pope should be re-established in that region, because it was a guarded secret. No one, as he fancied, saw aught but the relics, or heard aught save the muttered words. Who could doubt the miracle and the efficacy of the relics?

Alke was a student of philosophies as well as a protesting believer. Far in advance of the ideas of the Reformation upon these topics, had the Renaissance, which swept from Venice to Gaspar's cottage, lifted this woman. She had a true rationalist's belief in facts. She had that broader Christianity which, to the vision of a reactionary protestantism, is often rationalistic, because it holds every fact sacred. With a religious enthusiasm, she began to search for causes. Her creed she trusted would endure at least one more fact. It must endure it.

One night Gaspar had sat alone until daybreak. In the morning on which the peasant-woman saw Alke digging and tasting roots, she was possessed of the secret of the priest. At nightfall she had God's open secret in a fact. The root had been discovered. At the end of three days two other children had been cured, without relics or phrases or priests. The priests had suddenly departed ; and now the plague was stayed.

"Angel of the dawn!" again said the aged Barbé whom Alke had helped on his way to the communion, — "angel of the dawn!"

How great a dawn none knows, even at this day, lay in the soul of the least conspicuous child of humanity, who at that crisis conceived that a thoroughly Christian creed must have room for every fact, and that not even the new vision, which was protesting against the old, was ultimate. The historic blunder of Protestantism lies in the notion that the Reformation under Waldo, Wycliffe, Luther, and Calvin was complete in itself. The Renaissance is behind and within all thorough reformation; and not even Waldensian courage must be allowed to write a *ne plus ultra* upon the gateway of the mind. Perhaps the nineteenth century is learning, in the reconstruction of much dogma, that Luther's Reformation allowed too little place for the forces of the Renaissance.

Alke looked at the world, without and within, with these forces in her heart. "Poor girl!" Gaspar had said; "with this revolution in her bosom! But she has the grace of God; and that may make her happy, even here."

The Reformation — the Reformation which had the Renaissance behind and within it — had not only Luther within it, but Bacon, Cromwell, and Milton; and as a later blossom, Coleridge, Browning, even an Emerson. It gave the human brain the impulse of freedom; and its history has proved the conviction true that nothing is as safe as liberty. Protesting has not yet ceased; and protesting has come to be constructive rather than destructive. In this woman's soul the rationalistic Greek spirit had come, along with Luther's Latinistic, imperator-like self-respect. Therefore there were, even in her mind, germs of religious thought, and notions of the right of the soul to its own functions, which in theology have flung upon the nineteenth century such a constructive protester as Maurice, in politics such a constructive reformer as Lincoln.

How could she content herself with her environment, when such movements swirled in her brain? Could the grace of God and intellectual vitality suffice?

There is no such agony as sits at the gate of opportunity and lacks power, save that which waits with power before a wall in which opens no opportunity for its exercise and ministry.

"How useless," Alke had begun to say, "seem knowledge of language and enthusiasm here!"

It did not help her to be told by Gerard that France dreaded any movement which looked toward the popularizing of the Scriptures; but Alke connected the ideas. "These languages," said she, "are to be used in making the Scriptures an open book to all the world, and in explaining them to the nations. I ought to be helping it on."

As Gaspar, who had heard this conversation, looked at his daughter as she spoke of printing the Scriptures, the fingers of both his hands were partaking of the excitement of his mind, which was dreaming of setting the type somewhere for a cheaper edition of the Bible, as he had formerly helped to popularize the lines of Homer.

It was nearly 1526.

"Would that I could set the types!" said Gaspar.

"Would that I could read and correct the printed leaves!" said Alke.

But even this aspiration did not suffice. Nay; the grace of God, intellectual vitality, fine aspirations never will take the place of human love in the life of a woman.

Alke wandered out into the sunshine with the goats and her own restless heart. Near the tiny stream, where the grass had felt constant refreshing, grew the only stem of monk's-hood which Alke had seen, except the solitary specimen which her father had once brought to her from the high pastures. Its absence from this floral museum often seemed grateful to him. He disliked everything, even in Nature, which reminded him of a priest. The valley was far more tolerable to his sensitive enthusiasm because it refused to grow monk's-hood. Alke was saying this over to herself, while she held fast the copy of Luther's "Babylonian Captivity of the Church of God " which the young Reformer had sent to Gaspar Perrin. She sat upon a rock for a moment, with the rare blossom in her hand, and read aloud the concluding words of this heroic man : " I hear that bulls and other papistical things have been prepared, in which I am urged to recant or be proclaimed a heretic. If that be true, I wish this little book to be part of my future recantation."

Alke felt a strange longing in her heart.

"What is love," said she, " but this yearning to be loved by such a soul? What is it also, but to live for such an one?"

Poor Alke ! her name meant "yearning ; " and she had seen but few men, none of whom touched her girlish affections.

" I am too young to think of loving anybody," she added ; and then she gave herself up to that most exhaustive passion which visits the heart of an intellectual and affectionate girl, — the consuming desire to be allied with a noble and great soul. Dreams of the heroine she would be, if such a man as was Wycliffe should ever give her his heart ; visions of her ceaseless joy in suffering, if only she might go with a Hus to his couch of fire ; pictures of the rack on which her loveliness would gladly stretch itself, if only she could live in the dying for love and light, — these broke upon her as the soft air played upon her rosy cheeks, kissed her beautiful lips, and the monk's-hood blossom dropped from her hand. Love, abstract, ideal, but fiery and divine love had come with her opening womanhood. The girl had thus early blossomed into the glorious flower which yearned for its sunshine. For a moment it was as though she had found a gem, and had set it in gold. The gem she would not possess ; the setting would abide, and it would always demand a large and deep stone. To fall deeply in love with an ideal, suggested by some reality, makes the woman incapable of being satisfied with less than a hero. This was to be the fate of Alke.

She stooped to pick up the monk's-hood, and like a girl who has suddenly felt a woman's interest without losing the girl's ways of thinking, she said, —

"Well, I know I never could marry a monk. They cannot love. If they dared to love, it would be only to be excommunicated. They have sworn not to love."

Then she wondered how, if any monk had found surging in his soul these oceans of affection whose ripples began to affect her, he could ever help loving. She thought it would be wrong to try to imprison such divine feelings. Religion and love, she was sure, moved the world.

"No! a monk is under a vow; but Erasmus said to my father that human nature cancels vows. Yet" — and she crushed the monk's-hood blossom — "I could not love a monk, not even Salmani. They know no books but manuals of monkish prayer. They hate Master Erasmus, as my father distrusts him. They burn the heretics, and they killed Ami. They may kill my father!"

And she hurried to go home, taking in her left hand the little book, and in her right the flowers.

Why did she stop?

She suddenly remembered that Salmani was not blood-thirsty; that Martin Luther was a monk, and Catherine Von Bora had loved him. In her father's conversation, in her own conceptions, they two, at least, were saints. But Luther had been excommunicated?

She was bewildered, and sure of only one thing, that a strange yearning possessed her very soul. The problems of the heart were leaguing themselves with the problems of Alke's brain.

CHAPTER XIV.

SPIRITUAL ENVIRONMENTS.

Is it so, O Christ in heaven! that the highest suffer most;
That the strongest wander farthest, and more hopelessly are lost;
That the mark of rank in nature is capacity for pain,
And the anguish of the singer makes the sweetness of the strain?
SARAH WILLIAMS.

OUR information of the progress of events which affected Ami in the exciting months of the latter part of 1525, is meagre enough. What we have must be obtained from a conversation which occurred later, on the evening when Ami's old friend and teacher walked with him to the architect's rooms, where Ami was to inspect with care the plans of the palace of Villars-Coteret, which was at once the shrine and monument of the guilty love that the king bore to Mme. de Chateaubriand. Seldom did Ami have the pleasure of passing an evening with his friend, so constant were his duties to the court; and the old knight was as pleased with this attention as Ami had been to bestow it.

Nouvisset knew well the reverence in which Ami held the very name of the Queen Claude, whose heart had been penetrated by the last earthly agony, dying, as she did, with the early June flowers. The old man had a certain faith that the influences of the court had not entirely unmanned Ami, though he had begun to suspect that this youth, whom he knew Francis loved for his apparent susceptibility as well as for his excellence, had felt within him a manly shame at the mention of the name Chateaubriand. Ami had often seemed to dodge him in their conversation, when it approached her to whom Astrée was an adopted sister.

In confidence, Ami had once said that he was often far from being perfectly happy; and at certain moments Nouvisset had noticed with what fervor he asked curious questions about the pure streams and white snows near his childhood home. The old man thought he had discovered within this longing for the immaculate snows and crystal waters a noble revolt against the stained life of the court. Nouvisset himself felt that all the elegant splendor and magnificent pageantry of France about him, spotted with wrong and smeared with blood as they were, were but decorated falsities, when Ami's voice trembled with his own emotions, excited by the vision of a nearly forfeited ideal, and especially when his childlike simplicity dissolved the spectacle with one pure breath.

Each had been made the recipient of royal attentions that day. The king had remembered the Greek with a purse and a copy of "Faustus Andrelinus." The old knight and scholar had admired the copy which had been presented to Louis XII. when that monarch was travelling in Italy. Francis I. had obtained another through Grolier; and now, bound by Geoffrey Tory, bearing the salamander, the " F," the emblem of France, and the collar of Saint Michael, it was meant to complete the happiness of this gentle and faithful servant. Ami had been presented with a pair of golden spurs of most exquisite workmanship, bearing the initials of no less a knight than Gaston de Foix. Often had he wished to possess such a relic of the chivalrous youth whose consummate heroism never seemed so sure of remaining unsurpassed as when Ami felt that he stood amid the decaying splendors of knighthood on the " Field of the Cloth of Gold." At another and earlier hour the gift would have completed even his happiness.

" A happy day," said Nouvisset, " a very happy day it has been for us both ! " Ami was silent ; and with an evident effort at persuading, the scholarly old knight said, " Indeed, we are a favored and happy couple, Ami."

" I used to try to persuade Queen Claude that she was the happiest of human beings," said the young knight, deliberately. " I shall not soon forget my labors and their failures."

" Ami," said the old Greek, inquiringly, for he always loved gossip, " did you ever try to get her to love Mme. de Chateaubriand ? "

It was an unfortunate utterance ; or rather, perhaps, the name of Chateaubriand came in too early in the talk, and therefore the moment was unfortunate. Ami was indignant, then dignified, and then sensible. He had swiftly concluded that to show his anger would be to confess what he hated. He knew that the preceptor had not meant to link him unpleasantly with the Chateaubriands ; and if he seemed to take offence, the tale would be told. Terrible again did he find it to meet a fearless knight, and to be clad in armor so thin at certain points.

" No," answered Ami, at last, without giving any evidence that his mind had been a whirlpool ; " did you know Gaston de Foix ? "

The transition was sudden. Nouvisset had almost got his nose into Queen Claude's or Mme. de Chateaubriand's apartments, when unfortunately he was instantly confronted with the bleeding and disfigured corpse of Gaston de Foix on the battle-field of Ravenna. Again he lived through that awful day, seized the king's nephew as he fell, and heard Louis XII. say, as he was congratulated upon this triumph, "Wish my enemies such victories!"

Ami knew his teacher and friend perfectly. The last gleams of chivalry were dying away in France, as were some of the lights in the old Greek's brain. Ami knew that he could always, at least for a moment, stop the pursuing steps of this learned gossip, when he had started after plunder, by recreating some scene in which his chivalry had figured. He had tried it this time, had succeeded, and now, having had a moment to recover from his disquiet at the mention of the word "Chateaubriand," he felt prepared to humor his own mood of sadness and the inquiring appetite of his friend, by telling him all about the interview with the late queen.

As the old knight went on muttering to himself his curses on the Spaniards at Ravenna, Ami was thinking, —

"Oh, if I could only throw off this annoying feeling about the Chateaubriands whenever I meet my old teacher or whenever I see the name, I might find pleasure in him, as I once did. But I do love Astrée, though she is called *sister.*"

Love ought to sanctify everything, as it seems, to our easy sensibilities. But love is more honorable than we are; and love refuses, as more brightly the fires burn, to do aught but illuminate an offensive fact out of which exhale fever-laden memories.

Both minds finally got back to the ill-used queen, and Ami had the kindness to say, "Queen Claude was not happy, though she was the wife of Francis I. and the mother of a dauphin."

"Alas!" said the old courtier, "I was present in the Chapel of St. Germain-en-Laye on that day in May. I saw the black robes of mourning which they still wore for Anne de Bretagne. I knew it was a bad omen."

"Oh, you do not believe in omens!" said Ami, while his own mind recalled the event; and he rushed on to say, "The queen had a sincere love of purity, a just idea of truth, and she found herself satisfied with what I wish could satisfy others."

Ami had then, for the first time, said out loud to Nouvisset that the confessors and bishops, crucifixes and masses, abbots and popes, to which the queen had directed him in those moments when he believed so little and thirsted for goodness so deeply, had failed to satisfy. He saw the fine eye of Nouvisset gleam with curious intelligence, and heard him say with feeling, —

"Ami, did you see that burning of the hermit of Livry?"

There was indignation in the tone of voice; and for an instant the form of the old scholar stood out in the clear moonlight, as the statue of Bruno now stands out, the embodiment of freedom and reform, in the shadow of the Vatican.

The scene came back at once. Again Ami stood in front of the Cathedral of Notre Dame.

"I saw it. I see it yet. I shall never forget it," replied the younger knight, looking like a fearless Puritan born before the time; and as his voice grew more eloquent, he whispered: "That sickening smell of burning flesh; the dreadful tolling of the great bell; the white soul of the hermit shining out, surpassing the brilliance of the flame! Saw it? Yes. And, my knightliest of friends, I say to you what I dared to say to the Duchesse d'Alençon afterward, if this infernal kind of persecution must be carried on to protect the Holy Church, I would rather see the cathedral fall and bury in its ruins every false-hearted priest and wicked cardinal in Europe."

"That description," quickly said the old knight, "would include almost all of them. We must not wish to depopulate the sacred buildings. But, Ami," added he, "you have said enough to throw you into the same fire if Comte de Guise knew it; and as a knight, I tell you, think what you please, but hold your tongue."

"Oh," said Ami, and his face was white, "would that I had died with little Alke, if my fate be to smile on these outrages!"

"My boy," said the old man, who put his hand on his shoulder, "you can trust me."

"Ah, yes; I have trusted you this night with my heart."

"And tongue," added Nouvisset. "But answer me this, where there is no priest between us and the great God above,— answer me, Ami!" and he held up his tremulous hand pointing to the quiet stars. "Did you set the Duchesse d'Alençon to the task of helping Farel,— I mean William Farel,— did you help him to escape? You know he has gone to Geneva."

Silence like that above Nouvisset's hand reigned upon the lips whose heat had cooled perceptibly under the old knight's advice. Ami found himself confronted with a question which could be answered by a monosyllable; but never before seemed so praiseworthy and so convenient that masterly lying through half-truths uttered in royal presences, that elegant method of prevarication with which Ami had become familiar at court, but which had never pleased his conscience. The eye of the old knight never left its victim for an instant, while Ami's conscience, which just a moment before, in that dangerously free talk, had grown stalwart, thundered at the gates of speech for utterance.

Why should he be afraid? Because he had been afraid so long. Why should he not speak as his re-enthroned conscience demanded? Because he had so often silenced conscience in the courts of magnificent wickedness. He was afraid, but he did speak the truth.

"Yes!" he almost shouted; then bit his lip. But the

air was ambrosial; and Nouvisset thought he saw before him a youth whom the gods loved.

While the liberated conscience of Ami luxuriated for an instant in its new-found freedom, toying with its new crown, and the young knight's breast heaved with a self-respect he had never known before, the old knight quoted from Menander: —

ὃν οἱ θεοὶ φιλοῦσιν ἀποθνήσκει νεός.

Ami was not at all disconcerted at this prophecy of an early death. He recalled to mind what he had heard some one quote from Chaucer of England; and before he remembered where he had heard it, he had repeated the lines: —

" And certainly a man hath most honour
To dien in his excellence and flower."

When he thought of that hour in the course of which those lines were quoted by the man whom he now detested with an intensity greater even than that with which he abhorred the policy of the Holy Church, a pang of mingled jealousy and self-reproach seized his very soul; and it was not eased as the old knight laboriously said, —

"That sentence was quoted by that diabolical man, Brother Vian, and must be as false as he."

The irony in Nouvisset's voice was very keen. Where was the sorrow of Queen Claude, about which they had begun to talk twice in vain? Where were they?

Nouvisset had not changed from being the same elderly sceptic which he had found himself to be years ago, when he was the confidential servant of Louis XII. and Queen Claude was a girl. He had then lost all respect for the character of priests; he knew the Church to be foul, and the mass of her clergy to be ignorant and vicious, or shrewd and vile. He had then learned how little they really believed of the elaborate dogmas which grew longer as genuine faith decreased. He had seen with horror the ever-intensifying persecutions of the Reformers. He had beheld with terror the rise of a papistical party bent on the wholesale murder of those who would protest against the greed and villany of the clergy and the arrogance of the Pope. Day by day he had hoped to find the truth penetrating the mind of Ami. He had confidence that the Waldensian iron in his blood would some day feel the magnetic touch of these Reformers.

Of course he dared not tell Ami that his father and sister had not been killed. That would have been untrue to his king. He also had a dim notion that Ami and the world would be better off, if he remained the beloved subject of Francis I. He did not enter the fight against the Reformers, as others said, because he was old and laid by; and as he knew, because he honored their aims and wished them triumph. He did not fight for the Reformers, because he was a foreigner, had come to France only as a Greek mercenary, and did not desire to help to complicate affairs for his too weak and wilful sovereign. No; he was not in the fight, for he was hardly a Christian. His interest was in Ami, in knighthood, which might revive or die in the coming struggle, in elegant letters, in the Renaissance; and he never forgot that he was a Greek, that the culture of Erasmus and his predecessors who had initiated this great revolution in the brain, before it had touched the conscience of Europe, had been brought to Italy, where the Renaissance was now in its dotage, by Greeks from Constantinople. He would live and die simply a Greek, who had been of service to two French kings, — a Greek who had lost what faith he had acquired in the Holy Church, who believed in reformation by means of scholarship rather than by Masses or grace, and who was glad to see Ami terribly unsettled and indignant.

Ami, on the contrary, had gone a tremendous distance

in the experience and culture of a soul. He was more than unsettled and indignant. Conscience had been re-enthroned. Oh, how like an undisputed and regent power she sat in the soul of Ami again, when he discovered that he had actually told a human being of the feelings he had when the hermit of Livry was burned, and of the fact that William Farel escaped death and fled to Geneva through aid from the Duchesse d'Alençon and himself!

The fact that he had spoken seemed to have atoned for the whole past; and it was only when he had made that blunder in quoting words which to his mind had been actually soiled by the lips of Vian, that he lost sight of the heroic moment. Conscience was enthroned, truly; but when such passionate hate burns in the soul, the throne of conscience may prove inflammable.

Ami, beware that thou dost not lose the height which thou hast reached, in thy search for Vian's life!

CHAPTER XV.

A BELEAGUERED CASTLE.

He would not make his judgment blind. — In Memoriam.

NOW the conversation turned to Queen Claude and her sorrows with a graceful ease. Two great and moving energies had met in Ami's mind, — his indignation at the Church and his abhorrence of Vian, — and so nearly equal in power were they, that his mind was at rest, and ready for the topic which they had left. He was glad to begin again.

"As I said, the gracious queen really loved the true and good wherever she saw it."

"She would have loved to be loved, too, think you not?" said the old man, anxiously.

"Yes, oh, yes! Women are so like —"

"So like men in that respect," broke in Nouvisset.

"'T is true! So much does the human soul crave affection," said Ami.

"So much, my boy," added the old knight, "that a man, full grown and a knight, will often yield to those caresses of love which he did not at first respect."

Things of interest were getting far away from Queen Claude again, and they were getting perilously near to Ami's personal life. Could it be possible that his old friend and teacher suspected that his relations to Astrée had really so issued as to cause this genuine embarrassment?

Ami was perplexed at his own condition. Ashamed that, by the influence of Francis I. and Mme. de Chateaubriand, he had been led into what seemed to many, even to Nouvisset, an intrigue, he was also more deeply ashamed that he did not like to have any Chateaubriand lightly spoken of, so truly had the holiest affection sprung up within him in the midst of circumstances unsavory. Oh, how the clouds overlapped, though the sunlight did struggle between! Ami, however, instantly appreciated the situation; and he had so found the habit of being honest a pleasant one, that he replied, —

"So much, my honored friend, do we need love, that no unpleasant beginning which it may have, can drive it from the breast of a true knight."

The speaker was relieved.

"Ami, you have more trouble on your hands than you think," said Nouvisset.

"I have always found it so; and I find it harder than I supposed it would be, to tell you anything about the queen."

"Perhaps because," said Nouvisset, slyly, — "because we have other people and other facts in our minds. Even a queen, especially if she is dead and buried, has a hard time in expelling lesser people from the brain, if one really loves them."

There was no dodging this kindly thrust. It opened the steel coat-of-mail about Ami's soul, and Nouvisset could see his heart beat wildly.

"What can you mean?" said the young man, with no meaning whatever in his question.

Nouvisset was a knight; and, like a gentleman, he allowed his antagonist a moment of relief, which was still more pleasant to the younger knight when he found that the elder would not take an undue advantage, and when he heard him say, —

"You have spoken of 'the true knight,' and of what he

would not drive out of his breast. I am sure you did
not learn of those things from me. You are farther
along than my unworthy teaching has taken you. But
I know the king gave you that 'Book of the Order of
Chivalry,' printed by the English Caxton in 1484, — an
eloquent book it is; and you have read the words: 'Oh,
ye knights of England, where is the custom and usage
of noble chivalry that was used in those days?' Those
days, Ami, make a knight of to-day homesick for his
ancestor's coffin. Then you do not forget, I see, the
Augsburg folio, 'Consilium Buch,' and the inspiring
legends on the coat-of-arms. Oh, my boy, we wonder
that the forefathers of these velveted ninnies who would
ruin a virgin as they would kill a hare, do not rise from
their graves and snatch the armorial relics away from
unworthy men!"

The old knight looked like a living combination of the
hero and the saint, as he grew more eloquent. Ami was
silent. They had wandered away from the city, and
stood in the moonlight, under the mulberry-trees, while
the scholarly courtier spake on.

"I know not when I besought you to read good Sir
Thomas Mallory's translation of King Arthur's Histories,
and asked you to read again and again what Caxton
spake, 'Do after the good, and leave the evil; and it
shall bring you good fame and renown,' that you would
so soon find injustice, cowardice, hate, and even murder,
guarded by chivalry, at the king's court."

"My guide! did you not say something to me, a
minute since, about the danger of talking freely about
cardinals and their like? Is it safer to decry a king?
The king is my friend, you know, and yours."

These last words Ami uttered with a voice which had
become used to contrary emotions. He betrayed the fact
that with his love for the king, he had a conscience,
and a love for Nouvisset. No other man could have

spoken those words about the king's court with safety, though Ami knew the truth which they conveyed was indisputable.

"I know you, my boy, and I know Francis, King of France also. I am now an old man. I have not much to lose, but I would give up my life; if every knight in France were chivalrous. The word 'gentleman' is cursed with suggestions of a soft gentleness which seduces and damns."

The old man turned from the face of his companion; there was something in his eye brighter than the silver livery of battle. It was a tear shed over the decay of knighthood.

The young man was on the point of explaining what he meant when he used the phrase "the true knight." He had enjoyed speaking honestly to his friend, — he had never dared do so with the clergy, the dukes, or the king. Only once did he ever open so much of his soul to human eyes; and that was when he sat in the palace with the queen. Oh, if they could only get back once more to that topic, — the queen! Let them try.

"I meant to say," answered Nouvisset, "that to be a true knight in France at this hour is to be heroic and true, at a cost such as you cannot compute. I am proud of you; and God defend you!"

Ami felt happy; he scarcely knew why. His teacher and friend had certainly not meant to tell him that true chivalry would cut him off at court, or that it would bind him to Astrée, or that it would take the pain out of his soul. He had no time to extract the meaning from the seething mixture in his mind. He only felt as though Heaven were near, when he heard the words: "I am proud of you! God defend you!"

Involuntarily, as it seemed, and simultaneously, the two began to retrace their steps, and were soon back again, going into the city; but it was too late for any such thorough study of the plans of the new palace as the king had urged Ami to make. Upon discovering this, Ami said, —

"How thankful I am that the poor queen is spared knowing of this new building! It crushed her to know that she was unloved, and to feel often unhonored and even pitilessly neglected. This agony she has escaped by death."

Nouvisset knew well that Francis was making this elaborate expenditure to please Mme. de Chateaubriand; and yet he felt that he must not again throw Ami off the track by mentioning the name, if he was to obtain any of that kind of information about Queen Claude which would satisfy an old man who had always been a lover of gossip, and who was now amusing himself by writing his "Memoirs of the Court."

Suddenly Ami remembered this task which the old knight had set himself to perform for posterity; and he resolved that as they walked back to the palace, there should fall upon him an incessant stream of talk about the queen's affairs. The main facts Ami was sure the old chronicler knew; he would delight him with descriptions of insignificant but interesting things about herself and her ways. In much better spirits, therefore, than before, he began the colloquy again.

"The queen had many little things to make her happy. Of course, I do not mean simply her carriage, which you know was the first carriage in France," — Ami knew not that the second and a far richer one was soon to be given by her royal lover to Diana of Poitiers, — "and," continued the young man, "her cabinet, which was as rich and beautiful as her jewels were brilliant and rare, — that cabinet which I saw on that last afternoon at the palace, — a cabinet whose very key was adorned with half the history of chivalry, — the cabinet which was ornamented with exquisite gems, whose whole front, back, and sides were heavy with mother-of-pearl, ivory, and jasper, elaborately engraven — "

" And which," added the eager old man, delighted to produce a little scandalous information of his own, — "which, as I know, did not compare with the cabinet which the king sent by my own hand to Mme. de Chateaubriand, on the day after his visit to the tomb of Claude."

Ami was not to be thrown from the track, though he was astonished.

" Nor," continued he, "do I think as much as even she did, of the priceless scent-box which she opened so often on that afternoon of my visit, — a box on whose golden sides long ago Corneille de Bonté had graven the story of Daphne and Chloe — "

" A story which must have given great peace of mind to the queen as she thought about her lord," dryly interrupted Nouvisset ; and he proceeded to add : " You could hardly have expected her to be entirely satisfied with toying with that diminutive watch which, with her usual kindness, the king's mother had given to her after explaining that it was to take the place of the hour-glass which was very precious, — precious to the queen's mother, and therefore so abominable to Louise of Savoy. Ami, does the stately Louise of Savoy seem to enjoy this life now that the poor Claude has no further need of the Latin cross and the bejewelled timekeeper? "

" Oh," said Nouvisset, when he saw Ami hesitate, and remembered how well he enjoyed telling the truth, even after he had been pushed into it, — " oh, I know, and you know, that Claude was always a dove in the claws of a vulture, from the moment in which she became Queen of France until that other hour in which Louise of Savoy sent the glad news to Claude's absent husband that his queen was dead at St. Germain-en-Laye."

Ami felt that he would give his golden spurs and almost the last trappings of knighthood, to unbosom himself to this old friend.   While Nouvisset was an intolerable lover of gossip, he never told a secret.   Part of the interest of his singular character lay in this.   He had a marvellous appetite for salacious information, and an unsurpassed conscientiousness as to guarding it.   He was a Greek mercenary who had been a confidant at the court of Louis XII., and Ami knew that he had the secrets of a hundred human beings, and that his would be safe in that harbor; but after all, there was something so dear about his own secret that he did not want to have it left in bad company.   He was a knight; and his secret he really began to believe involved the destiny of one who was noble and true.

"Princess Claude," said he, with awful deliberation, "was a dove in the claws of a vulture. Did you ever think that an attempt had been made to rob less illustrious maidens of not less noble life-blood?"

"By the same beak?" asked the old knight, quickly.

"I see what I have done," said Ami.   "My very soul is aflame when I think I would have found and loved her as a pure man finds and loves his own, if I had not been used as foully as was Princess Claude; if she — I mean Astrée — had not been cursed with the scheming friendliness of Louise of Savoy and Mme. de Chateaubriand."

"What?" said the teacher, — "what?   Do you know that woman is the mother of the king?   Do you remember?   'The king is my friend, you know, and yours.'"

The repetition of the very words which Ami had spoken with two struggling motives in his tongue — "The king is my friend, you know, and yours" — unhorsed the young knight.   But they had been pronounced with precisely the same struggle on the lips of Nouvisset.   The old knight knew well that he had the boy where he must confess to all he cared to know of his life and hope.   Yet his simulation of indifference, with manifest anxiety as to the queen, and almost pretentious friendliness to the name of Francis I., must be adhered to for the moment.

With almost cruel suddenness, which, on the whole, was grateful to Ami, because it helped him out of the immediate crisis, the old man began to relate his own memories of the bric-à-brac, the toys, which the queen had possessed. It was a dreadful transition from the hot flame of Ami's soul, where crowns, diadems, and courts were being consumed in the fire of love, to the rooms of the royal Claude, full of the elegant pawns which Francis I. had given for love, — the cold sepulchre of dead affection bestrewn with embroidered grave-clothes. Both men had complete control of their faculties; and so far as outward appearances could testify, the transition was made easily.

"What an artist was that Luca della Robbia!" said the elder. "I never knew how much more Greek was he than that pretentious nephew of Andrea whom the king lauds to the skies, until I saw the white Madonna which Queen Claude asserted to me ever reminded her of Anne de Bretagne. A thousand of Giovanni's relievos, such as those in the sacristy of Santa Maria Novella which I saw when Florence was a camp, cannot equal one of Luca's medallions."

"No; certainly not in your judgment, Nouvisset, if it bear the arms of René of Anjou, or any heraldic devices. You are a knight!"

"Yes; but I am also a Greek, a lover of art, I trust. Knighthood is dead, except in my soul. Art is alive here!" and Nouvisset smote his breast. "And under that fellow Cellini, and old Palissy with his stained glass, and Leonardo, whom I wish the king could have persuaded to France; and Angelo, who is both heretic and architect, I am sure art is alive in this world which I am getting sorry to be leaving so soon."

The Renaissance rested like a glorious morning on the

old man's brow as he spoke these names, and as he
remembered that seven years before, he had seen in the
cathedral the two altar-pieces — one by Raphael, and the
other by Sebastiano del Piombo — ordered when Cardinal Giuliano was bishop of Narbonne.

"And you knew," said Ami, swept into that flood of
renascent life which broke forth at that time in any un-
suspected moment in the conversations of Western Europe, — "you knew that the beautiful gift which I have
to preserve from that melancholy hour is the vase of
lapis-lazuli which Benvenuto himself enriched with
pearls. At some time his Majesty will fetch Benvenuto
to Paris. But, God prosper him! things must become
more peaceful."

"I have seen it," answered the old man, forgetful of
the troubled king, — "I have seen it. It is most exquisite. You knew that the king himself conceived the design which Cellini worked out for Mme. de Chateaubri-
and, — that enamelled cup, whose edges, as I take it, are
too rough with diamonds which are cut to a point, and
whose sides one cannot hold without pain, for the finely
sharpened rubies upon it. But it was well conceived.
Mme. de Chateaubriand will find the cup very like the
love of the king, mark me, Ami!"

It was Ami's chance; he said sharply, "The king is
my friend, you know, and yours."

The old knight was unhorsed; and they were leagues
away from the topic, — the good Queen Claude.

"Nouvisset, why do you always run our talk to
Mme. de Chateaubriand?"

"Because we started out to inspect some plans for her
residence," answered he.

"How do you know that the palace of Villars-Coteret
is to be her residence?"

"Because I remember the night at Chambord when
you saw the beautiful Astrée, and that earlier night when

our Sire Francis I. saw the lovely Françoise de Foix, and when Louise of Savoy smiled on Jean de Laval de Montmorency, who is now thinking betimes of Mme. de Chateaubriand, when she thought of the ring which Cellini made — oh, I remember the tears in his eyes, brighter than the jewels of the king's mother, as the broken-hearted man, now called Comte de Chateaubriand, sat there behind the gentle Queen Claude, his wife at her feet, and the king eying her beauty."

"Why," said Ami, his heart sick within him, "what ring? Cellini made for what?"

"Boy even yet, I swear!" answered he; "and you never — you never knew of it? *You* carried the ring to Francis I., and saw him and M. de Guise compare and scrutinize them."

"I carried a ring, I saw it compared with another."

"And that new ring was a golden lie, — a cursed, elegant lie, full of wrong and shame, which brought Françoise de Foix from her castle to Chambord in spite of her husband's efforts to prevent it. You know what has happened since," said Nouvisset, with a wave of his hand.

"I only know that I am confounded at all this, — yes, I know of — "

"Of the intrigue, my son."

At that moment they had arrived in the street leading to the palace; and a swarm of chattering monks rushed by them. Strange faces also appeared, as they entered the familiar doors; and Nouvisset. who alone seemed to comprehend the situation, said, —

"Ami, be a true knight, until we meet again."

They had separated; and their thoughts would have been lost in the apprehension of strange scenes, if they had been such thoughts as men may lose.

CHAPTER XVI.

A DISCARDED FAVORITE.

> " Hateful is the dark-blue sky
> Vaulted o'er the dark-blue sea."

THAT conversation with Nouvisset was never finished. Notwithstanding this, however, Ami found out soon what all readers of French biography know, — the true story of that ring, — the vain effort of a husband to keep his beautiful wife from the eye of an ignoble monarch; the subtle invention of a ring exactly like one which he himself held, promising to send it to his home in Brittany only when he should deem it wise to welcome his beloved spouse to the court; the king's stealth in the sending of the fine imitation to the unsuspecting but weak Françoise de Foix; her sudden appearance before the scheming monarch, and the suffering of her mystified and suspicious husband : the unholy alliance ; the transformation of her husband Jean de Laval de Montmorency and Françoise de Foix into Comte and Comtesse de Chateaubriand, at the command of the dissimulating king; the ruined woman, the dishonored man !

Until Ami knew all these facts, he had not fathomed the murky gloom out of which he had seen shining his star, — Astrée.

"Oh, curses on the head of Louise of Savoy!" said Ami, as he remembered that the king's mother had planned it all, and had sought to make his own love for Astrée the den for such a brood of vipers. "Nouvisset knew that I could not successfully oppose her schemes and crimes, leagued as they were with the weakness of her son, — my best beloved! Oh, he was, he *is* my friend! Once more will I try to awaken the slumbering soul that may rule Europe."

Tears were in Ami's soul, and they were soon in his eyes. He went out into the fresh morning air. He never learned what many others could have told him, that the crowd of monks of the night before had been in pursuit of a luckless Lutheran, who happily had escaped them. He had learned enough, however, to convince him that critical hours had come. His heart was breaking for Astrée, when he took out of his pocket an exquisite little picture of his loved one, which, by order of his king, had been painted on ivory.

He now knew also what the appearance of those strange faces of the last night at the palace meant. The valet-de-chambre had made it clear that the king was about to exile Mme. de Chateaubriand. At last Louise of Savoy had become intolerant of her influence over the affairs of the king. Here was the guard of protection; and —

"Curses, curses upon her and the priests who grant indulgences!" cried Ami's heart.

The guard of protection waited to escort the Comtesse de Chateaubriand to a husband who would at least shelter the unfortunate woman.

Ami's heart sank within him. During the imprisonment of the king he had suffered as much of contumely as Chancellor Duprat and Louise of Savoy had dared to inflict upon him. The comtesse had served the queen regent, who had counselled with the chancellor, and accepted the advice of Parliament as to the suppression

of heretics.   Louis de Berquin, dear to Ami and to
Marguerite, had been seized for translating the writings
of Erasmus, and imprisoned in the Conciergerie.   Louise
of Savoy had made Ami charitable even toward the name
Chateaubriand by her cruel treatment of the king's
favorite, when the latter could not serve her.   Now that
the king had returned to France, saying, " Lo, I am king
again," the young knight had looked for better days.   The
sky, however, was very inauspicious.

The old knight, in his apartments, waited the orders
of the queen regent, who was sovereign over her son's
love-affairs.   Ami was commanded to appear before his
Majesty.   This knight was aware that some subterfuge
would be adopted to escape the force of convictions
which Francis I. never failed to honor in one way or
another.   The king saw that he must now appease
the conscience of his friend, — as deeply did he love
him as was possible in such a nature, — and he must
accomplish this by spreading a banquet before Ami's
intellect.

" He cannot be dull enough to miss the flashes of
Mlle. d'Heilly's wit," remarked his Majesty.   " She is far
more bright than the comtesse ever will be."   Then the
king repeated a saying which had already tickled the ears
of a court which was ready to welcome from the regent's
suite the new royal favorite, — " La plus belle des sa-
vantes, et la plus savante des belles."

" No," said the queen regent, as she thought of Ami, —
" no, my Cæsar ! If you must hold fast to a man who is
a nuisance, and who is rapidly becoming a heretic — "

" The astrologer bade me," said Francis I., with decision, " and I love Ami."

" Then make him easy," she answered ; " quote to him
the praise of the poet Clement Marot."

Francis I. was soon able to repeat those lines which
Marot had written of the king's new love : —

> " Dix-huit ans je vous donne,
>   Belle et bonne,
> Mais à votre sens rassis
> Trente-cinq et trente-six
>   J'en ordonne."

"Surely," said he, thinking of the wit which even Marguerite had loaned to her guilty brother, and which was now engraved in loving mottoes upon the jewels intended at first for the discarded Mme. de Chateaubriand, — "surely, Ami will help me to meet the tasks growing up with this revival of ancient learning ; and my Marguerite of Marguerites, with the sweet mademoiselle, will soothe his conscience with their scholarship."

A man who has no conscience is sure to make miscalculations with reference to one who has ; and Francis I. was therefore impotent with the Waldensian, when the concessions of friendship were forgotten. Ami was not strongest on the intellectual side of his nature. His power lay in the faculty for which Francis I. could spread no feast.

In the presence of conscience, the knight at once saw his Majesty's effort to conceal the topic of his heart with sentences which dealt with the affairs of the brain. So deep and tender was Ami's love for him, so hopeful had he become that Francis I. should be worthy of the title " King of Culture," that at first he resolved to acquiesce. Still, however, in despite throbbed the conscience within him. Ami was so made that if his intellectual powers played at all, they must be moved by a moral motive.

In that year it had grown increasingly difficult for Ami to acknowledge the spiritual dictatorship which Louise of Savoy had placed in the hands of the famous syndic Beda. Erasmus had said of Beda that such a man was no more fit to decide questions as to the future of the University of Paris, than was a wolf to sit in judgment upon the prospects of a kid. Ami was determined to recall Erasmus to his king.

Ami made no more audacious attack upon the party in power than when on the day upon which he saw the king willing to talk of learning, instead of allowing his Majesty to praise Mademoiselle, he thrust at him these words, —

"Erasmus is the only scholar sure to rule the future. Beda does not challenge even William Budé; he would not dare to challenge Erasmus."

"I have often wondered," replied the king, who was at once plunged into a most thoughtful mood, "that none of our divines has dared to lay hands on Erasmus."

Ami understood Beda, Syndic of the Sorbonne. Nouvisset had often put his self-conscious learning to shame. It was also true that no one so dreaded the sharp tongue and quick intelligence of Ami, as did that chief figure of Sorbonne orthodoxy.

"That knight Ami will make his Majesty think me a pretence or an idiot," complained Beda to Louise of Savoy.

No one had so completely demolished the schemes of Beda, which looked toward absolute control of the mental energies of France, as had Ami.

"I want to read to your Majesty," said Ami, one day, — "indeed, I must read to you, Sire — the letter which I have found out Erasmus wrote to Beda when the Syndic had succeeded in getting Friar Sutor's book afloat in Paris."

Francis I. had perused the Carthusian friar's work, at the instance of his mother, who was determined to be queen regent of her son's ideas of religion.

"Read!" commanded the king.

Ami read this passage from Erasmus: "What will be said by men of sober judgment, — and there are more to be counted everywhere who have no dislike for Erasmus,

—when they see such books issuing from the Sorbonne? Sound theologians are brought into contempt by the folly of a few."

"Did Beda answer that letter?" asked the king.

"Yes, and in most abominable Latin; and he called himself 'the poor Beda, who, like Saint Augustine, would seek to save the Church from error and scandal.'"

"What else did he say?"

"Oh, he told Erasmus that his writings on celibacy, the works and the feasts, especially those which concerned themselves with the translating of the Scriptures into the tongue of the people, and on praise of marriage, were looked at by the Sorbonne as vicious."

"And this controversy has gone on?"

"Yes, Sire! It has gone on until Erasmus has poured his scorn upon Beda, Friar Sutor, and the Sorbonne. He laughs at Sutor for saying that languages and literature are the Devil's devices; and he ridicules him when he says that to know Hebrew or Greek is heretical. And now, Sire, this book comes to you."

Ami placed in the king's hand "Guesses in Answer to Beda's Notes."

"What do you advise?" inquired his Majesty, looking at page after page.

"Beda must not continue to misrepresent your court, Sire. It will become the laughing-stock of Europe. Erasmus will set the whole world to sneering at France. Who can help a smile when he points out that Beda is like Cicero in the manner of beginning a sentence, and unlike him in not knowing the difference between the indicative and subjunctive moods? Who can respect Beda, after Erasmus has shown that in the little book, 'Errors of Erasmus,' there are one hundred and eighty lies, three hundred and ten calumnies, and forty-seven blasphemies?"

Francis I. smiled. "That is ludicrous, but serious,"

said he; and added, "But Beda says that Erasmus is in collusion with Luther."

"'I agree with Luther as a nightingale does with the cuckoo,'—that is his own saying," said Ami. "Beda says: 'The old theology must remain; but what are we to do with Luther, who is a wild boar, devastating the Lord's vineyard?'"

"What does Erasmus say to that?" inquired the king.

"'Theology must be scriptural and rational, be it old or new. The Church needs reform, Luther or no Luther.'"

Francis I. at that instant caught sight of his mother. Louise of Savoy was scornfully indignant, if her face was to be believed. She swept past; but she had overheard the whole conversation.

"Oh," said the king,—"oh that I were strong enough either to abolish the Sorbonne or to crush the whole brood of heretics!"

Ami knew prudence and silence to be identical at that time.

On the 16th of June—the biographers of Erasmus give us the exact date—a letter from the scholar had reached the King of France. Ami now read it to the king again. Erasmus, in that epistle, begged the right to have his works printed in Paris, the men of whose university, such as Sutor and Beda, were bringing great contempt upon it.

"It is most unjust," wrote Erasmus, "that they should be permitted to disseminate poison, and that we should not be permitted to apply the antidote."

Francis I. listened, arose, and walked in the direction which Louise of Savoy had taken. Ami knew now that the soul of the king was at a crisis of surpassing importance to his Majesty and to France. The king meant to be "the King of Culture" which he had been called. He had done much to limit the ignorant bigotry of

Beda. Could he — would he control with kingly might the college of the Sorbonne?

So much for the king; but where was Ami himself tending? Could he take the logical next step, pointing so distinctly toward an alliance with the Reformation?

Astrée and he sat in the evening under a splendid pavilion which had but a moment before made a rendezvous for the royal lovers Francis I. and Mme. de Chateaubriand, whose affections the guilty king had so completely won, from whom now he was about to part forever. The two moments, the two pairs of lovers, furnished a sad contrast.

This was the first scene, — that in which king and comtesse found agonies. In a moment of thoughtfulness about events very different from the one which would that night break the heart of her to whom the king was so frigid, his Majesty. had slowly said, —

"I am perplexed at the coming storm."

"There is not a cloud in the sky, or a breath of wind in the purple vineyards," was the soft answer.

The king quivered as she touched his flushed cheek.

"No; but Erasmus and Beda annoy me more than the Pope and the Emperor Charles."

Francis I. arose with evident impatience. They had never talked of Reformers and colleges. Why should he speak of such dry and prosaic facts now?

The Comtesse de Chateaubriand looked upon him with her sparkling eyes, her sickened heart beating violently, and said, —

"Let us talk of love, my king. I hope you are not concerned about those testy Reformers. Ami has Astrée's head full of whimsical notions of which lovers ought to know nothing. He has almost insulted your royal mother by what he dared to say about the indulgences. Astrée mopes about like a nun within a convent of skeletons. Ami tells her all that the puny Louis de Berquin has said, and then they pretend — Come nearer, sweet king ! — Oh, these Reformers trouble us ! They have made Ami and Astrée complain that things go not to the liking of some crazy monk in Germany, or some bold lover of Greek and Hebrew like Erasmus. — Not a kiss for me yet, noble sovereign ! Shall I kneel for it ? Ha ! I could not think you so agitated as to forget love. Alas ! as I was saying, Ami does not like my presence here, as I know full well. But — I know your woes, Sire — you would not forsake me ? That I know, beloved one ! You would not leave me, even if these notions of the Reformers prevail ? The priests do grant us absolution ; and they are the ministers of God. You doubt it not ? Alas ! I will call you, as does the queen regent, my Cæsar ! What is this ? Oh, Francis ! "

The mind of Francis I. was a tempest. Oh, what a deliverance — half heroic, half divine — if he could break with her on a difference about the Reformers ! It would please Ami, he thought.

The remembrance of Queen Claude, to whom he had been so false ; the recollection of the hour when he resolved to make France the seed-ground of the needed reform ; the love he had for the high-souled Ami, — all these swept upon him, as he arose again, weighted with a chain of guilt which made it impossible for his conscience to dream of reform. His magnificent form stood solemnly in the moonlight. The King of France felt that the higher sovereignties of his life and kingdom were slipping away from him. France seemed to shriek with the pale woman at his breast. The superbly attired monarch bore the fainting comtesse to her own apartments.

An hour had passed, and this was the second scene.

Ami and Astrée had found each other where the magnetic eye of Francis had given such ecstasy to the Comtesse de Chateaubriand until what she had deemed an unexpected manifestation of the king's conscience was discovered to be a blow which broke her heart. Here, where the fires of remorse and those of a new and guilty love had kindled and mingled in such a twisted flame as by the side of a languishing and discarded affection lit up that wreck of hope which Francis I. and his career had come to be, — here sat Astrée's purity and Ami's sacred faith. Did Astrée's liquid eyes realize how deeply Ami's soul had gone into their abysses? She knew Ami. His conscience, which had spurned the proposed intrigue, was her guardian. She was safe.

Did the very leaves seem to whisper as the splendid young knight drew her slender loveliness up to his beating heart, and gave to hers, in one long, loving kiss, the lips which had uttered such a protest against a wrong which priesthood and kingcraft would forgive? She felt herself to be in the circle of divine protection, and knew that no pope or emperor could so certainly preserve her. It was love's ecstasy within the fiery environment of an awakened conscience. Oh, how safe was Astrée! Their age allowed them to talk upon matters such as perhaps equally fond lovers in a finer moral atmosphere would have contemplated in silence. Besides the personal relations of Astrée — "An adopted sister; yes, only adopted," thought Ami — to the comtesse, the history of Ami's pure affection so unfortunately allied to the king's favorite allowed Astrée and Ami to express their sensitiveness as to her fortunes. They knew that while Ami was toying with the dark ringlets which fell from the head of Astrée as her head lay upon his heart, the King of France and the woman whom he had years ago stolen from her proud husband were yonder in the palace, passing through the agonies of their last interview.

"Let us be grateful," said the Waldensian knight, "that no foul memory stains our love, Astrée."

Astrée's eyes were two stars dipped in a silver sea of

tears; but Ami kissed every tear-drop away, one by one, as she piteously cried, —

"But what will become of her? Oh the heartless king!"

The protesting fire in Ami's blood now burned into furious pulses. He only said, —

"Astrée, by my soul, I do hate a condition of affairs in Church and State which allows a priest to sell to a king the right to steal his friend's bride, absolves him in advance, — for that use is made of abused indulgences, — absolves him from sins of unnamable infamy, and then stands by approvingly when he is ready to cast his victim into the dungeon or the grave, offering him pardons and indulgences at so much apiece."

"Love does not barter or steal or trade or grow weary," she said, as she nestled close to the strong young knight, like a bird which has just seen a winged creature like itself torn in the storm.

"No; nor does true religion sell its solemn authority for the debasing of souls," answered Ami.

Nothing could prevent the exile of Comtesse de Chateaubriand. Louise of Savoy was authoritative; Mlle. d'Heilly was happy. While in another part of the palace the latter was playing with the jewels which Francis I. had demanded of his former favorite, laughing also at the witticisms which gleamed from the exquisite cases, and laying her delicate hand of commandment upon the soul of his Majesty, Astrée, who had worked herself up into passionate self-sacrifice, had approached the dethroned Comtesse de Chateaubriand, where she sat like a beggared queen, moaning piteously, unbefriended, waiting for the valet-de-chambre to announce the guard.

"Oh, little one!" cried the dethroned woman, calling Astrée by the very name which she used when the in-

trigue was proposed to that innocent heart years before,
— "oh, little one, the saints protect thee! I bless thee
with hands which tremble because they have toyed with
infamy. Do you move away from me too? Oh, sister!
only '*adopted*'? O God! Child! I thank thee for wearing lilac-blossoms at thy girdle, — thank thee, little one!
Astrée, thinkest thou my blessing will curse thy pure
soul? No? Sister Astrée, I thank thee! Ah, I beg of
thee do not avoid my foul lips: they are parched; the
foulness is burned away. No? Astrée! Ami's kisses
will obliterate the stain I may leave upon thine.
I am a ruin. As the airs of heaven sweep over the
catastrophe, let the ruin and the winds teach thee, O
little one! The priests have nothing wherewith to
cleanse my soul. O Jesu! O Christ! Thou must save
another stained soul! Ami — Astrée! forgive me! Oh
that Louis de Berquin — only yesterday I was asking for
his ashes! — oh that Louis de Berquin or — Does
William Farel live, or Lefevre? Oh that each might
pray for my soul! Little one! Astrée!"

There was a noise outside, — dull, continuous, terrify-
ing. The infamous chivalry of Francis I. had accomplished its purpose. The guard had come.

Soon the speechless Astrée was conscious that Ami's
hand was gently pressing her forehead. The Comtesse
de Chateaubriand was on her way to the dark vault
beneath the chateau in Brittany.

CHAPTER XVII.

THE ZEAL OF HERESY.

Humana ante oculos fœde cum vita jaceret
In terris oppressa gravi sub religione,
Quæ caput a cœli regionibus ostendebat
Horribili super aspectu mortalibus instans.
LUCRETIUS.

BEFORE many days had gone, the queen regent, Chancellor Duprat, and Beda — the first a vicious and scheming bigot, the second her ignorant but able vicegerent, the third a pretentious persecutor of the Reforming scholars — had completely compassed their aims. The King of France having been offended and shamed by an interview with Ami, who steadily refused either to treat Mlle. d'Heilly, who was now Duchesse d'Étampes, as his queen, or to allow them to make his love for Astrée a shield for the royal crime, was ready to accede to a suggestion of the chancellor, inspired by Beda. This brought forth a simple scheme to send Ami upon an expedition to Florence and beyond even to Alexandria, for what Beda protested was the rescue of certain ancient manuscripts. The Italian ambassador had so described them as to leave no doubt in the minds of the scholars consulted by Francis I. as to their high value. For a share in the booty the Italian ambassador, on agreement with Admiral Andrea Doria, was willing to allow Francesco, whom Ami had loved as his companion at Chilly, to accompany him. With their eyes full of visions of palimpsests on which the Fathers of the Church disputed the right to territory with Homer and Æschylus, and especially with joy on the part of Ami, who felt that he must, at least for the present, withdraw himself from the court, these two young men were ready to set out. They had been provided with letters which would make their journey more charming than a royal pageant. One of the syndics of the Sorbonne was busy instructing Francesco in secret, who was to search for the Syriac manuscript of which both Eusebius and Palladius had made mention. He was sure that it would be found in one of the monastic institutions of the Scetic desert, perhaps in that of Saint Macarius.

Ami was talking earnestly with Marguerite of Navarre at St. Germain.

"The chancellor hates learning, and yet seems eager to behold a bit of Oriental vellum," said he, curiously.

"Think you that he desires the death of Sieur Berquin?" asked the Queen of Navarre.

"Beda loathes Berquin, who has been my teacher and friend, — my nearest friend, since the death of Nouvisset. I know you honor Berquin as you could not honor the Greek. The Syndics of the Sorbonne will rejoice at having us where we cannot confer for his protection. I am sorry, gracious princess, that Master Berquin is not a little less pugnacious. He may flame with uncontrollable enthusiasm for the Reform at a moment when it will be impossible to save him from the fierceness of the Sorbonne. Duprat is unable to read a word of Greek; and yet he wants Greek manuscripts. He is ignorant; and yet he knows that the ancient languages cannot be studied without giving an impulse to the Reform. Why does he want Francesco and myself to start to-day for more manuscripts? I cannot see a reason for it; but I feel that there is an intention to make away with Berquin."

"You are quite right about Sieur Berquin's lack of practical wisdom," quietly remarked the thoughtful princess. "It seemed almost impossible to save him before."

"Only your brother's love for you kept him from the prison, possibly the stake. This I have believed," said Ami.

"Will you speak to the good scholar ere you depart? Tell him of our love for him. Tell him that you leave your beloved friend the scholar in the hands of a loving king, who cannot always deny the Court of Parliament their privileges."

"The privilege, for example, of burning illustrious scholars and pious worshippers of God," interjected Ami.

"Tell him," continued the queen, "the whole story of his release. Ask him to consult with me before he acts in serious affairs."

"He will probably tell me that he consults with nothing but duty and Almighty God," said the knight, as he walked toward the balcony, not knowing whether quite to respect the inconsistent Marguerite. He added: "I do not know the whole story of his release."

"No one but myself could know it. Tell it to him, and he will allow me to guide him. It is this: When first, six years ago, his books were examined, the Inquisition found works of Carlstadt, Melancthon, and Luther. He was thrown into the square tower, after the commission had reported upon them. I did not know him then, save as a scholar and a man of piety; but, Ami, I knew that you had loved him, and that, since knighthood and learning had lost the active services of Nouvisset, Berquin had taught you much that the Greek could not teach. I wrote to the king, as my brother and as your loving friend. These were my words: 'Ami's tutor and friend is confined in the Conciergerie, and will be put to death according to law, if your Majesty does not interfere. Monseigneur, spare your loving Ami and your Marguerite.' The venue was changed. Duprat and the Chamber remonstrated. To this hour, no one knows who so persistently labored with the gracious king. John du Belay, Bishop of Bayonne, held the ground which I had gained with the sovereign. Chancellor Duprat quietly rebuked Berquin, instead of burning him in front of Notre Dame."

" Does not Berquin know of this?" asked Ami.

" Not a whisper. But you must tell him, also, that he ought to avoid being over-bold; also, that he must be willing to obey my counsel. Once again, after that, for your sake, did I save him. You had a helping hand in it all."

" Let me hear the whole story," said the knight.

" Four years ago Parliament was unsatisfied as to my mother's tolerance of heretics; and they reproached the king, who was then a prisoner at Madrid, with having given your teacher, Louis de Berquin, his freedom. They advised the queen regent to ask a commission of pontifical delegates. In January, as I now remember it, Berquin was again in the Conciergerie. He had dragged the name and fortune of Erasmus into the trial. I begged of my brother Francis his life for your sake. When the order to suspend came to Parliament, one cried out, ' The king is as badly advised as he himself is good ;' and they went on to condemn him. He could abjure his books, or be burned. You remember it, as I see. You told me he would not approve the sentence."

" I know the rest," interrupted Ami; "let me see if I have it not. I shall place it all before Master Berquin."

Ami proceeded to relate an occurrence the thought of which, he believed, would, in a crisis which the boldness of Berquin might precipitate, compel him to regard the advice of Marguerite so gratefully as to follow her counsel.

" I myself," said he, — " I intercepted the king, as he

approached Paris. He embraced me and said: 'Ami! I am King of France once more; and thou hast been faithful. I come back to my realm seeking to do all for one who would have kept me from the prison of Madrid.' Your letters were handed to him. I asked for the protection. Then the king wrote from Mont de Marsan his courageous letter. I say 'courageous,' because the principle that heresy must be controlled is one which an army of kings cannot oppose," added Ami, who felt that even precious heretics could tax their friends at court too heavily.

The reader may be willing to see some of the lines of that letter, the manuscript of which is now a suggestive memorial in the French archives. The king wrote: —

"We have presently been notified how that notwithstanding that, through our dear and much loved lady and mother, regent in France, during our absence, it was written unto you and ordered that you would please not to proceed in any way whatever with the matter of Sieur Berquin, lately detained a prisoner, until we should have been able to return to this our kingdom, you have nevertheless, at the request and pursuance of his ill-wishers, so far proceeded with his business that you have come to a definitive judgment of it. Whereat we cannot be too much astounded. . . . For this cause we do will and command upon you . . . that you are not to proceed to execute of the said judgment, which, as the report is, you have pronounced against the said Berquin, but shall put him himself and the depositions and the proceedings in his said trial in such safe keeping that you may be able to answer to us for them. . . . And take care that you make no default therein, for we do warn you that if default there be, we shall look to such of you as shall seem good to us to answer to us for it."

"Then," proceeded Ami, "he tried to get Erasmus to reply, but his prudence forbade it;" and the young knight added, "I cannot help wishing Erasmus were not so prudent, or Berquin were not so bold."

"Yes," said the beautiful Marguerite. "Then Beda —"

"Who is anxious to get me to the East."

"Then Beda," proceeded she, not without a manifestation of sadness at the thought of Ami's going, — "Beda made accusation against Berquin. The struggle between his Majesty and the court over Berquin's privileges in prison followed a letter which I wrote to my brother Francis. When I could take the scholar from the Louvre, and when he was in my service, I wrote to Montmorency these words: 'I thank you for the pleasure you have done me in the matter of poor Berquin, whom I esteem as much as if he were myself; and so you may say that you have delivered me from prison, since I consider in that light the pleasure done to me.' But I could not manage Sieur Berquin at all. He again attacked the monks and the infidelity of the Church. Erasmus wrote to him, begging him to cease. Again I pleaded with my noble brother the king. 'Poor Berquin,' wrote I, 'who through your goodness holds that God has twice preserved his life, throws himself upon you, having no longer any one to whom he can have recourse, for to give you to understand his innocence; and whereas, Monseigneur, I know the esteem in which you hold him, and the desire he hath always had to do you service, I do not fear to entreat you by letter instead of speech to be pleased to have pity on him. And if it please you to show signs of taking his matter to heart, I hope that the truth which he will make to appear, will convict the forgers of heretics of being slanderers and disobedient toward you, rather than zealots for the faith.'

"Once more," continued Marguerite of Navarre, "he was tried and set at liberty. Who could help standing near him? The grace of God was upon him. I should have gone with him through a thousand condemnations. But, Ami, bid him now hold his excited soul in peace for a while. If the enemies think him concerned in the

breaking of the images, Chancellor Duprat and even the
Queen Regent of France, my mother, will urge upon the
King his death."

June 1st had witnessed what the Catholics insisted,
with some justice, was a revolting infamy; what the
Reformers regretted to say was a too careless assertion
of their protest against superstitions.

The image of Notre Dame de Pierre stood at the
corner of the street, in the rear of the Church Petit
St. Antoine. It was especially reverenced by the devout.
That night, with the sounding of heavy hammers, the
image was broken. The head of the Virgin and that of
the child were cut off. The whole city was immediately
aroused with indignation. Even Ami was heard to say,
as he saw the King weeping, —

"The Reformers of France are as coarse as is Luther
himself."

At every roadway a man stood with a trumpet, pro-
claiming, by order of his Majesty, an offer of one thousand
golden crowns for the apprehension of the miscreants.
Every house was searched; processions of outraged Catholics visited the spot of the profanation. In ten days
the King of France, inflamed by the hot words of the
queen regent and Chancellor Duprat, marched with
bare head to the sacred place. The clergy and parish of
St. Paul followed his reverent figure. Cardinals and
nobles surrounded him. Each carried a white waxen
taper. The clarions and trumpets made a din of confused melodies; and the archers showed the purpose of
the realm to avenge the monstrous outrage.

With the awful memory of that scene, Ami could not
but feel a secret fear gnawing at his heart, as he parted
with the courageous zealot, — his teacher and friend,
Louis de Berquin.

CHAPTER XVIII.

SERVANT OF THE HOLY CHURCH.

" To paradise the gloomy passage winds
Through regions drear and dismal, and through pain
Emerging soon in beatific blaze
Of light."

WE last saw Vian at the home of Sir Thomas More. As he returned to Hampton Court, he felt a premonition that his relationships with one who had been so much to him were sure to end very soon. More had frankly told him that Wolsey's aims and methods did not commend themselves to his good judgment, and that he foresaw a rupture between himself and the cardinal near at hand.

" I shall not allow my affection for you, Vian, to deprive you from being of inestimable benefit to England. Nay, I love England too well to be cold in my desires that you should assist the Lord Cardinal in the establishment of his colleges," said More, who, even as speaker of the House of Commons, was beginning to avoid Henry's court.

Vian was soon under the spell exercised by a scheme which so thoroughly coincided with his tastes and opinions. Despite his desire for the publication of the English Bible, he had at length been persuaded that the England which he had come to worship had no place for

William Tyndale and his translation of the Scriptures. The common people could not read; there were none to teach them. What England appeared to require was presented in the idea of Wolsey, out of which Vian saw rising the beauty and wealth of Oxford. Wolsey's plan of building the new colleges had in no way neglected the men of "the new learning;" indeed, they were often selected as lecturers. It involved the destruction of the smaller monasteries, each of which, in Vian's opinion, nursed Romish despotism in England, and increased the difficulty in the way of that untrammelled intellectual life to the progress of which he was willing to devote his life. Vian was blind to the splendid pomp of Wolsey, which was becoming very offensive to those who could find in straying copies of Tyndale's translation a different conception of power. Vian was blind to this, because of his admiration of the cardinal's industry in turning the wealth of the monastic houses toward the new colleges. As Sir Thomas More grew more fierce in his opposition to a man who appeared to him only desirous to increase his authority by transferring power to these institutions of which he was master, Vian became enthusiastic in his praise, because it seemed that learning instead of ignorance, idleness, and iniquity should hereafter exercise rule.

"England will be less answerable to the Pope if there be more colleges," argued he.

Soon the time came when England's king was in need of an immunity from papal authority. Once again had a pope deceased; once again had Wolsey failed of election at the hands of the conclave; and Henry VIII. had met and loved the charming Anne Boleyn. Foxe and Gardiner had made a trip to the feet of his Holiness in behalf of Henry's scruples as to the legitimacy of his marriage with Katherine; but the trip was in vain. Vian, close to the sovereign, in his desire to make England powerful and independent, easily passed into sympathy with the king, believed in the necessity for a divorce, and of course, when he was not quite sure, bolstered up his belief in the righteousness of this cause for dispute by rejoicing in anything which might point toward a triumph for Henry and the cardinal.

"But for the fact that I am a Pythagorean, I had myself confessed that the daughter of Sir Thomas Boleyn is beautiful," said he to Wolsey, as he obtained the cardinal's instructions.

"Would that the king were a Pythagorean!" replied Wolsey, shaking his head sadly.

Vian was now quite sure that his suspicion that Wolsey was losing ground with Henry VIII. was well founded. However, he resolved to labor, in season and out of season, for the development of Oxford, which he had come to believe to be the task of his life.

Above the horizon another bright and steady star, somewhat overclouded, often baleful in its wandering rays, had risen. Thomas Cromwell had come to be Wolsey's accredited agent in the dissolution of the smaller monasteries. Vian's associations with this able man of affairs had made him stand in awe of this most astute and rigorous politician. Bent on the endowment of Oxford, Vian estimated Cromwell as a successful destroyer of monasteries with the same liberality that he used with More, years before, when Vian's mind was in need of a different kind of help. He had seen Cromwell persuade a displeased king, while he was learning to master the business of the State. He had beheld him "leaning in the great window, with a primer in his hand, saying of Our Lady's matins," as he placed in Vian's hand an order for the plate of a doomed priory or abbey. Our aims sanctify the servants which realize them. The great minister and cardinal was yet in his position of authority; now, however, more anxious to put down

heresy than aforetime.   Henry VIII. was smiling still on
Oxford, though intolerant of the scholars who objected
to the divorce.   Cromwell was pouring wealth into the
colleges, though he was cruel and rapacious.   Oxford
filled Vian's eye; and he therefore saw nothing else
clearly.

There was a time of awakening coming, as to the tremulous condition of Wolsey's fortunes; and the cardinal,
to whom Vian was so admiringly attached, would soon
require this monk, who was yet under his vow, for other
services.

In the proceedings in behalf of the king's divorce,
which had dragged through more than three years,
Henry VIII. had often become displeased with the cardinal; and Anne Boleyn had grown indignant.   Even
the cardinal had become alarmed.   Campeggio, the
papal legate, had shown by his own independence of
action that of the Pope Clement VII.   Vian saw, behind
the shadows, Katherine's nephew, Charles V.   Private information had reached the ears of Wolsey's friend that
Charles V. had insinuated to his Holiness that neither
Francis I. nor Henry VIII. had any loyal feeling toward
the papal see.

"Why," said Charles V., "even now, in the kingdom of France, are followers of Peter Waldo.   The King
of the French allows heresy in his realm, and is constant
at beseeching favors at Rome.   As for Henry of England,
his cardinal Wolsey would be pope even now.   He himself
will yield nothing to the papal tiara."

Six months thereafter, a papal nuncio, of courtly manners and signal ability, had placed the mind of the Pope
before Francis I.   Francis was in the midst of new em-
barrassments.   Marguerite — although now Marguerite,
Queen of Navarre — had encouraged the Reformers.
William Farel had escaped, going toward Geneva.   Lutheranism was growing, in spite of Duprat.   The King of

France had also allowed Admiral Andrea Doria to be insulted ; and at any moment he was likely to lose this Genoese ally.   Charles V. had not won Francis I. by the gift of Eleanor to be his wife ; the treaty of Madrid was broken ; Clement VII. distrusted him.

Anxious to attach the Pope to his threatened fortunes, Louise of Savoy had persuaded Francis I. to pledge an expedition of twenty young knights to proceed against the Waldensians ; and the satisfied nuncio was soon in England, negotiating with Wolsey.

August 20, 1529, Thomas Wolsey, Lord Cardinal, trembling upon the edge of complete disaster, ready to do anything to gain power with Clement VII., embraced Vian, gave him his blessing, and said, —

"You shall precede the French knights, who, through the messenger from his Holiness, will need your advice as to the method and time of attacking the heretics. Vian, I can do no other than this.   May God return you to us, as He will, doubtless, with honor ! "

Vian was prepared to prove his faithfulness to Wolsey, the cardinal's faithfulness to Rome, and his own valor.

CHAPTER XIX.

THICKENING CLOUDS.

Why are we weighed down with heaviness,
And utterly consumed with sharp distress,
While all things else have rest from weariness?
All things have rest: why should we toil alone?
  We only toil who are the first of things,
And make perpetual moan,
Still from one sorrow to another thrown;
  Nor steep our brows in slumber's holy balm;
Nor hearken what the inner spirit sings,
    "There is no joy but calm!"
Why should we ouly toil: the roof and crown of things?
                                        TENNYSON.

NINE months had elapsed since Ami had bid farewell to Astrée at the palace of St. Germain.

"Never was the court of my Cæsar so free from petty annoyances about reformations in the Holy Church! Never was his Majesty so untroubled with heretical scholars like Louis de Berquin!"

Louise of Savoy, truly Queen Regent of France in spite of Queen Eleanor, was speaking to her daughter Marguerite concerning the long absence of Ami, whom she appreciated as Queen of Navarre, and whom Ami appreciated as the one personal influence likely to put her brother into profounder sympathy with the Renaissance and the Reformation.

"He has been absent from us too long," said the latter, with a tender note of sadness. "Nine long months, and what dreadful questions have come!"

"None that Ami could have rightly answered," was the stiff remark of the queen regent.

"Ah, I know not, I know not; but I believe that if my brother had — "

"His Majesty, your sovereign!" haughtily interposed the queen regent, who had often been annoyed at the great influence of her daughter upon the court of her son.

"I love him, I honor him. I love him so much that I wish that Ami had remained in France. Had he remained and counselled, as his wisdom permitted, Admiral Andrea Doria would not have joined the hosts of Charles V., his Majesty's enemy."

"Andrea Doria was a base traitor, a lover of Genoa, — "

"His own dear city and home!"

"'T is true; but his loyalty had been given to the King of France."

"And the courtiers of France were allowed to break it," said Marguerite, firmly.

"Daughter and Queen, we must not quarrel. Ami will return soon enough;" and then the queen regent, in her most autocratic manner, added: "Astrée and your Majesty will behold the face of the young knight to-morrow."

The sister of Francis I. was full of rejoicing, and she hastened at once with queenly sympathy to inform the lovely Astrée.

Marguerite of Navarre neither overestimated the importance of the events of the last nine months, nor the probable influence which Ami would have exercised upon them. She knew how thoroughly her mother had laid her plans for his absence. She also was aware that the young knight was glad to absent himself from a court which had nothing but opposition to his statesmanlike propositions and his religious experiences.

When Beda, dreading his influence upon the king, had proposed to the queen regent to arrange the expedition to a distant monastery for the purpose of obtaining manuscripts, Ami was sick at heart at the dissolution of all prospects for untrammelled scholarship and wise reform, and sick even of the Reformers themselves.

The priesthood still regarded him a faithful, but erratic Catholic. He himself had come back to the opinion that Lutheranism, in its current aspect, must be dealt with more stringently. He had resolved, in his absence, to find a standing-ground for his own faith, that he might more wisely influence the faith of the king. What could afford a better opportunity for his mind to settle its future course than this lengthy bibliographical tour?

Letters had come from Ami to the king, which showed that his mind was turning with more loyal reverence to the Holy Church. In the light of these, the queen regent was more willing to have him with her son. Ami, she was now sure, would be less critical of the clergy, and less friendly to the foes of the Church, on his return. The University of Paris, the library of the king, and the peace of France might profit now at his early arrival; for he was laden with manuscripts.

"Of course, it is impossible for him to keep his hands out of our statecraft," said the wise Louise; and tossing her head: "But he cannot disturb our plans at once. He is cautious. He will have to take time to comprehend the events which have transpired;" and then she greatly comforted her orthodoxy and hope for peace, by adding: "He may, if he wants to prove his knighthood and serve the Holy Church, which some of his friends have so often reviled, — he may lead the secret expedition against the Waldensians."

She really chuckled at the idea of a Waldensian murdering a Waldensian.

True, significant events had transpired.

Ami was sure to find that the great changes of the last few months linked themselves with all the events which had succeeded the return of the king from Madrid, and showed how completely Francis I. had failed to comprehend his significant era. Some of those earlier events had accompanied Ami like ghosts. Nothing, however, so haunted him as the sacrifice and death of Bourbon, the old lover of Marguerite.

"Slay! slay! Blood! blood! Bourbon, Bourbon!"— the shout of the soldiers of the constable, when they learned of his death in sight of Rome,—had rung through the soul of Ami, as the latter stood in the damp cellars of ancient monasteries, seeking to read the red and yellow parchments.

Benvenuto Cellini, it was said, had then fired the shot which was fatal to a man of whom Francis I. had been jealous, to whom the mother of his Majesty had been resentful because he would not return a wicked love, and who, in spite of Ami's wise protests, had been transformed into a revengeful enemy of France.

Another matter had disquieted him. Louise of Savoy knew that Ami had left France fearing that the king would lose Andrea Doria from his service. And now Mme. de Chateaubriand's brother Lautrec had seen the king's old ally, Andrea Doria, blockade Naples, while his own army was stricken with famine and the plague. It would be impossible, as everybody about the court knew, for either Ami or the king to forget how often the sagacious young knight had besought his Majesty to respect the feelings of the admiral, and to honor the commerce of Genoa. The king's mother was sure that the news of

Andrea Doria's revolt might be kept from Ami until something could be done to regain the power thus lost.

The Spanish half of Charles V.'s dominion was now connected with the German half. Ami had often begged his royal friend to leave the influences of his favorites, even to break with a plan of Louise of Savoy, and thus to prevent the advance of the fortunes of his antagonist the emperor.

The treaty of Barcelona between the Pope and Emperor Charles had been signed in June. The shrewd Louise knew that Ami could not but feel a sickening sorrow when he should read " the Ladies' Peace."

The man whom none could trust, Duprat, who had meanwhile been made a bishop, had again brought France to shame by debasing the coin wherewith Charles V. was to have been paid for the release of the French princes. Ami had long ago described the real character of this minister so frequently and so truly, that Louise of Savoy, who could use Duprat so easily, called the Waldensian " a hateful nuisance."

Francis I. had been made defiant and theatrical by his captivity. Ami, with all wisdom and affection, had often urged upon him the lesson of obedience to law ; but now the Parliament of Paris was already impelled to say to the king, —

" We know well that you are above the laws ; still we venture to say that you ought not to will, nor should desire to will, all that you can."

Before his departure Ami had roused the hate of Louise, when he asserted the fact that Francis, in the treaty of Madrid, was about to imprison his own children to save his own freedom ; and now the world knew it. He had tried to translate for the ruler's ear the cry of the peasantry, who stared while the king purchased bronzes, furs, velvets, beasts, birds, palaces, furniture, and gorgeous jewels for his favorite, who had very soon become offensive as Duchesse d'Étampes; and even Marguerite had grown a little weary of this amateur statesmanship. The clergy were growing more corrupt and the people more ignorant, on a theory of popular misgovernment, which the young knight had often declared the basis of a public crime. The court was welcoming the Renaissance and trying to shut out the Reformation. Louise of Savoy was still more anxious than before for the presence of Erasmus, since he had quarrelled with Luther. She remembered that Ami had already told her fearlessly that France needed a William Farel, whom he had afterward rescued from her and Duprat. The German movement, under Luther, was fiercely hated; and now nothing so roused the ire of the queen regent, or disgusted her son, as the reflection that Queen Marguerite once nearly succeeded in influencing his Majesty toward Lutheranism.

Surely much had transpired. Marguerite of Navarre was quite certain, from the letters which she had read from Ami, that his protesting spirit had sensibly cooled while he had been rummaging in the monasteries. She assured her mother that he would be more tractable. She was quite as sure that he would be more able to influence her brother the king toward a wiser statesmanship, if Ami had meanwhile become a more devout Catholic.

As for herself, she was, it was true, still favorable to the Reform, still writing verses, still rejoicing with her brother's new favorite and helping their intrigues, still anxious to translate the Psalms and to hear the latest Monkish tale, — still the inconsistent, brilliant charm of the court.

She was, one evening, wondering with the king about the policy of the proposed secret expedition to exterminate some leaders of the Waldensians, when the king repeated to her what he had often said, —

" I have been accused by his Holiness of having heresy in my own realm whenever I have sought a favor at Rome.

I cannot protect the Waldensians who are in correspondence with Luther and Farel. I shall give his Holiness
twenty knights."

Francis I. had freely confessed his strong desire that
Ami should lead the expedition. Grave doubts, however,
arose in his mind. His Majesty thought Ami would now
be so agitated by what Francis had called "the unfortunate Berquin affair," that he would be uncontrollable.

" It will be well for him to prove his faith to the Church
and to you," said the queen regent. " Let him lead a
company of trained soldiers, each of whom is to look out
for himself, into the country of the Waldensians. There
can be no danger of his killing or encountering his own
friends, think you? His father must be dead long ago ;
and he lived in Piedmont, — leagues away from the well-
known spot where the leaders now write their heretical
letters to Ulric Zwingli and Martin Luther, and foment
discontent in our realm. His Holiness is right; and
you must exterminate the correspondents of these arch-
heretics. So long as these who are our French heretics
write to the German and Swiss leaders, and you know it,
we are in no wise worthy of papal benedictions. Ami
owes everything to yourself. Perhaps he is not ungrate-
ful. If Ami would have us believe him honest, if he would
serve the Church, let him lead the way. Wolsey's messenger, who will doubtless be a valiant duke desiring honor,
will precede him ; and he will send back to our French
contingent, as it follows him, such information about that
vile rendezvous for heretics as will enable the twenty
knights to strike and annihilate the heresy at a blow."

The eyes of Louise of Savoy were bright with a lurid
glow, furnishing a strange contrast with her pale, haggard
face. She hoped in her deepest soul that Ami would go
and never return. His statesmanship and her policies
could never live in peace together.

CHAPTER XX.

AMI AND THE DEATH OF BERQUIN.

If you are wise, repress your encomiums; do not disturb the hornets, and spend your time in your favorite studies. At all events, do not involve me, for the consequences might be inconvenient for us both. — Erasmus to Louis de Berquin.

ON the morning of Sept. 6, 1529, every ray of light seemed to linger in unwonted happiness upon the expanses of green which stretched away from the ancient chateau of Chambord. The gloomy old palace had, a short time before, been decorated anew in the name of a love which was now dead; but the Duchesse d'Étampes was enjoying the newly transformed archways quite as thoroughly as she had expected to relish the ownership of the mountings for Mme. de Chateaubriand's jewels, bearing the salamander crest of Francis, and graven with the amorous wit of the king's sister.

In this latter joy she was disappointed. She had seen the mountings of the case only as they had appeared in the form of ugly ingots, into which the elegant devices had been melted by the fire of Madame's resentment; but the duchesse nevertheless enjoyed the Moorish pavilion, in which she often sat with the king as much as though Francis had never been in love before.

Everything was astir. Wine was flowing in ruby streams into goblets glistening with artistic elegance. The king had been busily engaged with a minister of the court, who was inscribing upon the ivory tablet the names of those knights who were to comprise the secret expedition into the Alps. Precious stones emblazoned the messenger of his Holiness, who stood near and gave his invaluable counsel.

"We must be brief in our converse," said the king, who was always weary of business. "The huntsmen are ready; the animals are likely now to be best fitted for the chase;" and turning to the solemnly gazing representative of the Pope, "I would have you be seated at the banquet, after the sport, at the side of Ami, the young Bayard of France. He has just come back to us from the far East."

The messenger simply made an Italian courtesy.

In a short time the king was wildly engaged in the chase. The gay colors, the rapid motions, the splendid horsemanship made a brilliant spectacle.

At the window — on which Francis afterward engraved a distich on the inconstancy of woman — was to be observed another scene quite different. The persons visible were Ami, Astrée, and the old friend of Berquin, William Budé, the scholar and book-lover.

Erasmus himself had said of Budé: "Among many thousands of men you will not find any of higher integrity, and more versed in polite letters." Perhaps no two men in France more truly represented the spirit of reaction in the Sorbonne and the spirit of progress in sound learning, than Beda and Budé.

Until this morning Ami had not seen the king since the hour when he set out for the manuscripts of that remote monastery; and he knew nothing of what had occurred meanwhile, save that his love for Astrée was deeper and more sweet. William Budé had not been in the presence of his Majesty since the death of Ami's friend Berquin.

It was a great joy for Ami to meet with such a scholar

as Budé after so long a pilgrimage. The knight was full to overflowing of bibliographical lore. It was an unexpected feature of the day to find this broad and liberal scholar at his side, instead of Beda, in whom Erasmus had said " there are three thousand monks."

"Surely," thought Ami, " the king has grown more tolerant; I, on the other hand, have grown to be less tolerant."

He hardly knew how Budé would look upon his fresh hostility to the Reformers. However, he was bound to talk only of manuscripts. Ami had known him much as history knows him to-day, — a wealthy book-buyer at the first; then a patient and ambitious learner at the feet of scholars; then a friend of Nouvisset, of whom he had learned Greek; later, a traveller to Rome and Venice, reading manuscripts, and beginning to write his famous " Commentaries" on the Greek; and, later still, a laborer upon a book on the Roman *As*, which was to make him appear as a rival even of Erasmus. There was in his hand a letter from the great scholar, whom neither Astrée nor Ami had seen; and in his eye was a tear, as the young knight ended his monologue, which related to his journeys, the difficulties with monks and robbers, his discoveries in unfrequented cells, his struggles with ignorance, and the labor of reading with success a valuable palimpsest. Ami concluded his first enchanting tale with the query, —

" And how is Sieur Berquin? Would he were with us here !"

The scholar handed him a bit of manuscript. It was not ancient. They entirely forgot the bibliographical tour, as Ami read the following words, which were a copy made by Budé of the words spoken, April 16, by the President of the Court to Ami's friend Berquin.

Ami's soul was again being charged with fire from on high, while Astrée wept with Budé the scholar.

"Louis Berquin!" so ran the speech, "you are convicted of having belonged to the sect of Luther, and of having made wicked books against the majesty of God and of his glorious Mother. In consequence we do sentence you to make honorable amends, bareheaded and with waxen taper alight in your hand, in the great court of the palace, crying for mercy to God, the king, and the law, for the offence by you committed. After that you will be conducted, bareheaded and on foot, to the Place de Grève, where your books will be burned before your eyes. Then you will be taken in front of the church of Notre Dame, where you will make honorable amends to God and to the glorious Virgin, his mother. After which a hole will be pierced in your tongue, — that member wherewith you have sinned. Lastly, you will be placed in the prison of Monsieur de Paris (the bishop), and will there be confined between two stone walls for the whole of your life. And we forbid that there ever be given you book to read or pen and ink to write."

Here was an unexpected trial for Ami's new position. Could he be loyal to the hapless man whom he had loved, and to the other whom so lately he had sworn anew to revere?

"Did he appeal to the king?" asked the friend of Francis I.

"He was incarcerated at once. We might have saved him."

"And you did not?" said the knight, excitedly.

"The crowd gathered, — twenty thousand thronged the square and crossed the bridge. He would have walked surrounded with arquebusiers and archers through the street. But he appealed to the king."

Instantly the loving knight, who had been desperately working up his affections for Francis I., discovered the reflection on his sovereign.

"You are in his Majesty's chateau. Speak your contempt carefully, if at all. Francis I. is my friend. I am a knight," exclaimed he.

"And a lover of truth?" asked Budé, who, though thoroughly surprised, still thought he knew Ami.

The knight found himself where he had not been for two years, — where he dared not answer that question.

Things had indeed changed. He had determined to be a faithful, even a persecuting Catholic, if necessary. Again had his unspeakably intense jealousy of that English monk Vian driven him from any sort of desire to join with the Reformers. He had been changed by this evil spirit. At Florence, an English abbot who was travelling in Italy told him that only Wolsey, who was a politician without piety, believed in the orthodoxy of Vian; that the late Abbot Richard, of Glastonbury, had distrusted him and was glad to have the abbey rid of his presence; that probably before that hour Vian himself had fled to the Reformers and joined their ranks.

That information had been sufficient to rouse the most furious of the fires in Ami's soul. His jealousy had leaped again, like a hungry tiger, upon his growing love of the Reforming movement. This beastly and murderous passion had sucked almost every drop of the life-blood from his convictions. Even his conscience had found itself a drooping energy.

He hated the idea of walking in Vian's path, even if it led Godward. His whole soul had been a battle-ground. He had despised priestcraft, ignorance, fraud, infamies, indulgences; he had loved Farel, Berquin, Lefevre, and goodness. That was one fact feeding a Waldensian conscience.

He loathed Vian, who once supplanted him as a scholar in the eyes of Francis I., who also had once touched Astrée's hand with what he would now make oath was a villanous intent. That was the other fact feeding a devilish jealousy.

They had struggled for a while as he travelled on. Jealousy had won the triumph. He was ready soon to do something so bold, so decisive, so desperate in behalf of the Holy Church, that every bridge would be burned behind him, and retreat to his old position of sympathy with the Reformers would be utterly impossible. He had come back to France determined to put himself publicly, by some blazing act, where he would be compelled to remain a foe of the Reform, — above all, a foe of the detestable Vian.

Oh, how Astrée pitied him! She knew his heart so well. He had already told her of this purpose; she also knew that he loved the noble Louis de Berquin, and that the story of the silence of Francis I. while his old friend and tutor was roasting in flames, would well-nigh break Ami's heart. She did not know — no human being can know — the certainty with which jealousy, while it closes the pathways to heaven, can make the tenderest heart a thing of iron.

William Budé saw it all in Ami's transparent glances. He arose and said, —

"A knight trained by Nouvisset cares not to hear the truth."

It stung Ami. Vian, Nouvisset, Francis, Berquin, Astrée, — the names swept through his maddened brain as he touched his jewelled dagger, and found the soft, loving hand of that darling girl upon it.

"Never! never!" she said, with a delicate omnipotence, before which Ami faltered. "Never! Master Budé, forgive him! My Bayard and my adored one is still a scholar."

The humbled young knight begged for pardon and for the truth.

As well as he might after such an experience, did Budé tell him of the death of Berquin. Every fire died out of Ami's eye, and the dew-fall of grief was on his cheeks, until a thought of sympathy with Reformers, the conviction that it might lead to the company of Vian, and the furious jealousy of his untamed heart blazed there again, and licked up every tear-drop. Even Astrée's love trembled with fear.

"Berquin was unduly familiar with the men who committed the outrage with the images."

"Do you know their names? The chancellor does not; and even the inquisitors could not find them out," Budé calmly asserted. "Besides," continued he, "there was not a particle of evidence that your old tutor was aware of the event until the next day."

"Your old tutor!"—that phrase recalled some pathetic memories which sobbed in Ami's heart.

"You will vouchsafe me the whole story, Master," said Ami, somewhat less excitedly.

"Only four months after your departure,—Master Berquin kept you in his prayers, Ami,—he was arrested; and the speech which I gave you"—Astrée at this instant reached down, and with the hand which had released the dagger, picked up the crumpled manuscript and placed it in Ami's trembling hand,—"that speech was scarce uttered when Berquin cried out, 'I appeal to the king!'"

Budé was silent for a moment; and then he solemnly added: "I know this is the king's palace;" then standing up, he said, "But greater crimes have been done here than my telling the disciple of Berquin how this scholar died."

"You can tell me all; but I will honor my king," was Ami's remark.

"The King of kings and the Lord of lords?" inquired Budé, with sincere eloquence.

Astrée moved nearer to Ami, and put her white hand upon his shoulder.

The knight said nothing except this: "Proceed! the

ways of God are all cross-ways; the paths to heaven are
tangled."

"I have already said it, Ami! We might have saved
him. The gracious Queen Marguerite will tell you that I
begged Berquin, saying to him: 'Acquiesce; we can
save you later on, before the day of punishment. A second sentence is ready and pronounces death. All that
this sentence asks is a plea for pardon. Do we not all
need pardon?' I said. 'Acquiesce!'"

Ami, who had been bracing himself with reflection on
Vian, and with thinking how Vian might have loved Berquin, had the English monk been in France, anxious to
find a curse for a Reformer, inquiringly said, "And he
was still boastful of his heresy?"

"Not at all," answered Budé; "he was only a knightly
lover of truth. So knightly was he that at the last the
good Queen of Navarre wrote words like these to the
sovereign: 'I for the last time make you a very humble
request: it is that you will be pleased to have pity upon
poor Berquin, whom I know to be suffering for nothing
but loving the word of God and obeying yours. You will
be pleased, Monseigneur, so to act that it be not said that
separation has made you forget your most humble and
most obedient subject and sister, Marguerite.'"

"What was the answer?" inquired the agitated knight.

"The king made no reply. I have kept this copy of a
letter from Erasmus to his friend, and brought it to you."

William Budé then handed the crushed copy of the
speech and letter to Ami; and he began to read. Astrée looked over his shoulder.

The eyes of the three fell upon this passage in which
the Dutch scholar repeats what an eyewitness had told
him: —

"Not a symptom of agitation appeared either in his face or
the attitude of his body; he had the bearing of a man who is
meditating in his cabinet on the subject of his studies or in

a temple on the affairs of Heaven. Even when the executioner in a rough voice proclaimed his crime and its penalty, the constant serenity of his features was not at all altered. When the order was given him to dismount from the tumbril, he obeyed cheerfully without hesitating ; nevertheless he had not about him any of that audacity, that arrogance, which in the case of malefactors is sometimes bred of their natural savagery ; everything about him bore evidence to the tranquillity of a good conscience. Before he died he made a speech to the people ; but none could hear him, so great was the noise which the soldiers made, according, it is said, to the orders they had received. When a cord which bound him to the post suffocated his voice, not a soul in the crowd ejaculated the name of Jesus, whom it is customary to invoke even in favor of parricides and the sacreligious, to such extent was the multitude excited against him by those folks who are to be found everywhere, and who can do anything with the feelings of the simple and ignorant."

Ami cried out with pain. Not a syllable escaped his lips as he bolted past the knot of courtiers gathered without, deaf to the cries of Astrée, who followed him with her tearful pleadings.

CHAPTER XXI.

ANOTHER SERVANT OF THE HOLY CHURCH.

Which way I fly is hell ! myself am hell. — SHAKSPEARE.

IN a short time even Astrée had been forsaken by the tempest-tossed Ami. He was soon alone in the lower part of the principal fortress of St. Germain-en-Laye, whither he had fled in anguish of soul.

"Solitude!" said he, in his agony ; and he thought of the crowns which had been won and lost, the kingdoms saved and doomed, the revelations vouchsafed and withheld, when souls like his had found solitude. "Here," mused he, — "here is no mountain ; and yet Sinai with cloud and flame is here. Here is no desert ; and yet a John the Baptist may listen even here and detect the words, 'Repent! Repent!' on this damp air. Here is no Florence, with Guelph and Ghibelline in the street ; but Dante's 'Inferno' or 'Paradiso' is mine in this very cell. Here is no temple summit ; but here demons crowd to say, 'All these kingdoms are thine ; fall down and worship me!'"

The piteous wail of Louis de Berquin came in from between the stones ; so, also, did the compliments of Chevalier Bayard, *sans peur, sans reproche!* The struggling purity of a personal faith came in the scorched faces of countless martyrs, and looked at him from the wall ; so also did the affectionate wickedness of Francis I.

The Waldensian conscience, pure as a mountain snow-drift, bright as an Alpine dawn, hovered over his bursting temples; so also did the hands of cardinals and popes, and the traditions of an immutable institution. He was a passive, torn battle-ground.

The grandeur of the Holy Church, his obligations to the king, the fear of eternal torments, — all were now being driven back. The face of Louis de Berquin was scattering them as the dawn routs the night. It was Saul of Tarsus again, a moment after holding the clothes of those who stoned the martyr Stephen. The bloody face on whose wounds shone a light of transfiguration, was breaking his heart. Would that power win the victory?

At the instant when the tearful eyes again looked toward the eternal daytime, the foe which had grown despotic within his soul, and which had torn him and hurled him about so often, lifted its brutal throne upon the scene of the conflict. As into Saul, the hesitating persecutor, swept the pride of a Pharisee which turned him from sympathy to hate, so out of the lair in Ami, the questioning zealot, sprang with powerful ferocity the infernal passion of jealousy, turning him from pity to cruelty. He had just thought of Astrée, then of Vian, then of the career which should slake this burning hate. Jealousy had worked its damnation upon his jealous soul. He turned his back swiftly upon the morning; and, like Saul, he looked for the road to Damascus.

Astrée had found him; and she felt a stern purpose in his cold hand as she led him up the stone stairs.

He was immovable and unlovely, yet she loved him.

"I will hear of affairs of State when I return, — a knight blessed by the Holy Father and honored in this realm," he remarked to one of the ministers of Francis I.

The minister was more than delighted to learn that Ami had accepted so honorable a place among the twenty young knights, and who supposed he would like to hear of the treaties which had just been signed, and the gathering strength of the throne to deal with the Reformation.

No one cared to tell him that Andrea Doria had gone over to Charles V. Every one near Ami knew how often he had regretted the treatment which he foresaw would certainly make that chivalrous admiral an implacable enemy of Francis I.

Ami was busy with his own soul. "I go to make for myself a firm faith," cried he, as Astrée clung to him in the pitiful moonlight.

"Faith is not made by rash, passionate hate," she ventured to say, her eyes full of tears, her heart a living pain.

"I have no hold upon anything; I must grasp something in a desperate act. My soul has been mystified. I call myself a heretic, and from the deeps comes the word 'heretic.' I call myself a Catholic of Rome, and the echo from my vacant soul is 'Rome.' I never will be of the party of Reform. The accursed Vian has doubtless gone there, and is now as foul as he was false. I am his undying enemy, — you hear? Of his cause I will be an unrelenting persecutor."

"Oh, Ami, you do not look so tender and loving as is your wont, when you speak so !"

"Perhaps not; it is because I loved you that I hated him."

"What if he has not gone over to the Reformers?" she inquired, as he coldly moved aside. "Ami, my sweet knight, do not leave me. Let me kiss your lips, which seem so stiff and dry when you curse the monk."

It was an unsatisfactory kiss to both of them. Jealousy had even scorched Astrée. She knew it was burning Ami up. She must protest no more, for it seemed only to fan the flame.

"I said I would be an unrelenting persecutor, if need be, to kill that wretch who first — "

"I can never love a persecutor, Ami! You have taught me to love Him who said, ' Put up thy sword into the sheath,' " she answered, with ejaculations of grief.

"I care not for — " He was about to blaspheme, when, the banquet having been made ready, he was commanded to present himself before the king, and there he was invited to be seated by the side of the Pope's messenger.

On the morrow every detail of the march was explained, every plan of extermination made clear. Ami saw a great future in sight, — a future which had for him the career of a Captain of the Papal Guard. If this expedition should be successful, the position was his. Never did that ring which was given him by Leo X. at Bologna, long years ago, sparkle with such hope.

The next morning Astrée had been alone in her sorrow, save for the faithful priest, who was trying in vain to persuade her that Ami would return from that expedition against the Waldensians with a creed and with honor.

"And he will love me then," she said.

CHAPTER XXII.

TO THE MOUNTAINS.

We know not how to choose.   We cannot separate
Our longing and our hate.
LEWIS MORRIS.

FROM France to England hurried the nuncio of Clement VII.   Under the magnificent elms, near the palace of Henry VIII., Vian stood ready for his journey.   There he had said " Farewell " to his king.

The papal nuncio had supplied him with sufficient information concerning the desires of the Pope himself. His ardent admiration for the abilities of Wolsey's chosen messenger had constantly increased, as the latter spoke of the task before him, and opened unto this new agent of his Holiness the plans which had been matured at Hampton Court and Whitehall.

"Your Eminence has loaned to the service of the Church, at this juncture, a remarkably powerful man. His evident wisdom, strategy, and comprehensive understanding of what must be done to rid those valleys of heresy appear to surpass even his scholarship," remarked the nuncio to Wolsey, from whose breast hope had not yet quite gone.

"He is both a learned and a shrewd man.   I hope he may prove entirely successful," replied the cardinal, as he guardedly answered the Italian monk, careful to say nothing as to the state of Vian's faith in the Church.

"I shall accompany him to Calais; and one of the abbots of San Michele, intelligent of the plans of the trusted courtiers of the Pope, will guide him thence by a sure and short route to Susa, perhaps to the monastery beyond. Blessings upon you, my Lord Cardinal! With this farewell, and by your leave, I now gratefully withdraw from your presence. I shall be still more grateful to do you service at Rome."

At Rome! It was a skilful piece of flattery to the cardinal's ambition. The tiara of the Pope again came into the imagination of the butcher's son, — Thomas, Lord Wolsey. He seemed already within reach of the keys of Saint Peter. Desperate circumstances with Henry VIII. had made his hallucinations vivid.

The route to Dover, even to Calais, furnished no incident. Vian and the Italian were busy making maps which to-day seem only brilliant blunders. The state of the Church was spoken of, and the pardonable ambition of Wolsey was even applauded by the nuncio. Wily as the training of the Pope could make him, cautious as the crumbling condition of affairs would demand, cheerful because often Vian seemed somewhat morose and sad, the nuncio kept before the Englishman a vision of the cardinal at length to be created pope, and of Vian himself as his appointed vicegerent.

Not for a moment did the thoughtful Vian doubt that the success of this expedition might lift him into greater power in the Church. He knew not whether he desired it; however, he did not doubt his fitness, as he thought of others in power. No difficulty of belief, no carelessness of ceremonials, no utterance of his which could be rescued from a conversation with Erasmus, More, or Giovanni would be deemed of sufficient importance to keep him from an episcopate, for example, if Wolsey were in the chair at Rome, and his own service were needed.

At Calais the nuncio, who had already once or twice imbibed too freely of English wines, refreshed himself with a bottle of such very powerful port as to become quite talkative upon subjects hitherto held in abeyance.

"Some of the bishops are not sure of their faith," said Vian.

"Aha!" laughed the nuncio, "the cardinals most disturb his Holiness. Bembo, — ha, ha! — oh, Bembo would be the sort of pope to stamp out heresy. He refuses to read Saint Paul's epistles, lest his literary style should suffer. But he is very handsome. He will be more than cardinal some day. Even his mistress and children say it."

"How many children has this coming Prince of the Holy Church?" inquired Vian, his humor giving way before a sickened heart which pondered on the path before him.

"I know not, ha, ha!" replied the intoxicated annalist, as he proceeded to paint, as best he could in his hapless condition, the life of this distinguished religionist at Padua.

Vian was conscious of the influence of the Renaissance upon himself. He had, as we have seen, contemplated its astonishing power in Erasmus, Colet, and More. He had beheld Giovanni's good-humor and Richard Beere's horror at its steady advance in Glastonbury. Never, however, at that time had he considered it possible that even the Renaissance could produce such a pagan as was Bembo, secretary of the Pope Leo X. Indeed, history has kept this name as perhaps the most illustrious representative of that class of men whose intellectual powers assume a weird and unnatural grandeur, partially because of the absence of conscience, which leaves them at once isolated and ghost-like. Bembo was the fittest type of the humanity which held the reins of the papal court, whose servant at that hour was Vian.

"I can have all the freedom I want in the Holy Church," thought he, as he turned his fine face toward Padua, pushed his long locks back from his broad forehead, and remembered that Bembo's house was said to be one elaborate welcome to artists and scholars. Shelves of rare books enclosed the spacious rooms, in which were tables covered with coins and antiquities, or littered over with manuscripts — the oldest extant — of Virgil and Terence, Petrarch's poems, and the lives of Provincial Bards.

"I heard Luigi Cornaro read to Bembo his essay 'Della Vita Lobria,' and at his villa Lamprido repeated his lines. Aha! his wine — Bembo's wine — was not equal to that of Glastonbury," languidly mused the awakening nuncio; and he added, "A great pope would Bembo make, — a great pope."

"I heard Erasmus call Bembo 'that ape of Cicero,'" remarked Vian. "But it is impossible to get on in the Church without bishops and cardinals and a papal nuncio."

"Entirely so," said the Italian. "They would all be better Churchmen if they had more of the wine which strengthens your abbot at Glastonbury. Books and scholars make heresy; wine and swords make good papists."

In due course, on that lustrous morning in 1529, two tired travellers rode a couple of jaded horses into the town of Susa. One of them was an ignorant Piedmontese monk, who had outraged the other's conscience and intelligence at his cursing and bigotry, while he had chattered concerning the Waldensians; the other was Vian, who had come thither to perfect a scheme which would scarcely stop short of annihilating the more influential of a kind of human beings whom he now believed to be the only decent people in these regions.

These two had quarrelled all the way from Calais to Susa; and when the road from Mont Genevre came visibly near to that from Mont Cenis and the marshy valley of Susa appeared, so near was the place of parting that both men were relieved.

"His Holiness never had a greater fool on his errands," said this monk Torraneo to his own soul, as they pressed on through Susa and toward Monte Pirchiriano and San Michele, to which Vian had been directed at the church in Susa.

The Englishman had for a time tried to keep up the dignity of his position. But Vian had now ceased to quote Virgil and Hesiod to the ecclesiastical barbarian, and was intent on observing San Ambrogio, when he bethought himself that something ought to be done to make this monk more friendly to him.

"Everything," the nuncio had said to Vian, "depends on your appearance and bearing at San Michele. To that sanctuary his Holiness will ask the French King to send his knights from Paris. They will follow no leader who has not been well received at the Benedictine Monastery. You, as a Benedictine in the clothes of a gentleman, are there to consolidate France, England, and Italy against the heretics."

Vian was thoughtful and uneasy; the monk was disdainful.

"You do not know much about us," said the monk, testily.

"Do you revere the noble history of yonder sanctuary?" asked Vian, preparing to astonish him into admiration of that kind of intelligence which alone he had hope would be appreciated.

"It is better than the abbeys of England, — all of them. I am sure of that."

"It is a great and inspiring story which clings to it," replied the Englishman.

The monk was all attention. They were now ascending; and the grandeur of the building, the sublimity of its position, loosed the tongue of Vian.

"That ancient wall yonder, was the effort of the Lombard King to save his possessions from Charlemagne. Desiderius was his name," ventured Vian, with dogmatism.

"It was a long time ago! I did n't know either of them. The abbot knew Charle—whatever his name could be," was the monk's heavy reply.

Vian felt that he was gaining ground; but that, looked at from an historical point of view, the ground was not very valuable.

"Ah, Brother," said Vian, thinking how Giovanni would enjoy this innocent ignorance, "then you did not know Hugh de Montboissier, who did the offence for whose expiation the monastery was founded?"

"It was a long time ago; but I have heard the abbot tell of it, — how he came from Rome and saw one night the top of Monte Pirchiriano covered with fire — "

"No," said Vian; "that was the recluse of Monte Caprasio, Giovanni Vincenzo, who saw the summit wrapped in flames. You did not know him?"

"Why, no! The abbot told me I needed not to know even the name, if only I would return the beds to the chamberlain when the guests had gone. I have .done all these things; and," he added meditatively, "I cannot give you an order for more than two days' board. The ordinance says that is all."

"Fifteen days to persons beyond suspicion," said Vian, who remembered something of the reform of San Michele in 1478, who also now saw that the monk suspected him. "Giovanni Vincenzo returned to his lonely Caprasio," added Vian, gazing from San Pietro, which they had just reached, — an eminence more than one thousand feet above San Ambrogio.

"No; the prior never lets any monk wear his hair longer than two fingers broad," answered the monk. careless that Vincenzo died before the year 1000, and careful to notice the flowing beauty of Vian's hair.

When the level height of San Pietro had been reached, our travellers were so weary that they stopped upon its soft green grass to rest. The white glaciers of Mont Cenis made the eye ache with their piercing brilliancy; and it was a joy to look upon the valley of the Dora or the plains of Turin, in which sparkled the two lakes of Avigliana.

The monk, however, was still anxious for more information with which to dovetail his own slight intelligence; and Vian and he were soon before the ancient ruin which lay on their right, about which neither could say a truthful word. As they ascended the steps, however, the monk heard a tale which entirely convinced him that his companion was all that could be desired as an exterminator of heretics; and by the time the old Lombard doorway was reached, Torraneo's pride in things ecclesiastical burst forth freely. Seeing the lord abbot himself, he cried out, —

"I bring, my Lord —"

"Tut, tut!" said the imperious abbot. "Great is the honor which we mean to do this the accredited agent of his Holiness and Cardinal Wolsey; but you do not bring your Lord here! Torraneo, to the lavatory!"

Vian entered a very elegant apartment, and was received with all ceremony; while the monk who so recently had been turned into an admirer of the Englishman, worked aimlessly in the lavatory at cleansing his face and hands, while he pondered, as never before, on both the abomination of learning, and the facility with which the abbot always made him say what he did not mean to say.

Vian was an honored guest at San Michele. He had not come to study the abbey of La Chiusa, or the church of St. Lawrence, or the chapels of St. James and St. Nicholas, — not even the scenery which unfolded its magnificence before the beholder from that height. But he could not omit to notice the votive pictures and antique frescos. The pure Lombard architecture charmed him. The church, he saw, fastened itself into, and was partially builded from the living rock. From the level of the floor stretched an almost unequalled panorama. The valleys were green with verdure, through which lucent streams went singing seaward. As he was shown above to the great arch which stood at the top of the stairs on which corpses were placed in a sitting position, which the peasants crowned with flowers, he could not help saying, —

"This church built into the living rock is the coronation-place of death. Corpses sit between fragrant Nature below and the pure heavens above."

He turned away from the corpses, because he thought they made him heretical. Vian was right: every living heresy has been caused by the crowning of some skeleton.

The head of the house felt that he must be at least pleasant to Vian.

"It was entirely proper that the Pope should ask Francis I. to rid the valley of Lucerne of that pestilence. Lucerne is subject to his crown. He is always asking favors from his Holiness. Here is heresy in his own dominion," said the abbot.

"Cardinal Wolsey was also requested — "

"Yes; and right well was he asked to aid us in keeping the Church supreme. He desires the papacy?"

"I never heard him assert it," replied Vian.

"No; 't is like him. Every abbot in Italy has knowledge of him."

"Have you apprehended any Waldensians who bore letters to heretical persons?" inquired Vian.

"Look yonder!" answered the abbot, taking him to the window and pointing to a flying vulture which had just left the noisy companionship of a whole brood in the valley below. "That bird is flying off with the fellow's tongue, with which he refused to worship at the shrine. We caught him as he came through the valley going to Susa, brought him hither, found a letter from the wretch Martin Luther upon him, — a letter addressed to one Gaspar Perrin, — a villain who has the Waldensians meet at his house for conference. Into the vault, without food, we placed that varlet, until we deciphered the missive. He would not beg or worship, as we bade him. I commanded him to be thrown from the rock; and yonder — see the vultures there? No; near the tall pine! — yonder his cursed carcass lies."

Vian trembled, and said, "Shall I see the letter of Luther? It is important testimony."

"Ah! it proves these beasts to be foul with their correspondence with the adulterous monk of Erfurt. Here is the letter."

Vian read this passage, without betraying the fact that he was far from being calm: —

"To make the religious houses really useful, they should be converted into schools, wherein children might be brought up to manhood; instead of which, they are establishments where grown men are reduced to second childhood for the rest of their lives. . . . The hour is arrived, when we must trample under foot the power of Satan, and contend against the spirit of darkness. If our adversaries do not flee from us, Christ will know how to compel them. We who put our trust in the Lord of life and death, are lords both of life and of death."

He tried to escape the noble influence of the letter by attention to every ceremony, but in vain. It was

impossible for him to hear anything, as the cantor in-
toned the antiphon, "ad benedictus ad magnificat," save
the ringing sentences of the monk Martin Luther, as they
repeated themselves in his soul.

"I must depart by sunrise. Is the brother ready?"
said he to the abbot.

"You have chosen wisely. Fra Salmani is prepared
to go. I like him not. He has loved a Waldensian,
and lies under the suspicion of having purloined a
manuscript from the treasury at Turin."

Here was joy for Vian's tortured heart. He was to
meet, as his companion, a monk who cared enough for
manuscripts to have been considered guilty of stealing
one. Here was a lover also! Vian concealed his satisfaction, saying, —

"The French knights must not tarry, even if they
should come in three days. Let them follow my path."

"I shall bid them depart at once for the fortress of
La Torre, unless a contrary command shall come from
yourself. Sending letters is a perilous business. Witness
the vultures!"

CHAPTER XXIII.

VIAN AND SALMANI.

Out of the deep, my child, out of the deep,
Where all that was to be, in all that was,
Whirled for a million æons thro' the vast
Waste dawn of multitudinous eddying light, —
Out of the deep, my child, out of the deep,
Through all this changing world of changeless law,
And every phase of ever-heightening life,
And nine long months of ante-natal gloom,
Thou comest.

TENNYSON.

NEVER did a more lucent morning bathe San Michele with its splendors than that upon which Vian and Fra Salmani set out for La Torre. Never were two young men so sure of a delightful acquaintance. Wine and barley cakes, some salt meat and white chestnuts, loaded upon the back of Salmani, made Vian quite contented to be so far from the toothsome repasts of Hampton Court.

The route chosen carried them far from the paths and roadways which were likely to be travelled by Waldensians.

In the glow of evening, the two were approaching Fenestrelle. Twice, as they were upon the summits, did Fra Salmani point out the little village, with its cross, which was painted purple and crimson by the retreating day. It had been a day of revelation to both. Minds accustomed to work out problems for the most part alone found astonishing vigor as together, with an eager sympathy, they attempted to solve .their difficulties. The narrow defiles and almost inaccessible heights appeared to be easy of entrance or ascent, compared with the mysteries of faith and the barriers of dogma which confronted them.

"Then you are sure that the monks of Turin do not all of them share the ardor of your prior," said Vian.

"I am certain that in the whole monastery it was impossible to find one who knew this path and at the same time believed the Waldensians ought now to be put to the sword ; otherwise I should not have been chosen to conduct you. You were supposed to be favorable to burning them all in a slow fire," answered Fra Salmani.

"I was supposed to be a fiend?"

"Are there not such fiends in England?" asked the Italian monk.

"Cruelties have been practised to stifle the thought of scholars and pious souls ; but *I* have not practised them," answered Vian, who did not like to be taken for a torturer.

"The Church seems determined to burn the best she has."

"Do you think these Waldensians are good people?" inquired Wolsey's messenger.

"I cannot speak calmly," said the priest. "You have probably been informed that I am under suspicion. A manuscript has disappeared from our treasury at Turin. I am thought to love manuscripts more than the relics of the saints —"

"Pray what has that to do with the character of the Waldensians, which I want to know about?"

"In my case," answered the priest, with a blush on his cheek and a picture of Alke in his soul, "it has much to do with —"

"Well, well, I cannot understand this at all!" remarked Vian, impatiently.

Fra Salmani was also at sea. "What did you ask me?" inquired the embarrassed priest.

"What is the character — I mean, what are the habits of these people?"

"Ah! as I was saying, I knew one of them —"

"Only one of them! Then you know nothing about the subject," said Vian, with added impatience.

"I know one of them —"

"Who stole the manuscript from you?"

"No; it was not a robbery at all. She was not a thief."

"She? Ah! a woman, a woman, — by the stars, a woman; and you tell me you knew her, but that she was not a thief."

The priest was sorely tried. Everything seemed entangled. "You are quicker than I am. If you will be patient with me, I will tell you about the manuscript," said he.

"No, I want to hear about the woman who was not a thief — no, about the character of these Waldensians," said Vian, laughingly.

"Well, then, let me tell it in my way."

"Proceed."

"I was about to say that my observation was not large — "

"Confined to this woman?" asked Vian, with pitiless zeal.

"My observation is not large; but I believe the most pure and pious people I ever saw are these Waldensians whom you are come to slay."

Vian's eyes were set upon the calm face of the young priest.

"Will you hear about the manuscript now?" he said seriously.

"With your leave, Brother," answered Vian.

"I am under suspicion at the monastery. If you knew for what crime, you would think, perhaps, that I am too full of charity to Waldensians in my words."

"Where is the manuscript?" asked Vian, as he offered the young priest some wine and a barley cake.

"It will appear later in my story," said the Italian, who drank the wine and began to eat the cake with avidity.

"Do not let us lose sight of — of the woman," said the Pythagorean Vian, who had already explained his philosophical position to the priest. "Woman — that is, a noble woman — is the one fact which I cannot fit into my theories."

"This woman — this maiden, I will say in truth, was no debased man's soul reborn into this world, as your philosophy would say. She never could have been more lovely as an angel of heaven," said Salmani, offended at Pythagoreanism.

"And she did not steal the manuscript?"

The priest, being now refreshed, resolved to pay no attention to Vian's humorous queries. He saw a seriousness beneath them which he would trust; and he stood up, brushing the crumbs of cake from his garments, and said, —

"I only told you that I was under suspicion of having loved — "

"Why," cried out Vian, "that is just what you did *not* tell me at all. Oh, yes, I see now; you say you were under suspicion of having loved — the manuscript?"

"Not at all; I did love the maiden," replied the priest, hesitatingly but earnestly.

"So there was no suspicion at all on your part; and the prior was right about the fact that you did love the maiden. No wonder you are under suspicion, Fra Salmani."

" Your association with legal functionaries has made you — "

" Able to convict a lover of having stolen a manuscript," remarked the playful Vian.

" Now I will tell my story; and you will say I may overestimate the excellence of the Waldensians. Near the monastery, not many leagues from the spot where he was nearly killed years ago, lives the most intelligent of the Waldensians.   His name is Gaspar Perrin.   He was a printer in Venice; and he helped to set up the type for that very Euripides in your pouch. He lost his boy long ago; he was captured from him by the French cavalry and killed."

" The boy was killed? " asked Vian.   " Salmani, did you say the name was Perrin?   It seems to take hold of some memory within me.   I know a man by that name who desires my hurt.   But Gaspar Perrin's boy was killed? "

" He was killed; and only a daughter was left to him. I told you that this man was a printer at Venice for years. He knew all the scholars; and when he came from Ven- ice he brought many books with him.   He was over- proud of the girl, and taught her every page of his Latin and Greek books."

" Gaspar Perrin! that is the man to whom Luther wrote the letter which I saw," broke in Vian.

" The same, the same, I assure you.   He is the leader of the Waldensian mind in this region.   The prior has letters which William Farel and Ulric Zwingli of Geneva have sent to him.   They have been intercepted, and they show that he is in their secrets.   Farel and Zwingli rely on the Waldensians here to help them, if the affair should come to war."

" And the maiden and the manuscript? "

" Yes," resumed Salmani, " our law provided that the monastery should keep, if it obtained, the children of the heretics, and educate them in the Catholic faith. I was commanded to attire myself as a Waldensian youth, to watch the girl's paths, and to engage her in conversation until my fellows could seize her. When I found her learning, and saw her beauty, my heart was gone. She was — Oh, she *is* a lovely creature."

"Oh," said Vian, with kindled eye, "only a Pythagorean is safe in this wicked world. The Devil can catch a monk at any time ; but go on, go on ! Even a Pythagorean likes such a tale."

"I tried the patience of the prior, for I saw her often. I told him the time to seize her had not come. She did not think that I belonged to the monastery, for she often spoke of the wicked priests, and sang her hymns to me. As she grew older, she became more scholarly and beautiful. Once in a long while I would see her afar, and steal near, when Gaspar had gone, and she would read from Erasmus and Plato. Oh, such a celestial maiden !"

"And — " interrupted Vian, who was more excited than Fra Salmani.

"And at last I brought her a manuscript. I took it from the treasury of the monastery. It was not missed until Christmas Day. She had kept it secretly for months. It was a manuscript of Virgil."

"From the monastery of Turin ? " cried Vian. "And Erasmus ? "

"Yes," said Fra Salmani ; "she told me of Erasmus."

"This all seems stranger still," mused Vian. "I have heard Erasmus say that he was hoping to get a manuscript of Virgil from Turin. It seems a dream. And — "

"And I resolved to offer her my own soul and life ; but she said she loved only the Lord. I am sure she did not love me as I did her."

"For," added Vian, dryly, "you are sure you loved her more than you loved the Lord ? "

"No; I have been a true monk and faithful to all vows, except—"

"When you stole the manuscript and loved her."

"Alas, I wish she had loved me! She was truthful, and she did not love me."

A tear was glistening in Fra Salmani's eye, as he said, "I am sure the French knights would not kill a defence-less maiden, if they should chance to attack Gaspar's cottage."

Vian was thinking sadly of this wreck of love, while Fra Salmani did all he could to make him acquainted with the mountain passes and the safe path to the convent of the Récollets in La Torre. Vian's interest was not roused, however, until the Italian priest began to describe to him the morals of this persecuted people. As the earnest man, clad in garments which disguised the monk and identified him with these suffering mountaineers, stood out in the clear light and told the enchanted Englishman of their simple ways,—the virtue, the honor, the heroism, and righteousness of their hearts and cause,—it seemed impossible for Vian to take another step toward murdering them.

"What can I do," said he, "to make these noble people safe in the hands of his Holiness?"

"Francis I. has no nobler subject than Gaspar Perrin—"

Vian saw him stagger.

"O God!"

Fra Salmani, pierced with a single shot, fell at the feet of the English monk, writhed in pain for a brief moment, and, while Vian sought to bring the wine to his dying lips, in an agony which made him toss his body to the edge, Salmani fell into the chasm below.

"The heretic is dead! An arquebusier for heretics!" shouted a man with an ugly face, who had been posted at the defile to kill the Waldensian Barbé who was expected at that moment. As he looked down the chasm, he saw the pale face of Fra Salmani. He had murdered a monk of Turin, instead ! As the Barbé by another path wended his way toward La Torre, the most cultivated and honorable of unrequited lovers breathed his last amid the rocks and pines.

In a moment Vian saw that he could not reach the bruised body of his new-found friend. Flying from before him now was that wicked emissary of the Church, who had thought to kill an heretical Waldensian, but had killed only an heretical Catholic.

"Oh, the crime of killing him for speaking words of truth and mercy !" thought the troubled agent of the Pope, as he concealed himself between two rocks and opened his soul in simple prayer.

CHAPTER XXIV.

OLD EXPERIENCES IN NEW FORMS.

Blank misgivings of a Creature
Moving about in worlds not realized.
WORDSWORTH.

VIAN was not a man of deep religious nature. Prayer was not as easy to him as thought. The revolutions in which his life found its transformations were all approached on the intellectual side. His interest in the Reformation had been wakened by the Renaissance. He sought an unfettered mind rather than a clear conscience. But now he prayed to God, as never before.

" How reasonable is prayer like this ! " said the rationalistic monk, as he rose from his knees, and sought a place in which the night might be passed. He had no thought of going to Fenestrelle, at least at present. He would rather die in that melancholy place. In the moonlit night he rose and peered over the rock into the white face of Fra Salmani far below him, and came back to wait until dawn, with bitterest curses on his lips.

" The Devil is tempting thee, Vian ! " said his ambition and his regard for Wolsey.

If that were true, before two days of wandering amid the rocks and over the barriers had gone, Vian had in some measure vanquished the Devil, and regained his loyalty to the cause which he represented. Fortune favored him, when he resolved to be true to the cardinal, and when he reflected that he could not go back to England in shame. He found food, whenever he accepted a mission which he did not love; otherwise he was hungry and in peril.

Oh, Vian, on the night of the sixth day thou art ready even to persecute! The flesh is weak.

Through the early hours of the next day Vian hurried at a rapid pace toward some goal, — he knew not what. At last a glimmer of hope came.

From the priest whose body we left at the foot of the wall over which he had fallen into the clump of pines below, Vian had obtained such information of the country through which he was now to wander alone, as he had unduly calculated upon. For days he had been a lost man; but now he felt that at last he had come into the presence of what he recognized. As he approached Angrogna, he was at first puzzled at what he saw; then he found his mind quieted by the reflection that though he had without doubt travelled in almost an entire circuit around the spot from which he was to send back information to the French cavalry, and although he was not at all sure of the points of the compass, he was surely in sight of the Torrent of Angrogna. From one of the heights which he had just left, could be observed the mountain stream watering a charming nest of valleys, and running into the Pelice. Surely, the clump of buildings just· above was La Torre!

For a moment he stood half astonished and half assured by the presence of two strong but carelessly built forts, which were so located at the entrance of the passes to Angrogna as to be worth to their occupants a thousand troops.

"This," said he, as he nervously toiled along, — "this is what the priest called 'La Barricade.' Yonder is the broad wall of sword-like flints which, he told me, left

but one gateway for retreat. And yonder I see —
yonder ! it is that break in the mountains — the opening
for them. Through that they can easily escape to the
fastnesses."

He listened, as he looked up where crag piled itself
upon crag to create a perfect fortification for recalcitrant
Waldensians. He heard nothing but some sweet human
sounds and the bleating of herds, and his own soul
saying, "A grand race of fearless men must feed on
all this grandeur." The thought seemed so near the
borders of heresy .that he tried to suppress it, but in
vain.

He stopped an instant beneath the mingled shadows
of two trees, one of which was a twisted and ancient
chestnut whose limbs ran far toward a branching walnut
of equal strength and antiquity; he paused to listen
again, — not, as he himself fancied, for a band of Waldensians, but for the human tones which came out from
the billowing of the noisy torrent, like stars in a stormy
sky.

"It is so long since I have heard a human tone that I
could even listen to a Waldensian. Who knows but that
the soul of some ancient Sappho has transmigrated hither,
and now pays delightful penalties in these rocky fastnesses?" said the Pythagorean. "But I must not phi-
losophize now; for I am the chosen ambassador and
agent of his Holiness."

Vian straightened himself to his whole height, and tried
to grow murderous-looking, as he thought of his task, —
to plan the utter destruction of the Waldensian leaders.

He concluded to try the height above ; a safer path for
him was surely there, and he could see more of the
country. He toiled upward, thinking of La Barricade,
its strategic importance, the utter impossibility of a hundred French knights fighting successfully any kind of
heresy which might occupy it and hurl rocks from its

heights upon its invaders. He also thought of the delicious sounds which again reached his ear.

"It is no time for music. If Saint Cecilia were here, I could not stop. I am the favorite messenger of Thomas Wolsey, Cardinal; and I must see to it that heresy is extirpated. Oh, how I wish these heretics did not believe so many things which those Wycliffe letters have taught me to tolerate at Glastonbury! This thought entangles me. How quickly I would forget, if I could, that really the priest himself, Salmani, and what I have seen make me think that Louis XII. of France knew them best! He must have been heretical. Did he not say to his advisers, 'By the holy Mother of God, these heretics whom you urge me to destroy are better men than you, or myself, or any of my subjects'?"

Soon the eye of the messenger was following a strong bouquetin which leaped across a chasm before him with surprising agility. He had now reached a height from which could be seen the fortress of La Torre, whose dilapidation and romance still have their charm. The priests had told him how often blood had flowed down the sides of the knoll into the stream below. The thought came upon him that perhaps the best of this blood flowed from the veins of men who were guilty of simply asserting their right to their own thoughts.

Then the monk in him said, "That is heretical." At the next breath the Pythagorean wondered whose soul had been re-incarnated in the bouquetin, which Vian immediately guessed was a cross between a goat and a deer. What a Pythagorean problem was here! Whose soul was it? He must brush these contending thoughts from his brain, even if his heart were sick at the prospect of helping to butcher Waldensians.

Green spots surrounded with trees in richest foliage lay below him. The glistening snow was a living fire on the mountain-sides above him. Everything was sublime or lovely but his own purpose.

"These Barbetti — or *dogs*, as we would call them in Hampton Court — do not appreciate the grandeur of light and gloom in this varied landscape," said he to himself; and then, like a sweet dream, there floated to him again a song. It was like a bouquet floating upon a stream, — a cluster of mellow tones.

"No *dog* is that!" added the lover of music; and looking into the distance: "Ah! that is the college of the Barbetti yonder; that is the Satanic source of the heresies of this valley of Lucerne. There, in that cottage of Angrogna, live these foul Waldensian birds who fly out on this clear air with the heretical notions which threaten trouble for the Church." He was repeating the priest Torraneo's description, and he himself instantly qualified it by musing thus: "Perhaps that is the Oxford of this poor region without Oxford's tyranny. John Colet and Erasmus would be more welcome by its chancellor than yonder — " He looked toward England, and farther, even toward Lutterworth.

La Vachera, from whose inaccessible heights persecuted Waldensians had never been driven, rose sublimely as the lofty central point of the summits guarding the three valleys, and caught his eye, as he dreamed of Lutterworth, Wycliffe's letters, his childhood's vision.

That dear vision had strengthened itself in his mind as he told it to the enraptured priest Salmani. The very purity of the air, the limpid translucence of the streams, the unaffected genuineness of the awful heights, drove out the sounds of the bell which was tolling in the convent of Récollets, at which he must soon present himself; and then he welcomed instead the vision of his boyhood, and the softly penetrative tones of what now he knew was the voice of a woman.

That convent bell was to sound again, as the priest had told him, when the French knights were ready at the fortress of La Torre to sally forth to exterminate Waldensians. He had begun to hate its sounds.

"From San Giovanni to Valaro, if necessary, give no mercy to heretics!"

He read this order again. So also said the convent bell.

Vian tried to rid himself of the vision of his boyhood by repeating those bellicose words. The vision now perplexed him strangely; but it remained as firm as yonder Monte Viso. It was far more imperious than the solid-looking residence of the Count of La Torre, which he saw standing in the Place de la Torre, far in another direction. It had ruled the fresh daytime to the exclusion of Wolsey, Pope, and Pythagoras.

He would lie down to sleep. Night had been his salvation. The Devil came to other men when asleep; he attacked Vian's waking hours.

"And this *is* the Devil," he mused, as reaching the crag overlooking the valley he crawled upon the only path to a spot less rugged than all the region near; and there he tried to sleep himself into courage and safety.

The sun never looked down upon a more wisely clad sleeper. What he should wear that he might not be apprehended, and instead be successful in his task,— this had perplexed Hampton Court, Vian, and last of all, the guiding monk whose death at the foot of the precipice had left him now without any advice. He had taken up a gayly decorated hat, feathered, laced, and jewelled, and thrown it aside at Whitehall. As a monk he had never thought of making his appearance. He had not obeyed the Saint Paul's condemnation of 1487; and his hair, which had now grown so long as to entirely hide the tonsure, did not fit him to take a place at the convent of Récollets in La Torre, in the habit there used. Stole, chimere, rochette, cassock, alb, cope, and surplice, — even if he had been bishop of London, these would have been rejected. He had chosen to appear at Lyons as a legal functionary; but cap and coif, narrow

ruff and cape, long and ample sleeves, linen girdle and
gown, had then been cast aside. The wide sleeves and
slashed and puffed bonnet, plumed and ornamented,
which for a day on the " Field of the Cloth of Gold " he
had worn, made only a sickening memory as he tried to
catch a brief deliverance in sleep. Lutterworth — his
father came upon his memory as he lay there, clad as
his father would have been as a country gentleman. An
easy velvet cap was now his pillow; bright and ruddy
hose half covered his legs, which were constantly finding
a vigorous thorn-bush too near; his laced sturtops enclosed a pair of weary feet; his doublet was close-fitting,
made of silk and velvet, girdled about the waist with a
bright ceinture of satin and leather, and ornamented
with a few onyx stones, to which were affixed the pouch
presented to him by the queen, and a dagger which
had a jewelled haft, and was enclosed in a richly
ornamented sheath.

Sleep brought to him only a dream which concluded
in a revelation.

For a long hour in that dream did he wander over the
hills of his childhood. Lollards preached to him. His
father's name, hated at Glastonbury and Rome, became
the synonym for honor, freedom, and the ever-living
future. Priests blasphemed, raved, cursed; and the holy
meeting-places of his father's companions found in him
an orator struggling to the front in mobs of persecutors,
eloquent in his championship of the right of untrammelled thought. Wycliffe's letters were in his hand,
Wycliffe's arguments upon his tongue. The dreamer was
a fetterless proclaimer of a great Reform which lighted
up the whole sky. Amid it all, the one imperial centre
of it all, was his little mate. Again he kissed the sweet
lips, again she pushed back his flowing hair, again she
spoke to him, again he saw her unrivalled loveliness.

The dream melted away.

"There!" said the dream-ruled, yet half-awakened man, as he looked over the crag upon a graceful form whose face he could not see, "I have left childhood, hers and mine, behind! This is manhood; that yonder, — that is womanhood. Yes; but what — " and then, after a solemn pause in the solution of his mental problem, he whispered, "Is it she?"

Dream, an earlier vision, a reality, were confounding him.

As the returning consciousness of Vian began to make him realize that he had a dagger upon him, and that he was only a monk and a Pythagorean who had tried to sleep, he saw it all, — he thought he saw it all.

"The Devil seeks my soul. This is a Satanic temptation. Oh for the flogging-room of Glastonbury! Oh for the frown of Cardinal Wolsey!"

He was sure only of this, — that a form of unrivalled loveliness stood before him on the pasture below; and that he had heard, perhaps only in his dream, some sounds which seemed full of delicious wine, or tones which had once been heart-beats.

CHAPTER XXV.

VISIONS AND REALITIES.

Yet still that life awakens, brings again
  Its airy anthems, resonant and long,
Till earth and sky transfigured fill my brain
  With rhythmic sweeps of song.

BAYARD TAYLOR.

WHAT could this strange yet enchanting creature be doing? She was trying her voice, — playing with its possibilities, singing for the very joy of singing, — not as some court-born damsel in some tapestried room in Windsor Castle, but as a child of sky and mountain, flower and ice-floe, in the spacious opening in the mountain-chain, where the Architect of the universe had taxed omniscient energies to make a perfect audience-room in which that wonderful voice might utter itself.

Did the Devil choose this supreme test for the music-loving, vision-seeing monk? He had passed all other such tests triumphantly; but now he began to feel that in the vicinity of this matchless instrument on which this careless creature's breath seemed to play, so great was the contrast that they had not prepared him to meet this crisis successfully, — nay, they had somehow conspired to make this attraction resistless instead. Vian thought of the whining and mumbling which had been called music in the palace of the cardinal and at the court of the king, as these notes burst forth from that deep and yet many-toned organ; and the tired head of the young monk fairly ached to lay itself upon the breast which now filled itself with the fragrant air and breathed out roses, anemones, violets of dulcet sound.

He was, nevertheless, half disgusted with the sentimental instability which he at that moment discovered in himself. Was not this a female? He had never felt in that way toward an actual living woman. He caught his mind, as he divined with conceited wisdom, in the very act of falling in love. He lay there reproving himself, chastening his mind. It was easier to catch and chastise than to hold.

Where under heaven were some of the wise saws of Pythagoras that would annihilate such feelings as made him forget the thorn-bush which his leg had again touched vigorously? He knew perfectly well that he could have remembered them if only he could have stood upon his feet; but somehow he did not want to frighten this innocent nightingale away, for her sake. He could not rally to service any of the numerous advices of Abbot Richard Beere, who once helped him to get rid of that vision.

He remembered that Giovanni said once: "The Pythagorean view of woman is safer in the mind of a man who was never born for love than in the heart of Pythagoras himself, if he is accessible to the sentimental passion."

It was only a milestone. Vian's soul was running away rapidly; and he could only observe swiftly this and all other milestones, as he passed on.

One thing above all others had haunted Vian with possible peril, — the vision of his childhood. If only he could so fill his soul with Pythagorean philosophy and the recollection of his vows as a monk that this early and most beautiful vision might not obtrude itself, he could probably succeed in vanquishing the Devil.

"But why should I fight anything which has kept my character stainless? Only the vision of my little mate, — only this has kept me pure," thought he, truly.

Vian was glad that it must be impossible that he should meet her at this critical moment in his life, and especially was he glad to think that this strange attractive appearance should be only a poor peasant girl whom he could never really love.

This might be his soul's mate?   No !

"But I have seen many women at court and on great occasions like that of the 'Field of the Cloth of Gold,'" he was compelled to remember, "and I have then been sure that I should never see her in such circumstances as they were."

Uncomfortable as was Vian's position, — the thorn so close to his leg, and the sharp stones penetrating his knees and elbows, — he was now being made more uncomfortable by the vision of that never-forgotten child, who had grown with his own growth, who lived in his heart and life as sweet in her fragrant influence as the flower which blossomed under his dilating nostrils, — a vision which had been law and gospel to his spirit, and which now grew more and more definite as he tried to fight against it.

"That vision of yours has survived your reverence for monastic institutions ! " Giovanni had said to him, long months since. "The only thing which will destroy it is our philosophy ; and you will be a poor Pythagorean when you find your little mate."

Vian remembered that old Giovanni had made his heart burn often with the story which he told him of a black-eyed Italian girl whom he once loved, whose broken heart had long ago dissolved into dust beneath the sunny sky of Rome. In the tears which the old monk would try to hide as he told that tale of his own love, the career of a friar and the philosophy of Pythagoras were apparently washed away in the very presence of Vian.

"It seems that the Devil wants me to recollect all such things in this, my hour of trial," whispered Vian to his faltering heart.

Then the home of Thomas More — its companionship, its serene loveliness, its intellectual atmosphere — came swinging by; and he could see himself and his little mate keeping house together. "And Thomas More was teaching his mate music?" thought he.

As that fascinating reflection came and went, Vian found himself hurled, as by a tender but omnipotent energy, back to that June day at Lutterworth, when he gathered flowers for his invisible and adored one, and heard her sing. The vision was penetrated by the memory of certain fresh, sweet tones.

Abbot Richard had always said that the Devil would tempt him in this way. The very crag seemed to sink toward her. Vian was going down. He would make one desperate effort by repeating a prayer.

"Yet no prayer, no saints have kept me pure. I must not be false to that vision which has kept me; but I will be a monk and a Pythagorean."

The struggling man knew himself to be between two energies. Was one of them love? The other was certainly weakening in its grasp upon him.

Still the sweet-voiced peasant-girl — for Vian said solemnly and reproachfully a number of times: "She is only a peasant-girl. Heart of a monk and Pythagorean, be still!" — still she sang.

Notes that those rough old crags seemed to welcome, as some ragged and old mother embraces a long-lost and now luxuriantly clad child, found their way up the mountain-side, and in clearness outrivalled that pure air and yonder glistening snow far away; tones which rambled down to the brookside, and inserted their melodious currents within the ongoing liquidness of that urgent stream ; sounds which touched the earth in its beauty, dotted with the multitudes of flowers, and then swept upward as if the very gravitations had taken them to heaven for the song around the throne, — these conspired with her upward-looking face, into which he imagined the soft light dashed its kindliest waves, to make any man feel himself in the very presence-chamber of the Eternal Loveliness, with Saint Cecilia at the altar. But she was becoming more real than any saint. Now the peculiar quality of her tone enchained him. She had come nearer, and the tones were so rich, so unique, so like those of that day in June !

" Giovanni told me," said Vian to his agitation, " that Pythagorean ideas of woman would never be safe with poets and musicians, — with me." This last he said with such careless emphasis and so clearly that the maiden heard it. The lovely face turned toward him as the sounds ceased to make love with the sunbeams and the yellow dandelions which had opened their golden breasts to be stirred.

With unaffrighted air, she looked up to the crag. Vian was safely hidden from the glance of her eyes.

She had heard but a fragment, — she was not sure that she had heard anything at all. "'With me, with me?'" thought the peasant-girl, as she walked forward to pluck another blossom of monk's-hood which she had discovered, — "'with me'—

A solitary bird flew into air which was still resonant.

"That bird has his mate. I saw them feeding and heard them talk love in bird-tones only a moment since," thought she, certain now that the voice she had thought she heard was but the echo of her song, — perhaps the echo in her heart only of a longing for companionship. She did not dream that it was the echo of her yearning and her song borne back, not from the great bare walls of stone, but from the warm heart of an already ruined Pythagorean.

"With me?" she said it aloud. "With me? I could not love Salmani. Ah! I am mateless; but I will sing."

Vian, as he thought, was rapidly gathering himself together again. The Pythagorean was again able to recognize himself in his own thought, — considerably battered and much distressed, but yet a Pythagorean.

"And a monk," said he, silently but strongly, — Vian was whistling an old tune in a graveyard full of dead motives, — "a monk under a vow, under a solemn vow, — a vow that only such a base fellow as Martin Luther would break, — a vow of celibacy which saint after saint has adorned."

He felt a pang of regret at having found himself under necessity to call Martin Luther a base man, even in his thought, so much did he long for the liberty which the German monk had taken, so truly did he now sympathize with some of his doctrines.

Vian was confessing the despair of his position by bringing together his ancient monkish artillery, which he had long ago forsaken, and that of his Pythagorean philosophy which he would have been glad to think yet undestroyed by the experience of the last few minutes. He found no little difficulty in obtaining any kind of alliance, offensive, even defensive, between these irreconcilable powers. Even his Grace, Cardinal Wolsey, had never had such difficulty to make a compact between Charles V. and Henry VIII. If Vian took the view of woman, and of this woman especially, that belonged to a monk, he must so unduly twist his Pythagorean notions that they would be useless. If he persisted that Pythagorean ideas of all women were true, what was left of his monkish notions was a ruin. His soul had met that problem vainly. How could he look upon the Holy Virgin?

In the midst of the veritable panic created in his soul

by these foes, the thoughtless maiden began to sing again.
It seemed cruellest torture. Surely old Giovanni had never
made Abbot Richard suffer so with flogging. With that wild
grand freedom which a strong musical nature, surrounded,
by the mountains and thrilled with the experiences of
utterance, amid blazing flowers and glittering, distant
banks of snow, finds so fascinating and so inspiring, did
this voice pour out its treasured delight. The first tones
of this new song were volleys of flame, in which hid mis-
siles of destruction not to be resisted by a man standing
between two antagonistic philosophies, neither of which
would lend him help.

A happy idea came. It might be his salvation.

" It is the sense of freedom which she embodies," he
meditated. "It is a new experience to me ; I care nothing for her. I can care nothing for her, but I do care
for her kind of liberty. I love the untrammelled power
and richness in those melodies. I have lived amid
court saints. My mind has been hampered, my soul
has been limited. The whole of my life has been a genu-
flection at Glastonbury or a ceremony at Whitehall. I
want freedom, — the freedom of those tones. I want just
the liberty to utter the music of my nature which this
maiden has."

Vian felt firm ground beneath him again. Only one
danger remained. He had promised himself the sweet
peril of looking into her face.

" There can be no danger in that," said he, as he made
his place of concealment a little more comfortable.

As he turned over to avoid unpleasant contact with a
rough stone which was wearing its way into his Pythagorean philosophy and annoying his breast, very near to his
heart which had told the stone its secret in great agitation, he thought of his mission ; and a smile played upon
his face. It was a sickly smile of fancied power, and it
died in early life.

Where were Henry VIII., Cardinal Wolsey, the French cavalry, and his Holiness?

"And here I am," said he, "in this humiliated manner, lying stretched out on these stones on this crag, enslaved to a vision and what else the saints only know, — the trusted emissary of Thomas Wolsey. Well, he was a butcher's son. But he is now cardinal; and though he will not be Peter's successor at Rome, I am here to arrange the speedy killing of heretics. I am — "

He was just about to become a monstrous murderer of Waldensians before the French cavalry could arrive. He was unconscious of the significance of the act, in its revelation of his rising self-consciousness, when his ear caught the words which the maiden was singing, as she sat watching the goats. They were a translation of Luther's hymn: "Ein feste Burg ist unser Gott."

"The saints forefend me!" prayed the Pythagorean monk, who had long ago lost his respect for their abilities in that direction, but grasped despairingly whatever he could clutch in that bewildering moment, — "the saints forefend me! This is a Waldensian. Oh the curse of life!"

Vian did not know even then how deeply the Waldensian spirit had impressed him, how surely the life and character of the Waldenses, as he had studied them in these last few days, had wrought upon his liberty-seeking soul with an indescribable and potent charm. Neither did he realize, until that moment, that no murderous intention — for such it now seemed to be — could ever overcome the feelings which he had toward that beautiful creature.

"Oh for a quiet, untroubled, long look at her face! But, listen! she is a devout Waldensian." The words came distinctly, accompanied by richest tones.

Was it the voice of his mate?

"I would instantly slay any man who would harm that

woman," said the Pythagorean, "though she be a Waldensian? What is heresy, after all, but the assertion of the right to one's own soul in the presence of outgrown traditions? Who are the Waldensians, that I should be planning for their extermination? They are pure and thoughtful people, who have been truer to reason and the Scriptures than to priests and legends. There is more truth in that voice and in that song than in all the choirs of St. Albans and Glastonbury. There! she is taking off the wrapping about her shoulders! I would rather touch that garment than the shirt of Gildas; and I would rather stroke that sunny hair than Guinevere's at Glastonbury. Oh, how may I ever be able to behold her face!"

A kid whose mother had licked its little face while this maiden had been singing and the monk had been lying in exquisite tortures upon the crag above, had done what the Alpine goat's little ones almost never do, — it had wandered playfully away from the flock, until it stood for a moment, with eyes full of desperateness and ignorance, where it comprehended its peril, when, seeing no way of return to the piteously calling dam, frightened by the abyss which ran far down amid the rocks and pines, it leaped into a thorn-bush, where it hung for an instant, until, liberating itself, the crying little beast fell to the projecting crag below, and lay there bleeding, moaning with pain.

The instant of this confusion was a golden one to Vian. He carefully arose, escaping ear and eye of the maiden, and made his way over flowers and broken stones down toward the brook which flowed near the side of the mountain opposite the goat-pasture.

He had sworn to see that face.

Hurrying over the difficult defiles and purple soldanellas, never stopping to pluck a single star which throbbed upon the emerald beneath his feet, forgetful at last of Pythagoras and Abbot Richard, he soon found himself in the valley below, beheld by a woman's tender eye, which ruefully and sympathetically looked upward to an apparently inaccessible place on which lay the torn and agonizing kid.

Once she turned her face away. Vian grasped the long jewelled dagger which was the solitary memory of an intention which meant death to her. In an instant it flashed through the air, and as he saw it fall out of its rich sheath, he thought the word "Surrendered!" was written on its glittering edge.

As he came to her, the vision of the past and the reality of the present were one. With incredible rapidity did the scenes of childhood and youth return. He had been certain of meeting his little mate, somewhere, sometime.

Somewhere was here! sometime had come!

How fatal would be a shout of joy; yet joy was bursting his heart. As she spoke, down fell the defences of years and philosophies and fame. As everything else had gone into the grave except the vision, so now everything else was lost in her presence and tones. Her face was just like her voice. Emotions and memories stretched like tense strings over years of constantly growing fame. The past and present were united by them; blasts and zephyrs played upon them. The face filled his eyes with satisfaction; the voice had filled his ears with bells of annunciation. He was back again, with her, at Lutterworth, where the wild roses lived on the hillside, and where he had helped her to tread upon the smooth stones in the brook. He had sought for her in the castles; he now saw her in the dress of a peasant-girl, with the pasturing goats, — a Waldensian whom his plan would have murdered!

Never did loveliness beaming with sympathy for a little brute look so divine. Tears stood in Vian's eyes, as he heard this radiant being translate and re-utter the heart-break of the dam and the anguish of the kid. Kings fled from before his gaze, cardinals and popes went down forever, as what he supposed would be a woman's senseless shriek at the presence of a man turned out to be a modest but sufficiently effective welcome to any one who would appreciate her problem.

The maiden's character was entirely manifested. Tenderness was so allied with conscious power that false fears forsook her.

"Permit me to help you to recover the wounded kid," said Vian.

"Oh, the little thing is such a wanderer, — so like our souls, which wander and fall and are bruised," answered she ; her eyes deep as the sky, her beautiful face lustrous with a light from her soul.

Vian would have found in that kid a soul re-born, and in the dam some ancient mother, or perhaps a man whose deeds in the last life had been evil, if Pythagoras had not already abdicated finally in favor of this peasant-girl. The monk could think of nothing, although he did stop to repeat to his soul the sweet words of the maiden : "So like our souls, which wander and fall and are bruised."

Had the Devil come to him in the form of this angel of light?

He had banished all thoughts of the Devil. The atmosphere was celestial, not infernal. He could hardly bear to be absent from her lucent gaze, even to save the moaning kid.

"But," said he to his heart, "I must save the kid to save myself— and her ; " and he could positively feel the smile on his face, as he tried to climb.

Anybody would have known, by his awkwardness and blundering, that he was no citizen of the Alps. He essayed a pathless ascent.

There was a strange feeling in the breast of the maiden. The emphasis of life seemed suddenly removed from the kid to the rescuer. She was annoyed, then pleased, that she feared he might stumble ; and she felt her heart stop beating, and cold drops hung on her forehead when she fancied him whirling through the air down into the abyss.

"Have a care ! " she said, before she thought how it would sound in that vast gallery. To her bewilderment, the echo came tenderly back : " Have a care ! "

Vian heard both the utterance and the echo. If it had produced a commotion in her breast, there was a convulsion in the spirit of Vian. They had both forgotten the kid ; and Vian nearly forgot to hold fast, as he rounded a rough projection beneath which yawned a chasm filled with primroses and jutting rocks. He saw a picture of his mental condition, in that brief glance. He looked upward from between two perpendicular granites where he had pushed himself. He saw the blue sky peeping through ; then a great fleecy snow cloud, and then the wide solitude of heaven.

"Have a care ! " Oh, how lonely was he in that crevice ! He had never known what it was to be so sick for the sight of — a stranger, a female, a Waldensian peasant-girl.

Down below, with the kid's dam whose piteous vocabulary had hitherto been transformed into human speech by the maiden, upon a tableland, itself a greater crag, walked uneasily a lovely girl, who had forgotten the problem of the mother-goat, who instead was absorbed with her own problem, — a problem which she found made her feel uncomfortable in regions which neither manuscripts nor pastoral life had reached before. Oh, what a dreadful vacancy came into her life, when this noble being, upon whose face she had looked but a moment, passed upward through the narrow defile and out of her sight !

"I am thankful that you did not fall or get harmed in the defile!" was the outburst from the woman, when, intently looking up, she saw the fine head with eager eyes and radiant face emerge from behind the little cliff, and, like a splendid statue in dignity and upon such a matchless pedestal, Vian stood forth.

She had never seen such sinewy strength in the form of such grace and beauty.

When that compact and kingly man bent downward, and with inexpressible sympathy and carefulness put those white and delicate hands beneath the bleeding kid, and the maiden saw him lift the bruised one and put it upon his shoulder, its blood coursing down the velvet, while the heroic man steadied his body, and with a single glance of his fine eye swept earth and sky, she was sure that he was the tenderest and the truest of the sons of men. Like a soul at devotion, she stood transfixed before him. He looked down upon her, as the sun kindly withdrew behind a cloud. She was still silent. Her eyes then opened their measureless deeps. Tears were lying unborn within their mysterious loveliness. Her motionless form was eloquent; her silence was music itself.

She would speak, — if every rock echoed it. Love and religion must be one in such a soul as hers; and each must be expressive to exist. It might seem blasphemy, but it was only truth, and now it must be spoken.

"I can think of nothing," she said, "but the words about the Saviour bearing his weak and helpless on his shoulders!"

She was relieved. Vian swayed in the sunshine and peril.

"I have read it in the Vulgate," said he, knowing at once that he had made a blunder which might cost him everything in that vague, brilliant future which had just dawned. She was a Waldensian — and oh, how beautiful! He almost wished he had fallen into the chasm. "The Vulgate," — why did he say it?

"Have a care, have a care, I implore you! Trust not your steps to the gentians or lilac-colored bells beneath your feet! You will slip upon them! Oh, let the kid fall! Save yourself!"

Vian had nearly fallen over the precipice. That utterance had saved him; yet he held fast to the kid.

"'Himself he could not save,'" said Vian, as he tried to rest.

"I have read that also," answered the maiden, with firm loveliness, "but not in the Vulgate. I have read it with my father in English, — even in John Wycliffe's translation of the Gospels."

Wycliffe, — Lutterworth! The vision — this radiant woman!

"Oh, bewildering maiden, were you ever a child at Lutterworth?" This was the last gasp of Pythagoreanism.

The maiden made no immediate answer. She was evidently not offended.

"Ah, no!" she finally said. "You are of the great folk, as I believe; but I am a cottager's daughter."

"And your name?"

"Alke! I am Alke, Gaspar Perrin's child."

CHAPTER XXVI.

I have been here before,
  But when or how I cannot tell;
I know the grass beyond the door,
  'The sweet, keen smell,
The sighing sound, the lights around the shore.

You have been mine before, —
  How long ago I may not know ;
But just when at that swallow's soar
  Your neck turned so,
Some veil did fall, — I knew it all of yore.

Then, now, perchance again !
  Oh, round mine eyes your tresses shake !
Shall we not lie as we have lain
  Thus for Love's sake,
And sleep, and wake, yet never break the chain?
                                        ROSSETTI.

THAT night was full of perplexities for every one in the cottage of Gaspar Perrin. The more complete the explanation which each made, the more profound was the darkness in which these sincere persons tried to walk in friendliness. However, difficulties began soon to clear away. Vian had carried the wounded kid to the cottage door ; and Gaspar, noting his courtly air and dirty though costly costume, suspicious and a trifle worried at his presence, had, after the urgent entreaties of Alke, who always ruled him, invited the stranger to remain for the night.

The mountaineer had been expecting an attack from the Pope's legions since Christmas Day ; and every traveller had been carefully watched, oftentimes searched, as he passed to the monastery, before whose solemn steps the cohorts of their foes had so often been paraded.

Vian knew this to be the house that had been described to him as the secret meeting-place of the heretics. He had expected to enter it in a different state of mind, but he was not sad or offended. He had seen Alke.

In an hour after the arrival of Vian, the Waldensians had placed the cottage of Gaspar under the watch of ten vigilant guards ; and later in the evening, one of the peasants had produced a long dagger, on whose hilt was a jewelled cross and the arms of Leo X. He avowed to the Waldensian leaders that he found it in the valley below, where Gaspar's daughter had been tending the goats. The father was excited, and examined it with care.

" 'T is a premonition," said the Barbé. " The papal cohorts are coming. Not since Christmas Day have I seen an hour pass that I have not beheld strange preparations up yonder." He pointed to the monastery. Gaspar sighed and went into the cottage, carrying the dagger.

" Does Gaspar distrust the stranger? " asked an old man without.

" He is just now making himself sure. That man must give an account of himself. We will guard him well," answered an armed Waldensian.

Strange and often confusing emotions were swirling in curious agitation within the cottage. With a frankness and thoroughness quite characteristic of the man and his faith, Gaspar had told Vian of their creed, their hopes, their fears. Alke had been an earnest listener, betraying in this case a certain unaccustomed tolerance toward strangers which her father could not but dislike. Vian had asked her numerous questions about the curious manuscript which she had been reading on the day before on the mountain-side; and before long he had entirely captivated the stern father with his brilliant sayings, his seemingly inexhaustible scholarship, and his fine spirit. The honest, outspoken heretic had also charmed him.

Vian had felt that frankness ought to be met with frankness, and now that he had desperately fallen in love with this girl, he could and would lose everything else before he would lose her. When he touched her arm in helping her over the brook, he thought he detected a motionless response not altogether unfavorable to his hopes. He knew he loved her, at all events. Pythagoras, monasteries, Cardinal Wolsey, the French cavalry, his Holiness the Pope, — they had done nothing for his soul. They had nearly ruined his mind and conscience. He had long been a lonely sufferer, and they had granted him no relief. Here was the intellectual freedom which his father had at Lutterworth; here was the reality, — Alke, — the vision of whom had been his salvation.

What if he had been apprehended? He was willing to give up everything, and be a prisoner there with her forever. He would tell Gaspar Perrin his whole story, and he hoped to be detained at any cost. He would trust his life to the father of that maiden.

With breathless attention did Gaspar and Alke listen. Lutterworth, with the heretical Lollards; Glastonbury, with the struggle for liberty; the lights and shadows of Whitehall and Hampton Court, with the luxurious Wolsey; the constant tendency to go with the Reformers, and his love of "the new learning;" the recent expedition into those mountain fastnesses to prepare for the extermination of the Waldensians, and his constantly declining desires to persecute, — all these chapters in his autobiography came with a just and reserved eloquence, a candid vigor of expression, and an unquestioning trustfulness in the honor of those who, he was now told, were his captors, all of which entirely captivated Gaspar.

Alke wept and prayed, while Vian spoke.

So interested was the father in the story, so sure of its importance to the cause of the Protestants, that he noted not the big tears and the upward-looking eyes of love. He had so completely in his power the brains of the coming foe, that he could be gentle and even just in admiration.

"Lutterworth was the home of Master Wycliffe," said he.

Then Vian told him of the story of the Wycliffe letters which his father left to him, and how they increased the volume of heresy at Glastonbury, and the sorrows of Abbot Richard, whereupon the Waldensian went to the window; but Alke was more swift, and she placed the translation in Vian's hands. The atmosphere of the Reformation touched his forehead.

"We will protect you as never a Waldensian was protected by him whom you serve," promised Gaspar.

Soon Gaspar was talking without, with the members of the fraternity, who that night were to have held a conference at this cottage. Vian and Alke within were talking of manuscripts and looking love, instead of literature, into each other's eyes.

"Oh, divine companionship!" thought she, as Vian entranced her with quotations from the Greeks whose names were household words. "I have been so lonely in the world, except for my father. I am glad I could not love Salmani." And then she wondered what sort of feeling it was which gave her such exquisite uncomfortableness. She had never seen such a noble being as this. He appeared to be as scholarly as Erasmus and as human as Luther himself. She had never heard

such noble words as dropped from his tongue; yet
she fancied he could speak even sweeter words than
those, if he only would.

"I am anxious to know more about the treasures
hid in these monasteries," said Vian to Gaspar, as the
Waldensian entered and seated himself on a rough
stool. "How far is your prisoner from the monastery
of Turin?"

"A very wearisome journey it is to Turin," was the
answer. "Why do you ask about Turin?"

"Erasmus, whom I had the distinction to know when
a boy at Glastonbury, and later as a student, — Master
Erasmus told me of a manuscript of Virgil, which one
of your Waldensian maidens would have obtained for
him. A monk of Turin did love her. I could say
more of him, as I now believe. She refused his love,
and —"

Alke was crimson with blushes, and for the moment
Gaspar was tongue-tied.

"Oh, it is very strange! And you have told us truth
about yourself?" cried he, grasping the hand of Vian.
"Erasmus of Rotterdam —"

"Do you know him?" interrupted Vian, excitedly.
"Did you ever see the great Erasmus?"

"Get the Greek coins," shouted Gaspar to Alke; and
he added, as she brought the dull pieces, "Here they
are. Erasmus gave them to the child when she was
too young to know about them. He stopped with us,
not far from Turin, having lost his way in the snows. It
was a long time ago. We did talk together about the
Virgil manuscript at Turin. Lately, Alke promised Ani-
mo, the master's friend, that she would get the manuscript from Salmani —"

"Salmani? Is this Gaspar Perrin the printer?"

"The same," was the reply.

"The printer, with Aldus, of the Demosthenes?"

"Yes, I am he; and now I know you. For we have heard of you through letters from Erasmus himself. You are Vian,—Vian of Glastonbury! Alke, we have heard of the young Vian, the scholar!"

"The same," said Vian, with a good deal of joy at feeling so welcome. "And this, then, is the daughter of the printer, as Erasmus has called her,—the one who is to copy the Virgil manuscript. Oh, how strange!"

Gaspar had forgotten the guards without, until he overheard them talking at the door. They had been roused by the excited speech within, had heard the word "Erasmus" spoken clearly, and thinking a discussion had arisen about the Reformers, supposed they were needed by the cottager.

"Everything is right, good friends!" said Gaspar to them, as he opened and quickly shut the door.

On second thought, he deemed it best to give his friends without a little more information as to his guest.

Soon, therefore, Vian and Alke were alone again by a dim light, in which their glances could find each other's eyes, gazing meanwhile upon the freshly made and beautiful copy of the Virgil manuscript, which the Waldensian maiden had finished. Nothing could have added to the enthusiasm of Vian's love now, save this discovery that Alke was a scholar of no mean acquirements. The song of the Roman poet was as familiar to her as one of the mountain paths, and the quotations, which multiplied as the moments flew, were pronounced with charming accuracy by Alke's sweet lips. Hybla's honey lingered there, and the blue Ægean rippled in her smile. He thought how truly Erasmus had spoken of the beauty of an intelligent woman, one day when the scholar sought to destroy his Pythagoreanism.

"And you painted the commandment up there?" asked Vian, as he read above the homely door which led into an apartment that Alke called her study, the words which Aldus himself had placed above the door of his own study in Venice, —

> "Quisquis Es Rogat Te Aldus Etiam Atque Etiam,
> Ut Siquid Est Quod A Se Velis, Perpancis Agas,
> Deinde Actutum Abeas: Nisi, Tamquam Hercules,
> Defesso Atlante, Veneris Suppositurus Humeros.
> Semper Enim Erit Quod Et Tu Agas,
> Et Quotquot
> Huc Attulerint Pedes."

"I painted them," replied she. "You are the first who could read them, save my father and our Barbé. Those who can read are not expected to obey."

"Ah," said the proud Gaspar, who had just re-entered in a happy mood, "now that you have seen the copy of the Virgil manuscript, which Erasmus will have if he does not abuse Martin Luther, you must see the illuminations."

Vian thought Alke's face was sufficiently radiant; and often the color was very rich, especially if, in looking at the manuscript, he unwittingly touched her hand. Vian would have preferred to look only upon that face, but he was willing to inspect the illuminations.

"By daylight," said Alke; and then she felt a pang, because she had said something which for hours would part them. She tried to save herself from the pain of his absence, even for rest; but it was too late.

The cots were prepared. Gaspar's guards were assured that there could be no danger. Within a brief time the Waldensian was apparently in deep sleep. Vian's cot was near the window; he was not trying to sleep. Alke was wide awake thinking, until she fell into a dream of love.

CHAPTER XXVII.

AMI AND VIAN.

" The pathway of my duty lies in sunlight ;
And I would tread it with as firm a step,
Though it should terminate in cold oblivion,
As if Elysian pleasures at its close
Gleamed palpable to sight as things of earth."

SLEEP avoided Vian's eyes. He was soon outside, peering into the gloom which was now touched with promises of morning light. The night would have been a balm to any soul seeking only repose ; it was a vast horrible silence to one who looked outside of himself for a solution for problems so new, so unexpected. The love-lament of the ring-dove had died away ; the brown owl was voiceless, as he solemnly sat blinking at the moon-lit valley which he surveyed from his hole in the overhanging crag. Nothing was so noisy as Vian's heart, and it was far from being musical.

Was it a nightingale which disturbed yonder luxuriant mass of green, which looked so like fairy frostwork under the magic of the moonbeams?

"Nothing !" said Vian ; " it was nothing !" But his heart almost stopped.

Emerging now from behind a shadowy mist which made the sky away there over the cliffs look like a be-spangled bridal veil, the moon lit up the frowning bas-tions of rock with startling clearness. In his terror, Vian

could but stand astonished in the witchery of its brilliance.
The brown owl flew past him.

Crash ! Bounding down from the height immediately
above him, tumbling on with impetuous rapidity, borne
on from spot to spot by a momentum gained from such
a long, swift, unimpeded descent, came a huge rock, — a
fragment from the cliff above. With it came a shriek,
then a moan; and then the silence of death. Before
the report of the rupture which had released that jagged
edge from the height of the precipice, Vian 'thought he
saw a human figure there. Then as it broke off and fell,
the armor of a French knight glittered into the valley
below. An awakened eagle flew upward on wings which
seemed the pinions of death.

The French invaders had surely come. There now
stood or ran from spot to spot on the summit distinctly
visible, at least a score of full-clad men. With them soon
were priests from the monastery, each of whom was
making much gesticulation ; one of whom crawled to the
perilous edge from which the rock had been broken
away, and gazed after the unfortunate.

" I must call them at once, — Gaspar Perrin and Alke.
We are doomed to die by those swords. I shall die with
the Waldensians, — gladly let me die. I shall perish as a
Waldensian ! "

Vian did not need to waken those who had slept uneasily that night. Behind the trembling servant of Wolsey stood the hardy mountaineer, steadily gazing into the
pale purple mist which, like a passionless dream of death,
had floated up the valley as morning smote the crags.
The mist was disappearing like a mysterious memory.
In the eye of the intrepid man were a challenge and
the fiery prophecy of triumph, which made Vian pity
him.

Instantly another pair of eyes looked into Vian's. In
them were burning affectionateness which had not slept,

could not sleep, and an appealing wistfulness which made Vian wish he were clad with omnipotence, that he might protect the quivering Alke. In the tangled wilderness of his thoughts his purpose was making its laborious way. He was sure of only one thing.

"The glorious creature does love me!"

How did he reach that conclusion?

He felt Alke's touch of pitiful trustfulness upon the sleeve of his doubtlet, still soiled as it was with the blood of the dying kid. And in a moment he held her hand, which clung to his with such a desperate tenderness that he was transformed from feeling himself a quailing intruder in that home into being its hero. His heart beat with courageous regularity, and the pallor became a flush in his face as he said, —

"My little mate! many times before you had seen me, or I had beheld your face as I do now, had you made me heroic. In the vision — "

"The vision? What vision?" She released her grasp. "I have never seen you before. I do not believe in visions."

"Alas! hold me fast, Alke! It was a poor sinner's vision, — yes, a dream. I will tell you all here or in heaven!"

Vian and Alke looked upward, and saw the same sky, — a revelation of the infinite time and space which every true human love seeks, and never in vain. The dashing waterfall seemed but a murmur of love; the mellow light without a glare was its radiance; the echoes upon the sweet still air were its music; the dawn which was then making the peaks translucent was love's evangel.

"We are near unto God," whispered the Waldensian maiden.

"And unto each other," added Vian, who felt at once that the remark he had made lacked a little in piety.

Alke ran to the spot where her father stood filling his

great lungs with the morning, and then making the
morning and the mountains echo with his long, searching
clarion-call.   Every nook and torrent answered with a
sympathetic cry.   The scream of the eagle, bathing his
wings in the liquid dawn; the bleating of the wounded
goats which had just escaped death in the path of the
dislodged rock as it tumbled into the valley; and now
the shouts of the mountaineers, who had waited in armed
silence for the summons, added a weird significance to
each prolonged tone.

"Give the Virgil manuscript to the young man, —
to Vian!" cried out Gaspar to Alke, unforgetful of the
Renaissance amid the birth-throes of the Reformation.

Alke saw Vian hide the parchment within his breast;
and handing him the four coins which Erasmus had left
with her babyhood, years before in their old home, she
said with eager hope in every syllable, —

"It may be that they will spare you.   Here are Greece
and Rome, — the coins and the manuscript!"

"I care not to escape, except with something dearer
to me than all these.   Oh, were *you* not in my vision at
Lutterworth?   I know you were."

Action, not vision now, youth!   But all greatest action
is the doing of a vision.   "The French are here!"

"Courage, my children!   The French are come.
Every one is a knight!"

Gaspar had said nearly all that was in his heart, as the
mountaineers gathered about the cottage, and every one
spoke his name.

"Here are the letters," said Gaston Fuerdent; and he
gave into the hand of Gaspar a packet of letters from
Martin Luther, Ulric Zwingli, and Philip Melancthon.
"I have burned the letters of Farel."

"The Barbé commanded it; it is wicked to disclose
his plans," added Gerard Pastre.

All were agreed that Farel at Geneva had been overzealous, and had made too full a description of the plans of the Swiss Reformers.

"All are consumed," said a youth, — the son of Fuerdent, — who gazed with modest interest into Vian's eyes.

"An intruder I am aware I am," said Vian. "Perhaps I am suspected — "

"Be silent!" said Gaspar, before Vian could complete his remark.

"Be silent!" they all said; and Louis Savan relieved his mind by interjecting, —

"We would have been unprepared for the wretches for a week if you had not come. Now the victory is ours!"

He called the mountaineers to witness.

"We bless you!" they all cried out, as Alke stole up into quite significant nearness, and looked as if she would have said, —

"Vian, you are in the best place in the world for you — for me."

Every man inspected his arms. Old Henry Arnon grasped the jewelled hilt of a dagger, — the dagger which Vian had once thrown away. The Englishman looked at it with interest, and thought of the circumstances in which he parted with it. Wolsey would never see it again.

"Where is Wolsey, Lord Cardinal? Where is his Holiness? Where am I?" thought the young man.

There was a stiff old manuscript near his heart; but something else was much more near. Alke, pale with fear, stood alone by his side; while the rough men of the mountains looked upon Vian half as their deliverer, half as their prisoner. The powerful soul of the maiden was summoning every energy to say a word which lay upon her heart.

"Would you willingly die believing in the grace of God?" She had thus spoken it at last; and every sense

of danger fled from her soul.　She had been so true to
God and her own conscience, that she easily ascended
heights impossible before.

Vian confessed the omnipotence of the inquiry.　Love
and religion stood behind Alke's appeal.

" We are standing only for a moment together here, and
the next may see one or both of us before the great white
throne."

The words roused the drops of blood which a Wycliffite
father had put into Vian's veins, — so much did these
words remind him of Lutterworth, so much did they seem
to be a fragrant distillation from the spirituality which
blossomed in the Wycliffe letters.　Oh, so much more
clearly was Alke the real mate of those childhood dreams,
the soul of his life, that he half sobbed, and said hurriedly
as he saw the stir outside, —

" I trust myself to your Saviour's grace, but I never
was so anxious to live as I am now.　The vision ! — "

" Ah, Vian !　He must be *your* Saviour.　I cannot be
your priest."

" I am done with priests," said Vian, in a broken
voice.

" But you are not done with your Saviour? "　The
eyes of wistful fearlessness were full of tears.

" No, — oh, my mate, soul of mine ! — no ; I am just
beginning with Christ.　But I never wanted to live as I
do now."

" Because you are now prepared to die ? "

" I am prepared to live or to die — for you."

A gleam of polished steel flashed from the moss-
covered ledge not far from the cottage.

" Arm ! arm ! arm ! " cried Gaston Fuerdent.

" Conceal yourselves within ! " whispered Gerard Pastre, whose eyes lingered with Alke and Vian, as he turned
away.

" No," said Vian, — " no ; I must fight.　I *must*, — I

have imperilled you. I ought — but I could not have saved you."

The man's soul, conscious of having done all it could, was full of contrary emotions and opposing thoughts. But he could not be mistaken. The shout of the French knights pierced the silence of the cottage, coming over the clamor of the mountaineers.

Alke looked upon him with fond, yearning eyes. Vian dared to feel his heart crying for utterance. "I will tell her that I love her; I will claim her now as my own," thought he. "I may never again have the privilege."

"Hide the young man, Alke, child of my soul! Hide him!" commanded Gaspar, through the half-opened door.

"I shall not be protected at such cost, — the life of my little mate, so precious! I will die concealing you, Alke!" and he seized a sword provided for a critical moment.

"Oh, I must make you safe! Yonder is safety. Hide at once! I will cover you, — with my own body if need be," was the swift, eager response.

A thrill of pain, then a thrill of joy shot through the heart of what was once a monk and a Pythagorean, now so transformed. Silently Alke looked upon him with commanding love. Suddenly the stern manhood yielded a little.

"Cover me with your dead body? Oh, God! Oh, Alke!" said he.

"Yes, willingly, gladly!" answered she.

The fiery air was a thin but all-encompassing flame. At once a burning, half-frenzied kiss bound them to-gether for an instant, distilling into each heart the joy of a whole eternity.

"I shall fight without concealment," shouted the intoxicated lover.

"You shall be covered by my love," protested the

Waldensian maiden, as she wrapped the velveted man in
a coarse garment, dearer to him than the robe of a
queen.

Outside, the excitement was now intense. The invaders had gained the path and were hurrying near.

" I 'll warm it in the heart of a heretic," said a French
knight, as he touched the hilt of his sword.

" Did you ever smell the fumes of a roasted Waldensian ? " asked an ugly-faced priest, lumbering along after
the knightly leader, who appeared moody and was silent.

Vague memories were crowding into this French
knight's brain ; and he said to his heart : " Oh, faithless
coward ! Peter was the ' rock-man.' I am here for
Peter's holy successor. Harden, soft spirit within me !
Spare not a heretic ! Kill all, and then burn ! Long
live his Holiness Pope Clement VII. ! " shouted the
chosen friend of Francis I.

Around the edge of the mountain, where it met the
noisy stream, and where the shadow fell upon the Waldensians, — every man upon his knees, — Gaspar Perrin
was bearing their cause to the throne of a just God.

The French soldiery advanced in a solid company, a
priest at the side of the leader mumbling snatches of
Latin, as he held before them a gilt cross. The bells of
the convent were ringing. Gerard Pastre gave a signal
to a Waldensian. Down from the height above, like a
bolt from Israel's Jehovah, came a large rock, tumbling,
leaping, jagged with desolating energy. It tore its way
through the French soldiery with merciless force.

" Heaven is against us ! " shouted one of the dismayed
knights. The priest forgot his scraps of Latin, and with
white face aimlessly waved the gilt cross. It was all in
vain ; a nameless horror had broken upon them.

" Mother of God ! " groaned a dying knight.

" Holy saints and martyrs, pray for us ! " shrieked
another, over whose brilliant armor the mountaineers

triumphantly came, every eye blazing with a fierce joy.

Still the convent bell was ringing. The French were disorganized, panic-stricken ; all in retreat, save the fragment of their band, which had now entered the cottage and were laying it waste.

In the wainscoted room two men were in mortal combat. A pale but heroic woman lay on the floor. She was stunned, prostrate by a blow from the hand of the knight. Before that knight stood a hated man, skilfully handling a sword, as he had learned to do from Fra Giovanni at Glastonbury, and later on the " Field of the Cloth of Gold." But it was now for life or death.

" Villain ! " cried out the knight, as his sword seemed sure of Vian's heart.

" Wretch ! " shouted Vian, as he twisted the gleaming steel.

" Apostate monk ! I 'll kill you with your shameless love in sight ! " exclaimed the French knight, as he leaped at Vian, gasping, " Astrée ! Astrée ! " while his eye was aflame.

Backward and farther backward was Vian forced, into the very corner where Alke lay. Nearer and yet nearer to his heart came the touches of the fine sword which once Bayard had wielded. The knight, however, was growing weak, and the other knew it.

" I must not kill you, rather let me die," cried out the monk, as at length the sword of the knight fell from the hand of the wounded man, who muttered his overmastering rage.

There was a movement under the shadow. Alke had regained consciousness ; and rising, she flung herself upon the issue of the conflict with an aimless courage which looked piteously unto Vian. The bleeding knight was roused at the thought of the apostate monk and the woman — together here !

Overmastered by Vian, and yet spared !

" Spare not a heretic ! " rang again in his ears.

He could kill the woman, and that would kill the man, — the man who had been a hateful demon to him for all these years !   Even knighthood had lost its honor in the passion of whose tormenting fury this knight was but a charred ruin.

In an instant the French knight compressed all his hate in a dagger-point which glared toward Alke's bosom. In the same instant Vian's bosom felt its safety, as the desperate energy of the knight broke the dagger's point in the tough parchment of the Virgil manuscript lying next Vian's heart, unimpenetrable.

What was it that came like a death-damp to the knight's heart and hung like a horrible charm above her, as he struck at that woman?

As, in another dreadful instant, the knight thought of it, a blow, — Vian could not master himself now, — a swift, awful blow fell upon him, and he lay breathless on the floor of Gaspar Perrin's cottage, entirely unconscious, even when his dismayed followers seized his antagonist Vian, tore him from Alke's breaking heart, and placing him in chains, hurried away with their prisoner from the scene of such a disastrous defeat.

CHAPTER XXVIII.

There are flashes struck from midnights,
There are fire-flames noondays kindle,
Whereby piled-up honors perish,
Whereby swollen ambitions dwindle,
Which just this or that poor impulse,
Which for once had play unstifled,
Seems the sole work of a lifetime
That away the rest have trifled.

ROBERT BROWNING.

A SOFT film of lazy sunshine hung over the sides of Monte Vandalin. Even the little spurs toward Lucerne assumed an easy indifference in the delicious dreaminess of the air. Autumn was holding her last beautiful festival; and the winds of October paused at the threshold, that they might not disturb the fragrant calm. The hue of burnished gold was losing itself here and there in the red leaves which lingered with the sobbing breezes over sacred ground.

"Those red leaves are blood-drops. Heaven itself will not permit us to lose the memory!" said Alke, as she lifted the wounded and swollen foot of her father, and placed it upon a soft bit of lambskin, which she had fastened to the oaken stool upon which he was now resting it.

"No," answered Gaspar. "But we must remember something beside the sorrow, the blood, the dead. We are Christians; and, Alke — That noise?"

"It is only the soldier.   He has not groaned as he did yesterday.   Poor fellow! he looked into my face this morning when I gave him the cordial.   He sighed and smiled so piteously, — I wondered if he knew how nearly he came to striking that dagger into me; but Vian — Yes; the soldier, — he seems grateful.   He must be some great personage at the court of Francis.   Such armor — "

· "As I was saying," Gaspar pursued, "we are Christians. I do not mean by saying that, that we ought to be thinking of our cause and its righteous victory.   But, Alke — That muttering sound! "

"The poor man is saying something; I will go to him," she said; and she dropped the task she was trying to accomplish without, under the little festooned arbor, and hurried within to the French knight, who was restless with suffering.

"I do not mean that we ought to be quoting to ourselves warlike words from the Psalms to make us feel like Christians now."   Gaspar was talking to his own conscience, as he looked out into the scarlet vines, beneath which his eye discovered a shining helmet, another relic of that victory.   "But I do think Alke and I will feel more like Christians if we think of the Gospels and try — oh, how hard that poor girl is trying! — try to love our enemies."

Another long, plaintive groan came from the room in which the wounded soldier lay.   In a few moments, however, Alke came under the arbor and resumed her task.

"He is sleeping now," she said softly, "but he mutters such strange words."

Alke burst into tears.   Gaspar, with twinges of pain, moved his foot in his effort to get hold of her hand; reaching which, he pulled her close to him.   The start of agony communicated itself to the sympathetic Alke.   At once she was stroking the wounded foot with gentleness and love, while the tears fell upon the lambskin and moistened the dry blood-stains.

"Oh, it is hard to be a Christian!" she sobbed.

"Harder to be a burden-bearing or a forgiving Christian than to be a fighting one, my child!" added Gaspar, as he sought relief for himself and for her in moralizing just a little.

"Vian!"

They both heard the word "Vian."

Each looked anxiously into the face of the other, and saw only wonder struggling with forgiveness. Alke threw her womanly head upon Gaspar's breast, and cried, —

"I cannot go into that room, — I cannot! I have gone as far in being a Christian — "

"Be a Christian!" commanded the Waldensian, without a tone of cant in his words.

Alke looked up, submissive and sublime in her spiritual loveliness. "I will," said she. "It was only the slipping of my feet on the rocks. I did not fall quite?"

"No; you did not fall, my child. But this is a slippery and hard road for you."

"My father!" she whispered; and then she said in a womanly tone: "My father, it is hard here and now to be a Christian. That soldier yonder came leading a murderous band of cruel knights and priests upon our home. He loaned his beauty and his strength to the vicious monks, who harass our lives and spit upon the Gospel. His dagger — I will keep it for a memory — glittered at my heart. I cannot forget that cry, 'Spare not a heretic!' when he threw me to the floor, and — "

Alke stopped.

"Vian!"

Gaspar and Alke both heard it. The soldier, delirious with agony, groaned as he spoke that word, "Vian."

"How did a French knight know Vian, an Englishman? Wherever did he learn that name?" Gaspar's interest was quickening. "Alke, did they fight as do old foes?"

Alke had never thought of this remarkable circumstance, so much more remarkable had been her experiences. A dreadful uncertainty plied with the fearless wonder within her heart. Life had come to be an awful mystery, which in one golden day had dropped into another mystery more awful still.

"I know not. Ah! I remember too," she said, her eyes speaking with more of bewilderment than of discovery, — "I remember now, that when the conflict outside was at its height, and this young knight alone rushed upon Vian — " Alke could say no more. That frightful memory of her loved Vian, the horribly fierce eyes of the maddened knight, the desperate encounter, the heroism of Vian in saving her, the last look of Vian, as they led him away chained, — all came over her again like a ghastly reality. Gaspar pitied her; and while his breast was a turmoil of hate and love, he was half indignant when from the cottage the sound came again: "Vian!"

"That name again upon those cruel lips! Oh, it is too much!" exclaimed Alke.

She remembered that at the beginning of their contest in the cottage, indeed on the instant when the knight fixed his eyes upon Vian, he had hissed upon him as if her lover were another venomous reptile. As they confronted each other, the words "Apostate monk!" burned in the air. Some slumbering volcano of rage and hate seemed ready to burst out from the soul of the knight and belch its fury upon Vian.

To know this alone, however, was to know insufficiently; for not even the combatants knew the depth of those experiences of their own characters in that hour when swirling passions leaped and tossed themselves, obedient to the gathered impulse of years. Into the glare of those eyes which had looked upon Alke's lover in the home of his beloved, were come the passions which had been growing more furious since the days of the "Field of the Cloth of Gold;" the fiery jealousy which surrounded Astrée, the agonizing desperation which had risen out of a stormy soul in its search for a faith; the contempt which a knight of such temper and history felt for a recreant servant of a philosophy, a king, and a pope; and above all, the uncontrollable hate which was born at once when that trusted emissary was seen to have sunk the banners of France, England, and Rome within his love. All these were behind that last cry: "Spare not a heretic!" But now Alke knew it not, as again she heard him groan, "Vian! Vian! I say!"

Gaspar and she held their souls in patient silence. They had made the precept "Love your enemies" a fact of truest significance to the knight. It had not come without a struggle. An hour after that conflict Alke had thought herself a widowed soul. The rage and anguish which the faces of his marauding band exhibited when they thought their leader dead on the cottage floor, Alke was sure had been meted out to Vian, their prisoner. Great as was her affection for such a man, which years had grown and a single day had discovered, it was omnipotent after that scene. It wove ten thousand fancies, and bedewed with generous tears the memory of an idol which was now an ideal. So terrible was the grief, so benumbing the agony of that sudden separation, that at first Alke was ready to fly into the extremest passion of altruistic devotion. She had resolved to nurse the foe. The neighbors had their dead and dying to look out for. Alke had her hospital too, with its two patients, — her father, and the young knight whom Vian had perhaps fatally struck. For two days he had made no manifestation of returning consciousness. Her own suffering of heart was so keen that the presence of the merciless but silent foe of her own lover proved a means of restoring a sort of equilibrium. Gaspar had not yet looked into his face, for he was trying to be a Christian at Alke's expense. Cordials, gruels, and bandages had been applied to the soldier. The only gratitude expressed came as a muttered word which Alke could not understand, and that single smile which was so piteous as to afflict her heart. She resolved to be worthy of him whom she now believed to be dead ; and how could she more genuinely exemplify her faith in Christ than by being a Christian? She went on repeating the words, "Love your enemies," until this change came.

As a change had now come to the knight, a change had also been attested in Alke. As we have found her on this October day, the soldier is able to pronounce at least one word which she may understand, — Vian, — and Alke knows how hard it is to be a Christian.

Other words were muttered at nightfall, — "Astrée," "His Holiness," "Wretch ! "

That night Gaspar lay awake and listened for hours to such words as these. Indeed, he could not sleep, having heard the stricken man pronounce the first words. The exhausted Alke lay upon the couch next the window.

Soon the Waldensian found strangely tender feelings dominating his mind as he listened to the soldier's woful exclamations. They carried the mind of Gaspar away from these scenes. He was back again in Venice courting with the daughter of Count Aldani Neforzo as together they worked in their poverty. What a strange thing that that knight who would have murdered Gaspar's daughter should bring to him at this hour these dear recollections !

Still the words continued to pour forth from the suffering man ; still did Gaspar Perrin feel the old memories about his heart.

"No one," said the husband Gaspar Perrin, widowed so long ago, — "no one but she ever pronounced the words 'His Holiness,' with that lisping tone, — no one but Alke's mother." He felt again the grief of that far-away day, when he refused to pay for prayers for the dead.

"Vian !" sharply rang again the voice.

"It is the voice of Count Aldani Neforzo come to earth again," thought Gaspar, as he sat up and looked over to the cot by the door.

All became silent again. The pale reflections of the moonlight were travelling across the wainscoting; and as the disquieted Gaspar sat upright in bed, forgetful of his aching foot, he calculated that very soon the light of the moon would be falling into the face of the wounded knight, — the face which Alke had said was very beautiful.

Why cared Gaspar to steal a single look? He could not tell; he only knew that since he had heard that voice, it was impossible for him to sleep or content his wakefulness without the promise of a look upon that face. He had always studied faces, since Ami had been taken from him, and had unaccountable feelings with regard to this one.

At length the moment came when the light silvery glow rested upon the face. There was a careful movement in the bed by the cupboard ; and soon Gaspar was moving slowly, dragging his enswathed and bandaged foot after him, as he felt his way between chairs and stools toward the slumberer. Quite a picture it would have been for the crickets which chirped without the door, as the time-worn face of Gaspar came within the glow, and the tireless eyes looked upon the moonlit face of the knight. Gaspar shook from head to heel as he gazed ; but the night air was cold, as he thought.

Was it in the nostril, which, as the knight breathed heavily, made Gaspar feel that Count Aldani Neforzo, the grandfather of Alke, was again before him ? That forehead from which fell a wealth of light hair, a cloud of gold in the moonlight, — Alke's hair was so like it; and the lips, — they were such lips as Gaspar the lover had kissed in Venice, when he embraced the daughter of Neforzo. The soldier's hand was lying outside the coarse coverlet, — a long, slender hand, and the nails of the fingers, oh, he must not fancy it, — but they were like the mother's, the wife's, — so like them! A ring upon one finger, — a costly ring, with the papal arms engraved upon the emerald, caught the weird splendor; and the hand, which now moved with a twitch of pain, was so like his own, except the nails, — "so like mine," he said; "only mine are old and tired."

Gaspar was enthralled. "Oh, if this soldier would only open his eyes! Delirious as he is, he would not know me, even if— But I might—I might see their color," mused the serious man. "If Ami is living — yes, he would be about the age of this poor wounded fellow! I hunted in vain for his burial-place. This suspense, — it is intolerable. But I cannot sleep now, I have seen the soldier's face!"

Gaspar did not sleep. But when morning came and Alke saw that there were blood-drops on the floor, the Waldensian bade silence, for he had a plan.

"I will explain the presence of those drops of blood," he said. "Bring me word, Alke, at the moment when you find out the color of those eyes."

CHAPTER XXIX.

A GOLDEN DAY.

Facesti come quei che di notte,
Che porta il lume dietro, e se non giova
Ma dopo se fa le persone dotte.

DANTE.

"HE is awake now," said the careworn Alke, as next day she came close to Gaspar, who sat again under the arbor writing a letter to his friend the Reformer Philip Melancthon, in which he was relating the providences of Heaven, and telling him all about Vian, "the apostate monk," and this suffering victim of Vian's daring.

"Did you mark the color of those eyes?" inquired Gaspar, anxiously.

"I cannot tell it," was the reply.

"What! you? Alke, a painter ought to know blue from green, and black from brown," said Gaspar, a smile dying in anxious wonder on his face.

Alke had never seen the sea. She had read Homer and Virgil, and had listened to her father's descriptions of Venice; and she asked him, "Of what color is the sea?"

"Why," he began assuredly, — "why, yes; the sea — why, the sea is — " That was the color of the soldier's eyes. He could see that indescribable color in the eyes of Alke, as she looked archly upon her father's perplexity.

They had within them the oceanic green which is so soon blue, and the abysmal blue which grows restless with suggestions of profoundest darkness, — darkness which is altogether warm and beautiful. She did not try to describe them, for she saw her father understood her meaning. The sea, — he seemed at once to be looking out upon its tireless change and fathoming its liquid depths. Besides, there were Alke's eyes fixed upon him, — like the sea in myriad-minded revelation; and all that he desired to know he had found out. The knight's eyes were like Alke's.

"I suspected it — " Gaspar's manner betokened the formation of a still more complex plan. And then the hands which years ago held the lost child and had since worked so untiringly for Alke began to count each other's fingers, betraying to Alke the fact that her father, whose face was aglow with something more radiant than the autumnal sunshine, was enumerating years and probing another sensitive mystery.

In a few days the French soldier had become sufficiently strong to move about the room. He had not, however, taken a single step without the consciousness that the eye of this cottager was upon him. It annoyed his proud spirit.

"Of course," said he to his offended pride, "this espionage is most natural; for while I am a beneficiary I am also a prisoner. I — I have never been a prisoner before. My king has; but not I."

The kindness with which that womanly hand had dressed his wound scarcely permitted the knight to use such a word as "prisoner." He could hardly believe that she and the man, who was evidently her father, could desire to make him feel his imprisonment in this cottage which had been a hospital to him.

"Oh," whispered he at night, when Alke had almost broken his heart by her tenderness and care, "I wish I knew the name of these people ! Why do they call each other 'father' and 'daughter' in my hearing? What is it about that creature which makes my heart love her? Yet I do not love her as I love Astrée ! Would to the Mother of God, I had never thought of killing her ! " and then, with tears which Alke thought were tears of homesickness, he would sob himself to sleep.

When morning came there stood the fair child of these mountains close by his cot ; and once it seized him, — the thought that if his own little sister had lived, she might have been as sweet and beautiful ! Some day he meant to ask the father of this girl how far it was to Turin. He had a vague memory that once his own home was near Turin.

"But things with me are all so different now," mused he ; "and here am I, a friend of Francis I., in the home of a Waldensian whose daughter I tried to pierce with my dagger ! "

These thoughts made the hours horrible, — more horrible as they suggested the recollection of Vian. Oh, how the knight now began to despise his own jealous hate !

"I cannot fathom the silent, searching looks of her father," whispered the soldier, as the cottager once turned his gaze from the knight with a suddenness which bespoke a startled interest. "He has eyed me with the care of an officer or a student of curios ; " and then the knight smiled, as he saw the lovely woman piling together the pieces of his armor, illustrating at every movement her ignorance and her kindliness of heart. "Poor thing ! " thought he, "she has never girded a knight as Astrée has done."

Gaspar Perrin had now endured this silence as long as was possible. His calculations were surely correct.

Alke had not been let into his secret, and now there was no time. A single movement of the knight's head so matched a certain habitual movement of Alke's head, as she stood by the graceful soldier, that old Count Aldani Neforzo seemed to rise up between them to assure Gaspar.

"Sir," said Gaspar, "you are used to better fare than ours, I suppose."

"There is no fitter fare than starvation for a foe such as I have been," replied the other, with gallantry.

"Are you our foe?" inquired the cottager, who searched the face with tireless eyes.

The knight hung his head. "I could make a gift of my life, if it were mine, to take from you the memory of a knight striking at your child, — a woman. But I was consumed —" He was about to say something of Vian; but he was knightlier since his jealousy had fallen into the pit which it had digged and found its own abasement there.

"You are a knight, sir."

"Truly spoken, as I hope. I have longed for the true knighthood;" and the soldier thought of Nouvisset.

"Have you seen it in this cottage?"

"Ah, good friend! you perplex me. If yonder woman were but a man —"

"She would be of the chosen chivalry," flashed Gaspar, instantly.

The knight was silent, until the cottager asked, "Is there any chivalry save that which belongs to true Christianity?"

"None, none!" answered the soldier. The eyes, so like Alke's, were as tearful as hers.

Alke came nearer; and there swiftly passed over the soul of the knight a feeling which melted down all the iron barriers, and he dared to say, "If I were a Pythagorean, as was once the man who smote me here," —

he touched his wound, — "I should aver that I had been blessed in having known your child in some other life."

The supreme moment had come, — Gaspar knew it. Nothing was needed to confirm his suspicion that these two were brother and sister.

"I think, Knight, that the other life was the morning of this."

"Perhaps," said the mystified soldier, who then imagined that Vian had actually taught these folk Pythagoreanism.

"Sir," said Gaspar, drawing his stool nearer, as he unloosed his wrist-bands, and Alke placed his aching foot upon the lamb's skin, — "sir, you know not who looks into your eyes; but I will make sure of you before I tell you. Oh, God of memory, hear my prayer!"

The voice of the cottager trembled; his eyes were fountains. Even Alke was unnerved. The knight's white face was twitching with excitement. Silence was hushing their breath, until the eyes of the soldier saw before him two brawny wrists, bare and brown. They were stretched under his gaze. The arms of Gaspar trembled not.

What fastened the eyes of the young knight upon those white marks in that brown skin, — the livid scars, — sword-wounds of long years agone, but so plain, so white, so memorable!

"Do you remember your childhood?" cried Gaspar.

"My father! My own father! Oh, God, is it true?"

"My poor child, Ami! Oh, Ami!" The father's arms held him tenderly. "And little Alke! Oh, my dear children, my children!" Gaspar said it again and again, as they clasped each other in happy embrace.

The golden-stringed lyre was too delicate for such madly inspiring strokes. In a few days the young Barbé Gerard Pastre was praying at the bedside of Alke. The momentous transformations of the preceding days had issued to Ami in a fevered brain. He had become uncontrollable.

Now Gaspar sat wondering and weeping by the side of the cot on which the armor of the French knight — his own Ami — lay glittering. The bed by the doorway was empty. Ami had escaped them in his delirium.

The last words of characteristic sanity which he spoke to them were these : " I am a saved sinner ! The blood of Jesus Christ cleanseth from all sin, even from jealousy."

He had then rambled on in his talk about the Pope and Luther, and now for two nights and days the lame father and the faithful but exhausted Alke had prayed in vain for Ami's return.

CHAPTER XXX.

"UBI PAPA, UBI ROMA."

IMP · CÆSAR · KAROLVS · V · AVG ·
BONONIAM · DIVERTENS
IMPERII · INSIGNIA
A · CLEMENTE · PAPA · VII · RECEPTVRVS
HIC · QUOQUE · SANCTITATIS · ET · BONARUM · ARTIUM ·
DOMICILIUM · SUCCESSIT
SINGVLA · PERLVSTRANS · VNA · ET · SVSPICIENS.

SUCH is the record deeply graven on a single fine stone which is inserted within the strong wall of the large dormitory of the monastery of San Michele in Bosco. Three and a half centuries have gone ; but nothing of interest in the conduct, or of significance in the purposes of Emperor Charles V. has detached itself from that 25th of February, 1530, on which this powerful ruler received imperial coronation at the hands of the Pope. Significant as was his election on June 18, 1519, as the successor of Charlemagne, or the coronation at Aachen, by the Archbishop of Cologne, Oct. 23, 1520, each was naturally surpassed by the event at Bologna, when the King of the Romans and of Germany saw Clement VII. about to invest him with the world's richest diadem.

Charles V. had had an uneasy mastery. Francis I. was known to him as a courtly gentleman and a royal liar.

He had missed the discovery of the meaning of those
energies which had been operating in the Renaissance,
while he played with the eddies in the stream. He had
failed to comprehend the strength of the religious up-
heaval which at his own city and in his own court had
already made his affairs jostle uneasily. He had proven
himself a good foil for the intellect of Charles until he was
made his prisoner and slave ; and the Peace of Cambray
now admitted the French Sovereign into only an hour's
nervous friendship.

Henry VIII. was the only monarch whom Charles had
learned to respect, because he feared him. Directed, as
he seemed to be, by the genius of Wolsey, even he was
often manageable. The power of any alliance between
the English King and the Sovereign of France in the Low
Countries lay in their apparently pious and publicly applauded purpose of serving the Holy Father, and rescuing
him out of the grip of him who had made Italy bleed
beneath the Imperial arms. That purpose seemed forgotten. Henry's scheme for a divorce from Katherine
of Arragon, it appeared, could not but complicate his policies and embarrass his ambitions as a sovereign. Yet
Katherine's nephew, Charles V., was not blind to the fact
that it might lead to an alliance against the Imperial
standard.

Charles could not forget the negotiations at Amiens between Cardinal Wolsey and Francis I. That confederacy,
whatever had happened to the proposed marriage of Or-
leans and the princess, or to Henry's considerate but for-
mal renunciation of the French crown, had a strange
vitality. True, by relaxing somewhat of the severity of
the treaty of Madrid, he had not won either Francis or
Henry. This had simply irritated the emperor, and war
instead of a royal duel had come. Rome had been va-
cated ; Naples besieged ; and the Pope had acknowledged Francis I. as his emancipator. While Henry VIII.

had been unable to marshal England against him in the Low Countries, and Lautrec could not hold the French army because he failed to receive the support of his monarch, and Admiral Andrea Doria had revolted from a king who gave him compliments and an insulting court, attaching himself to the emperor who sent him to the relief of Naples, — all ending in disaster to France, the capture of Genoa, and the rout of the French army under Saint-Pol, — it was still evident to the wary Charles that jealousy of the Imperial standards was not humiliated either in France or England.

The Peace of Cambray had beneath it the empty treasury of the emperor and the weariness of the Spaniards. The emperor knew the Pope to be negotiating with both himself and the French King. Two women, even though one was the royal aunt of Charles, and the other was the mother of Francis, could not make such a protesting friendship inviolable. Even his treaty of June 20, 1529, with the Pope, was unsatisfactory. The white steed which his Holiness rode, and then sent to the Imperial commander, was not so burdened with testimonials of absolution for all who had plundered Rome, or with offers of ecclesiastical revenues, that he might not run away and find a road to the stables of the Supreme Pontiff.

Francis I. had sacrificed everything but his restless ambition and his facility at lying. Henry VIII. was in uninterrupted communication with him. The Pope had chatted with Henry's ambassador when the former was a prisoner of Charles V. at Castle St. Angelo, and had listened to the king's desire for a divorce from the emperor's aunt. Only the threats and promises of Charles V. had made his Holiness forget his obligation to serve the English monarch. Above all these in peril born of the fears of the army, were the Turk whose four weeks' siege of Vienna Charles had not forgotten, and the growing movement of the Reformers, whose progress Pope and ruler had affected to despise, but which they now saw must be met with a vigorous hand.

Nothing was, therefore, so natural as a desire for an alliance with the Pope, whom he had incarcerated and whose city he had sacked. Charles remembered that his grandsire Maximilian, at critical moments which he had not anticipated, repented that he had not obtained papal coronation. Enraged at Henry VIII., distrustful of Francis I., fearful of a coalition of his foes, and bent on the suppression of the Reformation, he would meet Clement VII. at Bologna as the King of France met Leo X. at the same place after the battle of Marignano.

Charles V. was ready to depart. Andrea Doria, the rebel against the French Sovereign, should command the flag-ship.

While the emperor *en route* was entertaining the husband of Lucretia Borgia, the Duke of Ferrara, at Reggio, Clement VII. was approaching Bologna. Charles had made a tour of magnificence. Attended by day by splendidly clothed men of State and the army, sleeping in palaces at night, received by cavalcades of cardinals, visited by ambassadors from the French King, his journey was interrupted only that he might be informed that his chancellor had been honored by the Pope, or that the gracious Pontiff had come near to Bologna; and on the 4th of November, he halted at the convent of the Italian brothers of the rule of Saint Bruno, close to the Certosa, outside the walls of the city. On one of its heavy stones to-day this record abides : —

A PERPETVA MEMORIA
CARLO V IMPERATORE
PER ESSERE CORONATO IN BOLOGNA
SI TRATTENNE
IN QVESTA ABITAZIONE
IL DI IV NOVEMBRE
AN. MDXXVIII.

As the emperor neared the convent, swiftly as a flash from the sun sped an arrow in dangerous proximity to his head.

The Imperial conqueror cried out: "Have I no safety here?"

"The safety of the Holy Church, the safety of all Italy!" replied one of the astonished cardinals who had attended his Majesty from Modena. He had not seen the arrow; indeed, it had escaped the discovery of all but the emperor. For him it was intended; for his heart its poisonous point had been prepared. The nervousness of the sovereign did not abate as the entire body of white-robed priests protested that such an occurrence was almost impossible. The illustrious companions of Charles V. made every search; attendants hastened to discover the guilty wretch; and the monarch was assured of his safety.

One of his company, however, ventured to utter his distrust of the monks.

"It could not have been a brother who had heard that mellifluous voice," remarked one of the monks, who, with many others, had spoken concerning the pleasing and quiet tones of a man whom all Italy had hitherto regarded with terror.

"It may have been a shot from one who saw that villanous underjaw and those protruding lips," whispered another, who was one of a larger number who had determined that no suavity of manner or gentleness of tone should lead them to forget that Charles had plundered Rome and made the Pontiff a captive.

Later in the day, when the emperor walked with Louis d'Avila, the historian, admiring the pictures and marbles with which popes and kings had enriched the sacred house, it was all explained.

A young man, suffering with a vicious sort of madness, evidently the result of disease, had been found near the

convent.   A bow, and a quiver lacking a single arrow, were
discovered with him; and he chattered incoherently in
French about that startling shot.   The pious and sympathetic monks, touched at first by the wretchedness of
his condition, then becoming wildly superstitious concerning his insanity, had sought to feed him; then they
had fled from him.   He had been last seen running toward the banks of the Savena, which was nearly a mile
away.

One of the imaginative brothers who longed to be rid
of unpleasant responsibilities, invented the story that the
madman leaped into the stream and was drowned.
Another, in sober truth, declared that his face was beautiful; and he was supported by one of the attendants of
the emperor when he averred that he possessed a valuable ring bearing the arms of Pope Leo X. and holding
an emerald.   Both grew excited when they asserted
they had seen him before, — one in Bologna, the other in
Florence.

At length the discharged arrow was found.   Its point
was poisoned.   The emperor himself trembled when he
read the inscription written plainly on a bit of parchment
and attached to it, —

"*Remember the Diet of Worms ! Forget not Katherine
of Arragon !   Be mindful of the Turk !*"

He read it again, and examined the missile.   It seemed
to his Majesty that all the problems of his life met in that
arrow.   They were loaded with disaster; yet it had missed
him.   What would have unmanned either of his royal
antagonists served to solidify the thought of Charles V.
Death had been escaped; he must be in Bologna on
the morrow.

Whence came the unexpected stranger?

For more than a week the maniac had entertained and
eluded the officers of Bologna.   No one knew his name,

the hour of his arrival, the meaning of his movements, or the reason of his sudden disappearance. He had been looked upon only as a pitiful beggar who bewildered all who beheld him by the remarkable combination of scholarly sanity and vicious insanity which he furnished. He had been in prison and out of prison; but the city was so interested in the pageant about to occur, so crowded had become every street, and so busy was every official, that his career in Bologna had at length come to be unnoticed. Thieves and cut-throats, however, had hunted in vain for the wearer of the emerald ring; an agent of a ducal family had sought to purchase it of the impecunious stranger; but he had escaped them all. Every street in Bologna seemed familiar to him; and he had related to a companion in penury the occurrences of the visit of Francis I. to Pope Leo X. at Bologna, with astonishing accuracy of detail. Flashes of reason illumined the midnight of his mind, as the lightning plays upon the blackness of the storm. The crowded city, with its loquacious and excited visitors intent on beholding such another spectacle as had fascinated Bolognese conversation since the appearance of Francis I., let him pursue his way, although his fits of madness would have indicated that his vicious schemes might be carried into effect at any moment. His ragged associates laughed when he declared that he would kill Pope Clement VII.; and the desperate bloodthirstiness of his plans only proved to them that he was harmless.

On the morning of October 23 he appeared clad in elegant garments. His bedfellow had been a successful robber, and was a Spanish fugitive. With him a bargain had been made for the use of some coveted garments for an indefinite period. The ring was accepted as a pawn, and the thief was delighted.

Adding his perfect mastery of the language to the impression made by the bright, rich clothing, the madman conceived himself able to find a way into the palaces and associations which were so soon to welcome the Supreme Pontiff.

As with such subtlety and intelligence he pursued his aims, the experience of a madman yielded to the sober tactics of wit. His physical condition was improving, and his madness was under control. When he felt the fit returning, he enforced silence upon his tongue and kept himself at a distance from his dagger. With superb self-mastery, his plan was consummated.

The hour at length came when the Holy Father was to enter the city. The insane man stood before the guard.

" He is a Spaniard, — an emissary of Charles V., King of the Romans and of Germany," cried one of the guard to another who was seeking to detain the stranger.

The madman thanked him in excellent phrase.

" That may be a Spaniard," quoth the irritated guard, "but he looks every inch a Frenchman."

" Nay, a child of our own Italy ! " interrupted a third, who detected the Italian blood mount to the stranger's cheeks as he went away.

" That man I have seen in Bologna, ere this," said the first. "And he is enough like the beautiful youth who came and went with the French Sovereign when he met Leo X. in our city, — like enough to him," — and he gazed upon the knightly form and abundant sunny hair, totally forgetful to regard the changes which intervening years must have made, — " like enough to that boy to be his father ! "

The old guard shook his wise head, and congratulated himself upon an existence on earth so long that he would be able to say, " I have seen two Popes receive two kings in Bologna."

" His language and his dress are of Spain. Let us not annoy the forerunner of the emperor ! " added an aged

Bolognese soldier, who had felt the weight of Charles V.'s sword at Rome, and with a wise terror thought of any interference with an Imperial representative.

The stranger hurried through the street, stopping not to behold the gleaming marble arcades or the noble terraces, anxious only to join in the magnificence of the entry itself. He had already slept in rags under the shadow of the ancient university buildings, and starved under the front of famous palaces, while masters of jurisprudence and eminent poets and illustrious scholars had passed by. Why should he now pause before a leaning tower or an exquisitely chiselled marble? He waited but for an instant in the shadow of the elegant Carisenda; and there he repeated the words of Dante, in which it has passed into imperishable literature, —

> " As seems the Carisenda to behold
>   Beneath the leaning side, when goes a cloud
>   Above it so that opposite it hangs;
>   Such did Antæus seem to me, who stood
>   Watching to see him stoop, and then it was
>   I could have wished to go some other way."

And then he said, as he cast a furtive glance about him, " Oh, Dante, if thy prophecy concerning the Holy Church is realized, how like a toy will appear yonder graceful Asinelli! But," he added, on suddenly seeing a man nearing the spot, " I am a Spanish gentleman, a friend of Charles V., — his emissary, if necessity shall require. Ha, ha! I must not think of Dante and the Church. I shall be mad again, — yes, mad! Oh God, this gloom! it thickens. I cannot kill the Pope, — no, not the Pope. I will kill the Emperor! Ha, ha! He would kill Luther if he had him again at the Diet of Worms. Yes, I will kill Charles. Ha! Oh, my bow! my dagger! The saints — ha, ha! — the saints defend the King of the Romans and of Germany! "

In his returning madness he fled to the place of concealment where the sleeping outlaw held the ring and the rags which he had forsaken. In an hour he had changed his garments, forgotten all about the entry of the Pontiff Clement VII., and lay panting with feverish excitement near the wall of the convent outside the defences of Bologna. He had found the bow and a quiver full of arrows, which, days ago, he had poisoned; and living on a morsel of food, he had awaited for ten days the arrival of the emperor.

The moment came. As he gazed upon his Majesty, the bow-string twanged; that arrow gleamed through the air.

On the 5th of November the king entered Bologna. He had given orders that the arrow should be brought with his armor; and as a significant memorial of the journey, he confided it to the guardianship of no less a person than Henry, Count of Nassau, High Chamberlain. Little did Charles V. dream that some of the ideas which attached to that arrow would make the name Nassau impregnable against oppression, when the nephew of that chamberlain should be known as William the Silent.

As little did the emperor dream that the interesting personage whom he now noticed as he entered the city, and took to be an elegantly attired Spaniard, was the madman who had sought his life near the convent on the day before.

There stood the excellently formed figure, as the emperor halted at the gateway. With unfrenzied eye, he looked upon Charles V. as he alighted from his white charger and mounted a dark bay genet. If any had questioned his presence, the stranger had replied like a knight and in faultless language.

The lucid hours of sanity had come again. He was master of himself; and he proposed to participate in these ceremonies. He had again donned the showy garments of a Spaniard, and was more at ease with kings than with ordinary thieves and beggars. His every movement or attitude was knightly.

The gate of San Felice had hardly opened, when an eye into which he had first looked years before, burned upon him with glowing recognition. Ten minutes later, as the cavalcade halted, and the rich gold brocade with which the emperor's genet was almost covered was arranged to hold more securely the damascened breastplates, a hand was affectionately laid upon the madman's shoulder. He trembled.

The voice shook: "Ami, Ami! what do you here? By all the saints — or is it his ghost? Ami!"

At last he had been discovered, recognized, called by name. He was stupefied by the sounds. "Ami!" He had not heard his name since the awful moment when in the desolated home of his father, Gaspar Perrin, his fever raged like a hell and the delirium came upon him. Life and biography were but a blank page until he discovered himself a wretched beggar in the streets of Bologna, — a city which he had remembered with dizzying reflections when he looked at the arms of Leo X. on his ring.

Ami's brain reeled with the shock attending the pronunciation of his name.

"Ami, Ami!" again said the voice, — a cry suppressed in a whisper. The poor man staggered. Without lifting his eyes from the helmet which the emperor had taken off as he kissed the crucifix which Cardinal Campeggio held to the royal lips, the discovered Ami turned to walk away with his ardent companion.

CHAPTER XXXI.

> " The soothing thoughts which spring
> Out of human suffering."

THE soul of the young man in the Spanish garb was a whirlpool. Memories, hopes, emotions of fear and of hate, feelings of chagrin and of despair, swirled in noisy tumult in his half-crazed brain. A hundred pictures of the mind suffused with a weird and melancholy light were torn to pieces and thrown about in confusion. He had seen faces that day which recalled his whole past as the friend of Francis I. and a person of distinction at the court. Here was a face, — the face sure to make everything incomprehensible.

There, an hour before these eyes had looked upon him, Ami had fancied Admiral Andrea Doria in that long retinue of gallant nobles and accoutred knights from Spain, Sicily, and the Netherlands.

What strange phantasy could it be? Ah! now it could not be a phantasy.

"Andrea Doria," persisted Ami, "was the chief ally of my royal friend Francis I. Andrea Doria in this procession? Andrea Doria with the light horsemen, — three hundred in blazing red uniform, — what can it mean? Andrea Doria close to Antonio de Leyva? What! the Admiral was the ally of France when Antonio tore from

Francis I. a whole division with its leader, on the field of Pavia !"

Surely the dreadful mania was coming again in a new form. " Andrea Doria followed by Bolognese youths, clad in velvet, riding on Turkish horses, or running at the side of Charles V., as he rode beneath a canopy of gold, his armor of steel and gold glittering like a flame, and the eagle-crest shining upon his helmet !" — it was the dream of the maniac Ami knew himself to be.

He raised his eyes, and looked, as he departed. He saw only the fragments of the crowd, — three thousand German foot, ten pieces of artillery, three thousand Spanish soldiers, and — Andrea Doria in the midst near the emperor ! Old gout-stricken Antonio de Leyva borne in a chair, commander-in-chief; and Admiral Andrea Doria —

" Oh, cursed malady !" cried Ami, as the newly found companion dragged him away.

There was no reply; the sick man stumbled along as far as possible, until at length he lay exhausted upon the ground.

Every remedy which love could suggest or pity imagine was applied. The crowd heeded not, but like a flood swept on. Here and there a streamlet separated itself from the main currents and worked its way to this place of interest.

" A Spaniard of the emperor's train !" said a wiseacre, as he walked on. " He has found purgatory in Bologna."

The eyes of Ami slowly opened. He riveted their gaze upon his solitary companion ; for the shouts of the crowd had attracted every one away from the spot except this loved friend of other days. Up into his face Ami looked with piteous emotion. Tears fell upon Ami's sunny hair from eyes which had waited unweariedly for a smile of recognition. What cared this man that yonder splendid pageant had occurred without his presence?   A kinglier power than Charles V. ruled his heart.

Love, which does not wait to comprehend the crisis, — love knew that the moment for complete devotion had come ; and in a human form love stood heroic, and of all else save its masterful duty forgetful.

The ashy lips of Ami moved.   The eager ears which had just heard the huzzas of the multitude were close to the trembling tongue ; and kneeling upon the very soil where years before stood Ami, as the proudest young knight of France, his friend heard the longed-for whisper, —

"Francesco ! It is Francesco !   In the name of Jesus Christ, I thank —   Francesco, do not betray me !"

The storm-tossed Ami had found succor in a fellow-sailor on life's unquiet sea, — a sailor whose stronger craft might seize his and condemn him as a pirate.   But Ami was safe.   Francesco de Robo loved the Church, but not the Sovereign of France.   He could not betray Ami, even for love of the Church.

Since these two men had met as fellow-servants to his Majesty Francis I., great changes had come to both. At Chilly the youths had handled the swords and books of old Nouvisset ; and the young Italian had grown into such favor with the king that he had been granted, at his own desire, a position of peculiar responsibility with Admiral Andrea Doria.   In all the tempests into which Ami's conscience had gone, Francesco had been sympathetic and true.   Oh, how those days of storm and shine, of brilliant wickedness and struggling hope, came back upon them, as with fast-flowing tears they embraced as restored lovers !

"Francesco," whispered Ami again, with a choking sob in his throat, — "Francesco, tell me, oh, tell me at once !   Where is my — "

He faltered; but the tongue of eloquent friendship spoke the dear word for Ami, — "Astrée."

Tears fell upon Ami's cheek from the eyes of Francesco, as he tried to kiss the forehead behind whose full beauty was a living agony. "I will tell you all, Ami, when you are in a condition to hear sweet news. The saints prosper your returning strength!"

"In the name of Jesus Christ!" slowly responded Ami.

Francesco was not oblivious that this phrase had been uttered by Ami but a moment before, and that it might denote an unimagined transformation. He knew it was not the hour for theological conversation. Louise of Savoy and Louis de Berquin seemed to be near, each looking scorn at the other; but Francesco was silent.

As Ami and Francesco waited alone for weakness to become strength, the huge pageant about Charles V. moved on. It had gone forward, leaving Francesco in a new life. Of all else he had made sacrifice to his love for Ami, whose condition perplexed him. A little wine and a short hour of sleep had so refreshed Ami, however, that soon Francesco had little difficulty in leading him to comfortable lodgings, where he left him, promising to return as soon as he could beg leave of absence from the Admiral Andrea Doria.

With a patience supported by affection and transfigured by hope, Ami awaited Francesco's return. The latter had found his way back into the centre of the moving spectacle, had paid due homage to the powerful admiral, and found it possible to pass the night with Ami.

"Oh," said Francesco, "this ostentatious glitter cannot miss me. I shall go where my life has some significance, where the crisis is genuine."

Fleet indeed were his feet, but fleeter still were the two tongues which that night related almost a complete biography of two souls. Ami had listened for so long a time for the sound of Francesco's footsteps, he was so weak and fearful of a return of his malady, that when Francesco entered he could hear the feeble voice of Ami uttering but two words: " Francesco — Astrée."

The staggering intellect had fastened its eye upon these two shining lights in its dark wanderings, and knew that each point of glory was within sight of the other: " Francesco — Astrée."

Not long did the conversation tarry with Andrea Doria's political position. Ami knew the steps which had led to the rupture. At length the schemes of Louise of Savoy and Duprat had united with repeated insults and the duplicity of the king; Savona had been fortified; Andrea Doria's beloved Genoa was robbed of her trade, and having revolted, he was about to be arrested by the minions of a king to whom he had given such important service, when he fled, sent back the collar of St. Michael to France, and joined the Imperial standard.

" Of course," said Francesco, who knew how earnestly the court strove to keep the intelligence from Ami while he was arming himself to kill Waldensians, — " of course I was glad to follow him as soon as I could." Francesco's lofty manner reminded Ami of Andrea Doria, as he had seen him commanding the galleys from Marseilles to Civita Vecchia, nearly four years before. " I was still more proud when he drove the French from Genoa and declined to become its doge. Andrea Doria is too great to be the servant even of Charles V."

" But he is at present in the procession of Charles V.? " mused Ami, not quite sure of the facts. " It is all so mysterious. You are still his companion, Francesco? Yes; it is confusing to me. But you love him; you did not love the king. — Love? yes, I loved Francis I.; but oh, Francesco, I loved Astrée! Let Andrea Doria follow Satan or Saint Paul, I am strong enough now. Astrée! — Oh, that awful pain is with me again! — "

Ami's head was in one of the loving palms of Francesco; while the young Italian stroked the burning brow with the other.   It soothed his soul: and Ami slept again, the lips moving now and then: "Francesco — Astrée!   Francesco — Astrée!"

If Francesco had been a student of mental physiology, and had been familiar with all the labyrinthine roadways in Ami's disordered brain, knowing each byway and the delicate strength of each bridge beneath which eddied such tangled currents, he could not have more successfully pursued his task of leading into the soul of his sick friend the long trains of information concerning events which had happened since they parted in Paris, on the day when Ami went forth to cement the friendship of pope and king in Waldensian blood.   Love tested every nerve, and love weighed every sentence before a word was spoken.   The result was that Francesco had soon told him of the feelings of Francis I. and his court at the turn things had taken with the cohort which Ami had led to La Torre; the certainty with which the king believed that Ami had been killed; the endless prayers which had been bargained for that his soul might have repose; the haughty exhibitions of sorrow on the part of Louise of Savoy; the grief of the Queen of Navarre; and the theory of many of Ami's friends that the knights had been careless in abandoning him, though they thought he had been mortally wounded, in a Waldensian's cottage.

"I could sleep now," he said, "if I knew that the anguish of another did not break her heart.   Tell me, does my Astrée live?"

"Astrée," responded Francesco, with a sympathy in his tone which seemed to feel the awful strain within the sick man's spirit, with a firmness of knowledge which instinctively realized that a quiver in his voice would start a panic in Ami's soul, — "Astrée lives, and Astrée loves you."

The dazed and happy man appeared to be looking into eternity, as he slowly said, "Astrée — Francesco."

" You are looking far away." Francesco was confident of Ami's strength.

" I saw her while you were saying she loved me ; the Holy Virgin by her side, lilies in her right hand, and the gate opening and closing. Francesco, is it true ? "

" Even so, Ami, even so. Oh, beloved of Astrée, noblest of knights " — Francesco kissed the flame in Ami's cheek, — " Ami, your Astrée is indeed a star, as you used to say. Her life at the court was as unsuited to her soul as an immeasurable earth would be to the presence of a glorious star from heaven. Her quickening beams never so illumined the world as since she has left it. When the news of your death in the mountains came, she said : ' He never so lived for God, for me, as now.' Her soul seemed at once transported to the eternity which she believed you had entered. An infinite sky adopted Astrée."

" The star ! " whispered Ami.

" And to complete her detachment from things of earth, she fled the court, the king, the eyes of her loving ones. The Admiral Andrea Doria alone knew her paths. Even he knows not where she may be now. Ami, be calm ! "

" My star is covered with thunderclouds," sobbed Ami.

" But she was landed in England, and was, a little time ago, safe in a nunnery in Somerset. Ami, I know you are glad Astrée is so far from the court of France — "

" In the name of Jesus Christ, let us give thanks and rejoice," was the only response.

CHAPTER XXXII.

FAINT YET PURSUING.

"*Evviva il Pontefice e l' Imperatore!   Viva Clemente e Carlo!*"

"I HAVE come where I have long desired to be, to the feet of your Holiness, that we may take measures together to relieve the needs of afflicted Christendom. May God grant my coming may prove to be for the good of his service and that of your Holiness, and useful to the Christian world!"

These words of the mightiest of civil monarchs fell upon the ears of the Supreme Pontiff, while Charles V. was on his knees before Clement VII. The Pope had at last yielded to the emperor's desire to kneel in adoration; kisses and tears had been freely interchanged; the attendant still held the tiara of his Holiness; the high chamberlain had placed in the royal hand the crowded crimson purse intended for the Pope. Both sovereigns had forgotten to remain pale, as at first, amid countless genuflexions; and after a fresh outburst of tears, Hildebrand's successor replied, —

"I thank God that I see you here safe, after your long journey by sea and land, and that affairs are in such a state that I need not despair of seeing, by means of your authority, peace and order re-established."

Never before had so many feet crowded into the street leading to the Basilica of St. Petronius; never had the eager gaze of the bell-ringer, who now had climbed into the high belfry, overlooked such a dense and motley throng. Workmen had carried to the temporary structure, within which these magnates were to meet for the first time, the gay colors of the house of Medici and ancient and elaborate tapestries. Twenty-eight cardinals, without a fear of those who had begun to be called Protesters, or Protestants, had borne thither their solemn dignity and obsolescent importance.

No one appeared to detect along the sky a single hint of that stormy glory which for the most part even yet lay smouldering in obscure and public places where the fire was gradually gaining command of masses of inflammable material, whence it would soon rush upward, commingling with the majestic splendor of the quiet stars. Only Charles V., — "Cæsar Imperator," — just as he rose from his knees and advanced to his seat on the left of the Pope, felt something in his breast which was the breath of the future whispering again the inscription on the arrow: " Remember the Diet of Worms ! "

In quiet and joy, deep as their love, Ami and Francesco had passed the day. The Admiral Andrea Doria had a vivid remembrance of Ami, and of his services at the French court. By the grace of the sailor, Francesco had been excused from attendance upon a scene at which a less generous and loving nature would have been present at any cost. Ami had rallied, and now talked with astonishing vigor. His friend could detect only a trace of the madness.

With infinite patience Francesco had awaited a moment of sufficient health in his friend for the relating of a story the very anticipation of whose details thrilled him. How should Francesco introduce the subject?

He was as much bewildered at the gate of San Felice

as Ami had been. The old friend could scarcely believe his eyes, when days ago, at the entry of Charles V., this attendant upon Andrea Doria saw standing near, the Ami who had been killed while crushing out Waldensian heresies. The day just passed had brought no order out of Francesco's confusion. He reflected that Ami had left the castle of Francis I. determined to find a settled faith. How had he succeeded? While Francesco had been answering the inquiries of the sick man, cautiously avoiding any straining of his feeble energy, a throng of inquiries starting in his own soul had almost paralyzed his tongue. One phrase which Ami twice used had fixed itself in the thought of Francesco.

"'In the name of the Lord Jesus Christ,' or 'In the name of Jesus the Christ,' — Ami, that is a new phrase with you, since we read Quintilian with Nouvisset, or recited from Saint Thomas Aquinas to William Farel."

"It is a phrase dear enough to William Farel," answered Ami.

"What do you know of Farel's whereabouts, man?"

"William Farel," said Ami, remembering Francesco's joy that night at hearing how Ami and Queen Marguerite had accomplished his escape, — "he is safe in Switzerland, and mighty is his power. Clement VII. will put no such crown upon the temples of Charles V. as God has put on the brow of our old friend."

"Ami, you speak like one of those who protest."

"In the name of Jesus Christ, — a name above every name in heaven above or earth beneath!" responded the Waldensian, his face radiant with unimagined light, his voice steady and resonant, his body raised upon his elbow, as he lay on a sort of cot. "In the name of Jesus Christ, I am what I am. Yes, Francesco, I am what I longed to be, when I lived in the midst of the infamies of that court; what I fought against being on the morning when we parted, when you called me 'the young Bayard,' —

when I went forth to kill my own people with the sword.
I am a Protestant!"

Francesco was dumb with astonishment; and eloquent with irrepressible admiration, he stood transfixed,
with the steady, seraphic gaze of that weak man upon
him.

"I know," said Ami, "that I have thrown my life before the sharpest of swords wielded by the knightliest of
men."

A tear stood in the eye of Francesco. Ami fell back
upon his cot, exhausted, fainting.

In a few moments Ami had been restored; but he was
a madman for the rest of the day. Again, that affection,
which was never so nearly omnipotent as when it must
travel in twilight and carry its burdens into darkness,
threw its ministries about the sufferer.

Through the entire afternoon Ami was quite beyond
control. By and by night brought such partial deliverance that the malady relaxed its severities. Ami fell
asleep, with Francesco at his side. The lips were moving,
and the words were audible.

" Astrée — Francesco ! I am a Protestant ! Astrée —
Francesco !"

Little did Ami think, at any previous moment, that of
the deeper lines in the spiritual biography of which Francesco had read so much to him, he had been kept in
ignorance. He knew, when they were together in Paris,
that of all men Francesco would be the first to understand him, if he should ever escape the fetid atmosphere
of the Church and cast his lot with the Reformers. Francesco knew more ; for he once had a hint that Ami had
sprung from a Reformer. Nouvisset, whose Greek temper and spirit had made both of them temperate in their
credulity, often preserved a studied silence when Ami
spoke of destroying heretics. The friendship of Marguerite had manifested itself in a correspondence in

which she had uttered every sentiment which made her such an ally of the Reform. Francesco's faith in the authority of the Pope had gone before Ami had left Astrée's side to fight for an orthodoxy which the former saw only as a vanishing-point. Now, as he sat there with Ami's feverish hand within his own, he too was a protester. But Francesco could not rest with a negative protestantism.

"Astrée — Francesco! I am a Protestant!"

"So also am I!" cried out Francesco, pressing the insane Ami with his lips, and seizing him, in his fresh, triumphant joy, with that wild, ungovernable freedom with which a strong river delayed by obstructions which at a given instant a baby's touch might remove, tosses a chip in its foam. He clasped the weak frame of Ami to his own breast, and was amazed to feel the sufferer straighten into his old knightly figure, remove himself a few steps, and say, "In the name of Jesus Christ!"

"Yes, yes!" Francesco knew that Ami's sanity had returned. "Yes, the hour has come; the occasion is here for me to declare it. The abominable mask has fallen. I believe every true knight in Europe is for the reform. It *is* in the name of Jesus Christ, Ami! They have crucified him afresh, and put him to an open shame. The new crusade is on. We will not try to rescue the grave of Christ from the Turk, but we will rescue the living Christ from the ecclesiasticism which has entombed him."

Of how much more enduring significance was this simple scene than that sumptuous display in the Piazza Maggiore, only the history of the human soul, beleaguered with doubts, dependent upon celestial certainties, flinging kings and pontiffs into graves, following the heroic and faithful toward the dawn, must tell. Charles and Clement were playing solemnly with the toys of yesterday; Francesco and Ami stood gladly reading the messages of to-morrow.

The hours passed swiftly, as Ami told of the march to
San Michele and on to the valleys; the attack of his
band upon the mountaineers; the discovery of Vian's
presence; the meeting of father and child, sister and
brother, after the fight with Wolsey's emissary.

What a combination, — Gaspar Perrin, Alke, Vian,
Ami!

During the conversation — for Ami's monologue was
turned into dialogue by the ardent curiosity and friendly
amazement of Francesco — often did the voice of the Waldensian falter; and Francesco stood like a living model
conjured into silence and made motionless by the tragic
incidents.

"Ami, you cannot now hate the man who saved you
from murdering your own sister, — you cannot, even
though his name was Vian."

"I can despise no human soul, now that I have known
the love of God," was Ami's answer.

"I know not all that you mean, when you speak of the
love of God. Would that I knew! Would that I felt
God's love as you do, Ami!" Francesco's voice was
unsteady with feeling. "But I do know that Astrée never
fled from your love for love of Vian."

"That I also know," quickly said Ami.

"I say to you, Ami, again, what once I said at the
castle, that Vian did not seek to rob you of Astrée. He
was as brilliant as another star, on the night when they
talked on the sward near the tent of the king. She could
not keep her own beams — star that she is! — from mingling with his. Ami, does the love of God crush out the
viper-brood of jealousy? Methinks I note a change in
your eye. It blazes not with angry jealousy, as once it
did, at the mention of one word, — Vian!"

"You had never said so much of my past sin," answered the Waldensian, "if you had known that it is dead.
Alas, it may be that he is dead! Poor Vian! I gave

him a ghastly and doubtless fatal wound. They took him away in chains, — my own knights, who forsook their leader, — though Vian seemed dying. Would that they had been less rough with so fine a frame, in which lived so lustrous a mind!"

Ami had determined to tell him of Alke's love for Vian at a later time.

"Ami, tears like these you never shed at Paris. Does the love of God find the purest fountains within us?"

"The love of God and the peace of God pass all understanding, Francesco!"

"I would that I knew it as you do."

Then the two men, with the same arms about each other which had lifted Nouvisset's swords so often, and without a word, found themselves kneeling down by that cot on which Ami had been such a sufferer. The silence was broken for a little time by sobs. Prayers which had only the language of tears, ascended to God; lips which had known only ritual, moved now with the one Holy Name.

"In the name of the Lord Jesus Christ," cried Francesco, "supplicate Heaven for me."

Ami began to pray aloud. No priesthood could have been more sublime; no ceremonial was so august as that moment presented. It was Ami's first prayer for another soul. Francesco held to him with desperate, loving energy. He seemed clinging to his guide with a death-like grasp, while walking over fathomless abysses.

"I am a sinner, Ami! Oh, Jesus Christ, I am a sinner!" cried the proud, struggling Italian.

"By grace ye are saved. It is not of yourselves; it is the gift of God."

"I beseech thy Grace, O Christ!" responded the suppliant.

"Believest thou on Jesus Christ?" asked Ami.

"I do believe; but I am slipping out of the hands of Satan."

"Thou art falling into the hand of God, Francesco!"

"It is the scarred hand of Christ! I do trust to be held," said the Italian.

Lips which had never borne another soul's destiny heavenward now became priestly, and were touched with fire as Ami prayed for Francesco. "Then, O God, thou Father of Jesus Christ, hear our prayer! O Son of God, be our Saviour! A child of thine, willing to know thy love, comes bringing himself to thee. Let not his sins come between thee and thy child!"

"They do not! Ami, my sins have not hidden me from God's love! They do not!" said Francesco, rising quickly, his face suffused with a celestial light. "Ami, I do know what the love of God is!"

CHAPTER XXXIII.

THE EMPEROR'S SERVANT.

"Brief rest upon the turning billow's height."

IT was in the early morning, that Ami and Francesco walked together far out from the Piazza Maggiore, upon which looked the windows of the palace occupied by the Pope and the emperor. Upon their steps the eye of Divine love seemed looking with infinite care. The world had been made new, while Francesco was kneeling with Ami in his humble lodgings. He had come to Bologna to be an attendant upon the crowning of Charles; he had been made an heir of God and a joint-heir with Jesus Christ, of a kingdom incorruptible, undefiled, and that fadeth not away. Every ray of sunlight which touched his path transfigured the planet; the sky was larger; the earth was encircled with hope.

Over three months had gone, since Charles V. arrived in Bologna. The coronation had not yet taken place; but Charles and Clement VII., who had the best of reasons for distrusting each other, had endured a prolonged festivity, had arranged various political schemes, and were now preparing for the august ceremony of coronation. Meanwhile a message from Ami had been sent to Gaspar Perrin, and one full of love had been received from Alke.

"The Lutheran soldiers pulled down the Pope's statue last night," said Francesco. "They went through the Piazza, pulling the head with a rope; and then they burned it."

"That is almost as wicked as a pope burning a living heretic," replied Ami, with a serious smile.

"Ami, we must belong to one army or to the other; and I should like to go into the army of the Reform, after this monstrous farce is over. This whole affair is as unreal as a mask."

"Behind the mask are ignorance and crime, superstition and lying," said Ami, with spirit.

"But we must stay until it is done. I shall go to the coronation with the admiral; and you will be with me. We shall see men with the faces of whom we may desire to be familiar. We are both young. We shall be as much in earnest, when this farce is over. Then, Ami, — then, as you say, to your father's home, and then to William Farel or Philip Melancthon. Your father knows both?"

"Yes; and Luther, too, as I believe."

This had been their matured plan for many days. Gaspar Perrin, who was in correspondence with the leaders of the revolt against Rome, had already sent news to William Farel, that the Reformers had gained a convert from the procession of Charles V. at Bologna. Ami had informed his father that it seemed wise — he knew not why — that he should remain and study the situation from this strategic point of view, and that soon this new and important accession to the ranks of the protesters would start with him for the cottage of the Waldensian. The letter of Ami closed with these words: —

"We are beholding a sunset. Behold the sunrise soon on your mountain-tops. You will discover it on the heights of the Waldensian's faith, before any may divine it in this thick, foul air."

It was the ardent flame of prophecy bursting from the breast of youth to gladden the weary eye of age.

The treaties between Pope and sovereign had been signed. The Pope had given to this obedient son of the Church the hat and sword. The bulls had been baited, and the horse-races were over. The university had been visited; and everybody was tired. The coronation-day was at hand. The emperor must be in Germany at once. Rome was too far away! "Ubi papa, ubi Roma" was repeated, as it had been for hundreds of years; and all was satisfactory.

The command of Andrea Doria brought both Francesco and Ami into the immediate service of the emperor. Even Charles V. admired the beauty and extolled the manners of the young knight whom Francis I. had had no thought of training for service at the coronation of his strongest foe. Ami was placed in a position of delicate responsibility. Francesco was sure that his madness would not recur; else to obtain such a place for him would have been to murder Charles. For hours, in the course of the tedious arrangements, the young Protester had the opportunity of studying the eyes, face, manners, and tones of the one giant enemy of the Reformation.

Ami received from one of the cardinals the guardianship of a priceless treasure. Ragged and half starved but a few days before, he had then beheld this same cardinal, as with his train he had advanced in solemn grandeur from the ancient cathedral of Monza, bearing this magnificent relic. It was the iron crown of Lombardy. There, enclosed in a gold crown which was made of jewelled rays, was this circle of iron, — a nail from the true cross. The cardinal showed Ami the blood-drop which had been almost lost in rust. Ami was silent with his thought. With his own fingers the first Christian king had placed that nail in his helmet, —so the cardinal assured Ami.

"Would so knightly a man as you are desire to kneel and kiss it?" asked his Grace.

Ami was courteous, heroic, silent. The cardinal crossed himself. His face was at first as red as his hat, then as white as the velvet on which rested the crown.

"Your sovereign will kneel to receive it! Your profane silence will be broken by the chatter of devils! These are cursed times, — alas! cursed times. Rome was sacked by him who will do penance for it to-day; but I know the curse for you!"

It was too late for the enraged cardinal to impeach the honor and loyalty of this strange attendant and guard. The Pope and the sovereign were in the chapel. Together, the dignitary and the guard walked within; but Ami carried only the crimson velvet cap which Charles V. wore, as he knelt to receive the iron crown; and he withdrew, content to let Clement VII. crown the foe of his old friend Francis I. without his even beholding the spectacle.

"This," thought Ami, "will seem to have been a dream of tawdry evanescence, when we find the kinglier souls who love God. I will not join in the procession, now that I did not kiss the iron crown! Oh, God of Jesus Christ, make plain my path!"

But there was no avoiding the procession. The most knightly figure in Bologna must stand close by the emperor; and, strangest of all, must obey his most curious whim.

"The arrow which missed my royal head, — where is it?" demanded Imperial Charles.

The chamberlain, Henry of Nassau, drew it from a jewelled quiver which had just been devised by the most eminent artist in Bologna. For nearly four months this artificer had been finding and polishing jewels, arranging them and fastening them upon a quiver of steel and gold, which was created to protect an arrow which had sped through the air, outside the walls near the convent, on the royal arrival. Charles V. looked upon the event as a pledge that the powers above held him in divine protection. He would not mount his white charger, until Andrea Doria and the Duke of Urbino, who stood waiting to hold the stirrup for him, had examined it and read the inscription, which was still clearly decipherable on the parchment attached, — "Remember the Diet of Worms!"

"That is enough," said Charles V., who did remember it. "Bear this with you, and fear not. Heaven with all the saints has rulers in close protection!" and then the emperor handed the gorgeous quiver to Ami, not at all interested in the solemn whiteness which made the young knight look like a ghost, as he received it.

The Pope's procession had already started. Ami could see it issuing forth in awful length between the halberdiers, pursuing its sinuous way like an immense serpent, rapacious, poisonous, omnipotent with its crushing folds, if ever its anger were aroused. He looked at the arrow. What a whirl of memories and hopes! Ami read the inscription, and whispered only this: "Remember the Diet of Worms!" Then he began to mutter it half audibly, again and again.

"I was not mad. No madman wrote those words. The only sanity is for Charles V. to remember that Luther is in the world. I was not mad. The sword which gleamed that day above the head of Martin Luther will cut off the head of that serpent." Thus meditated Ami, until the King of the Romans saw his hand touch the piece of parchment.

"Have a care of that arrow, and touch not the inscription!" commanded he. "Would that I knew the writer of those words! No madman was he." The emperor fell to talking with Andrea Doria at his side.

The wide bridge which had been formed from the window of the palace to the landing above the steps leading to the portal of St. Petronius, to make easy the passage of these dignitaries to the high altar, allowed six persons to walk abreast. The pressure of the papal procession had already begun to make the whole gallery tremble. Flowers and leaves fell from above down to the sumptuously carpeted floor, which was touched with the flowing edges of the fine tapestries and the magnificent velvet cloth, blue as the unclouded heavens above. Against these showed the rose-colored robes of the papal court. The purple-clad scholars, the cardinals in characteristic attire, archbishops in rich garments, the haughtily apparelled fathers of the ancient city, and the heavily armored standard-bearers of the Holy Church, helped to make the crowds of noble and titled ones which advanced before his Holiness.

It was a brilliant picture. Every largest thing was a broad splendor; every smallest a gem. Cellini had taxed his genius to create the very clasp which fastened the cope beneath that heavy jaw. Within the clasp was placed a gem whose every ray of beauty was a gleaming page of history. The state-chair trembled not, on the strong shoulders of the servants, who were so apparelled that at a distance they seemed only a red glare. The Pope's triple crown quivered above it all, like the point of an enormous flame.

Near enough to his Holiness to satisfy the demands of his position, always careful to be far enough away from the emblazoned heralds and finely dressed kings-at-arms of Francis I. to escape recognition, Ami beheld the emperor followed by officers of all grades, ambassadors of various powers, attendants without number, and cup-bearers, heralds, ministers, scions of royal houses, in mighty array. He saw his Majesty take the oath and receive the rochet. The eye could detect nothing but magnificence within the holy fane, as the great entrance welcomed the sovereign to St. Petronius.

Crash! and crash again! With the awful sound of a complete wreck, mingled with many shrieks and groans, drowning in a tumult of cries and prayers the uproar of the crowd around, fell a part of the gallery. A bounteous harvest of human beings also fell before the scythe-stroke of death.

No one had time to count the bruised and bleeding corses. The crowd was as steady as the emperor, when, immediately after prayer with the cardinal, as he entered, he donned the elaborately adorned cope and reappeared. The eagle was stretching his wings of pearls and rubies over the Imperial shoulders. The neck of the king was encircled with devices; but Ami saw only the Pillars of Hercules, and that significant phrase, "Plus ultra," — "More beyond," — which, since the hour of Columbus' great discovery, had taken the place of that ignorant assertion of the haughty past, "Ne plus ultra," — "No more beyond!"

As Ami saw it, he said: "'Plus ultra,' — 'More beyond!' Some spiritual voyager also will be here; and he will find some genuine fact on the other side of this our present faith, to balance with what we know. Then, in matters of the geography of the soul's life, 'Ne plus ultra!' will give way, on the crown of yonder Pope, to the glad assertion, 'Plus ultra!' — for there is always more beyond. Luther is a spiritual Columbus."

It was impossible for Ami to find Francesco, of whom he now thought, as these ideas entertained him. He would have so liked to hear Francesco, as he looked into the vista which had just then opened before his own mind. It stretched into spiritual realms far beyond, from behind the Supreme Pontiff, as there he sat before the three cardinals and the emperor, on the throne erected within the choir, through whose spaces reflections from the pontifical vessels shone, only to fade away as they touched the arras which Flanders had contributed to the hangings round about.

Somehow the figure of Henry IV., the predecessor of Charles V., standing in the snows of Canossa before the intolerable arrogance of Gregory VII., came swiftly before the eye of Ami, and vanished, as the emperor pressed his lips to the toe of Clement VII. It came again, when, after the anointing, the giving of the orb, sceptre, and sword, the placing of the half-priestly, half-kingly crown, the proclamation of high-sounding Roman titles, the clang of arms, the thunder of drums, the blare of trumpets, the roar of cannon, the shout "Evviva Carlo Imperatore!" he saw this performance repeated. Instantly Ami reflected that Charles V. was no Henry IV.; and that there lived in Germany one soul at least who in moral sovereignty surpassed them all.

What had kept Admiral Andrea Doria absent in the later moments of the pageant? Just a moment before he was not in his place; now he stood unattended nearest to the king. Ami missed Francesco.

He leaped to the conclusion that the populace had become anxious for the safety of the Pope and Charles V.; and that after the catastrophe at the gallery the suspicion of foul treachery to the emperor on the part of the Italians must have demanded the attention of the admiral. He had doubtless left Francesco, brave and true, to discover and arrest the progress of any movement against the sovereign. Ami did not overestimate the disorder and violence which lay imprisoned in the breasts of that Bolognese crowd.

While the Supreme Pontiff celebrated Mass, this self-respectful young Italian became more certain than ever that he was a protester. He was thinker enough to know that while the creed was being chanted by his Holiness, its definings were confining the intellect and hope of Europe; while the Gospels in Latin and in Greek were being chanted also by cardinal and prelate, the deeper harmonies and sweeter melodies within the misconceived words waited sadly for the lips and lives of

the common people to give them distinct utterance.
When the Pope granted plenary indulgence to all present, Ami reflected with indignant scorn upon the days
when Louise of Savoy offered her queenly hand to keep
him pure, while it was proposed that his mind should be
in league with iniquity. He threw out of his soul forever any such conception of the agony of his Redeemer
as would permit the Church to use Christ's superlative
merit to prolong a shameless infamy.

As the emperor and Clement VII. marched down the
great aisle, each holding the hand of the other, magnates
carrying their long flowing robes, an elegant baldaquin
borne above their heads, Ami thought of him who was
poor and lowly, who hungered and thirsted, who had not
a place for his head, whose crown was made of thorns,
whose white-robed ones have come up through great
tribulation.

They reached the open air. There stood this successor of Peter the poor fisherman, — the Vicar of Christ
Jesus, Clement VII.; an emperor bedecked with jewels
was holding his stirrup! This vicar of the man of Naz-
areth had given Charles V. the sceptre and orb which he
was to guard; Jesus had said, "My kingdom is not of
this world." This vicegerent of the Galilean peasant
had just crowned every devilish sentiment and Satanic
ambition which would serve the tiara of Rome; the
Redeemer had crowned his subjects, each a priest and
king, with moral power alone.

While Ami mused, the fire burned.

Was it strange that Ami should remember with joy and
hope the poverty, the heroism, the purity, the faith, the
simplicity and sublimity of Martin Luther, his father's
friend, as he saw that brocaded pontiff chatting pompously
with a scheming Cæsar Imperator beneath that glittering
canopy?

"Evviva il Pontefice e l' Imperatore! Viva Clemente

e Carlo!" shouted the multitude from balconies, windows, thronged streets, and crowded housetops.

"Where can Francesco be so long?" said the affectionate Ami, as he picked up a banneret on which flew the Imperial Eagle.

"You are wanted by Andrea Doria himself, when the procession reaches the banquet." The helmeted rider who thus spoke to Ami had signalled and had been allowed to approach the royal party.

In and out of this huge monotonous plain of ostentatious display, the silver stream of this friendship worked its way.

"What can keep Francesco so long?" asked this one soul, whose human love had been transfigured by the love of God.

The messenger shook his head and departed. The sceptre of Charles V., which for a moment was in the hand of Ami, had almost dropped from his grasp. The emperor knew not that the man who carried it looked upon those twelve Bolognese nobles who strained to bear the heavy baldaquin which sheltered his Majesty and the Pope as men who ought, at this crisis in the history of Europe, to be in better business. Emperor and Waldensian lived in the atmospheres made by different ideas. Each had thought of Luther at Worms; but through what various media had they seen him! It was not that one was Imperator and the other a servant. The difference lay in the fact that one was in league with yesterday, the other was in league with to-morrow.

As Ami beheld the gold chains of the Doctors of Laws who appeared in hoods of miniver, he seemed to see one of the last appearances of the chain as a limitation upon the scholar's soul. Clement VII. saw those chains as badges of subjection to the Church. The trumpeters made the air tremble. The drums kept the ears of the citizens weary with noise. The eye grew tired of the purple and crimson robes, the red fringes hung with pearls and gems, the red housings of the horses glittering with gold lace, silver maces, red hats on gilt staves, blue silk flags covered with lilies and golden lettering, white banners illumined by fiery crosses, and innumerable torches carried by illustrious men. Ami's heart was with Francesco. In the din and confusion he feared that his own madness might return upon him ; and now his lips moved again with the words : " Francesco — Astrée ! Astrée — Francesco ! "

At length to his weary brain the procession of Clement VII. and Charles V. became a confused mass of heralds, bishops, imperial eagles, Turkish horses, dukes, marquesses, counts, admirals, soldiers in red surcoats, colleges of cardinals in still more blazing red, tribunes in caps and cuirasses. Lorenzo Cibo, crusader and captain of the Papal Guard, carrying the image of the dead Christ ; the Gonfaloniere of Justice bearing a flag on which the word " Libertas " was written ; the sacrament carried on a horse on whose neck hung a silver bell, whose back was covered with gold and embroidery of silk ; the emperor, crowned and mantled ; the Supreme Pontiff, begemmed and adored, — these stood out from the rest of the long, rich pageant. Ami was tired out ; and the heart within him was aching with doubt. Where could Francesco be?

" Have you lost the arrow with the parchment, young man ? " said a knight who rode near, and was recognized at once as the chief attendant upon the chamberlain of the sovereign. As he spoke, he touched a large and jewelled lance.

In attitude and manner Ami was knightly enough, as he responded ; but his tongue was silent. The hated authority of both the Pope and the emperor looked at him for a long, painful moment.

" I will speak to the emperor, and satisfy his Imperial

Majesty," replied Ami; and then he tried to look contempt upon the knight. "Do you know the Admiral Andrea Doria? In the care of his friend and most chivalrous attendant, Francesco de Robo —"

"Francesco de Robo!" The knight's tone was full of intelligent astonishment and evident pain.

"Stop! May it please you to retire to another place!" urged Ami.

They withdrew from the procession, which had reached the great hall. For many minutes Ami's brain had been in chaos. Now lightning-like flashes of agony shot through his forehead. He was allowed to go: his face was like that of the dead; the King of the Romans would sleep a little before the banquet.

The knight seemed stern and cold, as the fevered lips of Ami opened to say: "The arrow which the High Chamberlain bade me keep safely, is in the safer guardianship of the best of young knights, Francesco de Robo."

The knight reined up his steed. "Young man, I know you well. By the soul of Bayard, — for I do not care for saints, — I charge you flee! Flee at my word, for your very life! You have been suspected of heresy; hence, of treason. The heralds of Francis I. in this procession have told of your history. Antonio de Leyva has a dagger in a murderous hand, waiting for your heart. Francesco de Robo was killed by the falling of the gallery! From his bleeding hand I brought this fragment of the arrow, — the quiver was stolen; and here is your ring which Francesco took from a robber. This piece of the arrow I shall give to the chamberlain. Take you the ring. Flee! flee at once!"

In a brief hour Ami was again clad as a beggar, and was in flight toward La Torre.

CHAPTER XXXIV.

WANDERINGS OF SOUL.

Spite of the mask eternal love doth wear
At times, that makes us shrink from it in fear,
Because the Father's face we cannot find,
Nor feel the presence of His love behind,
Nature at heart is very pitiful.

GERALD MASSEY.

"OH, what am I to believe? I could let all else go, if only I could hold to a faith in the goodness of this Almighty One. It is terrible that God is so powerful, if He is not kind!"

It was Vian, solitary and chilled, talking to his own soul, as he clambered up the side of one of the Alpine peaks in search of a spot upon which he could pass the night without the suffering which the unimpeded waves of cold air promised to his weary frame.

"Oh, why did an Almighty goodness ever permit me to see Alke, if having seen her she may not be mine? Omnipotent evil could hardly invent a more exquisite cruelty than this. To be trained by a vision which has every moral right to be revered and obeyed; to have been leagued with a dream which alone has made my existence valuable and my life worthy; then to have come to the glad moment when this vision, so desperately clung to, ceased being a dream and was henceforth a living reality, — a reality so surpassingly beautiful, so sacredly pure, — and in that same moment to have realized that the reality itself was quivering with yearnings to lose its life, and so to gain its life in my life ; then at last to find that the one deep and delicious kiss which made all that prophecy into history, marked the instant when we were hurled apart ! — this is a very crime against souls."

So strongly did the heart of Vian protest, in its unreasoning anguish, that his intellect was almost ready to say, " There is no God." He trembled as he remembered the last night's starless sky above him, threatening to become a permanent heaven for his soul. The wind shrieked amid the crags and pines ; and now and again the lightning bolt which leaped out of the scabbard of the midnight gloom seemed the sword of omnipotence which reached his heart.

" I know a bishop who is an atheist," he said ; and he laughed until the horror of it frightened him. " He was an atheist, because he never had a vision and had never loved. I may become one, because I have had one and have loved. By what opposite experiences do men reach the — " Vian could not say " truth."

The word " truth," like a solitary and hapless sailor, hung to the wreckage in Vian's soul. He must do something with it, for it seemed such a hapless thing. He asked the old question : " What is truth ? "

Four years and more, separated the evening of this day from the day of the attack and separation from Alke.

Vian was still suffering as a wounded man, — wounded in soul and body. The French knight Ami, on that dreadful day near La Torre, had given him a stroke with his steel which had lacerated the flesh of his shoulder ; and only the Virgil manuscript, four leaves of which had been run through by the point of Ami's sword had saved Vian's heart. In the haste with which he had been dragged away by the affrighted knights, nothing was done to provide against the loss of blood. The inhumanity of Vian's captors softened a little under the influence of the wine which they obtained from an innkeeper whose premises they raided for food; and the wife of the innkeeper was allowed to apply a plaster to the cut, and give some salve to their prisoner.

Vian had found out, before the French knights had gone far from the scene of their anticipated triumph at Gaspar Perrin's house, that they were actually panic-stricken by the complete victory achieved by the Waldensians. They were but a fragment of the contingent which Francis I. had loaned for the service of the Pope on that occasion; they were fearful of being pursued by the mountaineers, of whose daring and ability they had the most extravagant notions: they were leaderless, believing that Ami had been killed by Vian in the cottage; and where they were, or whither they were fleeing, they did not know.

Soon Vian, who appreciated the value of these features of their discomfiture to the safety of his own hopes, had begun to plan his escape. The night of Nov. 6, 1529, came upon the French knights, as they paused for rest in a narrow defile, into which fell the discordant echoes of a brawling stream that tumbled down over a confused mass of rocks. The guard had often slept at his side. He might fall asleep on that night. Amid the noises made by that furious cataract, Vian might make his escape. A storm was also coming on, and the very heavens seemed his ally. Never did the accordant tinkling of a thousand rills sound so melodiously as did the coarse plunges and ugly roar of that cataract. Never did Vian listen with such rapture to the growl of the thunder. Never quivered he with such fear and foreboding, as when the eyes of the storm-god were aflame in the dark, and in those flashes the cruel guard looked into his pale but determined face.

"Listen!" said the knight whom, for lack of a leader, each obeyed.

"A horseman!" ventured the prisoner.

"A Waldensian! you are praying?" said his guard.

Before Vian's silence had fully answered that query, a band of monks disguised as soldiers entered the defile, and exhibiting a gilt cross, found themselves welcomed by the hungry, frightened, and lost representatives of his Majesty Francis I. and his Holiness Clement VII.

"We are here to show you the road to your friends, who long to be back in Paris, where are no Waldensians, and to conduct you thither. We are also come to carry this false-hearted servant of the Pope to a suitable prison."

"Roast his flesh at La Torre!" cried out the guard. "I have seen better than he sizzle and fry at the capital."

"We have a strong prison many leagues from this spot. To that dungeon he shall be taken," was the answer.

For four years had the thick walls of one of the dungeons of the Holy Catholic Church surrounded the life and the hope of Vian. Silence as to the place on God's world in which his cell was located; silence as to the length or character of the tortures of which he was continually forewarned and many of which he did not escape; silence as to that checkered past, with its comedies and tragedies, its joys and agonies, its Alke; silence as to the future, which had now come to be inhabited with ghosts and doubts, — silence amid echoes of chains, cries of pain, whisperings of death, had oppressed the brain and presided over the heart of Vian for four long years.

At last one night Vian, who had feigned sickness, was visited by the guardsman, who had now made himself certain that the recalcitrant monk had no purpose of escaping.

The curious guard had brought with him Vian's coins and the manuscript; and he was determined to extract from him the story of their significance. Curiosity had made prudence forget herself.

Vian saw his opportunity. The silent walls could not cry out. He seized the arms upon the guard, who groaned as he received a blow from his own bludgeon. Every key which Vian tried, found the secret of the lock. Out into the valley he ran, and was free again.

When, at the opening of this chapter, we found him crawling upon the shelf of rocks which was sheltered from the raw wind, he had enjoyed five days of liberty; but he knew nothing as to where he was or whither he should go. He was free; and he would guard that freedom with life itself.

He had lost dates and days from his mind; but it was November, 1533.

Soon morning came. From gray to blue the sky deepened. Pale wreaths of dreamy white floated along the mountain summits. Resinous odors filled the air; and as the blue above grew more intense, Vian found his eyes, which for so long had even tended to confine his thoughts to the walls, running their new roadways into the unexplored infinities above him. A few chestnuts which he had kept for his hunger, at sunrise had sufficed to calm his fiercest demands; and carefully avoiding breaking open again the wound which had recently showed signs of healing, he had so turned his body that the full depth of the sky was above him; and Vian was thinking of Alke and the almightiness of God.

" ' What is truth?' Yes; I went to sleep, last night, with that question on my lips. Why need I care, if there is none almighty to be true? I do not care; for I am hungry now. Yet that is not truly *I*, who said I did not care for what truth may be, because I am hungry. *Truly* I? — what a strange thing is language! One puts words out of sight, and they rise again. *Truly* — Ah! we Pythagoreans believed the soul lived again;

but in actual life, it is the body. The idea dies; the word, its body, turns up again. I care not for *truth*, but I cannot talk long without that word 'truly.'"

A bouquetin went springing over him; and a gier-eagle swooped down near enough to find out that the ragged mass was not carrion.

"That bird thought it scented carrion. Well, I would be carrion itself, if I could honestly say I cared not what is truth! Who so made me, and for what? I know not. This I do know. *I* must confess an interest in 'truth,' whatever it is. Truth is to me what this light is to my eyes. What is truth?"

We have seen Vian, with the sub-prior of Glastonbury, struggling with the fear that intellectual and spiritual anarchy must surely come, if there happened to the Church and the Pope any such changes as the Reforming movement seemed to contemplate. Vian was a lover of order, organization, and strength. He looked with grave foreboding upon the prospect of an England without some sort of authoritative head and leader of religious interests. Yet he could never honestly acknowledge the supremacy of the Pope in his own brain, nor the right of the Church to condemn any man for refusing to believe the monstrous stories of saints and ceremonies.

Out of all that disaster into which his faith in Rome or in Pythagoreanism had fallen, rose one fact, so beautiful, so true, — Alke.

True, after a manner very common to mankind, Vian at Gaspar's home had accepted Jesus Christ as his Saviour; but Alke was far too prominent in the transaction to make the Christ, at such a crisis as this which involved the loss of Alke, a saving power in Vian's character and life. If ever he was to realize Jesus Christ as his Saviour, he must come to that realization through such an experience as would carry his intellectual nature; for Vian's regnant strength did not lie in his emotions or even in his conscience. His experience would certainly be as different from Ami's as were their souls.

Through many weeks of effort to avoid those monks and guardsmen who haunted the mountain paths for their escaped prisoner, he dodged their shrewdest guesses as to his hiding-places; and he also dodged the old forces of belief, which were even farther away than they from his real self. Alke — she, the little mate in his dream at Lutterworth — had led him into purity and honor; "now," said he, "she must lead me into faith and hope, if I am to reach either. But the one power which might make me true is denied me!"

He sobbed these last words, as one evening he stood so painfully alone in the desolation of the Alps, while the sinking sun was making the whole west a living flame. As against this sheen of intolerable red he stood gathering his rags about him, he seemed a black monolith whose edges burned with resistless fires.

"Ah, it is the truth which makes her true!" and Vian persuaded himself to strive to pray to it after a while, when night had entirely come. But it is easy to forget an abstraction, especially in the dream of such a personality as was Alke; and Vian went to sleep thinking only of her.

Every morning when the purple linnets flew into the crisp air, which was so stimulating to his thought and so exhaustive upon the poor supplies which he now dared to beg for his hunger, he looked upward to the snowy crests with these words in mind: "No man hath seen God at any time: the only begotten Son, he hath declared Him." But for many days the refulgent cloud which swept between the summit and Vian's eyes seemed big with prophecy of revelation.

"Why need I have a creed at all? Or if I need a creed, let the Church make it! Ah, no! the Church is composed of human beings, and" — he was thinking of

his dungeon and the tortures he had seen — "such human
beings ! They are inhuman.   These, notwithstanding,
are the men who keep the unity of the faith ; these
are the guardians of orthodoxy.   Oh, there never was
such heresy ! Besides, I have long ago renounced the
dominion of the Church over me."

So vanished the idea that the Church ever could
legislate a creed into his soul.

"Why need I believe?"   He was attempting to cross
an abyss at the moment, and he soon was saying : "I
should fail, if I doubted now.   Oh, I must have a faith
or perish ! "

For that winter he had hired himself to an ignorant
mountaineer, and had found out from him the direction
in which he could pursue his course to Basle.   Oftentimes as he looked out upon the snow, which lay like
a permanent enamel upon the fields, he believed that
spring-time might find living seeds beneath the cold,
glittering doubt which had overspread his soul.

Would spring-time ever come?   The fagots which he
gathered for his somewhat exacting employer had grown
and fallen in a vast amphitheatre which was now one white
splendor.

"Oh," he said once, "that I could hear Alke's voice
in this place ! " Then he amused himself with the notion
that as the mountaineers warmed themselves by these
fagots within the little home, so perhaps he was barely
keeping his mind at work with the relics of a once green
and beautiful faith.   But the peaks rose in such ghostly
procession and stretched their line so far toward the
north, and even the quivering orange which remained
for a moment against the battlemented sky-line faded
so soon, that his worn brain lost the significance of
its own ideas, and he sat looking out of vacancy into
vacancy.

"What is truth?"   Vian had said this so often in the

sharp air, as he had looked up to the frosty glory of a single crag, that the children called him, for want of his real name, "Truth." Oh, how often the little flaxen-haired girl who sat on his knee in the evening as he sang to her of the fathomless crimson of the Alpine morning, sent a sword into his soul, as she begged him to sing again, calling him "Truth!" "Truth!"

Spring-time at length glowed one day over the frozen mirror of ice, — a sky beneath reflecting the heavens above. The drifting clouds caught the prophecy of summer in the morning; and all day Vian saw it flickering in the great gallery builded of rock, which was always full of contending light and gloom. The illimitable gulf which lay below him was being disturbed by a venturesome stream, which hurried away from the dissolving slopes. Turquoise, beryl, and amethyst soon blazed forth where the mountains had been adorned with ice-covered flutings, like great lines of polished steel. Green edges appeared along the streams, and the awful monotony of trackless white was broken. Spring had come; and Vian, whose heart seemed bursting as they said "farewell" to "Truth," departed, going toward the north.

Provided with arquebus and flint, he found himself able to obtain game; and such other necessaries were purchased of mountaineers as made his progress far less painful than that of months before. All other problems were simple enough, however, in comparison with his problem of faith.

Long before Professor Tyndall, as he tells us, read Canon Mozley on "Miracles" in the Alps, did Vian find it possible to lose the personal God in the midst of Nature's sublimest spectacles. Long before Frederick W. Robertson wandered in the Tyrol, saying at length, though he had left much of the still unburied remains of English dogmatism behind him, "It is right to do right,"

Vian was asking himself, not "What is right?" — for his
conscience did not lead him, — but "What is truth?"
Long before John Henry Newman mentioned the mountain solitude as a spot for meditation and the strengthening
of faith, Vian was trying to find a seat of authority somewhere between the individual reason and the collective
Rome. "What is truth?" he still cried.

One day late in autumn he was skirting the northern
spur of an unknown range of peaks, and had just succeeded in avoiding an abrupt cliff, when he saw crouch-
ing before him a being so hideous, so debased, yet so
human, that his eye removed its gaze from him at once,
and sought to lose its memory in the distances above
him.

"That," said Vian, who had become accustomed to
hearing his own voice in the solitudes, — "that is the riddle
of this universe, — this pure blue sky, a vast infinity of
beauty, overarching that loathsome thing! Ah, the good
is too far away from the evil! The sky is not near
enough to the earth. Nay, if there were nothing but
what is below, no sky, we should not see such a monstrous thing! The wrong and the right, the bad and
the good, the earth and the sky— Horrible creature!"
and Vian looked up to heaven from the disgustful object
at his feet, and said, "O Almighty! — but art Thou
good?"

It was a cretin, such as the reader has doubtless seen
in his excursions through the valley of Aosta or the
Rhone.

This uncouth and distorted being was rolling in the
leaves, as appeared to be his habit on seeing a man
approach. His idiocy was most brutish. Great goitres
were protruding from his neck, and foul sores had eaten
their way over his scalp. His hands were like the talons
of a bird of prey. Gabbling incessantly in the patois of
utter idiocy, his mouth seemed the opening to a pit of

evil. He staggered toward Vian; and precipitantly did the friend of the late Cardinal Wolsey flee from him.

"Doubtless he has been brought out here to starve to death. Poor, hideous thing! What is truth?"

Vian was making the vain attempt to lose his reminiscence of the gibbering and foul cretin, when his eye swept across the vague blue mist, which lingered above the black rocks, beneath which grew the late crimson flowers. The haziness of his belief was sure of a sort of defence in that dream-like air. Wreaths of vapor were visiting the spires and pines; and just now he loved to look upon them rather than upon the sharp, definite grandeur which lifted the snow-clad pinnacles above. Every time he had seen the huge ledge flush with the waning day, "What is truth?" had thundered in his soul. Why did it now seem such a meaningless question?

"Ah!" said Vian, who pitilessly examined his own soul with Alke as a search-light, "I must not lose my interest in that question. What is truth? The truth has made her true; but I am not so clear-sighted as I was before that contorted and blear-eyed wretch crossed my path. Ha! could he have blinded me?"

Vian just then found in his mind one of the texts which he had learned from that Wycliffe New Testament. It came in response to his old query, "What is truth?"

"I am the truth!"

"Well," said Vian, as he clambered on, "Jesus Christ, who said 'I am the truth,' I have never seen or known, as I really believe, except in that hour with little Alke. We did not know him at Glastonbury. It was Mary the Virgin and the saints there. It is sure that many of the stories of these I cannot believe. They are untrue. How much may I believe of him whom I have not seen? Others *saw* him. Yes; but not as *my* Saviour. I must see him as *my* Saviour before what they saw of him can be believed by me. Ah! I remember another text, — now that I am resolved to go back and give these chestnuts to the poor brute. Would I had not to do this; for I could come to the truth if I should not see that mindless creature again !"

No, Vian; the truth lies concealed in the rags of the idiot. Whoso most needs any man, him does that man most need.

Vian climbed up and down, over the rocks, and waded a stream to reach the hunched and vacant-eyed cripple, who hobbled toward him in the glow of the sunset. *"He that hath done it unto the least of these hath done it unto me."* This sentence wreathed the unkempt head of the bleared cretin with an aureole.

"Unto me?" — Vian's eye was becoming more clear. "Unto me?" — he could now endure the suffocating smell. Yes; something was making Vian true.

"The truth made Alke true," — he had said that himself.

"Unto me?" — the senseless mass of flesh rolled his head from side to side, and falling among the leaves again, clapped his hooked hands.

Could Vian be mistaken? Something was lifting him up; and as he was lifted he saw more. "Is it the idiot whom I am seeking?" said he. "No; the Christ it is."

"Unto me?"

Something was actually saving Vian from his lower self to his higher self. Some one — the idiot or the Christ — was his Lord. He knew it was the real Christ.

"I do not need Rome or reason to tell me with authority," said he, as he fed the chattering clay. "This is a matter of fact; experience authorizes what I would tell Alke, if I could — Oh, how good is the Almighty ! The Christ, who is the truth, does save me."

On, over the mountains, fed daily by Vian's hand, grunting his gratitude and following him like a dog, did the cretin go. The hand which had touched that of Katherine of Arragon, and had helped to write Henry's attack on Luther, washed the cretin's head. The kindness which had saved Astrée at the " Field of the Cloth of Gold " showered its luxuriant blessings upon this creature, whom Vian regarded with more reverence than he ever wasted on the papal nuncio.

One day death parted the wanderers. The incurable malady had completed the paralysis of the cretin's frame, and in the delicious sunshine Vian covered the body. He knelt by the side of the pile of green branches, whose resinous odor made the only incense, and thanked God, and consecrated his soul anew to the service of the truth.

Vian's theological difficulties were solved in the beginning of his Christian experience. No one knew better than he how little an uninspired life can get out of an inspired book. Miracles and prophecies came to be the natural flower of a Personality who had made himself so real and had created such a gospel in Vian's soul. He often asked in after years that his tomb should bear this inscription : " He hath the witness in himself."

It is spring-time again, but it is also 1535 ; and we are in the presence of two men, — one a man of near middle age, whose brown hair has streaks of gray, whose forehead is even now seamed with two wrinkles which tell the tale of anxiety and hope, whose clothing is but a recent purchase by means of coins earned in the autumn preceding, at service under a respectable vintner, and whose heart is still full of hope ; the other is now old and feeble, his sunken cheeks denoting disease, his eye still keen and restless, his head tremulous, and his conversation threading the years of his own past and the possibilities of his guest's future.

One is Vian; the other is Erasmus of Rotterdam. They are in Basle; the Rhine gleams two hundred feet below the terrace. Limes and chestnut-trees have sifted the radiance which falls upon the paths which run toward the cathedral; and the old scholar, leaning hard upon the arm of his friend, has just promised him, as they look down upon the boats, that the letter to Henry VIII., which he has written for him, will certainly admit him at once to the king's service.

"It is a small payment toward the debt I owe to you for the Virgil manuscript," said Erasmus. "May Heaven give you Alke!"

The coins which Erasmus left with little Alke many years before were sufficient to have identified Vian, if the scholar had not known and believed him at the first.

Vian's tale made him a hero to the illustrious man.

Erasmus had detailed to him every circumstance which had wrought such changes in England as would make Vian welcome. Henry's rebellion against the Pope; the marriage to Anne Boleyn; his need of such help as Vian might give to the colleges, — these overshadowed the axe which had beheaded Thomas More, and the terror by which Thomas Cromwell ruled. Erasmus could not detain Vian, much as he loved him; and on the following day he bade him farewell.

CHAPTER XXXV.

AT COURT AGAIN.

We are never without a pilot. When we know not how to steer, and dare not hoist a sail, we can drift. The current knows the way, though we do not. — EMERSON.

IT was near the close of the year 1535, when Vian entered again into the service of the English crown. Before 1529 Wolsey was manager of the crown; since 1529 Henry himself had worn it.

Even Anne Boleyn, queen and beautiful woman, welcomed the returning exterminator of the Waldensians back to court with the words, —

"You have been a long while from us, and I fear the Waldensians still exist to trouble his Holiness."

"Your gracious Majesty," replied Vian, with graceful courtesies, "the severest trouble of his Holiness is not with the Waldensians, but rather with your royal husband. As for the Waldensians — " Vian was about to say that he hoped at least one of them still lived and loved him. The ringing laugh of the queen and the silence of Vian's aching heart showed him how nearly together humor and sorrow lie in the human soul and its experiences.

The main facts of the recent history of the English court had come to Vian from Erasmus at Basle. His new point of view had not diminished his interest in the trifles which associated themselves with events so decisive ; and his old friends—the retainers of Wolsey, whom Henry VIII. had spared or invited into the royal service —vied with one another in offering, as commodities serviceable in interesting converse, their accounts of Wolsey, Anne Boleyn, and the Pope, in exchange for the meagre sentences which allowed their eyes to look in upon the country of the Waldensians, the struggles of a soul amid the Alps, the last days of Master Erasmus at Basle.

The story of the most trusted retainer was a very sad one.

On the very day in September, 1529, upon which Vian, having left England to arrange for the destruction of recalcitrant Waldensians, was extracting some interesting opinions from the papal nuncio at Dover, Henry VIII. had left Woodstock for Grafton in Northamptonshire. At the former place, for more than a fortnight, the king had hunted stags with Anne Boleyn, over the same territory upon which another Henry had pursued with success the affections of the sweet Rosamond. At the latter place, September 19, his Majesty was staying with Anne Boleyn, talking over with her the already deep disgrace into which the illustrious cardinal had fallen.

" I love you, sweetheart, full well; but I cannot entirely discard so great a mind," said the king, who already knew that Norfolk and Suffolk together would make but a pygmy compared with the able but fallen statesman.

" No, my love and king ! but cardinals such as Wolsey are not free from the sentiment of revenge," answered Anne Boleyn, who was quite sure that her royal lover had a lingering affection for one who had fallen because he had served his master too loyally, and whom she desired her lover should hate or despise.

" I fear not ! " cried Henry VIII., with a sharpness which Anne Boleyn never forgot, until she too had fallen under that same haughty displeasure,—" I fear not ! I need him not. Some one else shall found the universities, if the revenues of abbeys are to be converted into scholars. The cardinal's secretary shall be the king's secretary. I shall distrust Cromwell and Gardiner no more."

The latter remark was especially pleasing to Anne Boleyn, for Sir Thomas and Norfolk had each expressed their admiration for his parts; and now that the king had distinctly substituted Gardiner for Wolsey in his confidence, she believed all would go well.

Before this, Wolsey, who knew full well that his end was nigh at hand, had solaced himself with the thought that in sending Vian upon such a mission he had at least commended himself to the favor of the Pope. Campeggio, who saw the cardinal September 14, had assured him that his Holiness could not forget such an act of loyalty, even though it came from his Grace in an hour of great extremity.

Vian had not touched the soil of France before he was informed that Queen Katherine herself knew of the disgrace of the cardinal.

"The ship is now in a storm which will plunge sailors and passengers to the bottom. Everybody is seeking a means of escape. The cardinal expects to be forsaken; the time-servers will refuse to go down in the wreck." This, also, the nuncio had said to Vian at Calais.

"Would I were with him!" was Vian's reply, as he had looked back toward England.

"No," said the nuncio, earnestly; "his friend and servant could not otherwise be so valuable to his failing fortunes as in doing what will commend his Eminence to the Pope."

Vian had felt, even then, that somehow the issue was not going to be a great triumph for either himself or the cardinal.

Before Vian had advanced a single step on that jour-

ney toward San Michele, even the servants of Wolsey
were made certain that all was lost. The court was a
thing of the past; the commission of the legates was re-
voked; Parliament was sure to impeach Wolsey. Nothing valuable was left. He had often looked upon the advance of the Reformation with favor; now the fact of its
progress held within it no comfort for him, for his most
trusted servant, Vian, was, at the moment of the disaster,
on his way to crush it among the prophets, — the
Waldensians.

"I am not sure that even his Holiness will look favorably upon me now," said the tottering minister, as he
grasped this solitary pillar of power.

On Sunday morning, September 19, Cardinal Wolsey and Cardinal Campeggio stood before the gates of
Woodstock. Only a single lodging was prepared, and
this was for Campeggio. However, Henry Norris, groom
of the stole to the king, provided for Wolsey. Then
came the interview with the superseded court. Norfolk
insulted, and Anne Boleyn reproached, the mighty ruin.
Henry VIII., however, seemed to feel the dignity of such
an august personality, when alone he stood with the man
who had served him with such incomparable ability, at
the large window, and in low tones discoursed of things
past and to come. When at night Wolsey took his way
toward Master Empson's house, the wrath of Anne Boleyn and that of Norfolk, who suspected that the cardinal
was restored to the confidence of the king, knew no
bounds.

The next day, instead of meeting at Woodstock this
man of eminent genius, as he had promised, the King of
England rode with Anne Boleyn to behold a piece of
ground which she desired to have for a new park. Now
Wolsey's heart was riven. Soon Campeggio was at Dover,
pausing on his way to Rome; and at the hour when Wolsey's beloved servant, Vian of Glastonbury, was uttering

love's sweetest and most broken accents to a Waldensian
maiden, Oct. 9, 1529, the greatest man of politics in the
sixteenth century had just forsaken his magnificent train
and the glittering insignia of office, with which, but a few
hours before, he had left Westminster Hall for the last
time, and was writing a piteous letter in which he called
himself, in words which upon the written page seem yet
to tingle with agony: "Your Grace's most prostrate,
poor chaplain, creature, and bedesman, T. Card. Ebor.
Miserrimus."

That sickening signature was read at the conclusion of
a letter which was addressed to Henry VIII., which any
student of English State papers will find in part as
follows : —

"Surely, most gracious king, the remembrance of my folly,
with the sharp sword of your Highness' displeasure, hath so
penetrate my heart that I cannot but lamentably cry . . . and
say, ' Sufficit ; nunc contine, piissime rex, manum tuam.' "

At length, at Leicester Abbey gates, November 26,
the pitiable cardinal stood, saying, " Father Abbot, I am
come hither to leave my bones among you ; " and three
days afterward, the man who had breathed into the island
the spirit which has made the Englishman of to-day self-
respectful, had closed his lips forever.

Over and over again had his old friends at Whitehall
told this story to Vian. It never failed to interest him,
though his position was changed.

Of course he eagerly devoured everything which helped
to complete the picture which was making in his mind
of the fall of the great cardinal, the advance of Thomas
Cromwell, and the development of the plan of breaking
up the monasteries, to which now he was more attached
than ever before ; for the future was widening out of that
immediate past. He soon found out that his sovereign
Henry VIII., who had welcomed him most heartily into

his service, looked upon the dissolution of the abbeys and other religious houses, not simply as an event most desirable for Oxford and Cambridge, into whose treasuries Wolsey had proposed to divert the revenues, but rather as an event which would so enlarge other personal privileges, and further convince the Papal See, against which His Majesty had rebelled, that England would make herself absolutely independent of a distinctively Romish policy.

"England against Rome," said Vian. He could not help thinking again of the Wycliffite letters. "Ah!" thought he, "I shall hunt Hampton Court over and over again, if need be, for those letters; and I shall show his Majesty that the heretic Wycliffe believed in England as ruled by Englishmen."

Before many days Vian had found an opportunity to read what he would never have thought of reading to Henry VIII., when, years ago, he was laboring with the king upon the attack upon Luther. His Majesty was delighted to get the fresh, sinewy phrases with which Wycliffe had combated the hierarchical notion of the State. "By my troth," said Henry, as he read Wycliffe's deliverances against papistical assumption, "he was a bold and just disputer. Would that he were alive at this hour! There be none so powerful as he in England, else I had not struggled so long alone."

"Your Majesty will let me say that Master John Wycliffe was in no wise more bold or more true than the followers of Peter Waldo, whom I went to kill. Ah, my king! I am right glad these hands shed none of that heroic blood."

Henry VIII. was all attention; but Vian, thinking it less serviceable to his cause to tell the story and repeat the faith of the Waldensians, than to appeal to the reason of the king on another and more practical matter, took a turn quite unexpected to his royal listener. "My king," said Vian, with persuasive force, "Master John Wycliffe coupled his notion of a freed nation with his labors for an open Bible. Never can the fancied authority of the Pope be so easily resisted as by the spread of Bible reading in England."

"But," laughed the haughty king, "did we not allow them to burn the books of William Tyndale, the translator of the Scriptures, when you were with Wolsey at Hampton Court? Have we not prohibited the reading of these Bibles?"

"Alas, yes! I knew not the worth of Scripture then, your Majesty; and had I known it, I could not have prevented it. It does argue great changes to think of your Majesty's court aiding a translation of the Bible for your common subjects. But, my king, you do not fear being inconsistent? Is it not true that we were once humble suppliants at the Pope's feet? Now your Majesty governs his own realm. Two years since, our Master Hugh Latimer was forbidden to preach in London; now we salute him as Bishop of Worcester."

The king smiled, as if he would say, "When you left us, Vian, our queen was Katherine of Arragon; now she is Anne Boleyn."

Vian's struggle in the mountains had made him bold. Life was going rapidly enough, as his heart knew. He cared nothing whatever about Henry's divorce. He was happy in the king's assertion of what Vian called "the English spirit," from whatever cause that assertion came. He had but one other desire which Henry VIII. could further toward fruition, — to realize as far as he might that dream which years before had come to him at Glastonbury, — England possessed of an unchained Bible.

Vian now knew perfectly well that if the Bible were to be sent into English homes at all, it must come to court with very different associations from those it brought in 1526, under Tyndale. The change of position toward the papacy on the part of Henry VIII. had not made the king or his courtiers more favorable to Lutheranism or disorder. Wolsey had died warning England against Lutheranism and a peasant war.

In 1526 Tyndale's translation of the New Testament, with the sheets of which he had escaped to Luther's city of Worms, had appeared in England, with the word "elder" instead of "priest," and "congregation" instead of "church." Now, in 1535, Vian saw that Henry VIII., who had made himself head of the Church of England, was certainly not more favorable than then to any novel idea of ecclesiasticism. Besides, Vian remembered that in 1526 six thousand copies of Tyndale's translation came back to England accompanied with Wycliffe's tracts; and although Vian had showed Henry VIII. that Wycliffe was a sort of prophet of his Majesty in asserting England's self-respect as against the Pope, he still remembered that there were many other Wycliffite notions to which the king would never assent. More — Vian's own great friend, Sir Thomas More, — oh, what a clouded memory he was to Vian! — had made impossible the success of Tyndale's translation in 1526. Now, England and Vian were to know him no longer; for he had perished in his opposition to the king but a few months before. And so strangely does a mind which is set upon certain ideas destroy its vision for anything else, that the king had little difficulty in convincing Vian, who sorely lamented More's death, that the great lawyer who had long ago become an opponent of an open Bible, had at length become an opponent of "the English spirit," which Vian had caught from Wycliffe and which he now found in Henry himself.

The universitie for whose support the monasteries must be sacrificed, were with the king; the possibility of the realization of Vian's hope of a Bible for the common people was with the king; the spirit of national independence of the Pope was with the king. It was an age of lights and shadows. Vian forgot to note the ambition or' cruelty of Cromwell, or the terror by which Henry ruled the people. He was intent on these three ends, and so Vian was himself with the king.

"I am sure," said he, to a friendly officer-at-arms, who had himself assisted at their destruction, — "I am sure that things may be managed so well that we shall never again behold a burning of Bibles at St. Paul's Cross. His Grace the Archbishop Cranmer and — I have almost called him *Master* Hugh Latimer — and the Bishop of Worcester will see to it. Ah! I knew a printer — "

Vian could not trust himself to speak of that printer, for he was none other than Alke's father, Gaspar Perrin. He walked forth dazed with the idea that the man whose closing life longed to identify itself with the printing of the Bible might have this streak of splendor in its sunset. But his mind could not dwell upon Gaspar. It soon rushed to Alke, — that bloody floor, and her face radiant with whiteness, — the agonizing farewell.

Vian was living over again that night of love and fear and that fateful day of murder and separation, when he was summoned into the king's presence.

"Once more," quoth the sovereign, "I am determined to spare no effort, my loyal and trusty Vian." The king's eyes sparkled with a light such as Vian used to behold in them when they were collaborators on the book against Luther.

The character of the light seemed the same, but upon what a different task was Vian now to be called !

The king dropped his crimson robe, and placed his bonnet, which shone with rubies and diamonds, by its side ; as he continued : "Scholars are a strange folk. More than once have I asked the illustrious Philip Melancthon of Wittenberg to be our teacher at Oxford ; but he has not been willing. Our book against Luther must have frightened him. Perhaps he knows now that we have no Pope ruling in England. I am about to bid you go and fetch him. Use all decent persuasion, Vian ; for my bonnet yonder would not purchase him. You who never killed a Waldensian " — the king smiled upon Vian — " may yet get Philip Melancthon in your tether."

With the blessing of the Primate of all England, and the promise of investiture with the Order of the Garter, Vian set out for Wittenberg.

" You are not a knight such as those whose legs bore the leathern band in Palestine ; but I am as powerful as Richard, even he of the Lion Heart, and I swear to you the garter if you have happy issue for my scheme."

These words followed Vian all the way to Wittenberg. But before him was the vision of his little mate at Lutterworth ; and by day and night it never left the sky save when the memory of Alke took its place.

CHAPTER XXXVI.

AN UNEXPECTED MEETING.

The heart is a small thing, but desireth great matters. It is not suffi-
cient for a kite's dinner, yet the whole world is not sufficient for it. —
QUARLES.

THE dull and sleepy town of Wittenberg had hardly
made itself ready for the glowing daytime which
was overspreading its towers and streets, when, by the aid
of a light which poured into one of the little upper windows of a room in Philip Melancthon's home, a man,
whose face bore signs of his having come close upon
middle life, roused from his sleep, took from his wallet a
letter, which was in the handwriting of Erasmus of Rotterdam, and began to read, as he had done the day
before many times. It was dated at Basle. The letter
was addressed to Gaspar Perrin. These were some of
the fragments upon which his eyes remained in fixed
gaze : —

"My own life is near its close. I can do little more. Well
do I remember when your hospitable kindness took me into
your cottage. It must be more than twenty years since you
told me that I had loosened an avalanche. Surely your
words were wise. Even now we know not where the avalanche may stop. Luther is contumacious and violent, and
in England the king is head of the Church . . . One thing I
may do — ay, two things — even yet. I thank you for the
manuscript of Virgil. It is better in my hands than in the

hand of the Capuchins. . . . I know this must astonish you.
. . . Where did I obtain it? . . . One night . . . he came
to my lodging . . . very ragged and weary. I recognized
him at once . . . long, brown hair, and noble grace of manner. . . . It was Vian, whom as a boy I had known at Glastonbury Abbey . . . the whole story of his love . . . had
placed the manuscript next his heart. The parchment saved
his life. He had made me sure with the coins, which I remember giving to your child . . . love for Alke knows no
boundaries. I pitied him, and asked much concerning his
years in the mountains . . . by faith a thorough Protestant,
— not like Luther, but like Melancthon . . . influence with the
King of England, to whom I sent Vian. Henry VIII. has so
changed his ideas with respect to the Pope that Vian will be
welcomed to his service . . . badly wounded, yet Vian did
not appear to cherish a tithe of resentment against his assailant . . . piteously said to me, 'May God grant I did not
kill Ami! I never had done him harm. He could not remain even as a prisoner in the presence of my sweet Alke
without being brought to the Saviour.' May this letter, my
last to any, find you in good health."

Philip Melancthon summoned his guest to the morning
meal at the moment when he was lying there, reading
the last sentences over and over again. This letter had
already thrown a bow of hope over Alke's storm-covered
life.

That guest in the room at Melancthon's house was
Ami Perrin, the Waldensian, who had already been with
Melancthon for a fortnight, and had been asked to become
secretary to the Reformer.

What was Ami doing in Wittenberg?

Since his return from Bologna, from which city he was
fleeing when we last saw him, he had taken his place as
the strongest adviser of the Barbés of the valleys; and
he was now on an embassy from the synod just held at
San Jean, to consult with Philip Melancthon with regard
to the attitude of the mountaineers toward the Swiss
Reformation under William Farel and Zwingli. Alke, who

had through these years conducted the correspondence of the Waldensians with Zwingli, Farel, and Luther, had not needed to ask Ami to take with him the letter from Erasmus when Ami set out for Wittenberg, for Ami knew her thoughts, and for his own soul's sake he desired to find news of Vian.

"I may get some news of him from England through Philip Melancthon," said the loyal brother, who had pledged his soul to omit nothing which by any chance could bring Alke's lover to this widowed soul.

"God bless you, Ami!" she had answered with trembling hopefulness.

That word, that face, that hopeful kiss of Alke's, which, as she touched Ami's lips with hers, seemed anxious for only Vian's lips again, had followed him ; and on the day of which we write in Wittenberg, even before the noon had looked down into the struggling old streets, there had entered into that quaint gabled house, which is still pointed out to tourists in Old College Street, the man whom Ami had wronged, whom he had tried to murder, who had once prevented him from murdering his own sister, — Alke's beloved Vian.

In the great arch at that historic window Ami was soon telling Melancthon such a tale of love, remorse, hatred, and hope as the gentle Reformer had never heard. For Ami at once had recognized Vian, as he looked down into the street and beheld the English gentlemen at the master's door. Instantly the Waldensian, who knew the gravity of the crisis, and who had unconsciously assumed the spirit and attitude of a French knight, had begged Melancthon to delay introducing him to the special messenger of Henry VIII. until he should have an opportunity of explaining the difficulties of the situation.

"Catherine, gentle one!" said the Reformer to his wife, who was passing into another apartment, "you

must hear this strange story ; " and handing her the letter
of Erasmus, Melancthon asked Ami to tell the story again.
But as the Waldensian began again, the excitement of his
mind was too intense.

" Perhaps you know what is sufficient to allow me, at
all costs, to make reparation to a wronged man, even in
your house. Oh, this mighty moment ! Believe me, my
friends, not even my own concern to do righteousness
unto Vian is equal to my anxiety to tell him of Alke's
abiding love. God help me ! "

" God guide thee ! " said Catherine Melancthon.

Ami had asked to meet Vian alone. The rain was
falling in torrents without, and now and then a thunder-
peal shook the town. Darkness had so far overspread
the sky that Catherine and her servants had lit the
lights within the room opposite the apartment for study.
Luther's Bible lay on the little table ; and a print
which represented the bold face of the Reformer hung
over the open fireplace, in which fagots were burning
brightly.

The introduction which Melancthon proposed was unnecessary, and was never entirely spoken. Vian, not
knowing that Ami was alive, having no such clear memory of him as that of his groans and pale face, having
been for all these years the victim of his horrible fears,
exclaimed, " Ami ! "

The Waldensian, not knowing but that his first word
would tear the hope from his sister's soul, and certain
only of this that he had cruelly wronged Vian, trembled
from head to foot as he uttered the one word " Vian ! "

Gratitude so throbbed in each voice that the abyss
between them was half bridged.

" What ! have you come to curse me, — me, who
never wronged you ? " said the Englishman, who stepped
into the full firelight, his doublet of velvet showing an in-
wrought design which involved the arms of Saint George,

and his face, in which Ami had a far graver interest, becoming the playground of agitating memories and passions.

"No," said Ami, once more as knightly as of old; "I, who have wronged *you*, have besought this interview—"

A thunder-peal crashed above the house, and Vian heard not the next words. The lightning which had preceded it was not more brilliant than was the emerald ring which alone gave Ami's dress a reminiscence of days at court.

"I offer you the hand and heart of a Christian," said he, advancing toward Vian.

"Without a stain of jealousy upon them?" asked the other.

"Even thus unspotted," replied Ami, whose plain costume made his manliness appear more chivalric. The meagre garments which clothed him, the white radiance upon his sad but noble face, the tears which glistened in his eyes more splendidly than did the jewels on Vian's collar, the solemn grandeur of his fine voice, had gone as one sweet, resistless appeal to Vian's heart.

"I can trust you," murmured he, as responsive tears came into his eyes, — "I can trust you if you have trusted Christ."

"With everything," added Ami, as Vian grasped his hand, — "with everything."

"There is *one* thing —" began Vian, unable to rein his hope.

"Ah! there are many," interrupted Ami, whose conscience must be heard, though every voicing memory should first cry out its appeal.

"Only *one* thing!" said Vian, as he paused and walked to the window, which rattled with the storm.

"The one thing?" observed Ami. "Yes; do you grant me pardon?"

"Ah, knight! friend! you have been pardoned long

since. I know the force of love's current; I have thought
that if I were once — "

"And are you yet a lover?"

"That is *the one thing!*" cried out Vian; "and I — "

The storm without was furious. An uprooted tree was
thrown against the house, and the window was broken.
Blinding sheets of rain filled the air without, and the
rain was blown into the room; but they heeded it
not.

"I loved the Waldensian maiden whom you sought to
kill. Forgive me! She loved me also."

Vian's eyes glared for an instant, but he regained
control. He kept it only for an instant.

"My sister, Alke!" exclaimed Ami. "She is my
own sister!"

"Wretch! But, oh! did you — "

"No; I knew not my own sister. Gaspar Perrin
was my father, *is* my father; and Alke — "

"What bedlam is this?" said Vian, as the storm again
broke in upon Ami's words, and the bewildered mind of
Vian struggled in the darkness which Ami had created
before him.

"On my troth, Ami, you have her eyes." The excited
lover looked back over the years into Alke's eyes, as he
gazed into Ami's. "On my life, those are her nostrils.
Knight, I believe it. But tell me — "

"And Alke loves you, Vian, — loves you even yet."

The door was opened at this unpropitious moment.
Catherine, — always a good housewife, — fearing the
desolation of such a storm, entered with as much of reti-
cence and courtesy as she possessed at such a crisis;
and Ami said at once, —

"We must beg pardon for our loud speech."

"It must have been serious talk to have made you
careless of such a gale as never before swept upon Wittenberg," she replied; and proceeding to ask the servants

to repair the broken window, offered Ami and Vian another room.

Neither Vian nor Ami cared what covered the floor or adorned the walls of that room. The conversation had too bold a current to feel the slightest interruption. Ami lost no time in telling him the story of his childhood and capture, his conversion, and the later movements in which he had been engaged with his old friend William Farel.

As soon as Vian's mind had grasped the main points of his tale, he cut short every detail, and begged to know all about Alke, whom he felt that he had never really loved until now. Her widowed life, her unceasing ministry, her passionate love for Vian, — these furnished a theme which Ami enlarged upon again and again. Vian forgot everything about the gentlemen of Henry's court, who were half exhausted in waiting below.

Would Melancthon go to England? Vian did not know that any one had asked him. The mind of this ambassador to the Reformer had lost sight even of Henry VIII. Alke lived, and Alke loved him!

Vian was now to proclaim himself a knight in deed and in truth.

"Ami, you were once a lover," said he, with a strange feeling that the ground upon which he had now ventured was once dangerous territory.

"I *am* a lover," answered Ami; and the emotions which throbbed in his heart trembled on his lips.

"May I ask you? — oh, I shall attempt to be as knightly as you have been, — does Astrée live?"

Ami was almost overborne. His own sorrow looked so sad, so desperate in the presence of Vian's joy. The old days of Amboise were upon him, — that hour at Chambord; the struggle in the stone apartment; the quivering, beautiful woman, who clung to him at last in spite of his evil heart.

"Oh, Vian," he sobbed, "she believed me dead; so also did you?"

"Yes."

"Evil days came upon her. She had no confidence in the character of the religious houses in France. She asked to be taken to England, and is now in a nunnery in Somerset."

"In Somerset?" The eyes of Vian were fixed upon Ami's lips.

"In Somerset."

"Does she love you still?"

"Ah, Vian, such love as hers never dies."

"By the power of Henry VIII., and by my soul, — give me your hand, Ami! — here I swear — and I can perform it, as God lives in heaven, Ami! — if Astrée loves you as you love her, she shall yet be yours."

"I can only bring to you her who waits your invitation, — the sweetest of sisters — "

"Alke! Alke!"

"I shall decline to become secretary to Master Melancthon. I am away to the mountains."

"And I first to the throne of Henry VIII. and then to Somerset."

CHAPTER XXXVII.

DELIVERANCE AND LOVE.

Love makes all things possible. — SHAKSPEARE.

HISTORICAL students — and those who care nothing for history have long ago deserted us — know that Henry VIII. was compelled to see Oxford get on without Philip Melancthon. Let us add that Ami never became secretary to the latter, and that very soon after the eventful day at Wittenberg, Vian, who had become a special commissioner of his Majesty for the suppression of the monasteries, had the joy of presenting at court his wife Alke. Ami had, by Vian's advice, become secretary to Master Miles Coverdale, in whose genius and industry Vian had at length so led the court to repose its confidence that before many months an authorized translation of the Bible should be the possible possession of every Englishman. Long since Ami and Alke had learned Vian's language from the lips of their father Gaspar Perrin, who many years before at the printing-press of Aldus had begun its study with diligence, and who now, a most capable printer even in his old age, had been of the greatest service to Miles Coverdale and his associates in giving excellence to the type in which the Scriptures were to make their appearance.

Gaspar Perrin had, with Alke's help, made the drawing for the well-known titlepage. The inscription, " Thy

word is a lantern unto my feet," was his suggestion; and
Alke presented his Majesty Henry VIII. with the conception beautifully painted on parchment.

Ami had redeemed his promise at Wittenberg. Could
it be that the eye of Vian had lost its vision for the separate personalities whose life was so bound up with his
own, in the perfect happiness he had found with Alke-
or in his interest in such tasks as the dissolution of the
religious houses and the translation of the Bible?

One who had been fortunate enough to go with Vian
to the Abbey of Glastonbury on an afternoon in 1538,
one year after his meeting with Ami at Wittenberg, would
have discerned within his conversation another plan,
much more personal than any of these. That plan involved the future joy of at least two human souls. How
could this man, into whose mind had gone the far-reach-
ing scheme of Henry VIII., turn aside from such grave
concerns to attend to a love-affair between Ami and
Astrée? The only answer is that Vian himself was living
in love's paradise, and knew something of the pressure
of love's commandments.

Never had the sixty acres of magnificent buildings
which constituted the stateliness of Glastonbury seemed
so noble and impressive as they did to Vian, when on
that afternoon the fine sunlight fell upon the old Nor-
man walls, and the shadows of the fleecy clouds lazily
moved over the soft green turf.

Here he had doubted and wept and prayed; and now
the whole splendid scene had become but an antiquity,
scarcely more potent to others than the vanished forests
in which the Celtic wanderers appealed to Her, or the
propitious winds which wafted hither the bark of Saint
Joseph and his company. But something had compelled
him to look ahead as he had seen abbey after abbey fall;
and a feeling of loyalty to the old walls which had protected

him had struggled into such supremacy, that, when it seemed possible that Henry VIII. should suppress even the most noble of the monasteries, Vian had devised the compromise which Parliament had adopted; and Glastonbury had escaped. He was glad for that act of love to the old abbey as he climbed Weary-all Hill and looked once more upon the Glastonbury Thorn. The white-throats seemed never so careless of their notes, which came in a squawk or a warble; but the chiff-chaff's tone was as mellow as the sunshine which Vian saw enwrapping a dark brown nightingale, that " creature of a fiery heart."

" They will sing over the ruins at no distant time," said he, sadly. " I will protect these walls as long as I may."

The tower of St. Michael's oratory, which still rises upon the summit of Tor Hill, was ivy-laden and sunlit.

" It is already yesterday gleaming upon St. Michael's. Really the only living thing is the ivy which clings to it. Perhaps all that is vital about any of these institutions is the memory or the love which covers over their hardness and unyielding grace."

Into the doorway of St. Joseph's chapel he looked, and Abbot Richard Whiting appeared.

" Ah, Vian, no one is more welcome than yourself to these venerable walls. You have protected us so often and so surely that it almost makes one forgive — "

" My heresy, Lord Abbot, is not beseeching for-giveness."

" Nay, we are the suppliants now," said the abbot, with painful regret. " Things have gone differently in France."

" France has declined the Reformation; but "— and Vian's prophetic voice almost pronounced the doom which history has chronicled. For France indeed did decline the Reformation; and France has been compelled to accept the Revolution. 1529–1789, — only two and one half centuries; and the world was taught again that statesmanship is the art of finding out in what direction Almighty God is going, and in getting things out of His way.

"I have, as his Majesty's special commissioner, a message to your Lordship," said Vian, assuming an authority over Richard Whiting which his heart did not feel.

The abbot read the document, examined the seal, and was silent while Vian proceeded, —

"You must understand that if, by his Majesty's kindness to me, I am able to postpone the suppression of this ancient house for some months, it must be because I now am made sure of the discovery and release of this affrighted sister Emelie under the Prioress Katerine Bourgcher of Mynchin Buckland Priory and Preceptory. I know her by another name. I must not be discouraged or impeded. I can save this abbey for months, perhaps, if the release is obtained at once."

Still the abbot said nothing.

"The authority of the king seems cruel to you? Ah! how rapacious have been the ignorance and superstition which have grown up in all our religious houses! We shall have no faith in England if we depend longer upon the incredible and the false. My Lord Abbot Richard Whiting, what think you? I have here a letter from our commission, which was sent to Hailes."

Vian handed to Abbot Richard the letter which now appears in the Chapter-House papers in the State Paper Offices.

This passage even to-day arrests the eye of the reader :

"Sir, we have been bolting and sifting the Blood of Hailes all this forenoon. It was wondrously, closely, and craftily inclosed and stopped up, for taking of care. And it cleaveth fast to the bottom of the little glass that it is in. And verily it seemeth to be an unctuous gum and compound of many things. It hath a certain unctuous moistness, and though it seems somewhat like blood when it is in the glass, yet when any parcel of the same is taken out, it turneth to a yellowness, and is cleaving like glue. But we have not yet examined all the monks; and therefore this my brother abbot shall tell your Lordship what he hath seen and heard in this matter. And in the end your Lordship shall know altogether. But we perceive not by your commission whether we shall send it up or leave it here, or certify thereof as we know."

The abbot read, and saying nothing, handed the letter back to Vian, who continued : "That gum in the phial was offered to pilgrims for years to be reverenced as some of the blood of Christ which fell from the cross of our Lord. English manhood can never build itself upon such deceptions. Our commission has gone to Kent and taken the Rood of Bexley."

"Oh !" cried the abbot, "it is sacrilege."

"Lord Abbot," replied Vian, "the profanity lies in defending such a fraud. For years the people have beheld its bending body, its twitching forehead, its opening lips, its goggling eyes. Even yesterday did Geoffry Chambers tear it apart at Maidstone ; and before the people who thronged the market he pulled out the wires and cords, and broke the wheels within it to pieces."

"Profanation !" exclaimed the abbot.

"Oh, England must be purged of these trickeries of monks ! Our room at London is filled with the villanous devices with which our monks have entrapped the people. His Grace hath said that what has been known as the blood of Saint Thomas at Canterbury is only red ochre. We have collected enough pieces of wood, each of which has been said to be a fragment of the true cross, to have made a great tree. The end is near. Our sovereign may displease many by his use of the revenues ; but rich monks must release lands and plate. I must not tarry ; this abbey has my pitiful love. As I have said, let me find the woman I seek — "

"She is a consecrated nun," interjected the abbot.

"And yet a woman beloved, — say not a word against her!" and the eyes of Vian were aflame.

In less than an hour the Abbot of Glastonbury, accompanied by the splendid train which reflected the last gleams of mediæval monasticism as its sun sank out of sight, was riding with Vian on the way to Mynchin Buckland Priory, Somerset.

Old Bathpole Road was lined with flowers as it ran under Creechbury Hill and toward the fields of the priory. Stoke and Orchard lay broadly basking in the filmy gold which fell out of the sky upon them; and the long shadows which alternated with the sunlight upon the ample meadows of Blackdown were still the shadows of a most beautiful morning. The demesne ponds were dappled by the soft winds, whose bosoms were filled with fragrances, as they came like tender messengers over the fields of Staple and Neroche, sighing themselves into whispers when they came close to the buildings of the House of Sisters.

"A noble history," observed the abbot, with pathos, as he began to tell Vian of the unique character of the institution, the Order of St. John of Jerusalem, the preceptory which was the finest example in all England of a hospitaller's commandery; adding that this was the only community of women which the order possessed, and that it had had but one prior.

But Vian cared little about Walter Prior, who had been dead for nearly four centuries; or Fina, who had departed this life in 1240; or the difficulties of the preceptor and prioress thirty years later. As Vian looked upon that never-failing source of revenue, the dove-cot, his mind went to Ami, whose love had as many wings of hope as then troubled the odorous air.

The abbot and Vian halted near the north side of the great church, which was surrounded by a picturesque group of buildings. A couple of sisters had just fetched some firewood from the adjoining park, which Vian had noticed was full of deer.

"So ill used are these sisters!" remarked the abbot.

"They appear to be more industrious than monks," replied Vian, with acidity.

The plinth mouldings, monuments, fragments of oaken wainscot, incised slabs, Lombardic crosses, altar-cloths, chalices, and copes, which even now are to be found in old buildings in Blackdown, Durslon, Staple, and West Monkton, were then all in place, helping to constitute the beauty of Mynchin Buckland. But Vian knew that the hour of their great significance had passed.

The abbot had introduced him. Vian had exhibited his letters of authorization; and with several officers who remained in the guest-room, he advised the abbot that he wished to be left at the priory, and instructed the prioress that he should demand that no pious service should go unperformed, and indeed that he should be allowed to inspect the house, without a single hint being given to any of the object of his search.

It was the day of the festival of Saint Mary, and two virgins were to be consecrated. Greatly to the annoyance and godly sorrow of the prioress, Vian demanded to be admitted after the introit of the Mass and Collect. The Epistle had not been read. Two virgins stood before the altar, each clothed in white, and each holding in one hand a taper, in the other the sacred habit. The bishop, who recognized Vian at once as the representative of Thomas Cromwell, trembled, as Vian turned his eyes away from him, and the virgins laid their habits at his feet. The bishop then blessed each habit.

"Receive, damsel, this cloke, which thou mayest bear without spot before the judgment-seat of our Lord Jesus Christ, to whom every knee doth bow, of things in heaven, and things on earth, and things under the earth, who, with the Father and the Holy Ghost, liveth and reigneth God, world without end, Amen!" This said the bishop to each one, after he had sprinkled the vestments with holy water. The Epistle and Mass followed. The virgins retired.

Vian's eye searched every face. Years had gone since he looked into her face, as he lifted her from beneath the overshadowing peril on the "Field of the Cloth of Gold." Still he was confident that a single look would not fail to discover her whom he sought.

The virgins returned, attired in the habits which had been blessed, each wearing the ring and veil which had been placed upon the altar, and bearing the paper of profession. They stood within the gate of the choir, each with the lighted taper in the right hand. In most delicious harmony these sentiments floated forth from their lips in the Latin words: "I love Christ, into whose chamber I have entered, whose mother is a Virgin, whose father knew not woman; whose instruments sing to me with measured voices, whom, when I shall have loved, I am chaste; when I shall have touched, I am clean; when I shall have received, I am a Virgin. Honey and milk from his mouth I have taken, and his blood hath adorned my cheeks."

"Come! come! come!" said the bishop.

"Ye daughters, hearken unto me! I will teach you the fear of the Lord. Alleluia!" responded the choir.

The virgins advanced. The antiphon concluded. They bowed to the ground, and then rose, singing, "And now we follow from our whole heart, and we fear Thee."

"Come! come! come!" said the bishop.

"Ye daughters, hearken unto me! I will teach you the fear of the Lord. Alleluia!" responded the choir.

Again the virgins advanced; again they bowed themselves; again they rose, singing, "And now we follow from our whole heart, and we fear Thee."

" Come ! come ! come ! " again said the bishop.

The virgins advanced.

" Ye daughters, hearken unto me ! I will teach you the fear of the Lord. Alleluia ! " responded the choir, out of whose harmony two voices lifted the strain, " Come unto Him and be enlightened, and your faces shall not be confounded."

" Ye daughters, hearken unto me ! I will teach you the fear of the Lord. Alleluia ! "

Vian thought he had never heard such music, save once in the mountains near La Torre.

The white-robed pair advanced, singing, " And we follow Thee with our whole heart, and fear Thee, and we seek Thy face. O Lord, confound us not, but do unto us according to Thy loving-kindness, and according to the multitude of Thy mercy."

The bishop prostrated himself, with his face toward the altar. His attendants did likewise, while the seven Psalms were being said, and the virgins were prostrate. Two clerks sang the Litany, and the choir responded. On reaching the verse appointed for the bishop, he rose and looking upon the virgins, said, —

" That it may please thee to bless and preserve our sisters in true religion."

" We beseech Thee," responded the choir.

Vian's eye was just then attracted to the form of one of the attending sisters whose face bore signs of intense suffering. Behind the anguish which still struggled there with the emotions which the scene and the music produced, there was a certain fadeless beauty.

The Litany was concluded ; the bishop sang " Veni Creator Spiritus," and the choir responded. One of the virgins advanced and made her profession. After she had made the sign of the cross, the other virgin did likewise profess.

Vian's attention was again directed toward the woman

whose eyes were now full of tears. He was sure they were black eyes, tender and brilliant within all her grief. She was soon standing near unto one of the virgins who had been consecrated. As the virgin on the right handed her the taper before receiving her veil, Vian found himself upon his feet.

"I will at least avoid a disturbance at this moment," reasoned he, with a heart which beat as unrestrainedly as did hers.

The face turned toward him. The eyes of dark splendor glanced once upon Vian's hesitation. He was back again in the dust-cloud on the " Field of the Cloth of Gold." It was Astrée.

Vian did not remain to behold the rest of the solemn ceremony. Arriving at the guest-room, he gave commands to his officers and awaited the coming of the prioress.

"I would see at once the sister who received the taper from the virgin who stood on the right of the bishop," said he to the prioress Katerine Bourgcher, at the instant of her appearance.

"Alas!" cried she.

"Yes; Sister Emelie — Astrée!"

"How do you know that name?" inquired the haughty lady.

"It matters not." Vian produced his Majesty's authorization.

"I have beheld that great seal and papers with the name of—"

Vian cut through the dignity of the prioress with the words, "I would behold the sister I have named, and at once!"

"This begins the end," remarked the prioress, in accents of lamentation.

"Yes," said Vian, "you have probably witnessed the last consecration of virgins within these walls."

"I spurn your prophecies; but I shall obey your most unrighteous demands."

"No parley here!" said Vian, as he advanced to speak to the officers. "I would speak to her immediately."

Soon Vian was seated in the apartment of the prioress. The door was opened; the prioress entered, retired, and at once the eyes of Vian fixed themselves upon another form.

"The monk Vian!" cried Astrée, as the old words of her lover Ami came back to associate themselves swiftly with the man who stood before her. "Deliver me from terrors viler and more cruel than death, O Vian, who once delivered me from death itself!"

The prioress entered in time to see her fall into the arms of Vian.

"For shame, for shame! I have always known your unfaithful heart," shouted the indignant prioress.

"The monk Vian!" sighed Astrée, as she revived, and Ami's words rushed back to her soul.

"And a monk, then? You are a monk! Oh, abomination of desolation, my house is scandalized!" shrieked Katerine Bourgcher, as she grasped her keys.

"Touch not this lady! Hear me! touch her not!" commanded Vian.

"I will not even behold such an unseemly spectacle. Avaunt, monk and nun!" hissed the prioress, in the name of her ritualistic virtue. But only the prioress retired from the room, adding, in muttering tones, "This is he whom she has loved more than her Lord. Oh, the foul one!"

"Astrée!" said he, with tender truthfulness in each tone.

"Vian!" answered the nun, as she gathered her thoughts into one.

"The whole story is told. I can tell you mine, — you will hear it as we journey along. You are wretched here?"

"I am."

"Because you love — "

"The memory of the knight Ami. You — oh, Vian, you forgave him?"

"The prioress believes that I am he whom you still love."

"Certainly; but I — "

"Yes, I know it, Astrée. I am only the special commissioner of his Majesty Henry VIII. I am come to deliver you."

"Merciful Jesu! and God bless you!" she exclaimed, as she kissed Vian's hands.

"I cannot tell you more, until — But you are safe with me; and — Officers are waiting my command. I will tell you all. Make yourself ready to depart."

Vian called for the prioress, who was irritable and sullenly silent. He commanded her to make Astrée's comfort sure in the prospect of a long ride.

Before that day's sun had lit the edges of Creechbury Hill, Astrée was riding with one of the officers who had come from London, by way of Glastonbury, with Vian. They rode together alone in the soft evening light. Vian had permitted them to loiter somewhat behind his cavalcade; for that officer was Ami.

CHAPTER XXXVIII.

THE END.

" Rest comes at length, though life be long and dreary;
The day must dawn, and darksome night be passed;
All journeys end with welcome to the weary,
And heaven — the heart's true home — will come at last."

UNIMPORTANT is every life, however endowed or compassed with privileges, until it passes into the service of important truth. Important as the infinite harvests which may be garnered from the triumph of any truth in men's hearts, does the least subtle, the least natively great life become the moment it has passed out of itself, and, through submission, into the use of organizing ideas.

A surpassing importance had entered the lives of Ami and Vian. The one had been freed from narrowing jealousies, because he had been captured by an all-dominating love; the other's mind had been emancipated from conventional limitations, because he had realized in a reasonable service the law of spiritual and intellectual liberty.

When at length they sat with Astrée and Alke by the side of the dust of Gaspar Perrin, who two days before had suddenly expired in the printing-room, they found the secret of power in the world. The mellow twilight was drifting into the apartment, and falling upon the face of the dead and upon the first copies of the English Bible, whose appearance marked the beginning of an era for the word of God and the English people.

" He was not a great man, yet his life had greatness in it," said Alke, reflectively, as she looked again upon the face and then into the red West.

" Only a printer in Venice, a believer in God's justice and truth, trusting his life to his faith ; a stainless radical, intent on finding and serving — "

" Intent on serving great truths, which always impart their greatness to him who serves them." Vian had rescued Alke's tremulous sentence from ending in tears ; and now she placed her hands gratefully in his.

" Truly ! " said the beautiful Astrée, seeking to console Ami, whose eye often found the white scar on the brown wrist now so motionless, " that is the greatness which makes his dust seem finer and more precious than that of Bayard. Bayard was the greatest in the annals of the old knighthood. Our father may be only one of the noblest in the annals of the new knighthood. It is with what seems greatest as it was aforetime, — ' the least in the kingdom of heaven is greater than he.' "

Ami and Vian had both been made ambitious to influence the world's history. The most eminent worshippers at the shrines of glory had taught them this aspiration and its language. Each had oftentimes found himself upon tossing seas, which made him only an incident amid the surge and foam hurled hither and thither by resistless power.

Had they failed to make their lives tell upon the future ?

In the battles of kings and cardinals, scholars and popes, in the swirl of the Reforming movement, each had, in some measure, kept his personality sacred. In the separate contest between the man and his circumstances, each had felt himself causative and free.

As near that calm sweet face — the face of an old man upon which rested the fadeless dawn of youth — they stood together, the awful oceantide which they had known came rushing in and told its tale. This completed career held the open secret of sovereignty. It had a greatness unto which no Abbot Richard of Glastonbury or Francis I. could approach. Gaspar Perrin was forever sure to have the regency which is obtained by loyalty to regent ideas.

Still would they ride upon these waves. Perhaps as drops of oil thrown out, they had, at Amboise and Paris, Glastonbury and Whitehall, made it possible for great waves to slip over each other so as to prevent a chaos more disastrous. Even yet wisdom and truth were inexhaustible. They had positions at court; and their relations to the Reformers would enable them to wield an influence to be measured only by the magnitude of the ideas which should rule them.

Softly and prayerfully did Astrée and Alke find their way amid the melancholy duties.

Ami sat reading the gospel of purity. His thirst for purity had carried him into the Reformation. He was reading it from the flowers which Vian, only the day before, had plucked from the Glastonbury Thorn, which for a week had been in full bloom. Astrée, who interpreted his mind, placed a single stainless blossom within the cold grasp of Gaspar Perrin.

Vian had been musing. He held the first copy of the English Bible in his hand. Only a short time ago Tyndale had been burned. Now the presses labored incessantly to bury from men's remembrance the hideous crime. By the favor of God the old Waldensian — the friend of Aldus — had been permitted to have his part in the new triumph. Vian's spiritual position had come to him by loyalty to that impulse generated within his bosom by the sight of the unchained Word of God.

Alke, who knew his soul, asked for the fresh volume ; and soon with the blossom from Glastonbury Thorn, the dead hand rested upon the printed Bible.

"Oh, deathless soul!" said Vian, as he looked again upon the transfigured face, "with purity of life and with the gospel of Christ, thou hast conquered!"

THE END.

SAVONAROLA,

HIS LIFE AND TIMES.

By WILLIAM CLARK, M.A., LL.D.

12mo, gilt top, 358 pages, $1.50.
Half calf or half morocco, $3.50.

PROFESSOR CLARK writes in popular style, thoroughly explains the intricate political system of Florence in its transition state, and succeeds in giving a well-rounded history of a man whose character will always be one of the most interesting in history to study.

The whole story is compactly and simply told in this volume, and in such a fascinating and charming way as to delight the reader. As a contribution to a proper estimate of a life that presents so many difficulties to the historian, this study of Professor Clark's is especially valuable. — *Living Church, Chicago.*

This is one of the best pieces of biographical work that have fallen under our eye during the present year. The author exhibits a thorough acquaintance with the history of the age in which the great Italian reformer's life was spent. All the information contained in the pages of the most trustworthy authorities has been critically examined, sifted, and condensed into this work. It is a pleasure to commend work which has been so excellently done. . . . The book is written in terse, forceful, and perfectly lucid English; the style of the author is strikingly vivid; and the reader obtains from the volume a very satisfactory conception of Savonarola's aims, deeds, and influence. — *Public Opinion, Washington.*

The book is a very careful study, kept candid and fair as far as it is possible for an enthusiastic admirer to be so. It is frank and full also in reference to authorities. — *Times, Chicago.*

The volume covers just about as much ground as the general reader is likely to want, and is the best popular book yet produced concerning one of the most interesting figures of the last half of the fifteenth century. — *Epoch, New York.*

EDUCATION and THE HIGHER LIFE.

By the Rt. Rev. J. L. SPALDING,

BISHOP OF PEORIA.

12mo, 210 pages. Price, $1.00.

READING these essays, one feels urged to purer thinking and
nobler doing. They incite to excellence of mind and to excellence
of soul. To one who feels pessimistic, narrow-minded, narrow-
souled, they come with joyous, faith-carrying words, which point
and lead to those higher truths of mind and soul which are free
from dogma of sect and creed, and which all lovers of the human
intellect and the divine intelligence delight to study. — *Public
Opinion, Washington.*

These essays are characterized by an elevation of thought, an
earnestness of purpose, which are well adapted to stir the soul to
nobler impulses and fuller consecration in the service of God and
man. . . . To all who are seeking mental and moral elevation, this
book will give many helpful hints. — *Methodist Magazine, Toronto.*

This is not a large work, but it is a practical and valuable one.
It is full of nuggets of golden counsel. It is impossible to read
the book without feeling that Bishop Spalding understands the true
nature of education, which is not simply to stuff the mind, but to
train it. We wish that the book might be read by the intelligent
youth of our land. It would tend to enlighten their minds as to
the best aims and purposes of life. — *The Observer, New York.*

The aspiring young men and women of the country will find in
these pages an earnest call to the higher life, — a summons to fix
their attention on pure and lofty ideals of character, and ever advance toward them with firm and courageous steps. — *Unity,
Chicago.*

The Bishop of Peoria enjoys more than a local fame as a
learned and eloquent man. There are many things wisely and well
said in this collection of essays. — *Living Church, Chicago.*

It is a plea for culture as a means toward attaining the·higher
life, and is a good word well spoken. — *The Inquirer, Philadelphia.*

Sold by all booksellers, or mailed, on receipt of price, by

A. C. McCLURG & CO., PUBLISHERS, ·

COR. WABASH AVE. AND MADISON ST., CHICAGO.

SESAME AND LILIES.

THREE LECTURES BY JOHN RUSKIN.

I. OF KINGS' TREASURES.
II. OF QUEENS' GARDENS.
III. OF THE MYSTERY OF LIFE.

12mo, 201 pages, gilt top.   Price, $1.00.

In half calf or half morocco, gilt top, $2.75.
In limp russia or limp morocco, gilt edges, $3.50.

One of the most popular as well as most valuable of Ruskin's works is "Sesame and Lilies," and this has been brought out by McClurg & Co. in a neat and handy volume of good print and excellent paper.   The publishers have wisely inserted in this volume Ruskin's admirable and thoroughly characteristic preface which he prepared for the new and revised edition of his works in 1871. The size, shape, and compactness of this issue make it an admirable pocket companion for desultory reading in the cars, in the woods, or at the shore. — *Evening Transcript, Boston.*

Other editions of this notable and popular book have been printed, but none so tastefully as this.   Of the book itself it may not be inopportune to say that it shows the author at his best, being devoted to life instead of art, and embodying Ruskin's earnestness and gift of language without calling attention to any of his oddities and hobbies. — *Herald, New York.*

It would be hard to find a better book to put into the hands of a youth — boy or girl — at that epoch of life when the spiritual and intellectual faculties seem to leap out with a bound from the chrysalis of the animal nature and determine their direction for life. — *Home Journal, New York.*

The book is one by all means to be commended to young women and young men who care for refinement of character and purity of heart and earnestness of purpose, and who are able to appreciate noble thought clothed in exquisite diction. — *Evangelist, New York.*

Sold by all booksellers, or mailed, on receipt of price, by

A. C. McCLURG & CO., PUBLISHERS,

COR. WABASH AVE. AND MADISON ST., CHICAGO

THE LAUREL-CROWNED LETTERS.

The Best Letters of Lord Chesterfield. Edited, with an Introduction, by EDWARD GILPIN JOHNSON.

The Best Letters of Lady Mary Wortley Montagu. Edited, with an Introduction, by OCTAVE THANET.

The Best Letters of Horace Walpole. Edited, with an Introduction, by ANNA B. McMAHAN.

The Best Letters of Madame de Sévigné. Edited, with an Introduction, by EDWARD PLAYFAIR ANDERSON. Each volume is finely printed and bound; 16mo, cloth, gilt tops, price, $1.00.

In half calf or half morocco, per vol., $2.75.

Of LORD CHESTERFIELD'S LETTERS, the *Atlantic Monthly* says:—

The editor seems to make good his claims to have treated these letters with such discrimination as to render the book really serviceable, not only as a piece of literature, but as a text-book in politeness.

Of LADY MARY WORTLEY MONTAGU'S LETTERS, the *New York Star* says:—

The selection is indeed an excellent one, and the notes by the present editor considerably enhance their value.

Of HORACE WALPOLE'S LETTERS, the *Philadelphia Public Ledger* says:—

These witty and entertaining letters show Walpole to bear out the promise of his fame,—the prince of letter-writers in an age which elevated the occupation into a fine art.

Of MADAME DE SÉVIGNÉ'S LETTERS, the *Boston Saturday Gazette* says:—

Accomplished, witty, pure, Madame de Sévigné's noble character is reflected in her writings, which will always hold a foremost place in the estimation of those who can appreciate high moral and intellectual qualities.

Sold by all booksellers, or mailed, on receipt of price, by

A. C. McCLURG & CO., PUBLISHERS,

COR. WABASH AVE. AND MADISON ST., CHICAGO.

LAUREL-CROWNED TALES.

ABDALLAH; OR, THE FOUR-LEAVED SHAMROCK. BY EDOUARD LABOULAYE. Translated by MARY L. BOOTH.

RASSELAS, PRINCE OF ABYSSINIA. BY SAMUEL JOHNSON.

RAPHAEL; OR, PAGES OF THE BOOK OF LIFE AT TWENTY. From the French of ALPHONSE DE LAMARTINE.

THE VICAR OF WAKEFIELD. BY OLIVER GOLDSMITH.

THE EPICUREAN. BY THOMAS MOORE.

PICCIOLA. BY X. B. SAINTINE.

Other volumes in preparation.

Handsomely printed from new plates, on fine laid paper, 12mo, cloth, with gilt tops, price per volume, $1.00.

In half calf or half morocco, $2.75.

In planning this series, the publishers have aimed at a form which should combine an unpretentious elegance suited to the fastidious book-lover with an inexpensiveness that must appeal to the most moderate buyer.

It is the intent to admit to the series only such tales as have for years or for generations commended themselves not only to the fastidious and the critical, but also to the great multitude of the refined reading public, — tales, in short, which combine purity and classical beauty of style with perennial popularity.

Sold by all booksellers, or mailed, on receipt of price, by

A. C. McCLURG & CO., PUBLISHERS,

COR. WABASH AVE. AND MADISON ST., CHICAGO.

MARTHA COREY.

A TALE OF THE SALEM WITCHCRAFT.

By Constance Goddard du Bois.

12mo, 314 pages. Price, $1.25.

THE same material drawn upon by Longfellow for his " New England Tragedies " is here used with greater fulness and with no less historical exactitude. The story has for its background the dark and gloomy pictures of the witchcraft persecution, of which it furnishes a thrilling view. It is remarkable for bold imagination, wonderfully rapid action, and continued and absorbing interest.

In short, it is too good a piece of fiction to be accepted as truth, which is to the credit of the author's imaginative powers; for " Martha Corey " is an absorbing tale. — *Public Ledger, Philadelphia.*

The story is curious and quaint, differing totally from the novels of this day; and the pictures of life among the early inhabitants of Massachusetts show that the author has been an untiring and faithful student for her work. — *Weekly Item, Philadelphia.*

The characters are well delineated; the language is smooth and refined; and from frequent change of scene and character the book is rendered very entertaining. The passions, love and hate, are carefully analyzed and faithfully described. It is a valuable little book. — *Globe, Chicago.*

An interesting tale of love and intrigue. . . . Miss Du Bois has given us a very readable book, and has succeeded where others have failed. — *Advertiser, Boston.*

The story of this book is pleasantly told; and as a picture of those sad times, when some of the worst and the best, of the darkest and the brightest, of the most hateful and the most lovable traits of human nature were openly manifested, is well worth reading. — *Illustrated Christian Weekly, New York.*

A story of marked strength, both of imagination and narration. —*Home Journal, New York.*

Sold by all booksellers, or mailed, on receipt of price, by

A. C. McCLURG & CO., Publishers,

Cor. Wabash Ave. and Madison St., Chicago.

THE BRIDGE OF THE GODS.

A ROMANCE OF INDIAN OREGON.

By F. H. BALCH.

12mo, 280 pages.   Price, $1.25.

THIS is a masterly and original delineation of Indian life. It is a strong story, charged with the elemental forces of the human heart. The author portrays with unusual power the intense, stern piety of the ministers of colonial New England, and the strange mingling of dignity, superstition, ferocity, and stoicism that characterized the early Indian warriors.

There is no need of romancing, and Mr. Balch's scenic descriptions are for all practical purposes real descriptions. The legends he relates of the great bridge which once spanned the Columbia, for which there is some substantial history, adds to the mystical charms of the story. His Indian characters are as real as if photographed from life. No writer has presented a finer character than the great chief of the Willamettes, Multnomah; Snoqualmie the Cayuse; or Tohomish the Seer. The night visit of Multnomah to the tomb of his dead wife upon that lonely island in the Willamette is a picture that will forever live in the reader's memory. . . . To those who have traversed the ground, and know something of Indian character and the wild, free life of pioneer days, the story will be charming — *Inter-Ocean, Chicago.*

It is a truthful and realistic picture of the powerful Indian tribes that inhabited the Oregon country two centuries ago. . . . It is a book that will be of value as a historical authority; and as a story of interest and charm, there are few novels that can rival it. — *Traveller, Boston.*

There is much and deep insight in this book. The characters stand in clear outline, and are original. The movement of the story is quick and varied, like the running water of the great river. — *The Pacific, San Francisco.*

Its field is new for fiction; it is obviously the work of one who has bestowed a great deal of study on the subjects he would illustrate. It is very interesting reading, fluently written. — *Times, Chicago.*

THE BEVERLEYS.

A Story of Calcutta.

BY MARY ABBOTT,

Author of "Alexia," etc.

12mo, 264 pages. Price, $1.25.

———

THE uncommonly favorable reception of Mrs. Abbott's brilliant novelette, "Alexia," by the public bespeaks in advance a lively interest in her new novel, "The Beverleys." It is a more extended and ambitious work than the former, but has the same grace of style and liveliness of treatment, together with a much more considerable plot and more subtle delineations of character and life. The action of the story takes place in India, and reveals on the part of the authoress the most intimate knowledge of the official life of the large and aristocratic English colony in Calcutta. The local coloring is strong and unusual.

A more joyous story cannot be imagined. . . . A harum-scarum good-nature; a frank pursuit of cakes and ale; a heedless, happy-go-lucky spirit, are admirable components in a novel, however trying they may be found in the walks of daily life. Such are the pleasures of "The Beverleys." To read it is recreation, indeed. — *Public Ledger, Philadelphia.*

The author writes throughout with good taste, and with a quick eye for the picturesque. — *Herald, New York.*

It is a pretty story, charmingly written, with cleverly sketched pictures of various types of character . . . The book abounds in keen, incisive philosophy, wrapped up in characteristic remarks. — *Times, Chicago*

An absorbing story. It is brilliantly and vivaciously written. — *Literary World, Boston.*

The author has until now been known, so far as we are aware, only by her former story, "Alexia." Unless signs fail which seldom *do* fail, these two with which her name is now associated are simply the forerunners of works in a like vein of which American literature will have reason to be proud. — *Standard, Chicago.*

———

Sold by all booksellers, or mailed, on receipt of price, by

A. C. McCLURG & CO., PUBLISHERS,

COR. WABASH AVE. AND MADISON ST., CHICAGO.

THE GREAT FRENCH WRITERS.

A Series of Studies of the Lives, Works, and Influence
of the Great Writers of the Past, by Great Writers
of the Present. Comprising —

MADAME DE SÉVIGNÉ. By Gaston Boissier.
GEORGE SAND. By E. Caro.
MONTESQUIEU. By Albert Sorel.
VICTOR COUSIN. By Jules Simon.
TURGOT. By Léon Say.
THIERS. By Paul de Rémusat.

With other volumes in preparation. Translated by Prof. MEL-
VILLE B. ANDERSON and Prof. EDWARD PLAYFAIR ANDER-
SON. 12mo. Price, $1.00 per volume.

In half morocco, gilt top, $2.50.

———

No writers of the century have exerted more influence upon English
and American thought than the writers of France, whether in fiction,
in criticism, or in metaphysics. . . . It was fortunate for Americans
especially that the scheme was conceived of having eminent French
writers of this generation prepare monographs upon the great writers
of past generations whose books are still the living thought not only of
their own country but of the age; and the translation of these monographs and their republication in this country is a literary event of considerable importance. — *Tribune, Chicago.*

When the reader has finished either of these volumes, he must certainly lay it down with the feeling that he has been admitted into the
intimate life of the great writer in whose charming company he has
been spending a few delightful hours, and that his knowledge of the
author's position in literature, and of his influence in the world, is sur-
prisingly enlarged and broadened. — *Nation, New York.*

These French monographs have a power of compression and light-
ness of touch which may well appear marvellous to American readers
not acquainted with the Gallic genius for biographical and critical
essays. — *Beacon, Boston.*

———

Sold by all booksellers, or mailed, on receipt of price, by

A. C. McCLURG & CO., PUBLISHERS,
COR WABASH AVE. AND MADISON ST., CHICAGO.

FACT, FANCY, AND FABLE.

A New Handbook for Ready Reference on Subjects Commonly Omitted from Cyclopædias. Compiled by Henry Frederic Reddall. Large 8vo, 536 pages. Half leather, $3 50.

In half morocco, gilt top, $6.50.

The motto, "Trifles make the sum of human things," could have no better illustration than this noble collection furnishes. It comprises personal sobriquets, familiar phrases, popular appellations, geographical nicknames, literary pseudonyms, mythological characters, red-letter days, political slang, contractions and abbreviations, technical terms, foreign words and phrases, Americanisms, etc. The work is compiled after a distinct plan, and with keen discrimination in regard to what is admitted and what excluded. — *Journal of Education, Boston.*

It is original in conception, and thorough in execution. It brings together, alphabetically, a surprising number of titles from near and remote sources, that are very necessary in reference when they are not indispensable to the general reader. . . . It supplements and enlarges the usefulness of every dictionary and all the handbooks the dictionary has suggested. — *Globe, Boston.*

It must take its place for the time being as the best work of its kind in existence, particularly as regards American topics. — *Sun, New York.*

There is much matter in the volume that has never before been collated. . . . Writers and readers alike will find this work serviceable and trustworthy. — *Press, Philadelphia.*

The book is one of the best compilations of its kind. — *Critic, New York.*

Sold by all booksellers, or mailed, on receipt of price, by

A. C. McCLURG & CO., Publishers,

Cor. Wabash Ave. and Madison St., Chicago.